The Journey is Our Home

Kathy Miner

About the Author:

Kathy Miner lives in Colorado Springs, CO, with her family and critters. She welcomes comments, questions and conversation about her book, and can be contacted on Facebook at Kathy Miner Books, or via email at kathyminerwriter@gmail.com.

Gratitude and Acknowledgments

As always, I owe an enormous debt of gratitude to my friends and beta readers: Candice Moriarty, Laura Martin, Cheryl Rose, Tammy Themel, and Annette Milligan. Thank you, truly, for your friendship and your input. Kim Bender and Nan Anders, my "in-loves," thank you both for your ongoing support, edits, and love. And Ray Hjelt, money could not buy what you have gifted me with: professional-level edits delivered with the love and investment of someone who has known me all my life. (I really wanted to use a dash instead of a colon there, but I forced myself to behave.) Blessings on you all.

Kate Crosby, you came through with Cass' name just when I needed it most, and Leona Nolan-Mayo, you were there with information on arrows just minutes after I asked – thank you both. David Perry, you're the BEST when it comes to inspiration; your encouragement got me going and kept me going. I owe you a beer, my friend. Carol Browne, I very literally couldn't have written the sections on sailing without your advice and corrections, and I am so grateful. Dorman Gray, you are The Man, always there with information when I need it, always willing to share your intelligence and expertise. I appreciate your input, your world view, and especially your friendship. And Jesse Reynolds, my love my honey my sweet, you came through so many times, with gamer language and Game of Thrones references, and with the Grindylow for the win. Thank you, son o' mine.

Max and Phyl Miner, if there is anything admirable in any of these characters, it began with you two. You gave me the strongest of women and the most honorable of men to model from. Thank you for your brilliant edits as well as for your never-ending support.

Kristy, I have no words, and it's not because I spent them all in this book – we both know I have an endless supply! Ha! What I don't have are words lyrical enough to thank you, to express how much joy your involvement in all of my books gives me. You make me better in every way.

And finally, I want to thank my Rob, my Casey and my Kaya. I had to use all the juggling and balancing skills I possess to get this book done, and my family suffered for it. From the outside looking in, writing seems like a glamorous and exciting profession. Those on the inside know it's countless hours of staring at the back of someone's head, someone who is there but really not there, and hearing "Just a minute, honey..." over and over again. I'm sorry, my loves, for the toll this one took on everyone...but kind of thrilled, too. Half of this book was written in a busy Autism treatment center, the other half in the eye of a hurricane. There was much gnashing of teeth. There were many hysterical tears. Does this mean I finally, FINALLY qualify as a suffering artist? After a ridiculously blessed life, it is ABOUT TIME. Hey, that gives me an idea for a story...

ONE
Naomi: Woodland Park, CO
July

For the third time, Naomi set the log on its end and centered the axe head on it. She tightened her shaking hands until the axe stopped wobbling, pictured Martin in her mind, lifted the axe into the air, and tried to do as he did.

Didn't work.

The axe glanced off the log again, jarring her shoulders and back, and Naomi discovered she was snarling. Out loud. From where she'd put him on a stay fifteen safe feet away, Hades whined. For once, she didn't pause to reassure the big, watchful Rottweiler, to send love. She had nothing left to give Hades, couldn't comfort him, because she couldn't comfort herself.

Piper was gone.

She, Jack and the other travelers had zoomed off shortly after dawn this morning, waved off by the entire community, the sound of their motorcycles a shocking roar in the soft, rosy morning. Everyone, even the elderly and those with tiny infants, had gathered to see them off. Jack had been their leader, and although he'd spent the last several months delegating his responsibilities and had grown steadily more distant from everyone since Layla's death, he had led them through the early days following the plague and he would be missed.

No one had stepped up to take his place yet, and there was a shifting, anxious restlessness in the community as a result. Jack's responsibilities could be divided and shared, but who would lead them? Who would they look to when danger threatened and swift decisions were called for? Who would speak for them, as more and more outsiders found their way here? Naomi was acutely aware of the collective anxiety and was equally aware of how often eyes turned to her now, how often people asked her the questions they used to take to Jack.

Today, though, she couldn't care less.

Today, her only surviving child had once again struck out on her own. But unlike that long-ago, other-life day when she and Scott had moved Piper into the dorms at the University of Northern Colorado, she couldn't call to chat, to hear her daughter's voice and know she was safe. Couldn't Skype, couldn't hop in the car and make the two-hour drive to see her. Couldn't turn her attention to Macy and Scott, filling the empty ache with the rest of her family. Today, she was alone. No longer wife, no longer mother. Just taking the next breath hurt more than she could believe.

She might never see Piper again. Her daughter had disappeared into the morning mist and might never be back. There had to be somewhere to go with the emotions boiling in her chest, the regret making her heart boom, the grief making her vision ebb and pulse with light. Something she could do, some way to let it out. Back at the cabin, she'd cleaned everything there was to clean, rearranged every room, and then put it all back the way it was in the first place. The harder she worked, the harder she tried to not think, the more frantic she felt.

She had refused to join the rest of the community to see them off, turning her face away from Piper's goodbye this morning at the cabin, refusing to *feel* the tears her daughter had been choking back. Fifteen minutes later, she'd been running, running as fast as she could manage with Hades on her heels. Piper had taken the ATV, and when Naomi finally arrived on the edge of the gathering wheezing, staggering, breathless, she'd heard the collective call, the voices raised in fare-wells and safe-journeys, the startling roar of the bikes. Too late. People stared at her wild self, at her halo of snarled hair and the tears she couldn't stop, and a few of them tried to approach her, to offer comfort. She had snarled at them, just as she was snarling now.

Too late. Too late to kiss her daughter's soft face one last time. Too late to give her the protective amulet she'd fashioned, patterned on the one Layla had given her last spring. Too late to wrap every bit of love and mother-energy she had left in her broken-down heart around her girl, as if that would have made a difference. As if anything would make a difference. Her daughter was heading into a violent, desperate, unpredictable world. She may as well have jumped off a cliff.

Naomi centered the axe head on the log again, glaring fire at it, then swung the axe up and brought it down with all her strength. It bit this time – bit deep and stuck. She jerked at it, then jerked again, yanking and cussing.

"Naomi! What in hell are you doing?"

She ripped the axe free and swung around. Martin was standing beside Hades, hands propped on his hips, face dark with irritation. He took a half-step back when she turned, his eyes widening slightly, his body falling into a defensive posture. Oh, the gratification of that. The ferocious satisfaction his wariness brought her. Hades tensed as he picked up her mood, shifting into a silent crouch, his body taut with the potential of menace. Naomi hefted the axe, saw Martin's eyes flicker to it, to Hades, then back to her, and she exulted.

"Show me how to do this," she snapped. "Now."

Martin's eyebrows rose slowly. He stared her down for a handful of heartbeats. Then, he moved to join her. "First, put the log lower, on the ground – here, on this bed of wood chips so you don't damage the axe head. You need your full range of motion, to make up for what you don't have in upper-body strength. Feet apart. Hands apart." He accompanied his words with nudges of his own feet and hands, and then pointed at a crack on the log. "Hit it right here."

She listened to every word he said and did exactly as he told her, striking the log precisely, feeling the axe head sink deep again. Amazing, how much easier it was. Martin grunted approval and helped her lever the axe head free. "Again. Same spot."

She split the log on her second strike, and he set up another without a word. They fell into a silent rhythm, broken only by the "chunk" of her axe and the increasing huff of her breathing. She lost track of the number of logs she had split by the time he reached for the axe.

"That's enough for now."

He took hold of the axe, but Naomi refused to let it go. As she'd worked, the burning in her gut had eased, replaced by the burning in her arms and shoulders. Her stomach clenched at the thought of stopping. Stopping meant thinking. "I'll finish the pile."

"No, you won't." He popped the axe out of her hands with maddening ease. "Best way to get hurt splitting wood is to keep working when you need a break."

She grabbed at the axe, missed. "I don't need a break." She grabbed again, and felt the snarl boil up her throat once more. "Give it back to me. I said give it back!"

"Naomi."

She looked up. Exasperation and a sad knowing on his features this time. As soon as their eyes met, the dam broke.

"I didn't say goodbye!"

The words wailed from the depths of her. Dimly, she heard him sigh before he maneuvered her to sit on one of the large, un-split logs. Huge, tearing sobs felt like they'd rip her chest apart, but she couldn't begin to stop them, rocking back and forth with the force of her misery. Martin up-ended a log beside her and sat, letting her cry it out. Not until she was swiping at her streaming nose and hiccupping brokenly did he touch her, his big, warm hand landing on her shoulder and squeezing. She looked up at him through swollen eyes.

"Well. I bet you won't make a dumb-ass mistake like that again, will you?"

The old, soft Naomi would have been crushed and outraged, cut to the bone. The hardened thing she'd become barked out a laugh and shrugged his hand off her shoulder. She shook her head, lifting her t-shirt to scrub the tears and snot off her face. "Thanks, Martin. You always know just what to say to make me feel better."

She tipped her head back and stared at a summer sky so blue it looked like a painting. A steady, increasing breeze picked up the wisps of hair that had escaped her braid; there was monsoon energy in the air in spite of the blue sky. Before the day was out, she was sure, they'd have thunderstorms. Where would Piper and the others take shelter, she wondered? The tears welled up again. She let them flow this time, gentle cleansing instead of violent catharsis.

"The ironic thing," she said to the sky, "is that I've been acting just like her. Just like Piper used to act when she was a teenager. Not talking to her unless I had to, refusing to look at her." Her throat tightened up, but she kept choking the words out. She needed to get this out. "I thought she'd see how hurt I was, that she'd change her mind about going. Or about letting me go with her."

"You could have gone with her. If you had really wanted to go, she couldn't have stopped you."

"No, she couldn't have. But she didn't want me to go."

She swallowed and turned her face away; no need to remind Martin of the words Piper had hurled at her. He had been there when she'd done it. There had been plenty of witnesses to that mother-daughter throw-down.

They had been gathered at the church to begin working through the practical details of the travelers' departure. Weeks before, the call had gone out in the community for people willing to travel with Jack and Piper. Ed, their former neighbor, had been the first to volunteer, showing up to the meeting with his scruffy dog at his side.

"Maybe I'll swing down to Texas after we get Jack settled," he had said. "See if I've got any family left other than Rosemary, here." At the sound of her name, Rosemary had lifted adoring eyes to Ed's face, and his hand had dropped to rest on her head. "As long as I can bring my best girl, I wouldn't mind seeing what's going on in the rest of the world."

To everyone's surprise, Owen Weber had also stepped up. Layla's death and the loss of their unborn child, so soon after the loss of his wife and children in the plague, had brought the quiet giant of a man to his knees. His eyes had been haunted, hardly lifting from the floor as he spoke in a voice rusty from disuse. "I can't stay here. I have people in Minnesota. Might be I'll head there when we've found your sister, Jack. But I can't stay here."

Naomi had glanced nervously at Jack, but if he was feeling anything other than compassion, he didn't let it show as he nodded his acceptance. The meeting had progressed with a discussion about mode of travel, and as opinions were offered and expanded on, Naomi had been aware of the ever-increasing tension emanating from her daughter, a tension that had been building steadily since Piper had announced she'd be leaving.

They had argued about that, of course. Naomi had said everything she could think of to dissuade her, but Piper would not be moved. Eventually, Naomi had been forced to admit her daughter's reasoning was sound: Piper wanted to put distance between Brody and her, wanted to help Jack find his sister, wanted to expand on the historical record she'd started during her time with Brody's group and start creating connections between the scattered communities, like theirs, that had to be out there.

Naomi had come to understand those reasons, especially the first of them. She had also assumed she'd be going with them, and began to plan accordingly. As the weeks had passed, though, Piper had grown increasingly tense whenever Naomi spoke of the trip, increasingly silent. Naomi had ignored it. Deep inside, though, she had known what those silences meant. Piper had confirmed her fears, breaking in as Naomi had been lobbying for travel on horseback.

"Mom, stop!" Piper's words had burst out of her, and she had closed her eyes for a moment before going on in a calmer tone. "It's not going to happen. I should have said something sooner, but I didn't want to hurt you. You're not going with us."

It had taken Naomi long, breathless moments to get her voice working. "I am going," she had insisted. "Of course I'm going, Piper. I have to. We just found each other again."

"I know, and I'm sorry. But we need to travel as fast as possible on the way there, and horses just aren't practical. You've never driven a motorcycle, and –"

"I can learn! I learned to ride a horse, didn't I? I'm not like I was before, Piper. I'm stronger now, more fit, and I –"

"Mom, I don't want you to go!" Again, the words had erupted out of Piper, and again, she had modulated her tone, meeting her mother's eyes steadily. "I'm sorry it hurts you, but I don't want you to go."

An awful silence had followed Piper's quiet words. The reactions of the others had been telling: Jack, Ed, and Owen had all looked down. Naomi could *feel* their respect and their sorrow for her pain, but none of them spoke up in support of her. Martin's eyes had been steady on Naomi's stricken face, and his hand had found hers under the table. He had known this was coming, Naomi realized. Whether he had guessed or Piper had told him didn't really matter, because he didn't argue with Piper, either.

"It's not…I just…" Piper had hemmed and hawed in very un-Piper-like fashion, and Naomi had *felt* the swooping roller-coaster of her emotions: terrible guilt warring with a powerful yearning. For freedom. From her.

"Mom, this is just something I need to do on my own. I just need...some space. Some distance from...everything."

Naomi had risen from the table where they had all been seated. Too hurt to feel angry. Too frightened for her daughter to feel humiliated. Martin had started to rise with her, but she'd stopped him with a raised, shaking hand. She had left the room without another word. Preparations had gone forward without her input or involvement, and the confrontation had never been spoken of again. Until now.

Martin handed her a handkerchief before she could swipe at her face with her t-shirt again, and she took it, murmuring a thank-you. Somehow, he always had a clean handkerchief, even now, when laundry was a much more difficult chore than in the time before, and people were becoming accustomed to going about daily life much grubbier. Naomi blew her nose, then returned her eyes to the sky, wishing she could pull that cool blue inside her and soothe her heart with it.

As hurt and frightened as she had been by Piper's decision, she was still a good mother. And a good mother did not smother, stifle, coerce or manipulate her children. Not ever, not even in these times. "I could have gone with her. You're right. I could have insisted on following her or guilt-tripped her into staying."

She looked at Martin, feeling empty and angry and lost. "But then what? Do I follow her around for the rest of our lives? Do I cling to her forever? Refuse to let her go? When it was time for her to go to college, she couldn't wait to get away, to get out on her own. She hasn't changed, and she never will. Piper has been walking away from me since she took her very first steps."

"She loves you. You know that."

Naomi heaved a deep sigh. "I do. And it's not an angry thing anymore, thank God. But Piper is a seeker. She has a gypsy's soul. The plague, everything she went through – none of it changed her basic nature. She is who she is. I could feel how excited she was to go, all tangled up with her guilt over leaving me." Her throat tightened. "I miss Macy, so much. She was a homebody, like me. Scott and I used to joke that we had one of each. Piper started asking for her own apartment when she turned 16, and we'd have been nudging Macy out on her 30th birthday. Now, I don't know who I am. I don't know who to be without being a mom to my girls."

Martin snorted softly. "So. Empty nest syndrome on steroids, then."

Again, he surprised a bark of laughter out of her. "Yeah."

A soft, chuffing bark drew Naomi's attention, and she turned to meet Hades' worried gaze. Unless she was in physical danger, he stayed where she put him, though it distressed him terribly to see her cry. Naomi clicked her fingers twice, releasing him from the stay, and he shot to her side.   The big dog pressed close, rumbling softly in contentment under her stroking, scratching hands.   As always, contact with one of the dogs calmed and comforted her.

She looked around for perky, golden, butterfly ears and bright eyes, blinked in surprise at the impressive pile of wood she'd split, then looked at Martin. "Where's Persephone?"

"With Grace."

He looked away as he said it. Naomi frowned. She'd been so caught up in the boil and turmoil of her own feelings, she'd been oblivious to all else. Her frown deepened as she examined his familiar profile, seeing the subtle lines of strain that only someone who knew him well would see, *feeling* the undercurrent of distress in him.

"What's wrong?" Worry made her words sharp. Martin's daughter, Grace, had become so precious to her. "Has something happened? Is Grace okay?"

"She's fine. She's at the library with Anne, like always. She'd sleep there if I'd let her." But he still wasn't looking at her.

"Then what are you so worried about?"

He did look at her then, a sideways glance of annoyance. "It can wait."

"If something's wrong with Grace –"

"God, this intuition thing can be such a pain in the ass," he muttered. When she started to argue, he glowered at her. "I said it can wait. You've got enough with Piper leaving today. I'm trying to be sensitive here."

"Oh. I see." To her amazement, she felt the corners of her mouth twitch, and a laugh bubble up. She set it free, then laughed again when his frown grew darker still. "Come on, Martin, you can't blame me for not catching on. When have you ever worried about being sensitive before?"

"A guy can try."

He looked gruff and embarrassed, and Naomi felt her toes edge closer to a cliff she'd been sneaking up on for some time now. As always, the realization sent her into nervous motion. She stood up and stretched, feeling the pull of new muscles in her neck, shoulders and arms. In the time before, the sensation would have dismayed her; she'd have headed straight for some ibuprofen and a heating pad. Now, that ache meant strength to come, a new skill learned, and she had learned to love it.

"I guess I'd better stack this. If you help me, I've got some herbal tea Verity gave me chilling in a jar, down in the lake."

"Herbal tea from Verity? That could be dangerous." Martin stood up and started helping her stack. "Does it have mind-altering properties?"

"Just a blend for relaxation and calming, she said." Naomi frowned, considering. "Guess if we start seeing angels, we'll know she lied."

"Any cookies to go along with it?"

A smile lifted her mouth again, and this time, her heart. Martin might be blunt, plainspoken to a fault, and sparing with his compliments, but he was forever angling for her cookies, and his praise of them was extravagant. It stroked her ego and satisfied her nurturing soul. Small moments of joy. Breath by breath. This was how to survive now.

They worked until the newly split wood was stacked, and then took a break to sit side-by-side in the Adirondack chairs Naomi had set up under a huge old cottonwood tree. Naomi produced the promised tea and the gingersnap cookies she'd baked yesterday with mixed intentions, half-planning to send them with Piper, half-planning to eat them all herself in an orgy of self-indulgent self-pity. This option was better. She'd splurged and traded for some of the spelt flour Ignacio had just started harvesting and grinding, and the result was delicious. She closed her eyes and leaned her head back, listening to Martin hum appreciatively as he munched, enjoying the peace of the summer morning.

With her eyes closed, she could *feel* Piper, her bright and burning girl, there in her chest. Hades pressed against her leg and laid his big head in her lap. She curved an arm around him, using the comfort he gave her to send a pulse of love and apology along the connection between her and Piper. Experimentation over the last couple of months had taught them that Piper might not get the message right away, at that exact moment, but it would be there waiting for her when she chose to focus on the bond. It wasn't the goodbye Naomi should have given her, but it was better than nothing.

A rustle overhead, followed by a series of low, chuckling notes, made her open her eyes. The raven she called Loki perched on a branch just a few feet above them, glossy black feathers sleek and handsome. He cocked his head inquisitively at her, eyes darting to the last cookie on the plate. She picked it up, broke it into pieces, and stood. "I'll share. But it'll cost you."

She reached up, and felt a thrill when he took a chunk of cookie without hesitation. It had taken her weeks to get him to take food from her hand. She fed him several more pieces, then withheld the last. "Your mission, should you choose to accept it, is to keep tabs on Piper." She focused on Piper, on her bright hair and way of moving, on the sound of her voice and the lilt of her laughter, then offered the impressions to Loki and imagined him watching her daughter. Loki ruffled his feathers, head tilting from side to side in interest. As always, she could *feel* his intelligence and curiosity, could sense the surprisingly sophisticated structure of his mind. "Just report back to me from time to time. I'd really appreciate it."

"Do you really think he can understand what you're saying?"

Martin's voice startled the young raven. Loki launched off the branch with an irritated "Kraa!" and flapped away, flying low over the lake and disappearing into the trees on the far ridge. Naomi watched him go, then sat back down. "No, I don't think he understands my words. But he may understand my intent." She smiled wryly. "Not that it'll do much good. Even if he did follow Piper and keep an eye on her, I don't speak raven."

She changed the subject. "So, I'm pretty sure you had something other than 'teach a crazy woman to chop wood then listen to her cry' on your to-do list this morning. What am I taking you away from?"

Martin shrugged, and she detected frustration in the movement. "Not much. Thomas and I need to talk. He wants to increase our perimeter security, and I don't think there's any way to do that. Not here, anyway. The area is too wide-open, and there aren't enough of us to pull off the patrolled boundaries he has in mind."

"He's still angry about Piper and her group walking in and taking control."

"Yeah, he is. We're more prepared for that scenario now, but he still thinks we could mount a defense against a larger hostile force, and I think it's dangerous to think that way. Our best chance is to clear out if we're faced with superior numbers and fire power. We need bolt holes, places we can shelter and hide until the danger passes. Thomas and I need to reach a meeting of the minds on it so we can have a community meeting and give folks instructions."

"Hmm." A frown creased the skin of her forehead. "We've lost so much. It's understandable folks would want to stand and fight, defend what little we have left."

"Understandable, but stupid. It's not worth it to die defending things that can be replaced. Food and shelter are important, but people are irreplaceable."

"I agree." She raised a stern eyebrow. "But telling people they're stupid isn't a good way to get them to listen to you or to do what you want."

Martin made an impatient sound. "Sugar-coating it wastes time. I say it like I see it. You know that."

"I do. That's why you should let me do the talking when the time comes. You and Thomas get your ducks in a row, and I'll talk at the community meeting, let people know what the recommendations are. They need to know we understand, and that the choice will ultimately rest with them whether to hide or stand and fight, but we can't take care of each other if we're all dead."

Martin's lips lifted. "You're plenty blunt yourself, in case you didn't notice."

"You've rubbed off." It felt so good, to focus outside herself and her heartache over Piper. "Do you know how Rowan's doing with Quinn and that medicinal herb garden? Or where Alder's at with his solar panel project?"

They talked for the better part of an hour, discussing ideas and problem-solving. Now that people were starting to come to grips with the fact that life would never return to the way they had known it, it was time to look to the future, time to think beyond basic survival. People all over the community were starting to buzz with excitement over the projects that were taking shape, and the collective energy that was beginning to build was one of innovation, determination and hope. These people would probably never see another open gas station, but how could they adapt vehicles to run on alternative fuel? Before the plague, the green movement had been thriving in Colorado. Many homes in the city already had solar panels installed, and Alder was determined to salvage and install panels on every occupied home before snow fell again. And the world-wide-web might not be resurrected in their lifetimes, but how could they collect, organize and preserve the knowledge they were already in possession of?

Grace and Anne were knee-deep in the latter project, working together every day to gather books from the community, add them to the library's collection and catalog them. Alder had installed a solar panel array to run the lights and a single computer at the library, but Anne was also creating a physical card catalog to back up the digital files. Some of the older teens were helping with the project, though Naomi had heard rumblings of problems there. Grace shared her father's predilection for straight-talk and had very little patience with the giggling frivolity of the other teenage girls, especially the ones who persisted in casting Bambi-eyes in Quinn's direction.

Thoughts of Grace and Quinn made her slip a sideways glance at Martin, wondering at his earlier disquiet. Had he started to suspect that the solemn-eyed baby girl with Quinn was Grace's daughter? As always, the secret weighed heavily on her heart. Not for the first time, she regretted promising Grace she'd keep it.

Since the Woodland Park survivors had split between Carroll Lakes and Ignacio's group on Turkey Creek, weeks could go by without the whole community coming together. Even at the larger gatherings, Quinn was adept at avoiding Grace, and, therefore, Martin. It was possible Martin hadn't gotten a clear look at the baby, who resembled Grace to a startling degree. But what if he had? If he asked her straight out, Naomi had decided, she would tell him the truth. He would be furious, Grace would be furious, but Naomi would not lie, and not just because Martin would *know*. That baby was his granddaughter. He had a right to be a part of her life.

Naomi had watched Quinn from a distance, little Lark perched in the crook of his arm, shadowed by the young tweens who had arrived with Piper's group – Elise's twins, Sam and Beck. Like Grace and Quinn, Elise's children had seen things children shouldn't see on their journey here. If Piper hadn't told Naomi that Beck was a girl – Becca – she wouldn't have guessed. The three had become inseparable, and didn't mingle with the Woodland Park kids. Naomi wished there was a way to reconcile the tension between the two groups, but she suspected only time and experience would resolve the situation. The kids here had lost loved ones, had suffered the loss of the life they knew, but the kids from the outside had experienced the violence and depravity of a world in transition. Quinn and Grace, Sam and Beck, would be forever marked by what they had seen and survived.

Martin gave a mighty stretch, then looked over at Naomi. "Why so quiet all of a sudden?"

She blocked the guilt that wanted to rise – too easy to detect in these times, and she didn't want to explain herself. "Long night. Tired."

"Naomi." He waited until she looked over at him. "People are looking to you to take Jack's place. You know that."

Naomi rolled her eyes. "They should be looking to you. You had command experience in the Marines. The only thing I ever led was a PTA meeting."

"You can trot that self-effacing shit out all day long, it's not going to change anything. Résumes and past experience don't mean squat. People are starting to trust what they *feel*, more and more, and this community's instincts are pointing at you."

He was right, and she didn't need him to tell her this. Nor did she want to talk about it. Not today. They sat in silence for long moments, listening to the wind build into small gusts, watching birds flit about the business of a summer day, ripe and in full bloom. Then Martin slapped his thighs and stood up. He held his hand out to her.

"What do you say we go get drunk?"

She snorted and swatted at his hand, squinting up at the sun. "Get drunk! It's not even noon!"

"Total breakdown of society, Naomi. Those rules no longer apply."

She gazed up at him, at his outstretched hand. Then she stood up and took his hand, knowing it put her toes on the edge of that cliff. Exhilarating. Terrifying. "I've never been drunk."

Surprising Martin was a rare thing, but she'd managed it. "You're shittin' me."

"Nope. Not unless 'tipsy' counts."

"It certainly does not. You are way overdue, then. Rite of passage." He laced his fingers through hers and squeezed. "And I happen to know where a bottle of whiskey is that has your name on it."

Naomi wrinkled her nose. Whiskey. Probably pretty different from the white wine she had occasionally enjoyed in the time before. "I thought Rowan confiscated all the alcohol for her tinctures."

"She thinks she did. What she doesn't know, and all that." He gazed down at her, then tugged her a little closer. "Are you going to faint again if I tell you I plan to kiss you one of these days, sooner rather than later?"

Naomi's heart gave a great and painful lurch. "I'm not sure. Probably not before. Maybe after."

"Hmm. That could work in my favor. C'mon." He pulled her along, moving towards her cabin door. "You can settle the animals, then –"

He broke off. His head snapped around, scanning the skies, his forehead creasing in concentration. "What the hell?"

She heard it, too – a deep, steady "thump-thump-thump" she hadn't heard in over a year. The sound seemed to be coming from everywhere. She and Martin stepped farther into the clearing by the cabin, turning in circles with their heads tipped to the sky.

The helicopter seemed to explode from behind a ridge, the heavy throb of the rotors a surreal battery against their ears. It was flying low, coming at them fast. Martin shoved Naomi to the ground, crowding her against the cabin wall. She reached out and snagged Hades around the neck, yanking him to her side. Martin watched until the helicopter was almost on top of them, then spun around, covering his face with his arms, shielding Naomi's body with his. It flew close overhead, buffeting them with air, dirt and noise.

When it had passed, Naomi staggered to her feet. They stood together in the clearing by her cabin, watching the helicopter continue north, then swing in a wide arc and head due east. Not until it was no longer visible did Naomi find her voice.

"My God! Where do you think it came from?"

Martin's face, so young a moment ago, so old now, remained tipped to the sky as he answered. "Fort Carson, I'd bet. It was a Black Hawk." He spared her a bleak glance.

"That whiskey's going to have to wait, honey. We need to get everyone together. This changes everything."

TWO
Grace: Woodland Park, CO

By the time her father arrived at the library, Grace had coaxed Anne out from under the reference desk, but the older woman wasn't yet coherent. The helicopter had flown over Woodland Park several times, sweeping over the town in a way that suggested a search pattern. Grace had run outside as soon as she realized what she was hearing. Once, the Black Hawk had passed over so low, she'd been able to see the pilot and co-pilot, their eyes hidden behind aviator sunglasses, as well as the shadowy forms of two crew members behind them. Every instinct had told her to hide, and it had taken all the nerve she possessed to stand her ground, but she needed information. Giving in to her fear wouldn't serve.

Anne had tried to follow her outside, but her terror had been too great. When the helicopter swung to the north and faded out of hearing, Grace re-entered the library to find Anne weeping and rocking, hands over her ears, huddled under the desk while Persephone danced in anxious half-circles around her. Grace knew Anne had suffered a terrible experience on Fort Carson – her dad was certain "Anne" wasn't her real name – and the sound of that helicopter must have brought it all back. Grace found a bulky sweater hanging on a hook in the tiny kitchen area – it had probably been there since the librarian who owned it died in the plague - and wrapped Anne in it. She had just managed to get her to take a few sips of water from a coffee mug when her father walked in with Naomi on his heels.

His sharp eyes assessed and analyzed. "She okay?"

"Not really." Grace moved aside so Naomi could take her place. Anne leaned into Naomi's embrace, shuddering and shaking, trying to gulp out words. Naomi rubbed her back and just listened, doing what she was so good at, doling out comfort and reassurance. Persephone climbed into Naomi's lap, licking her chin once in greeting before turning her attention back to Anne. The little dog had an infallible instinct for the person with the greatest need; between her and Naomi's warm mothering, Anne would be set right. Grace pretty much sucked at anything maternal-ish, so she left them to it and moved to join her dad.

"It was a Black Hawk, wasn't it?"

"Yes." His forehead was creased with concern. "I don't know that much about them, but I didn't see any external fuel tanks. If I'm remembering correctly, their range is about 300 miles…"

"320 nautical miles, depending on payload." Grace gestured for her father to follow her to a nearby table where her pet project was organized. "It has a combat radius of 368 miles, and can carry from eleven to fourteen fully equipped combat soldiers – sources vary on that – or twenty lightly-armed personnel."

She looked up to find her father gazing at her with an expression she saw too often on his face these days: a mixture of anxiety and pride. "What?"

"Nautical miles?"

"Equivalent to 1.15 miles. It's an ancient measurement, actually –"

"I know what a nautical mile is." He looked down at the stacks of books and papers, then picked up a yellow legal pad and started to flip through her notes. "What I wonder is why you know."

Grace clenched her hands into fists to keep from snatching the notes away from him. She hated it when people touched her stacks. They might look disorganized, but she had a system and knew where everything was. The papers and books were part of a physical matrix that fed and supported her mental one. Shifting even a single paper disrupted both systems. "I've studied what materials we have here on the helicopters that were part of the Combat Aviation Brigade on Fort Carson – mostly kids' books and archived newspaper articles." She gave up the battle and twitched the legal pad out of her dad's hands, flipping to the correct page before returning it to its proper orientation. "It was logical to assume the gang would eventually try to get them in the air."

Again, with the anxiety and pride. "Logical," her dad agreed. He stuck his hands in his pockets and nodded at her project. "There's more than information on helicopters here. What is all this?"

"Projections. Predictions." Grace shrugged. "Guesses, really, based on what I've studied of military strategy, what I know of the gang, calculations on when they would run low on resources in the city and begin to look farther afield."

"And how does the helicopter we just saw impact your calculations?"

"They're running a little behind what I thought they would be, but it's still bad news." She paused. "Really bad news, dad."

"I know."

The front door of the library opened, and Thomas, her dad's second-in-command, hurried in. Not even a minute later, the rumble of a pair of ATV's announced the arrival of Andrea and Paul, a sister-brother duo that were heavily involved in the community's security. Rowan was moments behind them, her eyes honing in on Anne, who was still hiccupping with sobs in Naomi's arms. Last to arrive was Ignacio. He usually represented the folks that had congregated on Turkey Creek, and he had Ethan with him.

Grace nodded to herself – that was good thinking. Ethan had military experience. He had come in with Piper's group but had stayed when the rest of the group left, settling near Ignacio's ranch with his woman, Elise, and her twin children, Sam and Beck. From what Grace had heard, the twins and Quinn were besties now. The three of them were Ethan's faithful shadows which made her wonder if he had brought them with him this morning.

As always, her heart leaped up to lodge in her throat at the thought of seeing Quinn. She leaned to see around Ignacio and Ethan, hoping, dreading, but they were alone. Her heart sank in both relief and disappointment. She had also heard that Quinn was only rarely seen without Lark balanced on his hip or cradled against his chest in a baby sling. Seeing the baby would take more of her resources than she could spare right now. The arrival of that helicopter signaled a huge change for them all, and it was her job to make them see that.

They gathered around her table, and her dad spoke, skipping even his usual abrupt greeting. "We saw one Black Hawk with what looked like a crew of four. We were at Naomi's cabin – they came from the south, then circled over to the east and disappeared."

Murmurs of confirmation went around the table, and Ethan spoke. "It was probably a combination training flight and reconnaissance mission, checking us and other small communities out. The Air Force Academy is due east of here – I'm sure they, whoever 'they' are, wanted a look at that, too."

Grace nodded her agreement, but maintained her silence. She and her dad had discussed it, and it worked better if she spoke as little as possible, only answering questions directed specifically to her. Some of the adults were still struggling with the concept of an inexperienced girl providing so much of what they perceived as guidance and leadership, and Grace was the last person that could clarify for them. She provided information, data she had gathered and organized. It was up to her dad and the rest of the adults to decide what to do with that information.

Her dad nodded as well, then turned his gaze to Grace. "What can you tell us?"

Grace picked up the yellow legal pad and flipped a few pages, though she didn't need it. She had these numbers memorized. "We can't confirm exactly how many aircraft were on Fort Carson before the plague hit, but when the Combat Aviation Brigade reached full strength, it should have included around a hundred helicopters – a combination of Chinooks, Black Hawks and Apaches. The last newspaper article I could find that mentioned actual numbers was two years old. At the time, there were six of each aircraft on the post."

Grace paused, then looked up at her dad. This was hard information to deliver, harder to hear, and it helped if she pretended it was just the two of them. "Even if they never added more helicopters, even if it were just those eighteen, they could still move enough personnel into our area to outnumber us by four-to-one. Both the Black Hawks and the Apaches have a cruising speed of around 170 mph. They could take off from Fort Carson and overwhelm us in under 15 minutes. A single Apache helicopter has enough firepower to destroy both of our settlements if it's armed with Hellfire missiles and Hydra rocket launchers, not to mention the 30mm cannon. Dad, those Apaches are the most sophisticated attack helicopters ever created. They're just about indestructible. And they might have dozens of them."

Total silence met Grace's pronouncement. Long moments later, it didn't surprise Grace at all that Naomi was the first to breach the stunned hush.

"Okay." The older woman's face was lined with anxiety, white with fear, but her mouth was set in a determined line. In times like these, it was hard for Grace to reconcile the lean, no-nonsense Naomi with the soft, fluttery mother Piper had told her about. "Okay," she repeated. "Let's start at the beginning. First, are we assuming this is the gang?" She turned to look at Ethan. "Or might someone else be responsible? Brody and the men with him – are any of them pilots?"

"Tyler is a mechanic, and, if I'm not mistaken, he also had his pilot's license. At the very least, he would know the rudiments of getting a helicopter into the air. And it would surprise me if Brody didn't know at least a little about it as well." Ethan frowned. "What's less likely is that they would reveal their capabilities. Brody played his cards tight, and he always tended towards the covert. This doesn't feel like something he would do."

Andrea spoke. "Could it be help from the outside? You know, like the National Guard or something?" Before anyone could answer, she grimaced. "Scratch that. They would have landed, spoken to us for at least a few minutes, and asked what our needs were." She looked down and swallowed hard. "It's stupid, I know, still hoping the cavalry will ride in."

"Not stupid," Grace said. "Dangerous. The people supporting the gang in Colorado Springs aren't all bad people. They're just desperate for someone to help them, which makes them easy to control."

Andrea spared her a resentful glance. "I know that." She shifted her gaze to Martin. "But why should we proceed from the assumption that they're hostile? What if we had a helicopter? Wouldn't we check things out first, too?" She looked down at the table in front of her, and though Grace didn't *feel* things as the others did, Andrea's longings were easy to read. "We're safe here. It's a waste of resources to be constantly focused on defense."

Grace pressed her mouth into a tight line and folded her hands together, squeezing until her knuckles turned white. But keeping her lips zipped didn't do much good when Andrea could so easily detect the frustration Grace had refrained from giving voice to.

The older woman glared at her. "We are safe! The people that have come from the Springs haven't caused any trouble, and we don't have enough for that gang to bother with – not enough people, and not enough resources. I'm sick of having to be suspicious of everything, all the time." She closed her eyes, her shoulders drooped, her voice dropping to a whisper. "I'm just so sick of always being afraid."

A deep silence followed Andrea's words. Grace's eyes darted around the gathered faces, where she read sympathy, understanding, agreement. Oh, this would not do at all.

She pushed to her feet. "I get that you feel that way, but here's the thing: You're not safe. None of us are. What we thought of as 'safe' in the time before doesn't exist, and it probably won't again, not in our lifetimes. Believing you're safe is the most dangerous thing I can think of, if you want to survive."

Her father flinched, and in spite of herself, she met his gaze. His dark eyes were filled with emotions that were easy to read – guilt, sorrow, pain – and when he spoke, his words were meant only for her. "I hoped that you were starting to feel more secure."

Grace didn't know what to say to make him feel better, so she told the truth. "It's a relief that this is happening, Dad. I knew it would, and waiting for the other shoe to drop was nerve-wracking. There's no such thing as 'security.' This community and everything we've built could be destroyed in a matter of hours. The majority of us would likely die in an attack, and those of us that didn't die..." She swallowed. "There are worse things than dead."

"I hate that you know that."

"I know." They might have been alone in the room. "But I do, and I can't pretend that I don't."

"I should have kept you safe. It's a father's job to protect his daughter." Before she could protest the impossibility of that belief, he pulled out his mind-reading trick and answered her. "I don't really care that it might not have been possible for me to keep you safe, even if I'd been with you right after the plague. Calling it 'impossible' doesn't change how I feel."

He swallowed the rest of what she suspected he wanted to say, out of respect for her privacy. Almost everyone knew Grace had been through something, but very few knew exactly what. And even her father didn't know all of it.

"I'm sorry." She dropped her gaze. She didn't know how to comfort him. She really did suck at this stuff. So she took refuge in what she was good at. She focused on the group one at a time and delivered her data.

"If my predictions are correct, the gang will invade in eight to twelve weeks. They'll let us do the work of summer – growing crops, putting by provisions for the winter – then they'll come in sufficient numbers to take it all, supplies and any people they have use for." She couldn't maintain eye contact any longer, flipping through her notes to hide her gaze. "Women and female children, especially. They might offer a place to people who want to work for them, but it's more likely they'll just massacre the rest of us – no chance of bothersome retaliation or rescue attempts that way."

During the silence that followed, she looked around, reading reactions as best she could and noting the people who were still making eye contact with her, especially Ethan, who was nodding. He spoke when her eyes met his.

"I agree with Grace's assessment. One of the first rules of survival is to defend what you have. You have to prepare for the fact that someone else is planning to take advantage of your planning. They know we're here, they know you survived the last winter, they know we're busy getting ready for the next one. With a group our size, they'll infiltrate with spies, if they haven't already. They'll know just how to hit us when they do, the locations of our stockpiles, and what our defenses are."

"I don't agree! Why are we listening to a traumatized little girl, anyway? Of course she thinks everyone in the outside world is hostile – everyone knows she was –" Andrea bit off her own angry outburst, her face twitching with the effort of controlling herself. Then, she simply slumped forward on the table, hid her face in her crossed arms, and began to cry quietly. Her brother's face was almost comical with alarm as he scooted his chair closer to her and began to pat her back awkwardly.

Her father had leaned forward protectively as soon as Andrea started in on Grace, and he leaned back slowly, taking deep breaths. Grace recognized the expression on his face; he had a handle on himself, but just barely. Andrea's outburst had further eroded the stability of the group's dynamic. Not for the first time, Grace wondered if the increased intuitive *knowing* was an evolution or a step backwards for humanity. And also not for the first time, she was grateful it hadn't happened to her. How did people even think, with all that emotional garbage going on?

Back in control of himself, her dad picked up the ball. "It's pretty obvious we need to hope for the best but prepare for the worst." He looked at Grace. "Do your predictions include recommendations?"

Grace nodded, but had to push past dread to speak. No one was going to like hearing what she had to say. "We need to leave."

Her voice sounded tentative, even to her, so she tried again. "We need to leave," she repeated, with conviction this time, "Relocate. As far away from any major metropolitan area as we can get."

This time, instead of silence, her pronouncement was met with a soft, despairing, collective sigh. With the exception of her father and Ethan, every person around the table seemed to shrink into themselves, and Naomi's face was pale with shock.

"Leave? You mean for good? Forever?" Her voice was a thread of sound. "Leave our homes, and our dead, their graves? Gracie, there has to be another way."

Grace reached across the table, tapping a stack of books on disaster preparation. The top two were from Naomi's private library. "You gave me these books," she said softly. "They were your husband's, and you said you'd read them." She held Naomi's gaze. "You know what they say. Survivors should join with like-minded people and get as far away from large cities as possible. It's why Jack and the others planned their route the way they did – to avoid populous areas."

Naomi's eyes flickered to Martin. "But what if we hide, when they come? Your dad and I were just talking about this." She leaned forward, her expression shifting from stricken to determined. "We create bolt holes where we can hide on a moment's notice. We cache food and supplies in secret locations, so we can survive while we rebuild, if they do raid us. Why couldn't that work?" Her gaze shifted to Ignacio, who nodded at her. "That could work."

Grace looked down and trapped the words she wanted to say behind tight lips. She had the deepest respect for Naomi, and she wouldn't shred her argument, not in front of all these people. She was profoundly grateful when Ethan gave the answer she didn't want to voice.

"Naomi, I'm sorry to say I just don't think that'll work. Ya'll have been lucky here. The geography has protected you from being overrun, but it won't last. Even if they didn't have the helicopters, they would come. They'd find a way to open the pass, or stage a larger invasion from Rampart Range Road. As the crow flies, we're less than 20 miles away from them. It's just not far enough."

With the sensitivity he was becoming known for, even among their newly sensitized community, Ethan zeroed in on Ignacio and Andrea, whose faces were set in lines that mirrored Naomi's determination. "You have to understand the mindset. They're not builders. They don't innovate or create, and they certainly don't cooperate with outsiders. They take, control, and use. What they don't need, they destroy. It's all they know."

Under the pressure of his gaze, Andrea's face twisted, and her tears broke free. She gazed back at him, her voice jerking with angry, hiccupping sobs. "Then what's to stop them from finding us after we move? Do we run forever? Do we just become nomads? When do we take a stand and defend our homes?" Her eyes shifted to her brother. Paul's face was rigid, but his eyes mirrored her grief. "Our people helped found this town, over a hundred years ago. We've been here for generations. This is our place, where our roots sink deep. I'd rather die defending it than abandon it."

Her despair was so potent that it touched even Grace, and the effect it had on the others in the room made the polarities obvious. Naomi and Thomas were nodding their agreement. Ignacio reached across the table to pat Andrea's hand, clucking and shushing as he would with one of his horses, and Paul reached to hold her other hand.

By contrast, Ethan, Rowan and Anne were making troubled eye contact and shifting in their seats. Her father was glaring at the table top, but he looked up at her when he felt her gaze. She saw in his eyes the same knowledge that had brought her to this recommendation and knew he agreed with her. His next words, though, surprised her.

"I grew up military, and spent most of my adult life deployed, or stationed somewhere I didn't have a lot of choice about. I don't have the kind of roots you're talking about, Andrea, and I don't think Ethan does either." He glanced at Ethan, who nodded confirmation. "We all need some time to think through the ramifications before we come to any kind of a decision. In the meantime –"

Thomas' angry voice cut him off. "There's nothing to think about. If people want to stay, they stay. If they want to run, they run. Simple."

Martin's eyes narrowed, and he drew a deep breath in through his nose. His jaw tightened, but again, he surprised Grace with his moderate tone. "It's not simple, and that kind of aggressive attitude doesn't help. Take some time to think it through before you –"

"Don't tell me what to do!" Thomas' chair screeched on the floor as he shoved back from the table, obviously ready to stand and storm out. "And you can damn sure stop telling me what to think!" His eyes cut around the circle. "We've got a choice to make. Either we run and hide with our tails tucked between our legs, or we make a stand. We may lose some people, but if we fight back hard enough, they'll decide we're not worth it and move on to easier prey. They're bullies, pure and simple. You stand up to a bully, they back down. That's the way the world works."

"But they're not bullies. You're not analyzing the situation correctly." Grace's voice shook. This was a catastrophe. Without Naomi and Ignacio's buy-in, the community would stay put, and they would be slaughtered. She was certain of it. All eyes swung to her, and she pressed on. "Bullies are about bravado. The leaders of the gang – they're predators. They're trained killers, all of them. Like Ethan said, they don't know anything but 'us and them.' They only understand cooperation as it benefits them, and their idea of community is extremely limited. It's like that kids' movie, with the ants and the grasshoppers..."

She broke off and looked down. What a stupid example, serving only to remind everyone how young she was. Her heart was pounding with anxiety, and she really thought she might throw up. She made herself look up, viewing the group through prisms of tears. "Please listen. Please. They'll come, and they will show no mercy. We're a different species to them. They learned to disassociate so they could go to war, or so they could survive their childhoods, or whatever. They don't think of us as people. They don't think of their own supporters as people. They call them 'sheep' and they know just how to control them."

A mocking voice echoed up out of her memory, and she flinched, swallowing the burn of bile in the back of her throat. "'Feed 'em and fuck 'em.' That's what they do," she whispered, staring at the table, seeing leaping flames and contorted faces. "They control by giving with one hand and beating with the other. They protect and provide during the day, then spend their nights raping and killing, where everyone can see. They make sure everyone can see." Her eyes met Thomas'. He was staring at her, horrified and fascinated. "They create and feed off fear, but they don't feel it. They're not bullies. They're subhuman. The world doesn't work the way you want it to. Not anymore."

She left then, walked away from the stunned silence, so grateful she couldn't *feel* their pity. Her dad started to rise to go with her, but she waved him back. She needed some time alone to find steady ground, and they needed to argue this out. She had said everything she could say, and she was sure her continued presence would be a hindrance rather than a help. And while she could hardly stand to imagine what would happen if they decided to stay, their decision wouldn't affect her own long term plans. Nothing could alter those.

Heading for the door, she whistled softly between her teeth, and Persephone shot to her side. Grace held her arms out and the little dog leaped without hesitation. Cradling the dog's sturdy warmth close, Grace pushed through the library doors and stepped into the midday sunshine.

A crowd had gathered, which wasn't surprising. People were clustered in groups of five or six, hands flying in excited, agitated gestures as they talked among themselves. Grace spotted the tight cluster of Woodland Park kids and ducked her head, veering in the opposite direction. No love lost there, and at least on Grace's part, no desire to change that. She buried her nose in Persephone's soft, musky fur and wove through the crowd, keeping her eyes down. On the edge of the crowd, nearly home-free, a pair of familiar boots made her freeze mid-stride.

Her eyes snapped up. Quinn was as frozen as she was, staring. Lark was drowsing against his shoulder, and oh, how she'd grown. Before, the baby had made Grace think of Benji, but she had changed. She might have come to life straight from Grace's baby book, so much did she resemble her mother. Lark's sleepy eyes blinked, then slid her way as Grace watched. The impact of her dark eyes stole what little breath Grace had left. Such ancient eyes, so sad. So knowing. Those eyes saw straight into Grace's heart and knew all. Knew her. Lark lifted a chubby arm and stretched it towards Grace, her fingers splayed like a tiny, yearning starfish.

Grace's head went light. She stumbled back a step, then two, and bumped into someone. The contact broke the connection between her and Lark, and Grace looked up, ready to murmur an apology and get the hell out of here. Seeing her father's face made the world spin.

Her dad steadied her, though his eyes were locked on Lark. In his face, Grace saw not shock, not surprise, but longing. He gazed at the baby for long, long moments, then looked down at his daughter. Grace's face felt numb, and she realized she hadn't taken a breath since she first locked eyes with Quinn. She sucked in a huge lungful of air, then another, but it was too late.

Too late. The words echoed through her head as woozy black narrowed her vision to a pinpoint.

Too late. He knew.

Dimly, she heard her father's voice calling her name, but her legs folded and the black became complete.

THREE
Piper: On the eastern plains of Colorado

"Jumpin' Jack flash, it's a gas, gas, gas..."

Piper segued into a through-the-teeth whistle for the guitar riff that followed, bopping her head along with the beat as she set out the supplies they would need for dinner. Behind her, Jack made a sound halfway between a laugh and a huff, and she allowed herself a brief, smug smile. When she turned to look at him, though, her face was a perfect mask of innocent neutrality. "Did you say something?"

"Nope." Jack's face, too, was inscrutably neutral, though there was a light in his eyes that could have been either irritation or amusement.

Interesting, either way.

Beside him, Ed was grinning, and even Owen had a little smile playing about his lips. She'd been at this all day, singing snippets of songs featuring the name "Jack." It would appear all three of them had caught on, though Jack had yet to rise to the bait. A worthy foe.

Jack gestured to the food she was setting out. "Are we eating dinner cold, or do we want a fire?"

Piper looked around, scanning the evening sky before turning back to her task and answering his question. "Let's stick with cold food. I know we haven't seen anyone all day, but I'd rather not chance a fire. Not until we get a better feel for being on the road."

"Works for me. I'll help with something else, then, since I'm on fire detail. But first, I've gotta see a man about a horse."

Piper suppressed a grimace while he disappeared around the edge of the hill they were camped on. Announcing bathroom breaks was just one of many safety practices they had been taught to implement, and it never failed to make her uncomfortable. Privacy was a luxury she had been denied completely during her time with Brody, and letting three men know when she had to tinkle made too many feelings stir in the depths, feelings she didn't want or need to think about.

Ed, too, scanned the skies. "Looks like it's going to be a clear and quiet night. I'll get the sleeping bags and pads out, but we'll skip the tents."

With Rosemary trotting at his heels, he went to get the job done. At the base of the hill, Owen moved from bike to bike, checking tire pressure, oil and fuel levels, going about his duties in characteristic silence. They all had tasks to complete, some of which would rotate – Piper had KP duty today, but tomorrow Jack would take over - and some of which were permanent assignments, based on each person's experience and aptitude. Owen had the most mechanical knowledge, so he would maintain the motorcycles. Ed had been a gardener and carried a book Anne had grudgingly given him on foraging for edible plants. He was learning to watch for flora they could augment their supplies with. Jack had declared himself "talentless unless it's time to sing Kumbaya," but had learned to dig a Dakota fire hole with admirable speed and skill.

Piper had the medical training she'd learned from Ruth, and though she wasn't as supernaturally accurate as her mother, she was a superb shot. She'd be ready, when her skills were needed, in whatever capacity. She didn't consider it a weakness to hope that she'd have little call for the former, and if called upon for the latter, she'd be aiming at game, rather than at a human.

The echo of a man's sobbing voice, begging for mercy, floated up out of the depths. She swatted the memory away as she would ward off a persistent hornet – with annoyance and just a touch of fear – and focused on assembling their dinner. She loaded plates for all of them with boiled eggs, apples and sliced, fresh vegetables from Verity's ridiculously abundant garden. Then she repacked the food they weren't eating in the saddle bags on the motorcycles. Constant readiness to leave was another on-the-road safety rule. If they should need to abandon a campsite in a hurry, leaving supplies behind could cripple them. They had too far to go.

They were headed for Jack's hometown of Pewaukee, Wisconsin. The hope was that Jack's sister, Caroline – Cara, as he called her when he forgot to be stuffy and formal – would have returned to familiar ground in the wake of the plague. He also needed to confirm whether his parents were alive or dead, though he was as sure they were gone as he was convinced his sister was alive. Piper didn't question his certainty; not only did she have the same kind of connection with her mother, but she could *see* the bond-line connecting Jack and his younger sister, a thin but vibrant green arrow pointing them unerringly to the northeast. It was the only bond-line Jack had left, other than the vibrant, opalescent one connecting him to Piper.

That one, she preferred not to think about. So she stuffed it down with all the other things she preferred not to think about these days and occupied her mind with finding another "Jack" song to poke at him with. There was a method to her childishness. You could learn a great deal about a person by watching how they dealt with irritation, and the better they all understood each other, the better they would work together when they ran into trouble. That they would run into trouble was certain; Piper had lived it, and Jack dreamed of it, almost constantly these days.

Between the two of them, the nightmares were relentless. Jack had been the first to broach the subject when Martin had been drilling into them the necessity of adequate sleep. Jack didn't know if he talked or called out, he had said, but he suspected he did. Martin had nodded, then had turned to look at Piper, a single eyebrow raised in expectation. Apparently, Naomi had been tattling.

"Okay, fine. Yes, I have nightmares, too." Martin's other eyebrow had joined the first, and she had scowled.

"And my mom says I talk. Sometimes I scream. What do you want me to do about it?"

"I want you to be smart. In the military you're trained to go without sleep, but none of you have had that training. Nothing is worse than trying to run wired and tired all the time. You get stupid, and stupid will kill you faster than your worst enemy ever could." His eyes had flicked between them. "Check in with each other, every morning. If you didn't get enough sleep, say so. If you think the other one's lying about it, say so."

At that point his eyes had locked on Piper. "Don't try to tough it out, and don't worry about being the 'weak link' just because you're the only woman. You've got nothing to prove, Piper. Ethan will tell you the same thing. If any one of you can't carry your part of the load, it's better to be honest about it rather than dropping it out of exhaustion."

Martin and Ethan had helped them prepare for the 1,000 mile trip, and between the two of them, Piper couldn't imagine a single disastrous scenario that hadn't been anticipated and planned for. In addition to the supplies they had packed in the saddle bags on the bikes, they all carried backpacks with emergency food and water, along with survival gear and additional weapons. Rather than extra fuel, they carried fuel treatment and filters, as well as hand-pump siphon tubes for salvaging gas from abandoned vehicles. They were hoping to make it as far as possible on the motorcycles, but Ethan believed they were at the outer limits of finding usable fuel. It had been over a year since the plague, and even fuel stored under ideal conditions had degraded. The filters and fuel treatment could only do so much, he had cautioned. Besides, as they headed into more populous areas, the noise of the bikes might attract attention they didn't want. It was possible they would be on foot by the time they reached Pewaukee.

With any luck, they would find Cara there and convince her to return with them to Colorado before snow flew again. Piper seriously doubted it would be that easy, but it was as good a place as any to start. According to Jack, Cara's last known address was Saugatuck, Michigan, an artsy resort town on the Lake Michigan shore, but she had moved around a lot. Once they got closer, she was hoping Jack's bond-line would serve as a guide. Between here and there, however, there was a lot of ground to cover.

For tonight, they were camped a few miles outside of Limon, just as they'd planned. Rather than risk the congested Highway 24 and subsequently the city, they had headed west and south out of Woodland Park, swinging through burned-out Cripple Creek, then Victor. Twice, they saw smoke rising from homes, but they didn't stop. From Victor, they had curved and crept their way down Phantom Canyon Road to Highway 50, then east to Penrose. From there, they had scooted across the southern edge of Fort Carson, traveling off-road at times in order to stay well north of Pueblo, and had zigzagged north-east on country roads, ghosting by the tiny plains towns of Hanover, Truckton, and Rush.

They had seen more smoke here and there, and had all sensed eyes on them more than once, but, still, they did not stop. Establishing contact with other people wasn't their primary objective at this point, not until they were on their way back home. Avoiding others, both Martin and Ethan had emphasized, was one of the most important safety precautions they could take. In times like these, people were trouble.

The only planned exception was a stop in Limon. Grace and Quinn had grown up in the small, close-knit ranching community, and Martin had lived there during the years he'd been married to Grace's mother. Grace and Quinn had experienced some trouble right after the plague, a run-in with a father-son duo, but everyone involved felt this stop was worth the risk.

Limon wasn't ideal, in terms of distance from Colorado Springs or Denver, but if there was a community here, they might prove to be valuable allies. A hub for travelers in the time before, Limon sat at the crossroads of Interstate 70, U.S. Highways 24, 40 and 287, and State Highways 71 and 86. The survivors living there might have useful information for travelers. With Martin, Grace and Quinn's names as entrée, they hoped to make contact.

If they judged the situation and the people they met to be trustworthy, they would encourage them to connect with the people they'd left behind in Woodland Park. Piper had been taking meticulous notes in an atlas she'd brought for the sole purpose of marking human habitation. If the people in Limon wanted to send runners, she'd have information on safe passage for them. Maybe they would stay a few days, and she'd have a chance to add to the record of events she'd originally started so long ago, before Noah's death, before Brody. Hopefully, someone somewhere else was doing the same thing, and eventually mankind would be able to patch together a record of what had happened in these dark times.

Owen was the first to join her, sitting down on the camp stool next to her and stretching out his legs with a sigh. There was a stillness about Owen that Piper found restful. For all his intimidating size and obvious physical power, he carried about him an aura of gentleness, and he was one of the few men she was completely comfortable around. Piper handed him a plate, and he thanked her quietly before beginning to eat. Ed was a few minutes behind him. As he sat, he made a shooing motion at Rosemary.

"Go on, girl. Go rustle up your own grub. There are rabbits all over the place."

The dog was off like a shot, zipping into the tall grass that hadn't been flattened by their activities. Piper handed Ed his plate, and he, too, began to eat. Piper waited for Jack, too thoroughly trained by her mother to start eating before everyone was "at the table." Around them, the huge bowl of prairie sky was deepening to blues and purples as the sun approached the horizon. Piper gazed towards the west, where she could still see the mountains of home, craggy and dark and familiar. Sometime in the next couple of days, if all went as planned, she would turn around and no longer be able to see them. The thought brought with it both exhilaration and sorrow.

A rustle behind her announced Jack's return. He sat down on the last camp stool and accepted the plate Piper handed him with a cheerful thank-you. Then, he bent his head and closed his eyes in silent prayer. He'd done the same thing at lunch. Piper waited until he lifted his head and began sorting through the selection on his plate.

"That's still important to you? Saying grace?"

The corner of Jack's mouth twitched up, a wry half-smile. "It's important to me now."

"It wasn't before?" Piper might never sit in a classroom again, but she'd be a sociology student for the rest of her days. People had always fascinated her, the choices they made, the beliefs they embraced and decided to defend. She had never been close to someone who had chosen a religiously-centered life before. Jack didn't seem to mind her endless questions, so she kept right on asking them. Besides, it limited their relationship to a form she was comfortable with: Piper as scientist, Jack as bug.

Owen finished his food and handed his empty plate to Piper, nodding politely. Then, he returned to the bikes. Ed, too, finished eating and handed over his plate. He left Piper and Jack to their conversation, stretching out on his sleeping bag and tipping his hat over his face. He had first watch, so getting a nap was a smart move. Piper bit into one of her eggs as Jack answered her question.

"Before the plague, it was a habit, something I didn't think much about. I grew up in a religious home, and we always said grace." He took a bite of crunchy red pepper and made a sound of appreciation. "This is from Verity's garden, isn't it? I can always tell. Vegetables and angels. Such a weird combo to excel at." Then, he went on. "After the plague, I stopped praying at all. No grace, no daily devotions. Nothing."

Piper waited to see if he would continue. When he didn't, she probed. "Why? Were you angry at God?"

"Of course. Everybody was angry at God then. A lot of people still are. But I've been angry at God before. That wasn't why I stopped praying." His voice and manner were easy. Peaceful. This was something he'd come to grips with and settled in his mind. "I stopped praying because for the first time in my life, I didn't want to stop sinning."

When it was clear he didn't intend to go on, Piper prodded again. "Care to elaborate on that?"

"Nope." There was no rancor or defensiveness in the single word, nor in his demeanor. But his eyes flickered to Owen, and she knew with certainty that she would not be allowed to cross the line he'd just drawn.

She hadn't known Jack well before, but both her mother and Martin had commented on how much he had changed – a "kinder, gentler Jack," as Naomi put it. The Jack Piper was getting to know was smart and compassionate, quick to see the humor in any given situation, and obviously still grieving a woman who hadn't been his own. Sooner or later, she planned to finesse that story out of him. But while grief for Layla may have broken and softened his intensity, he was still no push-over. Piper shifted tactics.

"As I understand Christian theory, you could have kept right on sinning and just asked for forgiveness. Isn't that one of the basic tenets of your religion? That people will inevitably sin but will always be forgiven as long as they believe in Jesus?"

Jack's lips twitched again, this time into a knowing smile. Obviously, he saw right through her shift to general theory gambit. "Sure, that's an accurate description of the Christian faith, in its simplest and most basic form." He pointed a crispy, raw green bean at her. "A question for you: Do simple and basic relationships satisfy you?"

It was her turn to smile at how neatly he'd turned her question. "Not really."

"Well, there's part of your answer. Another question: Do you accept less from yourself than you know you're capable of?"

That question bothered her, stirred the depths again, but his honesty required her to meet it with her own. "Sometimes," she admitted. "But never for long. Eventually, I reach a point where I have to reconcile. There's always a reckoning."

"Exactly. A point where you have to pay the piper." He blinked at her, his face so perfectly innocent, she was wildly impressed. "So to speak."

Piper grinned. "Have you been waiting all day to use that?"

"Yep."

She laughed, and crunched into her own vegetables. "Well played, Jumpin' Jack. Well played."

They ate the rest of their meal in companionable silence. When she had finished eating, Piper stood up and stretched, taking the time to work out the unfamiliar kinks brought on by hours spent on a motorcycle.

If they decided not to stay in Limon, they would ride just a little longer tomorrow, and perhaps longer the next day. Both Martin and Ethan had cautioned them against a "sprint" mentality. It wouldn't serve them to rush headlong into danger. Better to take longer and *feel* their way along, letting their intuition – a concept nobody scoffed at anymore – guide them safely. With that in mind, she walked to the top of the hill they were camped on to see if she could perceive anything about where they were headed tomorrow.

The town was a distant smudge on the prairie, a suggestion of straight lines against the soft curves of the rolling plains. She settled cross-legged on the ground and opened up her senses. She didn't see any smoke, and she was too far away to make out individual bond lines, but the little town was suffused with a glow that told her people were there, working and living together. She should have thought to grab her binoculars.

Moments later, Jack joined her, settling down beside her and handing her the binoculars she'd just been wishing for. "Can you *see* anything from here?"

She took the binoculars from him, wondering if she should be freaked out, and decided not to be for the time being. "Just a subtle light. What about you?"

"Not much, but a faint sense of community. Bonds forged in hardship. They'll have each other's backs, and they'll be suspicious of outsiders."

"Which is smart. I'll be suspicious if they welcome us with open arms." Piper lifted the binoculars and scanned the town. There, a thin trail of smoke, and another a short distance away. Probably cooking fires. "Unless they've posted warnings or we *feel* something off, we stick to the plan: Leave the bikes outside of town and walk in, let them see we're armed, but put out our best 'not a threat' vibes. As long as they don't shoot first and ask questions later, we should be okay."

"Here's hoping."

Jack leaned back on his elbows and crossed his ankles. Down at the bottom of the hill, Rosemary slid out of the tall grass bordering the camp, a limp rabbit in her jaws, and curled up next to Ed to consume it. She was almost as efficient a hunter as little Persephone, and though Ed didn't have the same depth of connection as Naomi did with her dogs – he claimed not to have any intuitive skills at all – the bond between man and dog was obvious. Owen finished whatever he'd been doing with the bikes, and like Ed, reclined on his sleeping bag to rest before his watch.

Piper nodded in their direction. "So. Ed has been open about the fact that he hasn't changed like the rest of us, but what about Owen? Any idea what's going on with him?"

Jack's face closed behind that neutral mask he was so good at slipping on. "No idea, but he probably wouldn't confide in me." He glanced at her and smiled tightly, with just a hint of razor's edge. "We've never been best buddies."

She returned the tight smile. "I'll bet not." She knew she was pushing, but couldn't think of a reason not to. "Can I ask a personal question?"

Jack eyed her for a long moment. "If I say 'no,' you'll just circle back to it later. So fire away."

"Was the baby Layla lost yours?"

She catalogued and analyzed his physical response. A sharp intake of breath through his nose. Widened eyes. Dilated pupils. And pain. All over his face and bleeding off him in waves. She was pretty sure she knew his answer before he gave it.

"No, the baby wasn't mine. Is that what people think?" He closed his eyes and held up his hand. "Never mind. Doesn't matter what people thought, of her or of me." He opened his eyes again, and this time, Piper didn't have any problem reading what he was feeling. "Too far, Piper. That was too far."

"I apologize." But was she really sorry? She honestly wasn't sure. "I could promise it won't happen again, but I can't leave a mystery alone."

"It's not a mystery. It's my private life. It's also my past." His eyes locked on hers, and for the very first time, she *felt* the power at his disposal. "Leave it alone."

His command rendered her reluctant to speak, reluctant to ask any more questions. Reluctant, but not incapable. "Holy shit," she breathed, when she was able. "So that's what people were talking about. What all can you do with that, do you know? I heard you can make people do things, but how far does it go? How long do the effects last? Can you make someone do something that's in conflict with their core values? Can you -"

"Piper. Stop." He didn't put any power behind his words this time, but the weariness in his voice made her comply. "I can appreciate your endless curiosity, I really can. I'm interested in what makes people tick, too, and the changes in humanity fascinate me. But I can't answer all your questions, and there are ones I won't answer. I have hurt others with what I can do. I hurt myself, betrayed my own core beliefs." He pinned her with his gaze again. "So unless you're ready to bare your soul about everything you've been through, unless you're ready to trade the dark truths you've learned about yourself for my ugly secrets, you need to respect the boundaries and leave it alone when I say to."

Now she was sorry, truly. The ache of remorse in the center of her chest surprised her with its intensity. The bond-line between them coalesced into what looked like a solid cylinder of white light, though she had no earthly idea why.

"I apologize," she repeated, holding his gaze. "And this time I mean it."

"Well, then, this time I accept." He looked away, and she felt him withdraw from the connection between them. It both relieved and frightened her. His voice, when he spoke, was deliberately light. "I'll make you a deal, Piper. If we find ourselves hanging upside down over a pit of lava with no way out, and no hope of survival, I'll tell all."

She responded in kind. "I appreciate your thoughtfulness, Jack. It's good to know you won't let me die curious."

He waited a few beats, then shifted them farther away from the topic. "You've got third watch?"

"Dead of night," Piper confirmed. They both knew the schedule forward and backwards, but the words helped rebuild the buffer between them. "One of the short shifts. I relieve Owen, and you relieve me, is that right?"

"Yep. I get to see the sun come up." He stood. "Speaking of, I'm going to try to settle in, get some sleep. Martin said it would be tough, the first couple of nights."

"Jack." She held up the binoculars. "How did you know I wanted these?"

He shrugged. "Just knew. Does it bother you?"

Piper looked away. "I'm not sure yet."

Jack gave her a brotherly pat on the shoulder then headed back down the hill towards their camp, whistling as he went. It took Piper a moment to recognize the tune, and when she did, she couldn't stop a crack of surprised laughter. She sang along with his cheerful whistle as she followed him down the hill.

"Little ditty, about Jack and Diane…"

FOUR
Jack: On the eastern plains of Colorado

Waves, grey and huge, rolling against a sky filled with battered black clouds. Jack felt the pitch of a boat under his feet, felt the burn of wet rope against his palms, turned to see flames, painfully bright against all the grey and black. Too close, too close, had to get farther away –

"Jack."

He sat bolt upright, holding his breath until his surging mind and darting eyes could orient him. The prairie. Near Limon. Deep in the night, the only illumination a waxing crescent moon in a sky glorious with stars.

Piper's voice again, from a few feet away. "You're okay. It was just a nightmare."

"Just a nightmare," Jack repeated hoarsely. "Just a dream." And not even a bad one. They were all unsettling, so detailed and real, but he hadn't even died in this one. He released the breath he'd been holding, and took the time to draw several more calming breaths before he spoke again. "Is it my watch?"

"Not quite – you've got 15 minutes to go. Do you think you can go back to sleep?"

"No." He unzipped his sleeping bag, checked his boots, and slid his feet into them. Ed slept on, Rosemary curled up next to him, but Owen's eyes were open, sparkling faintly in the scant moonlight. Jack stood. "I'll be right back. Then you can get some rest."

He moved well away from their camp to relieve himself, shivering as the soft but steady wind cooled the sweat on his body. Before they had embarked on this journey, he and Piper had taken an exploratory camping trip, checking out the area north of Woodland Park, the town of Deckers and the surrounding resort camping areas. In the five nights they'd been out, they had become familiar with each other's sleeping patterns, including the signs of encroaching nightmares.

It had bothered him at first, a vulnerability he wouldn't have chosen to share, but Piper's piteous whimpers had quickly relieved him of his pride. His dreams were harbingers, warnings of danger to come. He was certain of this. Piper's disquiet rose from the abuse her body and mind had suffered, from her damaged heart. She was so tough when awake, so capable and formidable. It hurt his heart to hear her secret pain.

He picked his way through the tall grass back to camp, shrugging into a jacket as Piper slipped away for a moment of privacy. When she returned, she curled up in her sleeping bag, snugging the mummy bag around her head. She didn't ask about his dream, and he wouldn't ask about hers when he had to rouse her out of it. He walked the perimeter of their camp twice, then settled down on the campstool they had set up on the rise above their sleeping area, watching over her sleep with a protectiveness he knew she would reject if her eyes were open.

He didn't understand yet what Piper was to him, or might be in the future. He had dreamed of her, had recognized her the moment their eyes met, but all that told him was that she would have significance, that she would have a role in his future. Nothing romantic or sexual had stirred between them, though a friendship was unfolding, something he very much enjoyed. They had similar senses of humor, similar interests in people and what motivated them. He enjoyed talking to her, admired her grit, and was glad to have her as one of his companions on this journey. For now, their relationship was all he wanted it to be.

Besides, given what Piper had survived, she might not ever want a romantic relationship, much less be capable of a healthy one. He didn't know all the details – he didn't think anyone did, not even Naomi – but he knew enough. Her ordeal hadn't broken her, but it had twisted her, body, mind and soul. She made him think of the troubled kids he had known, with a veneer of anger defending the deep, deep hurt. She took refuge in being strong and in control, just as Gracie hid behind her intellectual capabilities. He felt a vast tenderness for both of them.

And there was Layla, still in his heart. He sensed her sometimes, a soft brush of air, her distinctive scent, the faintest echo of her laughter. Jack glanced at Owen, wondering if she visited him, too – her lover, father of her child. He had asked Verity about it once, and she had confirmed it. Layla did visit now and again. Something left she was still "invested in," in Verity-speak. A task she wanted to see completed. Layla's visits were both comfort and torture. Most of the time, her absence was a raw hollow inside him.

The night was holy with stillness, pure, a perfect time to open his heart to God. What the future would hold for Christianity he couldn't begin to guess, but he felt like he'd lived through fire and come home. Layla's death had broken him in ways he couldn't have imagined. For the first time in his life, he had understood the gaping hollowness of loss. Jack had looked around at his community with eyes that could finally see and had been completely humbled. These people had survived the deaths of lovers and children, of parents, spouses and best friends. And they had persevered. Their strength was astonishing.

He had also recognized some truths about himself, truths that still made him wince in discomfort, even here in the dark, alone with this spectacular sky and the wind rolling soft waves in the prairie grass. He lifted his face to the stars and marveled again, as he always would, that God could love such a flawed and un-lovely man.

As badly as he had treated Layla, he had treated his own sister worse. He knew, now, that Verity had been right. He'd failed the lesson the first time God had given it, when Cara had needed him. He'd failed again when Layla could have been both teacher and lover. Now he had a chance to come full circle, to re-unite with his sister and be the brother he always should have been. To be the man God had intended him to be.

Jack watched over his companions through the dark hours, walking the perimeter occasionally, standing to shift from foot to foot when he got too cold or too sleepy. Shortly before dawn, Piper twitched violently in her sleeping bag, then went still. Jack held his breath, hoping she would settle, but her legs started to thrash, and she started moaning softly, an anguished, "I'm sorry, I'm sorry, I'm sorry." He moved to crouch beside her, resting his hand firmly on her shoulder.

"Piper. Wake up. You're safe."

He moved back smoothly when she shot upright, a dance they'd already done too many times. Both Owen and Ed started awake, and Rosemary whined. Jack held a palm out, letting them both know it was okay. Ed settled back down, murmuring soothingly to his dog, but Owen stayed as he was, raised on an elbow to watch, his forehead wrinkled in concern.

Piper's breathing was ragged. She fought her way free of her sleeping bag, then scrambled a few feet away. Jack heard her retch, a pattern he'd learned to expect when she sobbed her regret in her sleep. He kept his distance, letting her finish in as much privacy as he could give her, getting a bottle of water and a soft cloth from the pack on his bike. He handed both to her when she returned. She accepted them wordlessly, and he walked the perimeter again while she swished out her mouth and wiped her face. She had laid back down when he returned, but he knew she wasn't sleeping. Owen, too, was still awake, lying on his back with his head resting on his stacked hands, staring at the stars above. Jack dragged the campstool closer and sat down.

"How long 'til dawn?" Piper's voice was husky, but she had regained control.

"About an hour, maybe less." He knew she didn't want to go back to sleep, but she needed to. She had only been asleep a few hours. He started talking. "Did I ever tell you how I came to be named 'Jack?'"

He actually *felt* her smile in the dark. "You didn't."

"Well, I'll tell you, then." He settled back, crossing his legs at the ankle, and pitched his voice to entertain and *soothe*. "My mother was probably the biggest fan of *Little House on the Prairie* of all time, both the books and the TV series. Michael Landon made her swoon, which was why my father put his foot down, emphatically, when she wanted to name me 'Michael.' He put the kibosh on 'Charles' as well, so they agreed on 'Jack,' which, if you will remember, was the name of the dog."

Piper shook with soft laughter in the dark, and he smiled. He could *feel* the tension easing out of her, the loosening of muscles that would permit her to return to sleep. He glanced at Owen, and to his surprise, could see the lighter white of the man's teeth in the dark as he grinned. Jack went on.

"When my little sister came along, she started at the top with 'Caroline.' She always hoped to add a Mary, Laura, Carrie and maybe even a Grace, but it wasn't meant to be. Cara and I were it for them."

"My mom wanted a big family, too, but she kept miscarrying after me." Piper's voice was starting to sound sleepy. "Macy was a surprise tag-along. We loved her so much. She was such a gift."

"We felt the same way about Cara. Dad told me Mom lost three babies between us, and he was ready to call it quits. She begged him for one more try, and they had Cara. I was nine. I couldn't believe how much I loved her."

His throat closed and he stopped speaking, surprised both by the memory and by the power of it. How could he have forgotten? Baby sister, so cute, so little and silly. And here was Piper, never to see her baby sister again. He cleared his throat and went on.

"We never called her 'Caroline' – well, my mom did when she was mad – but she was always 'Cara' or 'Care-bear' or 'the baby,' which she hated. She started going by a different name when she ran away, and, when I saw her years later, she said she'd had it legally changed." He made himself relax the sneer that had twisted his face. "Cassandra something-or-other. She didn't want us to find her. She was only sixteen when she took off. She kept it as a stage name, for her work as a psychic. I hated the name and everything it represented, so I refused to use it."

"That's interesting – like the Cassandra of Greek mythology?"

"I didn't ask why she chose it." Jack was quiet for a moment. "Why didn't I ask? It must have been important to her."

"If she went to the trouble to change it legally, it's safe to say the name has great meaning for her. In Greek mythology, Cassandra was the daughter of King Priam of Troy. Apollo wanted to seduce her – or as my mom used to tell it, Apollo 'wanted her favor' – so he gave her the gift of prophecy. When she turned him down flat, he cursed her so that no one would believe her prophecies."

Jack winced. "Well. That would fit. I take it one of your many pets was named 'Cassandra?'"

"A chinchilla." Piper yawned, and settled deeper into the sleeping bag. "Do you know which name she would be going by now?"

"I hadn't thought about that. Won't do us much good to ask around for 'Cara' if she's known as 'Cassandra,' will it?" Jack grimaced. "Crap."

Again, he *felt* her smile. His G-rated profanity never failed to amuse her. "Watch your mouth, Pastor."

She turned away from him with another jaw-cracking yawn, and curled up. Jack stood to walk the perimeter again and found Owen watching him. "We'll find your sister," he said. "I'm sure of it."

Then he, too, rolled over and settled into his sleeping bag, leaving Jack to wonder at the other man's certainty. Owen spoke so rarely, it was hard not to read importance into everything he said. Maybe, like Piper's Brody, he had a sense of the future, of what was to come. No, Jack corrected himself. Not "Piper's Brody." The man had taken enough from her. Linking them, even in his mind, was offensive.

Dawn finally warmed the eastern horizon with pink. Jack set up a campstool to shade Piper's face from the rising sun, then sat down and watched the prairie wake up, smiling as meadowlarks sang and dove for their breakfast, and insects whirred and dodged. Little moments of joy, as

Naomi always said. In this hard new world, all you could do was swim from one island to the next.

The community would do well with Naomi leading them, he mused. He was sure of it, even if she wasn't. He wondered if they would decide to stay in the Woodland Park area or if they would relocate to a more remote and defensible location but the wondering was academic. His future lay in a different direction. He hadn't said as much to Piper or the others yet, but somehow he knew he wouldn't be returning to live in Colorado. Something beyond Cara was pulling him home.

To Jack's relief, Piper slept several hours past dawn. He, Owen and Ed had already washed and eaten when she roused around. The three of them made themselves scarce to give her some privacy, and Jack walked to the top of the hill again, planning to see if he could detect any activity in Limon through the binoculars. Ed joined him.

"What do you think?" Rosemary ranged all around them, fresh as a daisy, ears perky with interest in the bright morning sun. "Or should I say, what do you *feel*?"

Jack smiled and lifted the binoculars to his eyes, scanning for a moment before he answered. "It looks and *feels* quiet. Hopefully, we won't need any of Martin's strategies."

"Well, hope for the best, plan for the worst." Ed shot him a sideways look. "If he said that once, he said it a thousand times. So we walk in armed, Owen in the lead, then you and Piper, with Rosemary and me bringing up the rear."

Jack nodded. They had worked out this type of approach with Martin. "If they want to get aggressive, we identify the leader, I start talking, and Piper aims for the strongest bond-line he or she has while we back out."

Ed smiled. "Our pretty-as-a-picture secret weapon." He shook his head. "Never saw anything like her and her mother for shooting, and who would have guessed? First time I met Naomi, she was bringing a plate of cookies to my front door, hair and makeup done just so, a sweet, pretty lady. She might even have been wearing an apron. And Piper. In my mind, she's still a cute little tomboy with skinned knees, a hot temper and a ready fist." The smile fell away from his face, leaving him looking old and haunted. "And now here we are. Never could have imagined it."

Jack nudged him gently away from the past. "We should confirm the plan with the others and get moving. If this doesn't work out, I'd like to put some distance between us and them before night falls."

Ed nodded, and whistled for Rosemary. She came tearing out of the tall grass instantly, tongue lolling, and glued herself to Ed's side. He touched her head, then looked up at Jack. "Wouldn't hurt for you to do some of that praying you do, Pastor. I'd hate to see us meet trouble on our very first stop."

By the time they joined the others, Piper had washed up, changed her clothes, and was working on finishing her breakfast. Her short blonde hair stood out in wet spikes around her head. She looked up, her sharp eyes the exact shade of green Jack knew so well from dreams. The expression on her face was all determination, no fear.

Piper's vulnerabilities belonged to the night. During the day, she was a Valkyrie.

Owen joined them, and Jack went over what he and Ed had discussed. He watched Piper as he talked, noting the faint circles under her eyes, noting also that her movements were brisk and that she was eating the last of Verity's vegetables with enthusiasm. She nodded occasionally as he talked, but her gaze darted and swooped with the movements of the birds all around them. When a red-winged blackbird trilled its distinctive song, she smiled. Then, her eyes narrowed. "I don't believe it. It can't be."

Jack followed the direction of her gaze just as a raven fluttered to land on the handlebars of Piper's motorcycle. The big bird cocked his head to the side when he saw them looking at him and croaked, a sound familiar even to Jack's unpracticed ear.

"Isn't that the raven your mom calls 'Loki?'" When Piper nodded, a dumbstruck expression on her face, Ed grinned, Owen shook his head in amusement, and Jack laughed. "Well, what do you know. You wouldn't let her come, but she managed to send her spies just the same. A post-apocalyptic GPS tracking device. Only Naomi could have pulled that off."

Piper looked away from Loki, her expression a complicated mixture of irritation and love, with just a touch of fear. She closed her eyes for a moment, resting her hand over her heart, then gasped softly. When her eyes opened again, the moss-green was magnified by tears. "She sent a message. She loves me, and she's sorry. Damn it, mom."

She surged to her feet and took refuge in movement, rolling her sleeping bag and stowing the rest of her supplies. Loki watched them all curiously as they moved about the camp, then croaked again and flew off to the west. By the time they were ready to leave, the sun was approaching mid-morning and they were all anxious to get on the road.

Once again, the bikes seemed dangerously loud when they took off. They rode slowly, bumping across the prairie until they reached State Road 71, one of the numerous roads that led into Limon. There weren't many vehicles here, nothing like the congestion they'd seen in other spots, especially when they had crossed I-25. They increased their speed, Jack in the lead, with Piper right behind him. The vehicles they passed had clearly been ransacked for supplies, but there were no bodies inside. Jack slowed his bike as they passed a wide-open minivan, and nodded at the grass-covered mounds alongside the road.

"Look at that. Someone buried the people who were inside."

"Respect for the dead is a good sign," Ed commented. "Tends to go hand-in-hand with respect for the living."

They slowed again when they started to pass occasional houses. Piper pulled up alongside Jack and signaled – her instinct for people was the most sensitive – and they pulled off at the now-deserted Tamarack Golf Course. They cut the bikes' motors, and Piper rubbed the back of her neck.

"They know we're here. They must have watchers stationed outside of town. There's no one in our immediate vicinity, but I'm sure they're converging on us. I know we planned to leave the bikes before we were detected, but it's too late."

"So what do you think?" Jack asked. "Should we just ride on, try to get closer to I-70?"

Piper thought for a moment, then shook her head. "No, let's leave the bikes here and walk. It will seem less threatening. Besides, none of us can shoot very well from a moving motorcycle, and you can't hocus-pocus 'em if they can't hear your voice over the bikes. No sense in negating our only advantages."

Jack nodded, then made eye contact with Ed and Owen, who also nodded agreement. "It's as good a plan as any. If worse comes to worst, we scatter and make our way back here."

They pushed the motorcycles behind the small club house, then donned their emergency backpacks. Jack and Ed carried shotguns, Piper the same AR15 rifle she'd had since her time with Brody's group, while Owen was armed with the hunting rifle he'd had since he was a boy. They headed back out to the main road, the crunch of their boots on gravel the only sound. Falling into the formation they'd agreed on, they walked towards town. Jack's senses were so painfully wide-open, he could feel his companions' anxiety as his own, even Rosemary's.

They began to pass more and more homes, and the sensation of being watched increased steadily until Jack's skin was crawling with it. Out of the corners of his eyes, he began to detect movement behind the houses they were passing, but still, no one challenged them or stepped into the open. They'd been walking for about fifteen minutes when Jack decided he'd had just about enough of the cat-and-mouse routine.

"This is as good a place as any, Owen. Let's see if they want to come out and talk."

Owen stopped and rolled his massive shoulders, scanning from side to side. Piper and Jack took up positions back-to-back behind him, facing out, while Ed turned to watch the way they'd come.

Jack spoke over his shoulder. "What can you tell us, Piper?"

"Their bond lines are all around us, like a grid," Piper answered. "I count eight in our immediate vicinity, a lot more radiating north of here."

Jack called out. "Are you willing to talk to us? We're friends of Martin and Grace Ramirez and Quinn Harris. We just want to talk."

They waited. In the silence, a meadowlark sang, and Jack could hear Piper's breathing, swift and light. Finally, a man's voice called out. "Tell us about Grace and Quinn."

Jack turned his face towards the unseen speaker. "They're both part of our community now. Teenagers. They traveled from here together to look for Grace's dad, Martin Ramirez. They were the only ones in their immediate families to survive."

A few more heartbeats of silence. Then a man stepped out from behind a house on Jack's side of the road and began walking towards them. He carried a shotgun low across his hips, but his finger was on the trigger. Owen stiffened, and shifted his rifle towards the man. The man stopped walking, squinting at them. Then, he spoke.

"You could probably get a shot off, but you'll be dead before me. There are twenty weapons trained on you right now."

"More like eight," Jack kept his voice easy, confident, in spite of his tension. Underneath the "easy," though, he layered just a little *power*. "We aren't looking for a fight, but we will defend ourselves. We're just passing through, and we wanted to see if there was a community here, make a connection for our own people. If you're not interested, we'll just go on our way."

The man scrutinized them a moment longer, then called over his shoulder without taking his eyes off them. "Bernice? What's the call?"

A woman's quavering voice answered from out of sight. "I think they're okay, Brian. Everything he said was the truth."

Brian snapped a question at Jack. "Do you intend us any harm?"

Jack pitched his voice to carry to the hidden Bernice. "No, we don't."

A moment passed, then Bernice's voice warbled out again. "Truth."

Brian's shoulders relaxed, and he took his finger away from the trigger. "My name is Brian Weaver. We've learned to be wary of strangers."

"I'm Jack. This is Owen, Piper, Ed and Rosemary." He nodded to them in turn. "We don't intend to stay. We're headed east to look for family, but if our communities could connect, we might be able to help each other in the future."

Brian gestured for them to walk with him. "Why don't you join us for our noon meal? We can trade information."

Jack glanced around his circle of companions and got a brief nod from each. By earlier agreement, he, Owen and Ed slung their firearms over their shoulders, while Piper kept hers cradled in the crook of her arm. As they walked, Jack noted people stepping out from behind houses and buildings, making eye contact with Brian, then fading back at his nod. An elderly woman emerged from behind another house as they passed, approaching with a gait that was both spry and hitching.

"I'm Bernice," she said, in the wobbly voice they had heard before. She held out her hand. "I approve all of our newcomers."

Jack took her soft, papery hand between his own. So many senior citizens had died in the plague, and the Woodland Park community had come to view the few surviving elders as treasures. "Bernice," he said, taking the time to really *connect* with her rather than falling back on what Layla used to call his "smarm." He squeezed her hand warmly before letting her go. "The friend I mentioned, Martin Ramirez, is very good at knowing when people are telling the truth, too."

"I knew Martin's first wife, Lena, though I don't recall ever meeting him. Deployed all the time, as I remember, then they divorced. I used to golf with Lena's mom, every Tuesday. She sure adored those grandkids, Gracie and little Benji. She passed a few years before the plague, and I'm glad she didn't live to see it. Sometimes, I'm sorry I did."

"We wouldn't know what to do without you, Bernice." Brian moved to the old woman's side, tucking her hand in the crook of his arm. Their eyes met, and Bernice nodded. Brian looked back at the travelers, his eyes once more assessing. "Have you changed? Since the plague?"

Jack returned the scrutiny, *feeling* his way forward. He and Piper had talked at length about the fact that different groups of people would have different attitudes towards the apparent shift in humanity and about the need to proceed with caution. "Everyone who survived has changed, in many ways," he hedged.

Before Brian could respond, Bernice made an impatient sound and swatted Jack's arm. "Don't get slippery, young man. We appreciate straight talk here, and you won't come to harm, no matter your answer. Are you psychic or not?"

Jack bit the inside of his cheek to control what might be misinterpreted as a disrespectful grin. "We call it intuitive, ma'am. And yes, many of the people in our community are different, including me. I feel what others are feeling, like their emotions are mine." Telling all wasn't necessary, he decided, and left it at that. "People here have changed as well?"

Brian answered. "A lot of us, not everyone. Intuitive – that's a good way to describe it. Bernice here *knows* when people are lying or being deceptive. I'm not as sensitive, but I *feel* things more strongly than before, like what used to be a hunch is now a sure thing." He looked past Jack. "What about the rest of you?"

Piper spoke. "I can see the connections between people."

Ed chimed in next. "My wife used to say I couldn't catch a hint with a butterfly net, so I guess evolution left me behind." He inclined his head towards Owen. "Our friend here is the strong and silent type and keeps his own counsel."

Jack approved of their friendly but carefully edited descriptions. "What about the children here? Have the majority of them changed, too?"

Brian nodded. "All of them, much more so than the adults." He smiled crookedly. "We've had a time, trying to figure out how to handle some of the little ones. They say whatever they're thinking, and they know things they shouldn't."

Jack let his grin show this time. "We had an interesting classroom conversation about Viagra that was started by a five-year-old girl."

"Classroom?" Bernice's gaze was sharp, interested. "I was the high school principal, before I retired. You're a teacher, then?"

"A youth pastor, before. Anything I needed to be after, including a teacher."

Brian's laugh was wry. "I hear that." He gestured for them to start walking again, keeping the pace easy for Bernice. Jack and Piper walked beside them, Ed and Owen a short distance behind. "I used to sell insurance. Fat lot of good those closing skills are doing me now."

He looked at Piper, and though he was subtle about it, his eyes performed a thorough sweep. Jack could *feel* the other man's interest, and Piper's sudden tension. "What about you, Piper?"

"College student, before. University of Northern Colorado." Her voice was clipped, almost unfriendly, and Jack had to resist the urge to step in, to soften the interaction for her. She wouldn't thank him for it. "Now I just shoot things that need shooting."

Brian's eyebrows shot up, but instead of discouraging his interest, Piper's words spiked it. "Is that so? Your daddy taught you to shoot, did he?"

"My mother, actually." Piper pointedly focused on Bernice, not quite the cut direct, but close enough. "Do you know about the gang that's in control of Colorado Springs?"

Bernice's face tightened. "We do. We've got some folks that are refugees from that mess. Denver is pretty bad, too, but not as organized, from what we hear. A lot of smaller gangs, fighting each other for resources. We're more concerned about the group in Colorado Springs. They're the most likely to cause us trouble in the future."

They walked up a gravel driveway and past a two-story farmhouse, stopping in front of what appeared to be a long, low adobe bunkhouse. Brian gestured at the open doorway. "Here's lunch. After things settled down, we all gathered on this end of town to consolidate resources and watch each other's backs. We do a communal meal here at noon, Monday thru Friday. Keeps everyone in touch, keeps us all accounted for."

He led them inside. The interior was dark and cool, thanks to the thick walls of the building and the strategically opened windows which allowed the ever-present prairie breeze in. About twenty people were already seated at long tables, which were set up cafeteria style. As one, they looked up, eyeing the newcomers with interest.

Once again, Jack was aware of particular interest in Piper, this time from a pair of young men seated on the far side of the room. Piper stopped walking, her eyes darting around the room, her discomfort with the attention they were getting obvious. As he watched, her chest started to heave, and her hands turned to white-knuckled claws on the rifle she still held. Her eyes swung around and locked onto Jack's.

"I can't breathe."

She didn't say the words, didn't even mouth them, but he heard her voice as if she spoke directly in his ear. Her terror nearly swamped him. Jack shored up his shields and smiled smoothly at Brian and Bernice. "Excuse me just a moment, would you?"

He caught Ed's eye and tilted his head towards Brian. Without missing a beat, Ed stepped into his spot and picked up the interaction, belying his earlier claim that he couldn't take a hint. "If I could trouble you for a bowl of water for Rosemary? She feeds herself, but water would sure be appreciated..."

Jack moved to take Piper's arm, steering them to an unoccupied corner of the room. Owen went with them, then turned his back, using his big body as a shield to give them some privacy. Jack looked down at Piper's white, rigid face.

"What is it?"

"It's just like the mess hall, at the camp at Walden." Her eyes were glazed, locked on a vision from the past. "This is just like when Noah and I got there, and they were all staring at me. I don't want them to stare at me. I don't want it!" The words spilled out of her in strangled, gasping rushes. "This was a terrible mistake - we never should have come here!"

Jack pitched his voice to cut through her panic, layers of *calm* and *logic* and *soothe*. "This is not just like Walden, and if you take a deep breath, you'll be able to *see* why. So take a deep breath." He put a punch of *imperative* in his next word. "Now."

Her chest heaved at his command, and her eyes opened wide in surprise. Jack nodded. "Good. Again." He waited until she'd hauled in three deep breaths, then said, "Better. Now look around and tell me what you see. How is this different than Walden?"

Piper did as he asked. "The bonds extend outside this room. They're not as isolated." Her eyes flicked among the tables, and interest began to replace the panic. "They're all bonded to Brian, but even more so to Bernice. She's as much a leader as he is, and she's beloved by all. She's the center of a web of love, green lines everywhere, and they go both ways." She looked at Jack. "Nobody loved Brody. They were all dependent on him, but most of them were also terrified of him. His lines were all red, and they only went one way – from the group to him." Her eyes dropped, and a frown creased her forehead. "Well. Except for one." Then she looked back up, and her eyes narrowed. "You used your voice thingy on me again, didn't you?"

"Sure did. I'll apologize later." He inclined his head towards the young men, and Brian. "In the meantime, how do you want to play this? We can pretend you and I are together romantically, but if that would make you just as uncomfortable, it'll never work. If I can *feel* what you're feeling, chances are good someone else here can, too."

Piper frowned. "Which is a weakness I don't intend to advertise."

She thought for a moment, then started to talk her way through it. "I don't need to lie. If they ask, I just say I'm not interested. This group is civilized enough to accept that answer. They're just looking. I can handle that." Then her spine straightened, her shoulders squared and the Valkyrie met his gaze with narrowed eyes. "But if they try to do more than look, Jack, I'll beat the shit out of them."

"I'll help."

Owen's voice was a rusty rumble, startling them both. He smiled down at Piper, and when Piper smiled back, Jack was shocked by a bolt of white-hot jealousy, piercing his chest like a spear. He blinked, hard and fast, stunned. Where had that come from? Then, he tuned in to what they were both feeling, and the stabbing tension in his chest eased.

Owen reached out to bump Piper's shoulder with a huge fist, his smile turning into a grin. Big brother to little sister. "Actually, I would just let you handle it. Maybe take some bets on the side."

Piper laughed. Buddy to buddy. "Deal, but you split the take with me 50-50." She looked down for a moment, swallowed, then looked up at both Owen and Jack. "I'm sorry. I got blindsided. I'll try not to let it happen again."

Owen ducked his head and nodded. Jack managed a smile, still trying to make sense of his own reaction, and gestured towards the waiting group. "Atta girl. Let's eat."

They returned to Brian, Bernice and Ed. Brian's eyes asked questions, but he didn't give voice to them. Instead, he led them to the food spread out on a buffet table, and they all helped themselves to homemade tortillas, an abundance of fresh vegetables, and to Ed's special delight, strips of grilled steak. Brian gestured to the food.

"Most of us have been ranchers for generations, and now we're all gardeners, too. I'd guess we've had an easier time than most adapting." They all sat down together as more people filed in and began serving themselves. "The refugees out of the cities have told us food is a constant issue. They're fighting over roast cat and whatever canned stuff they can still find, when all they'd have to do is grow or raise their own. I guess people will either learn or starve."

"How many survived the plague here?" Piper asked.

"Twenty-eight, including Grace and Quinn," Brian answered. "But we've grown since then. We have folks from Denver and Colorado Springs, a few from Pueblo, travelers from parts east of here, and three babies born this summer. We now number eighty-six."

He looked down for a moment. When he looked up, his face was both determined and sad. "There's something I need to come clean about. My dad and I saw Grace and Quinn, right after the plague. They came into town looking for food. At that time we were scrambling, trying to make sure there was enough for everyone. Some folks were trying to hoard, strangers were coming through and stealing anything they could get their hands on. It was a free-for-all."

Piper's face hardened. Jack knew she had tucked Gracie under her wing, and though she teased her uber-maternal mother about being a broody hen, she was as protective as Naomi in her own way. "You're the ones who shot at them."

Brian didn't flinch away from the judgement in her gaze. "We are. We were trying to disable their truck, but my dad was startled and his shot went high. They must have thought we were trying to kill them. We planned to go talk to them after a few days, but when we went out to the Harris ranch they were gone." Brian swallowed hard. "It haunted my dad to his dying day. I lost him over the winter – pneumonia. It would mean a lot to me to apologize to those kids for both of us, but especially for my dad. It would help him rest easier, crazy as that sounds."

Ed answered him. "It doesn't sound crazy at all. Quinn and Grace ran into some trouble after they left here, and it might give their hearts some peace to know you didn't intend to harm them. Grace, especially, needs to know that there are good people left in the world."

"You could travel to Woodland Park yourself," Jack suggested. "Make contact with the community and talk to the kids at the same time. Or, if you can't be spared here, you could send a runner with a message."

"I'll make plans to go. No one here is indispensable. We try to double up on all our duties and tasks, and we share information constantly. So much knowledge has already been lost." He shook his head. "We're sitting on top of a huge alternative-energy plant, but there's no one left alive who knows how to run it or how to maintenance the wind turbines. We've been trying to figure it out, but we're so busy just living I'm afraid we'll lose the incentive to try, along with so many other things."

"When you get to Woodland Park, ask for a man named Alder," Jack said. "He's our chief mechanic and jury-rigger, and I think those turbines might make him drool."

"Alder. I'll remember. Well, then, enough about us." Brian leaned forward, arms folded on the table. "Where are you headed, and how can we help?"

Jack outlined their plans while Brian listened, his face showing increasing concern. When Jack finished talking, Brian shook his head. "I hate to tell you this, but from what we've heard, you're headed from bad to worse. We had a group arrive early this spring from all over back east. Three of them started in Pennsylvania, and they picked people up as they went. Seventeen of them made it here, but not before they ran into all manner of trouble. Word is, everything east of the Mississippi River is hazardous. Too populated. One fellow wouldn't have made it out of Chicago alive if not for his dog – she was a retired police dog, if you can believe it, and she fought to the death to protect him."

Ed glanced down at Rosemary, his face sober. "None of that sounds promising. No word of any organized effort to help folks or any attempts on the part of the government to get the country back on its feet?"

Bernice snorted and shook her head. "Sweetie, you've been around the block – maybe not as many times as me, but still. Those shysters won't pop their heads up until the dust has long since settled. We're on our own."

Jack took a deep breath and blew it out. "I appreciate the information, but I've got to do what I've got to do." He looked at Ed, Owen, and Piper in turn. "But if I haven't said it before, I'll say it now. You can stop, any time you want to. None of you are obligated to follow me into danger." All three of them just stared back at him blandly, and Piper rolled her hand in a "get on with it" gesture. Jack finished anyway. "Just think it over."

Around them, people were finishing with their food, but they weren't leaving. Cards and board games came out, and a teenaged girl produced a guitar, learning chords under the direction of an older woman. Near the open windows, a trio of battered recliners were all occupied by people reading, and a group of men and women at an adjacent table all held knitting needles or crochet hooks.

Brian's eyes flickered to Piper yet again. His glances had grown more and more lingering as the meal had progressed, in spite of the fact that Piper had met his attempts to draw her out with cold-eyed disinterest. "You all are welcome to stay a few days, if you like, and get to know us. Who knows?" He waited until Piper met his gaze, then gave her a smile so beautiful and charismatic, it had certainly clinched many a sales deal. "You might find something here you like and decide to stay."

Two things happened at once: Owen seemed to swell to twice his normal size, and Piper bared her teeth, the expression as feral as Brian's had been charming. Seated side by side as they were, the combined effect was magnificently intimidating. Brian's eyes widened so suddenly the effect was comic, and Jack couldn't stop a bark of laughter.

He clapped Brian on the shoulder and stood up. "We'll take you up on part of that offer, Brian. Maybe Owen can take a look at those turbines, and I'll bet Piper would like to talk to those folks from the east coast. But I think we'll be moving on after that. In the meantime, how about if I sing for our supper? Could I borrow that guitar?"

Bernice beamed and clapped her hands. "Dinner and a show! Traci!" She waved at the teenager holding the guitar. "Bring that over here, honey!"

Traci did as Bernice asked, and Jack thanked her. He strummed and tuned for a moment, then looked up to find his traveling companions all gazing at him with varying degrees of surprise.

"I didn't know you could play guitar," Ed observed.

"Or sing," Piper added, looking just a little nervous. Beside her, Owen remained silent, but his skepticism was plain to see. Piper went on. "You can sing, right? This isn't going to be like when your drunk buddy gets up to karaoke and thinks – mistakenly – that he's got a gift, right?"

Jack rolled his eyes. "Hello? Youth pastor, remember? I've got skills. It's a pre-req."

He looked around the room, and felt completely in his element for the very first time since before the plague. "Hi, everyone. I'm Jack. My friends and I truly appreciate your hospitality. You want to do a good old-fashioned sing-along?"

One of the knitters called back. "Could you sing for us?" She rested her elbows on the table and tilted her head to the side, gifting him with a flirty smile. "It's been so long since we were entertained by a handsome man."

There was some grumbling from the men scattered around the room at that, but Jack nodded. "Sure. How about some musical advice?" He caught Brian's eye and winked, then strummed the plaintive opening notes of his favorite Bonnie Raitt tune, "Nobody's Girl."

"She don't need anybody to tell her she's pretty..."

Piper's face bloomed a satisfying red, and Jack smiled as he sang. How he had missed this – he hadn't played or sung so much as a note for over a year. He finished the song, and the room burst into applause. People started calling out requests, and if he knew it, he sang it. He coerced them into a few sing-alongs, and when his voice was raspy and his fingertips numb, he announced the last song.

"This one is for one of my friends. Piper, give 'em a wave." Piper rolled her eyes, pink-cheeked, but did as he asked. Jack looked at the two young men craning to get a better look from the back table, nudging each other and mouthing her name. When they realized he was staring at them, their cheeks, too, flushed with color. "Remember that first song I sang, guys? Refer back."

Then he struck the bouncy opening chords of the Ray Charles classic. "Hit the road, Jack, and don't you come back no more..."

Piper's laughter rang through the room, and Jack realized he couldn't remember the last time he'd felt so happy.

FIVE
Cass: Sailing on Lake Michigan

The specter lifted out of the heaving gray water as Cass was fighting to control her mainsail in the rising wind. The summer squall had blustered up out of nowhere; likewise, the ghost that was now hovering just off her starboard bow had risen from the unseen depths, and there she would remain until Cass acknowledged her.

"A little busy right now!" She shouted the words over the gusting wind and the slap of water on her small hull. "Just carry on with your haunting until I get this handled, 'kay?"

The ghost – a woman with dark hair – seemed to nod, which was interesting. Cass spared her darting glances as she worked to keep her boat from heeling by spilling wind from her mainsail. The spirit lingered for a few minutes then faded; Cass was certain she hadn't seen the last of her, but at the moment, she had her hands full trying to keep her craft under control and upright.

By thee gods, she was not going to get swamped by a little Lake Michigan temper tantrum. If it was her destiny to end this incarnation on the Great Lakes, so be it, but no less than the Witch of November better be the one to come for her. She grimaced and cast a nervous eye to the lowering skies. Yes, it was July, but her sailing skills needed a lot of work before she threw that challenge out to the Universe.

"Just kidding!" She hollered at Fate, just in case she'd been listening in, too. "I'd rather not meet her, thanks all the same!"

Not that she hadn't come a long way. A year ago, she wouldn't have known what a mainsail was. Veda had spent the long winter and spring teaching her as much as she could about sailing, and Cass had devoted hours to studying the *Sailing Fundamentals* book she'd salvaged from the Michigan Maritime Museum in South Haven. Theory and experience, however, were two very different things.

She'd been fooled by the big, white, fluffy cumulus clouds that had gathered on the horizon, for example, masking the black nimbus clouds behind them. By the time she'd accurately assessed the situation, it was too late to make a run for shore. Better to weather the storm in big water than chance the breaking waves of the shallows where she would either capsize or run aground.

As quickly as it hit, the squall line passed. Cass watched the line of rain retreat, feeling her heartbeat slow, feeling for the first time how desperately cold she was. "Stupid, stupid, stupid," she muttered. When she was sure it was safe, she unhooked her safety harness, used a bungee-cord to secure the tiller, and headed below to change into dry clothes and the weather gear she should have been in before the squall hit. As she changed, she went back over the weather pattern in her mind, noting the signs she had missed, resolving to do better next time. She returned to the deck, where the sun was already making a watery reappearance.

"Long foretold, long last, short notice, soon past," she said to no one in particular. She'd spent so much time alone during the last six weeks, she'd gotten into the habit of speaking aloud, often in the form of a back-and-forth commentary. Besides, given her talents, she never knew when someone would be around to hear her. The ghosts rarely answered back in the conversational sense, but from her earliest memories, she had talked to them. Once she'd passed the age of imaginary friends, the practice had gotten her into worlds of trouble.

As if summoned by her thoughts, the dark-haired woman rose from the water again. Cass checked her sails, let her hand rest on the still-secured tiller, and relaxed back in the captain's chair. She took a moment to say a prayer of protection, to center herself, and to shift her mind to a neutral, receiving state. Then she opened to whatever communication this spirit wished to make. The woman seemed to be gazing at her with curiosity, and for the first time, Cass noticed that her hands were curved around a softly rounded belly.

"You were pregnant when you crossed over?" Cass waited. After a moment, she felt as much as heard a soft, *Yes*. Again, she waited. Information could come to her in many ways. She might see, hear, smell, feel or even taste a communication from a spirit. Sometimes, an overly enthusiastic entity might hit her with a multi-sensory onslaught, what Cass called "information via firehose." This woman was more respectful and seemed content to let Cass ask the questions.

"Is there a message you want me to deliver to someone?"

Yes.

"The baby's father?"

No.

"Okay. Someone else, then?"

She waited, but the woman seemed to be struggling to stay connected. Unless Cass sailed directly over a restless shipwreck, she didn't often encounter spirits on the water – one of the reasons she spent so much time on her boat now. These days, the spirit presence onshore was overwhelming, both visitors from across the veil, and those poor, earthbound souls that didn't yet realize their physical bodies had died. This woman was of the former group, and it made Cass wonder where she had come from.

"Did you die here, on the lake?"

No.

"Hmm." Cass frowned. "Can you show me where you're from? I sense that's an important part of your message."

In answer, a brisk breeze stirred the air around them. Dry air, scented with pine and something fresh and indefinable – Cass had a strong impression of a high mountain meadow. As soon as her mind made that connection, she saw a distinctive, white-capped peak and recognized it from pictures.

"Pikes Peak? Is that Pikes Peak?"

The woman's *Yes* was so faint, Cass could barely detect it. She faded immediately, leaving Cass unsettled. That had been Pikes Peak; she was sure of it. She waited a few more minutes, hoping the woman would return, then got up to tend to her mainsail again.

A stiff breeze had followed in the wake of the squall, noticeably colder than before, and she adjusted her sails to catch it. Just before the squall hit, she'd spotted the Point Betsie Lighthouse on the Michigan shore, and unless something else unexpected arose, she should be able to make South Manitou Island by late afternoon. The wind cooperated beautifully, sending the 26 foot MacGregor flying over the water. Of the boats left abandoned in the marina, Veda had chosen it as a "good beginner boat" for Cass, something she could handle alone, although it was no beauty, nor was it as stable as a larger, heavier boat would be in rough conditions. Faults aside, Cass loved it, and sailing solo was an unexpected joy in troubled times. The absolute peace, the intimacy between her, the boat, and the lake, and the sense of freedom from the problems on land all combined into a deeply satisfying surprise from the Universe.

For a time, the endless adjustments of sailing kept her from wondering why a spirit from her brother's home in Colorado would seek her out. There were rules – or as Veda liked to say in her best pirate accent, "More what you'd call 'guidelines' than actual rules." Typically, spirits stayed connected to the location where they had either lived or died. Occasionally, a spirit would attach itself to a living person, and even more infrequently, a very strong entity could traverse great distances to interact with the living. If the dark-haired woman truly was from Colorado, she must have been a force to be reckoned with in life. And she must have something very important to convey.

Like most of the other natural-born mediums Cass had met, she'd learned the rules only after a great deal of confusion and fear. Her childhood had been filled with a series of escalating shocks, as she began to realize the people around her weren't experiencing what she was experiencing, and her adolescence had been a swift spiral down into hell. What a relief it had been to learn that she could control her interactions with spirit, that she could call the shots. Veda, her mentor in all things, had taught her.

"It's like that Julia Roberts character in *Pretty Woman*, you know? The hooker that landed Richard Gere? It's like her hooker rules: you say who, you say when, you say where."

Cass had nodded, though she hadn't known. A movie about a prostitute who got the guy wasn't approved viewing for a minister's daughter. Veda was a movie fanatic, and even though she frequently used films Cass had never even heard of to illustrate her points, Cass usually got the gist. She learned how to block unwanted interactions, learned how to protect herself with white light and prayer, learned how to create a barrier between herself and endless interruptions from the spirit world. It was like putting her phone on "Do Not Disturb," and the reprieve had saved her life.

Now, years later, she could look back on her younger self and marvel that she hadn't gone insane. By the time she was ten, she had stopped talking about the spirits that came to her. By the time she was twelve, she was using alcohol to cope with the pain of her fall from adored baby of the family to accused liar and chronic trouble-maker. The booze had the side benefit of blunting the spirit activity she experienced, or she was certain she wouldn't have made it through adolescence alive. On her thirteenth birthday, some kind of door had been thrown open, and spirits came from everywhere to badger her: *Help me contact my wife – I need to tell her I'm okay, so she can stop grieving and get on with her life. You need to get in touch with my kids – I told them not to sell my house, and I meant it! Tell my brother I love him – it's not his fault, and I know that now...* And so it went, on and on, day and night. Ironic, that even now she credited alcohol abuse with saving her life.

Just after her sixteenth birthday, she'd walked out her parents' front door and out of their lives. Jack had been in seminary then, but even when he was home, they didn't talk. Cass had been so finished with their disappointment, their distrust. She'd spent a few months on the streets in Milwaukee, picking pockets and busking for cash, but a brush with the cops had set her in motion again. She'd lifted a fat wallet down by the marina, and following an intuitive hunch that couldn't be blunted by alcohol, she'd bought an expensive ticket for the ferry to Muskegon, Michigan. There, in the Lake Express lobby, she'd met Veda.

The older woman had looked like a rotund circus tent, draped in layers of fringed and brightly colored fabric, and she'd checked her watch as Cass had approached. "Spirits called that one to the minute, didn't they?" She stuck out her hand. "I'm Veda, and I have to tell you, the spirits have been buggin' the dickens out of me about you for quite some time."

Cass had taken her hand automatically – you didn't shed sixteen years of deeply ingrained courtesy overnight. The contact had made her scalp tingle with warmth, quite a pleasant sensation. "Spirits?" she'd managed, and Veda had smiled.

"Ghosts, specters, souls, or the dearly departed, if you like. I prefer 'spirits.' Much more dramatic. And your name is? There's some confusion in the ranks on that."

Cass had avoided giving out her name in case her parents had been looking for her and had made one up on the spot when it couldn't be avoided. In that moment, she had known two things. First, this woman would see through any subterfuge and wouldn't take kindly to a lie, no matter the justification. And second, it was time to leave the past behind. "My given name is Caroline Kiel. Cara. But I would like to be called Cassandra from now on."

"Ah, Cassandra. Cursed by the god who couldn't seduce her. A strong choice." With that, Veda had spun on her heel and marched away. "Well, come on then, Cass. Time to go home."

For Cass, that was exactly what Veda became. Home. Wherever Veda was, with her crystals and Tarot cards, her fringed scarves and her books on palmistry, there Cass found safety. Instruction. Security. And love. They had moved around fairly frequently, up and down the Lake

Michigan shoreline, following the ebb and flow of tourism and the vagaries of their profession. Veda had introduced her to the metaphysical community, and Cass had finally found acceptance, then success. By the time she was eighteen, she was a highly sought-after medium. She earned her GED, and started taking college classes on investment strategy in her spare time. Earning her way in the world with the gift that had cost her so much was deeply satisfying, as well as profoundly healing.

It hadn't been a linear path out of the dark, for sure. She'd floundered around trying to define herself, as all young people must – even psychic ones. She had tried to embrace Wicca for a while, but never resonated with the many rules and rituals. Then she'd gone through a "slutty gypsy" phase, which Veda had certainly not appreciated, followed briefly by an "antithesis" phase where she wore only tailored business suits and gave readings with a cool aloofness she thought came across as "professional."

Finally, she'd settled into what she thought of as her Truth, a place where the trappings were irrelevant. What she wore and how people judged her outward appearance didn't matter. She had been put on this planet by the Divine, at this time, for reasons she would learn as the adventure unfolded. This understanding had shaped her practice as a medium and psychic counselor. She loved nothing more than showing a soul in anguish how to free itself from the expectations of parents, friends, lovers, or society in order to embrace the unique being the Universe had created. Just as Veda had freed her.

It wasn't often, Cass knew, that you got to settle a karmic debt and pay it forward at the same time. She had asked Veda once what had possessed her, taking in an angry, confused teenager with a drinking problem. Veda had smiled. "You know I don't hold with future casting for myself, but you and me, we were foretold. Our souls planned this path together. And I can't tell you how grateful I am. You're the daughter of my heart, sweet girl, troubles and all."

With fair winds, Cass would be back on Beaver Island late tomorrow, basking in Veda's warm and colorful company, suffering through a cup of her truly terrible tea, and sharing all she'd learned on her journey. She was sailing in familiar waters now, and her heart soared with the joy of it. She recognized the steep green and golden point that marked Sleeping Bear Dunes, and adjusted her heading to the northwest. Flying in front of the benevolent wind, she was tying up at the dock on South Manitou Island in less than two hours. Cass and Veda had sailed from Beaver Island to both North and South Manitou numerous times while Cass had been learning, and the sense of homecoming brought tears to her eyes.

When she had finished securing her boat, she grabbed some overnight supplies and headed onto shore. Uninhabited by year-round residents since the 1950's, the island had boasted several campgrounds, a lighthouse and weather station, some abandoned homes and farm structures, and a seasonally manned ranger station in the time before. Cass headed to the station now, scanning for evidence that anyone had taken up residence since she'd last been here, finding none. The station hadn't yet been staffed for the year when the plague struck, and Cass and Veda had stayed overnight there a few times this past spring. Cass trotted up the porch steps and slipped inside, finding it just as they'd left it – dusty, but still habitable. She settled her things, then went back outside, feeling energized.

She had enough daylight left to hike to the ancient white cedar forest on the south shore. Some of the trees there were over 500 years old; it was one of the holiest places she'd ever been, and she never missed a chance to visit and recharge her core. She jogged back to her boat to grab her daypack and change her deck shoes for her hiking boots. Then, she headed out. After so many days on the boat, the rhythm of walking felt heavenly. The late afternoon sun was softened by a high haze of clouds, and the brisk and friendly wind cooled her as she strode along. She lifted her face to the sky, smiling, then laughing aloud in simple joy and thankfulness.

She'd seen so much trouble in the last six weeks, so much misery. She had left Beaver Island in late May, sailing down the Michigan shoreline in short hops. South of Whitehall, the mainland was a mess. Too many people, too few resources, even in some of the farming communities. The larger cities were hazardous on many levels. Unstable chemical storage was starting to toxify ground water and give rise to fires, and packs of both feral dogs and predatory humans ruled the deserted streets. There had been a mass exodus, she had learned, of survivors on the heavily industrialized east side of the state to the less populated west coast. The burden on already overburdened communities was complicated by a cultural clash between urban and rural sensibilities, a tension that had carried over from before the plague. In time, the city slickers and the country hicks would make peace, but the ongoing conflict was sure wreaking havoc in the here-and-now.

Cass had reason, over and over, to be grateful that Veda had acted so quickly when news of the plague broke a year ago spring. The older woman had grown up in Charlevoix, and had visited Beaver Island frequently on family vacations. She and Cass had been on the last ferry to make the run to the island, lugging all the worldly possessions they could carry in huge, overstuffed bags and suitcases, every penny of money they'd saved between the two of them stuffed in Veda's ample bra. Cass had felt silly about it at the time, sure Veda was over-reacting. She sure didn't feel silly now, especially when she saw the struggles people on the mainland were dealing with. Beaver Island wasn't perfect. The winters were long and brutal, and only eleven of the island's permanent residents had survived. More survivors had trickled in over the last year, and their community now numbered twenty-nine. They had turned one group away on Veda's say-so, but in comparison to the mainland, they'd seen very little trouble.

Cass's intuition had steered her past Muskegon, and sent her on her way swiftly after a brief stop in Grand Haven. She stayed a couple of weeks in Holland, and spent even longer in Saugatuck, one of the places she and Veda had lived the longest. Wherever she stopped, she gathered as much news as she could and bartered her skills for supplies that she could either trade on down the line or take back to the island with her. More than ever before, her particular psychic talents were in demand, as grief-stricken survivors sought confirmation that their lost ones were okay. Over and over, Cass shared what a lifetime of intimacy with spirit had taught her: That all beings were made of energy, and energy could not die – it simply changed forms.

"Your beloveds are still with you," she had said, too many times to count, "Just not in the way they were before."

Sometimes what she shared gave peace. Sometimes it didn't, which was no different than the time before. At least now she didn't have to spend as much time "proving" that she really was in contact with the spirit world, what with the changes so many people had gone through. When her protective measures failed, when the pressure of so many departed souls overwhelmed her, she would retreat to her boat, find a quiet cove or deserted dock, and spend a few days alone. Even so, as Cass traveled, word of her talent began to precede her. A small crowd of folks in South Haven had heard of her, and even more in St. Joseph. She didn't know if the living or the dead were responsible for spreading the word.

She had intended to circle down around Chicago and continue up the Wisconsin shoreline, but the survivors in St. Joseph had warned her against going any farther south. Rumors of people disappearing from communities, especially children, had been trickling in via travelers from the area. Who was behind the disappearances and for what purpose people were being taken, no one yet knew, but speculation was running wild. In addition, fires were raging unchecked from Gary, Indiana to the north side of Chicago. Cass wasn't yet an experienced enough sailor to strike out across open water, and there was no reason to chance it. There was nothing left for her in Wisconsin.

When the plague exploded into an official pandemic, she had called home for the first time in eight years. Her mother had answered, and as soon as she heard her mom's hoarse voice, Cass had known. Like Veda, she avoided future casting for herself. Even with her clients, she preferred to work with the past, for healing, and with the here-and-now, for positive change. But sometimes, the flash forward was so inevitable, she caught a glimpse. Her parents were both sick, her dad desperately so, and Cass knew with certainty neither one would last the week. She had talked to her mom for hours, had listened to her sob in grief and fear, had told her a carefully edited version of her whereabouts since she'd left home, and had asked about Jack, whom they hadn't been able to reach. They had talked until her mom fell asleep. After listening to her raspy breathing for a long, long time, Cass had disconnected the line, knowing she would never speak to either of her parents again.

A few days later, she had felt them both brush her heart on their way across the veil. Her mom had lingered for just a few minutes, her dad a little longer, his spirit touching her with love and forgiveness and acceptance, gifts for which she would have given anything while they were alive. The contact had brought her long-wounded heart some peace, but it hadn't been enough. Just not enough. Even with her first-hand knowledge of the eternal nature of the human soul, her still-human heart had longed for their physical presence, for a last embrace, a smile, a tender touch. She had cried inconsolably in Veda's arms, and even now, the memory brought tears to her eyes.

Cass lifted her face to the breeze. Her thoughts had carried her past the weather station and around the southern end of the island. The sun was easing towards the western horizon, the long summer day sliding into a long summer dusk, when she paused on the bluff that overlooked the partially submerged wreck of the Francisco Morazan. No lives had been lost when the freighter had run aground in foul weather more than a half century before, so other than the thriving colony of raucous cormorants, it was quiet. Around the decaying hulk, the waters of Lake Michigan sparkled and rippled with deceptive gentleness, the wreck itself standing testament to how dangerous and changeable the lake could be.

From the bluff, the trail wound into the Valley of the Giants, one of the few stands of virgin timber left in the state. Cass slowed her steps as she entered the gently rustling shade, then stopped and tilted her head back, breathing in the earthy richness and ancient peace of the towering cedars. Places like this were her church now, all the cathedral she could ever need. She pulled her daypack off and sat down, relaxing into a cross-legged position on the cool sand of the path. Pressing a hand over her heart, she sent her gratitude to the Source for this place, for the fact that she was alive and here, listening to the birds sing their songs of eventide in the vibrant green canopy high above.

The dark-haired woman returned to her there which didn't surprise Cass in the least.

She *felt* the woman first, as a shift in the energy around her, a shimmer in the air and on her skin. Cass closed her eyes, centered, protected, and opened. When she opened her eyes again, the woman was right in front of her, lovely and laughing. Her dark hair lifted and flowed around her head as if she was under water. Cass smiled, and got right to the point.

"Did you know my brother, Jack?"

Yes.

The answer was immediate. Cass nodded, then took a deep, steadying breath. If Jack had crossed over, he hadn't made contact with her. She had to ask, although she was reluctant to do so. Maintaining a neutral mindset was much more difficult when there was a personal connection. "Is he there with you, in the spirit world?"

No.

Cass tilted her head to the side, considering, remembering the curve of an unborn baby. "Can you show me how you knew him?"

A series of images kaleidoscoped in front of her eyes: Jack, sitting behind the steering wheel of a car, looking as stuffy and insufferable as she'd ever seen him. Jack, wretched with sweat and fever, delirious, calling for their mother. Jack, laughing in the middle of a group of kids, his face alight with fun and love. Jack, his eyes dilated with desire, demanding and aggressive and overwhelmingly sexual. Jack, his face torn with grief and love, his strong arms keeping her warm as she made the passage, his voice following her across: "Love is as strong as death; its jealousy unyielding as the grave. It burns like blazing fire, like a mighty flame."

"Gah!" Cass threw up a hand and squeezed her eyes shut. "Okay, give me a minute to assimilate." She grimaced, muttering, "Some of that, I really didn't need to know." After a moment, she cracked her eyes open. "What's your name?"

In answer, she heard an unmistakable guitar intro and Eric Clapton's voice. "Your name is Layla?"

Yes.

"Was your baby Jack's baby, too?"

The woman's regret preceded her soft *No.*

Cass nodded. "Okay. So not his baby, but you two definitely had an interesting story. Is it him I'm supposed to deliver the message to? Because I have to tell you, that could be challenging."

Again, a soft *No,* and this time, Layla lifted her hand to point directly at Cass.

"Me? The message is for me? Well, that's a first." She leaned forward, suddenly filled with anticipation and a strange certainty that destiny was shifting, like sand, beneath her feet. "What's the message?"

A tarot card flashed in front of Cass' eyes, the first of the major arcana, a young man striding out on a journey with a bundle on his back: The Fool. And music again, a guitar and Jack's voice this time, singing an old Ray Charles tune. Joy burst in her heart like sunshine.

"Jack's coming home!"

SIX
Naomi: Woodland Park, CO

Naomi had just finished wrapping and packing the last of the ginger snap cookies when Hades' low chuff alerted her that someone was approaching the cabin. Seconds later, the distinctive sound of a small creature zipping in through the dog door made her turn. Persephone launched into the air and Naomi caught her, laughing in joy and welcome as the little dog bathed her chin with love, love, love and dog saliva.

"There's my sweet girl! Who'd you bring with you?" She blended her senses with Hades, something she did almost without thinking these days, and had the answer to her question. "That would be Martin."

She walked to the door, still cradling Persephone and smiling when she opened it. The expression on Martin's face made the smile die instantly. "What is it? What's wrong? Is Grace hurt?"

Martin shook his head and stepped past her into the cabin. Naomi pulled the door shut and set Persephone down, reaching to grasp Martin's cold hand. "Are you hurt? Sick? What's wrong?"

Martin shook his head again and laughed, though there was no humor in the sound. He pulled his hand away and scrubbed both palms over his face. "I never have to worry about how to introduce an issue with you. Before I'm hardly thinking it, you want to know what's wrong. It's kind of irritating, to tell you the truth."

"Well now that you've brought it up, you have some irritating habits yourself." Naomi closed her eyes for a moment, and imagined a large, warm hand smoothing the bristles from her spine. "But that's a topic for another time. Sit. Talk."

"Yes ma'am." Martin's edges were all still there, but he belied the sarcasm by complying with her first request, at least. He sat down at the table, folding his arms and staring down at them. Naomi watched him for a second, then set about fussing. She always had a kettle warming on the wood-burning stove, so in just a few minutes she had a mug of steaming, fragrant tea in front of him. She sat down across from him with her own mug and waited.

He didn't make her wait long, nor did he tiptoe around. "The baby with Quinn. Lark. She's Grace's daughter, isn't she?"

Naomi felt a moment of breathlessness, then reached across the table to grasp his wrist, pulling his hand free so she could weave her fingers through his. She sent his heart a warm wave of comfort before she nodded. "Yes."

He nodded as well, squinting as he gazed at her. Long moments passed before he spoke again. "You knew. She told you."

"She didn't volunteer the information. I guessed, when we first found her, back at my old house. When I helped her bathe, I could tell she'd recently had a baby." Naomi waited, letting him work through this at his own pace. She had known this day would come, and welcomed it, now that it was here.

Martin turned his head to the side. "I saw her the day Piper and Jack and the others left. Went over to say hello to Ignacio, and Quinn was there with her. With Lark. I knew, the instant I saw her."

He returned his eyes to hers, and they were filled with torment and wonder at the same time. "She looks exactly like Grace did, just the spitting image of her. But it was more than that. I could *feel* her connection, both to Grace and to me. Naomi." His voice broke, his eyes suddenly swimming. God, how it twisted her heart to see this strong man's tears. "Grace is that little girl's mama! Why aren't they together? And I'm her grandfather! What am I supposed to do with all that?"

They weren't Naomi's questions to answer, and she knew it. "Have you talked to Grace yet?"

"No. Not yet. She's been avoiding me for days. I think she knows I know." He breathed for a moment. "Did she ever plan on telling me?"

"I'm not sure. She's still so fragile, I haven't pressed her on it." She squeezed his hand. "I'm sorry I kept it from you. She asked me to not say anything. She's terrified of what you might do, of losing you like she lost the rest of her family."

Martin wiped at his eyes impatiently, then frowned. "Why is she afraid of what I might do? Does she really think I'm that harsh? Christ, her mom was pregnant with her when we got married. I'm sure Grace did the math on that long ago. I'm not in a position to do any judging."

He paused. His eyes narrowed, and Naomi saw the instant the terrible knowledge took root. His voice, when he spoke, was pleading. "Isn't Quinn the father? Or her boyfriend, William?"

Oh, God. This, she hadn't seen coming. Naomi drew in a deep, steadying breath, and reached for Martin's other hand. She shook her head, holding his gaze, flooding him with all the comfort she could summon. "No, Martin. Neither one of them."

He knew, then, and his face went sickly white. "Oh my God. Oh, no. Not that, no."

Naomi *felt* his heart stutter, then pound. He slumped forward on the table, burying his face in his folded arms. She scooted around to kneel beside him, rubbing his back in long, soothing strokes. "Just take deep breaths. That's it."

She rubbed his back until his pulse slowed, leaning her cheek on his shoulder. She waited, and when he lifted his head again, she took his chin and turned his head so he would meet her gaze. He needed to hear this. "She survived it. She survived, and we've got her now, safe and sound."

She didn't promise that Grace would be okay, because she didn't know if it was true. Grace had survived being gang-raped, but she would never be the same. Nor would Piper. Both their daughters had been brutalized, and sometimes, it made Naomi wonder why the whole damn human race hadn't just died out. What was it all for, if they couldn't rise up out of the ashes of the old world as better people? What was in the dark hearts of those people that they sought to damage and exploit?

She shook off the bleak thoughts and concentrated on Martin. He looked so much older than he had just a few minutes ago. His eyes gazed at a distant horizon as he assimilated the information, and she knew the moment he went to the place Grace had dreaded. His face smoothed into a cold, hard mask, and every bit of light in his eyes died. This was the face of the Marine, she knew, the face he'd worn for combat. For killing.

He sat up straight and pulled away from her. "I couldn't understand why she would abandon her own child. Now I know why." His voice was as cold and controlled as his face. "What Ed's friend at Bear Creek told us about – it was like that, for her. They raped her, and they would have killed her, if she hadn't escaped. Those men need to be put down, like the diseased animals they are."

He turned bloodshot eyes to Naomi. "I shouldn't have stopped you that day, with Brody. I should have let you kill him where he stood. I should have helped you kill him. And I'm going to kill the men that did this to her, every single one of them."

Naomi overrode the instinct to soothe and comfort, giving instead some of the hard reality Martin was so fond of dispensing. "That is the most selfish thing I've ever heard.   And your reaction is exactly why Grace didn't confide in you."

Martin's nostrils flared, and the wave of *menace* that rolled off him had Naomi stepping backwards before she was even aware of moving. Hades was suddenly there, a low growl rumbling in his chest, crowding his big body between them. Persephone barked sharply, then whined, then barked again, as if trying to get Martin's attention. He didn't even seem to notice. His chest heaved, and he bit out words. "How is wanting to defend my daughter selfish?"

"It's too late to defend her," she shot back, and he flinched as if she'd slapped him. "She has lost her mother and her brother, and William. She's estranged from Quinn, when any fool can see how dear they are to each other. Most of all, she longs for that baby girl, but she doesn't know how to handle what she's feeling. You've seen the way she carries Persephone around, like a baby. Just like you do, when you're missing little Michael."

Naomi felt her chin begin to wobble and fought to control it.   He didn't need her tears, her softness or compassion right now. He needed truth. "If you leave her to pursue some sort of vengeance, which could very well get you killed, you will be abandoning your daughter. You'll be leaving her completely alone in this world. And it will be so much worse than losing everyone else, because you will have *chosen* to leave her."

He stared at her, and she could *feel* his rage as if it was her own, a combination of impotence and anger. He knew she was right. He stood up so fast, the chair he'd been sitting in tipped over to crash on the floor. Again, he didn't even seem to notice, pacing back and forth in the space beside the table, faster and faster, raking his hands through his hair in ever-increasing agitation.

Naomi stood up and retrieved the axe from where she kept it, just inside the door. Without a word, she handed it to him, then followed him outside to the woodpile.

She sat in one of the Adirondack chairs nearby, Hades beside her, Persephone in her lap, watching as the hard work slowly wore the desperate edges off his fury. He paused to peel off his t-shirt, hardly missing a beat as he tossed it to her. His familiar scent lifted from the damp folds, and Naomi turned her face away, unnerved by the slow, hot curl of desire, the first she'd felt since Scott had died. Of all the timing. She kept her eyes closed after that, unwilling to either act on the feeling or lie to herself about it, listening to the rise and fall of the wind and the steady chunk of Martin's axe.

He split and stacked an enormous pile of wood before he wound down. Naomi was drowsing by that time, leaning her head back against the chair, Persephone curled up on her chest. She blinked sleepily when Martin retrieved his t-shirt from her lap, and watched as he paused to mop his face with a clean handkerchief before he slid the shirt back on and pulled a chair over to sit beside her. He looked calmer, but his rage was banked only, still simmering just beneath the surface.

"Would it be worse, do you think, knowing exactly what happened? Or is what I'm imagining more terrible?" He asked the questions in a low voice without looking at her.

"I honestly don't know. Piper didn't tell me details, but I *felt* things. When I touched her, sometimes." She was quiet for a moment. "I try not to think about it."

"How am I supposed to look at her or talk to her and *not* think about it? I can't just pretend it never happened. And I sure as hell can't pretend I don't know."

"No, you can't. But she would hate it if she saw it in your face every time you looked at her, just like Piper did. Neither one of our girls deserves to be defined by what happened to them. They're not victims. They're survivors."

Martin grunted. "Semantics. Words. They don't help me. They don't tell me how to keep it from eating me alive."

"There's always more wood to split." He shot an irritated glance at her, and Naomi reached out to rest her hand on his forearm. "Here's the thing. If you can't figure that out, if I can't, how are our girls going to? We're the parents. We've got to show them the way."

"Shit." Martin shut his eyes. "I know you're right, in my head. I can hear your words and understand the logic of them, but I can't feel it, here, in my gut." His hands opened and closed in white-knuckled fists, pressing against his stomach. "All I can feel is how badly I want to hurt them. I want to make them scream before I crush their skulls."

"I know. I know exactly what you mean."

He tipped his head back against the chair, staring up at the sky. After a moment, he held his hand out to her, and she curled her fingers with his and squeezed. He squeezed back, then tugged their joined hands to rest over his heart.

"It's not the baby's fault, though. Lark isn't to blame. Grace can't think that." He lapsed into silence again, and Naomi didn't try to fill it, giving him time and quiet to think it through. Finally, he spoke again, his voice stronger, surer. "I want to be a part of that baby's life, to help raise her. There are two people left on this Earth who share my blood, that I know of. She's my granddaughter." He looked at Naomi, and the wonder was back in his eyes. "Lark. It's a pretty name, don't you think?"

"It's a lovely name for a darling, sweet baby."

His lips curved, a precious moment of real pleasure, real pride. Then he sobered once more. "Grace will come around. She's a mother now. She'll learn to love her baby, I'm sure she will."

For the first time since their conversation began, Naomi felt a chill of trepidation, for both of them. "Martin, you can't decide that for her. You see Grace when you look at Lark, but you can't know what Grace sees."

His jaw set at a stubborn angle. "I'll help her see. Like you said. I'll love little Lark, and show Grace the way."

Naomi smiled, even though Martin, of all people, would see the lie of it. "I hope so. For all of you, I hope so."

He looked away, his jaw flexing and relaxing for a moment, then returned dark, intense eyes to hers. "You were wrong about one thing, though. Grace wouldn't be left alone. She would have you."

Naomi smiled. "She's stuck with me, whether she likes it or not. Now, do we need to postpone this trip? I was just about to head over to Ignacio's to get the horses. We can put it off, if you want time to talk to Grace."

Martin frowned. "Let's see how it shakes out. Like I said, she's been avoiding me for all she's worth. I'll talk to her tonight, and make the call after that." He blew out a big breath of air. "I know it's been quiet since we saw that first helicopter, but my skin's crawling. We need information, sooner rather than later. And we need to know about the conditions on Rampart Range Road, whether a large group could move on us via that route."

"Okay." Naomi hesitated, then went with her gut. "Do you want to come with me to Ignacio's? You could talk to Quinn. If he's okay with it, you could introduce yourself to Lark."

Martin looked down at his hands, and Persephone chose that moment to step delicately from Naomi's lap over to his. He scooped her little body to his chest and buried his nose in her fur. Then he tucked her against his shoulder and stood up. "I do want to go, but there's something I need to do first. I'll meet you back here with the ATV, say in about twenty minutes?"

"Sure."

As usual, he didn't say goodbye but just went on his way, Persephone's perky ears just visible over his shoulder as he strode along. Naomi watched until they disappeared over a rise, then sighed. Heartache loomed dark on the horizon, for everyone involved. In a perfect world, Grace would heal, and open her heart to her daughter. She and Quinn would raise the baby together, whether they did so as friends or as a romantic couple. Martin would help, and Ignacio, and a constellation of others, including Naomi herself. She shook her head. In a perfect world, little Lark wouldn't exist.

But she did exist, the product of her mother's suffering and her grandparents' young love. Who could say what tragedies and accidents, what strokes of fortune, good and bad, went into the creation of a person? She doubted they would ever know who Lark's father was, but what if that little girl was the finest thing he ever created, in spite of the violence of that creation? There was no way to twist her mind around the complexities of it, to see the balance. Maybe "perfection," then, lay in trusting that a balance did exist, that life was somehow unfolding as it should, even if she couldn't see it from her limited perspective. Naomi shook her head again and laughed softly to herself. She was starting to sound like Verity. And that was pretty terrifying.

Hades heaved out of his spot in the shade and ambled over to her, resting his head in her lap and gazing up at her, his back end shifting from side to side as he wagged what little tail he had. Naomi smoothed her hands over his big head, then leaned to scratch his chest, making him rumble happily. He hooked his jaw over her shoulder and squeezed, pressing the side of his head to the side of hers. As always, his version of a hug made her smile, made her chest ache with the joy and warmth of him, wrapped around her heart. Naomi had loved animals all her life, and had enjoyed close bonds with many, but Hades was different. He had become as foundational to her as breath, as the pulse of blood through her veins. She laughed and sat back, ruffling his ears, which made him grin his big, drooly grin.

"You and me, we are peas and carrots. Our relationship, I understand."

She rose and headed inside. She was packed and ready for their trip, though she couldn't say she was looking forward to it. Martin had been meaning to travel over Rampart Range Road, the way Quinn and Lark had arrived, and they would combine that scouting mission with a visit to the people at Bear Creek. She and Martin already had an in with the group, so they were the logical people to go. Whether or not they would learn anything about the helicopter they'd seen was questionable. Naomi doubted it, but they had to try.

She had tried and failed to avoid thinking about Grace's recommendations for their community. The thought of leaving this place rendered her breathless. This had been Scott's family home. Macy's fragile bones lay in this soil. And most importantly, Piper would return here when her wandering days were done. Leaving would mean severing the only physical link she had left with her gypsy girl. Naomi's hands moved automatically through the motions of preparing vegetables and dried venison for a soup she would set to simmer for dinner, even as her mind rubbed over and over the justifications she'd already worn smooth. Valid reasons, all. Except for one thing.

That one thing had come to her in the middle of the night. She had opened her eyes, disturbed perhaps by the movement of an animal outside, or Hades twitching in a dream, but as soon as she had focused on the dimly lit ceiling, a soft voice in her mind had asked a question: What's best for you, Naomi?

She hadn't been able to answer that question. Not then. Not now.

A sudden thump beside her made her jump. Ares prowled towards her, looking for a handout and ignoring the "no cats on the counter" rule with arrogant disdain. Naomi hissed and shooed him down, then waited a few minutes before she "accidentally" dropped a sliver of venison on the floor. Hades' ears shot to full attention, but he'd long since learned to keep his distance from the rangy tomcat. Ares spent as much time out and about as he spent in the cabin these days, and wore the scars of his survival with imperial pride. Only during the worst of the winter snows had Naomi needed to supplement his diet. She stroked along his spine, then moved to give Hades a taste of venison as well. Outside, she heard the sound of the ATV approaching, so she cupped Hades' chin, met his eyes, and touched his mind with a silent command to "Stay."

She stepped out of the cabin just as Martin pulled up. He kept the ATV idling, and Naomi narrowed her eyes as she walked towards him, trying to analyze what was different. Not until she caught an unfamiliar scent did she figure it out.

"You shaved?"

"Twice." He rubbed a hand along his jaw, which usually sported a light stubble. "When Grace and Benji were babies, their mom got me in the habit. I don't have much of a beard and I've gotten lazy about shaving, but I don't want to whisker burn Lark, if I hold her."

Naomi looked down and swallowed hard, overwhelmed by the sudden need to cry. Scott had done the same thing when the girls had been tiny, shaving as soon as he'd gotten home from work. Their little heads had always smelled of his aftershave when Naomi put them to bed. She climbed onto the ATV behind Martin and secretly wiped her eyes behind his back. "Let's go."

She used the trip to get a handle on her feelings, focusing on the scenery streaming by: the huge, grey boulders in the forest along Rampart Range Road, the slow decay of the deserted buildings in town, the wide-open sky above Highway 24 when they left the city. By the time Martin pulled up at Ignacio's ranch, she had achieved a measure of control. This wasn't about her, and no one involved needed her emotions thrown into the mix.

Ignacio appeared in the doorway of the barn, and lifted his hand in welcome. Martin parked and shut off the ATV, and together they walked into the dim, dusty stable. Ignacio had returned to currying Ben, who nickered when he caught sight of Naomi. Shakti stuck her head out of her stall as they walked past, chuffing a hello. Naomi hugged Ignacio first, then leaned into Ben's shoulder, wrapped her arms around his neck, and shut her eyes. He folded his head around her while she soaked in the warmth of his beautiful, enormous heart. After a moment, Ignacio's hand landed on her back, light and warm.

"What's wrong?"

Naomi opened her eyes and smiled at her friend. "Don't ask Martin that. He'll accuse you of being 'annoying.'"

Martin shot her a look which reinforced that very opinion, then turned sober eyes on Ignacio. "Is Quinn around? And Lark?"

It didn't surprise Naomi a bit when Ignacio understood the implications of Martin's question immediately. "Go slow and careful with the boy, Martin. He'd die for that little girl, and his deepest fear is that someone will take her away from him."

"He told you, then? That Lark is Grace's daughter?"

"He didn't tell me anything. I have eyes, don't I? He's pretty near as defensive about Grace as he is about Lark – won't tolerate so much as a single word against her. He and the twins have churned around with the town kids about it more than once."

Martin nodded. "I owe him, then." His voice strangled thin with emotion. "For taking care of both my girls."

Ignacio nodded towards the house. "They're inside. Quinn was going to feed her lunch then put her down for a nap."

Naomi straightened. "Do you want me to come with you?"

Martin nodded, which surprised her, and held out his hand. When she took it, he squeezed so hard she yelped. He murmured an apology and loosened his grip, and she could feel that his hands were shaking. By the time they reached the door that led to the mudroom and the kitchen beyond, he was sweating. He gestured for her to precede him. Naomi knocked softly, then stepped inside.

Quinn was seated at the kitchen table. Lark was tucked in the crook of his arm, drinking from a bottle, her dark eyes locked on his face as he murmured to her. They had both grown since she'd last seen them, which made her want to cry again. Quinn looked up and smiled when he saw her. Then his eyes flickered behind her, and the smile vanished. He stood up, and the boy vanished as well. In his place, a hard-eyed man stood holding a sleepy baby, all the muscles in his face tensed and tight.

"I won't let you take her away from me," Quinn said. "If Grace sent you, you tell her I'm sorry, but it's too late. Lark is my daughter now."

Naomi took a deep breath, and spared just a moment to long for the time before, when they could all pretend that this was just a casual visit for a little while, and ease up on Martin's reason for being here gently, slowly. But, no. All of the social niceties she had so excelled at were useless now, and Quinn, it would appear, could be as direct as Martin. Well, she could be direct, too.

"We don't want to take her, Quinn, and Grace didn't send us." She stepped to the side, and reached back to pull Martin forward. He hadn't taken his eyes off the baby or made a sound since they had stepped into the room. Naomi turned back to Quinn. "Martin just wants to know his granddaughter and help you in any way he can. She's some of the only family he has left."

"She's the only family I have, period." Quinn's arms tightened around the baby, and she started to squirm and fuss. "We don't need any help."

Martin's eyes shifted to Quinn. "Did you know your grandpa when you were a boy, Quinn?"

Quinn flinched, and looked away. "Yes."

"Did you love him?"

Quinn scowled at the floor, and the boy was back. "That's not fair," he muttered.

Naomi tilted her head to the side. "It is fair," she said gently, insistently. "Martin wants to give his love to Lark, just like your grandpa gave his love to you." She let that sink in for a moment. "He's not trying to take anything away from you. He wants to add to the love and support around his granddaughter."

Quinn shut his eyes, his expression pained. Then he opened his eyes and stared at Martin. "What did Grace tell you?"

"Nothing. But I know, about how Lark was conceived."

"It's not her fault!" Quinn burst in before Martin could finish speaking. "And I won't have people thinking that, do you hear me? Lark didn't ask to be born. What happened to Grace isn't a part of her. I won't let it be!"

Lark's fussing escalated into fretful crying. Without missing a beat, Quinn shifted the baby to his shoulder, rubbing and swaying in a baby-soothing dance as old as time. He glared at both Martin and Naomi, his expression as fierce as his hands were gentle. "People suspect, you know, about Grace and Lark. You can't hide something like that, not with the way people have changed. They think I'm the father, that Grace abandoned both of us. For Lark's sake, they can keep right on thinking that. I won't have them talking behind her back, calling her 'bad blood,' or worse, telling her someday about the ugliness she came from. I'll die before I'll let that happen, do you understand me?"

Martin hung his head for a moment. When he lifted it, tears were running freely down his cheeks. He shrugged to wipe them on the shoulders of his shirt, but didn't try to hide them. "As far as I'm concerned," he said hoarsely, "I couldn't ask for a better father for my grandbaby. I can't promise I'll never interfere because I'm a man of strong opinions, but I swear to you I will never try to take her away from you." He held out his hand. "On my honor, I swear it."

Quinn measured him, the man once again in full possession of his features. Finally, he reached out to clasp Martin's hand. They shook, hands locked. Then Quinn returned to patting Lark's back. For long moments, the only sound in the kitchen was the baby's softly diminishing fussing. Then, Quinn shifted Lark in his big, confident hands and offered her to Martin.

"Would you like to hold her?"

Martin's face twisted. He took the baby without a word, turning away as he tucked her against his chest. Naomi could see his shoulders shaking, and she turned away to give him some privacy in this intensely intimate moment. She looked up at Quinn.

"Thank you."

He nodded, his face reddening softly in the dim light of the kitchen, all boy again. "Yeah." He met Naomi's eyes, his own eyes troubled. "So Grace never told him? Nothing at all?"

"No." Naomi paused, searching for words that were both gentle and truthful. "She's so confused, Quinn. She doesn't talk about it, but I can *feel* it. Her instinct is to love Lark, but she can't separate the baby from what she went through. I don't know if she'll ever be able to."

"I know." Quinn glanced over his shoulder at Martin and Lark, then lowered his voice for Naomi's ears only. "We went through so much together, Grace and me. I wanted us to be a family. I wanted her to learn to love me, like she loved William. Like she'd love a husband." His face flushed red again. "You know what I mean."

"I do." Tenderness for this sweet boy just swamped her. She touched his forearm, fingers light. "But I don't know if she'll ever be able to feel that way for any man. Not for a long time, at least."

"That's what Ignacio says." Quinn hung his head. "I didn't tell him what happened to Grace, but he knows. You know how he just figures stuff out, without you saying anything. He says when a horse has been broke badly, with violence and fear, sometimes it's damaged forever. Its trust is broken." Quinn looked down again, and his voice shook. "He says Grace is like that. He says her trust in people was broken, not just her trust in men. No one stepped up to help her when those men were hurting her. Night after night, and not one person even tried."

"You helped her. She said you saved her life."

Quinn shrugged. "Only after she got herself away from them. I didn't rescue her or anything."

"There are many ways to rescue someone," Naomi said. She looked over her shoulder at Martin. He was holding Lark in the crook of his arm, and they were gazing at each other, transfixed. "You were there for both Grace and Lark when they desperately needed you, and I know one person, at least, who is very grateful."

Martin looked up and met her gaze. "Come look at her eyes, Naomi. Have you ever seen such eyes?" He turned to the side as Naomi approached, tilting and tucking his shoulder into her as she leaned close. Together, they gazed down at the baby, who regarded them both with an ancient solemnity. "It's like she looks right into you. Like she sees into your soul."

"Hello, Lark," Naomi greeted her softly. "Bitty baby bean."

The baby smiled at Naomi's playful tone, proudly displaying two teeth. Both Naomi and Martin beamed back at her, then smiled at each other. Martin leaned his forehead against Naomi's for a moment, his dark eyes inches from hers, and Naomi felt the connection between them deepen and wrap around her bones.

"Thank you," he said softly. "For helping make this happen."

Then he bent to kiss Lark's downy head, rubbing his freshly-shaven cheek against the baby's face. Lark reached up to pat his cheeks, and their eyes locked once more. Watching them fall in love, Naomi went right over the edge of that cliff herself. For both of them.

SEVEN
Grace: Woodland Park, CO

Grace scooted in the door of the cabin she shared with her dad right on the razor's edge of curfew, which wasn't all that different from the time before. In those days, she had taken great pleasure in slicing it as thin as possible, always managing to avoid triggering the consequences by the narrowest margin. Curfew, then, had been "9:00 pm on a school night, midnight on the weekend." Curfew now was "before dark," which was considerably later during the summer than during the winter, but she still had that narrow margin down pat. The last sliver of brilliant orange sun slipped behind the mountains just as she closed the cabin door behind her.

Often, her dad had already gone to bed by the time she returned home. He was up before dawn most days, and adequate sleep, he always joked, was one of the fundamental human rights he'd fought for during his years with the Marines. Just like in the time before, she was expected to check in and let him know she was home, and Grace headed through the small living room on tiptoe to do just that. A light flared by the dark fireplace, and she squealed, clutching her chest where her heart pounded.

"Dad! Geez, you scared the crap out of me!"

Martin adjusted the wick on the hurricane lamp he'd lit, then settled back in his chair, just gazing at her, not speaking. Instead of slowing down, Grace's heart picked up speed. Oh, this did not bode well. Not well at all. For three days, she'd used every trick in the book – faking sleep, rushing out the door for a nonexistent meeting with Anne, staying out as late as she dared – all to avoid the conversation she feared was inevitable. And imminent.

Rather than let him take the lead, she launched with the first thing that came to mind. "I'm glad you're up, actually. Anne and I have been researching possible locales to check out for relocation, and I think we've narrowed it down to two. Anne likes the idea of Crested Butte, but I think Pagosa Springs is a much more viable option. She has friends in Crested Butte, and that's swaying her opinion. Pagosa Springs, though, has a much more temperate climate, and it's –"

"Grace."

She faltered for a moment, then pressed on. She could feel something huge rising up in her, something terrible that would change everything. "It's nearly 2,000 feet lower in elevation, which means a longer growing season, and then there are the hot springs to consider –"

"Grace, stop."

"Dad, just let me finish, okay?" She was nearly babbling now but couldn't do anything about it. "It's really important. People need to understand the consequences of staying here. They need to think in terms of isolation and defense, just for a generation or maybe two, until the danger passes. Then..."

Her dad stood up and walked to stand right in front of her, and her voice faded into silence. He hesitated, then put his hands on her shoulders and squeezed. "I know about Lark. I know she's your daughter, and how she was conceived."

Grace's insides went cold and still. She stared up at her father for what felt like a lifetime. Then she pulled her shoulders free and backed several steps away from him. She couldn't stand being close to his warmth, to the sound of his breathing. His face was twisted, but she couldn't identify the type of pain he was feeling. Remorse? Disgust? Guilt?

"Gracie, I am so sorry. I should have known, but I didn't want to. I convinced myself Quinn was the father. Or maybe William, I thought, before he died. Naomi said—"

"She told you. After I asked her not to." Grace latched on to the betrayal, fanned the flames of it, and anger began to warm the ice inside her. "She promised. She broke her word—"

"No. That's not how it was," he interrupted, voice firm. "I guessed that Lark was yours. How could I not, Gracie? Do you have any idea how much she looks like you? I asked Naomi, and she confirmed it. She also told me I was wrong about Lark's father."

"Don't use that word!" The simmering anger flared and snapped. "Don't *ever* use that word! She doesn't have a father. Whichever one he was, he was a rapist, and a murderer. A sub-human, unintentional sperm donor."

Martin flinched. He gazed at her for long moments, then held out his hand. "Will you sit down, so we can talk it out? I know I'm not as good at the talking stuff as your mom was." His voice choked off for a moment, and his eyes shone with sudden tears, but he pressed on. "But I'm what you're stuck with. I can get Naomi, if it'd be easier to talk to her."

Grace didn't want to sit, and she sure didn't want to talk. She folded her arms across her chest and took refuge in cool intellect, in orderly logic. "I don't want to talk about it, to you or Naomi. Not ever." Because she sounded petulant, even to her own ears, she took a few deep breaths. She was proud of how much calmer she sounded when she continued. "Research doesn't support psychotherapy as an effective approach to restoring mental health, and it follows that 'talking it out,' especially without the benefit of an experienced professional –"

"Gracie, sweetheart, you can't outsmart this."

She stopped talking. He took a step towards her as he continued, ducking his head to meet her gaze.

"You can't think it right, or research it right, or create one of your scary cause-and-effect, future-scenario-probability spreadsheets. You can't figure this out with your brain. I know I'm not the most touchy-feely guy, but even I know this. You have to feel it, work your way through it, so you can heal."

His words shredded her defenses, left her naked and vulnerable, feelings which were not to be endured. She backed up several more steps, glaring at him, hunching her shoulders and wrapping her arms as far around herself as she could get them. "I am healed. I'm fine. My life is just fine the way it is, and I don't need anything to be different."

"I held Lark today."

Her legs wobbled. When Martin moved towards her, she held out both hands, stopping him. "You...you what? What did you say?"

"I held Lark. She's beautiful, just as sweet and pretty as you were. And I talked to Quinn. He's open to us being a part of their lives."

A low buzz started in Grace's ears. She couldn't think fast enough to get ahead of this, and the sensation reminded her of that basement room, of trying to make sense of the kind of violence she hadn't known existed. She remembered how hard she'd tried to think her way out of the same fate as that long-dead girl, and how completely she'd failed. What had that girl's name been? She couldn't remember, and felt sick to her stomach.

Her dad went on, a forced optimism in his tone that made her want to put her hands over her ears. "Quinn is determined to raise Lark as his daughter, and he doesn't want her to ever know the truth. I have to say in this instance, I agree with him. When you're ready, we'll go together to see them again. It can be after Naomi and I get back, or we could postpone the trip if you want –"

Grace shook her head, and couldn't seem to stop. "No. No, no, no. Who said you could do that? What gave you the right, to talk to him, to see her, any of it?"

Martin's jaw tightened. "She's my granddaughter. That's what gave me the right." He stared at her for a moment, his eyes bleak. "Gracie, I understand why you don't want anything to do with her right now. But if you just gave her a chance –"

"You understand? What makes you think you understand, Dad?"

She turned away from him and gathered herself. Here it was. The confrontation she had done everything in her power to avoid. He thought he had this all figured out, but what she had to say was so much worse than what he had in his head. She turned back to face him. Fast, she needed to do this fast, like ripping off a bandage.

"I won't have anything to do with Lark, Dad. Not ever. I don't feel for her what a mother is supposed to feel for her child. I don't love her. I won't ever be able to love her." She held up a hand before he could interrupt. "And before you ask, yes, I have factored in the trauma of her conception and birth. Do you really think I didn't research this? There's no doubt those are factors, but here's the thing: I'm no different than I was before. I haven't changed like the rest of you. I didn't take the evolutionary step. My theory is that I'm deficient emotionally –"

"Deficient?" Martin shook his head, his forehead furrowed in angry confusion. "Jesus, Grace, you're the least 'deficient' person I know." She tried to interrupt and he plowed over her, voice rising, temper slipping. "No. I'm not going to listen to your bullshit theories. You think you've thought this all out, but you're your own worst enemy. You're trying to use your head to protect your heart, which is maybe the stupidest thing I've ever known you to do."

Time for another angle. "Dad, do you remember the first time you had sex?"

Martin dropped down on the sofa and covered his face with his hands. "For the love of all that's holy, Grace. What the hell?"

"Do you?"

"Of course I do! What does that have to do with anything?" He saw where she was headed too late to call back the words, and his face went pale before she even started talking.

"I don't. I was unconscious. I'm not telling you this to make you feel worse. Just hear me out. I was a virgin before those men raped me, but not because I was such a 'good girl.' I thought it through when I started dating William, and I didn't think sex was a good idea. I had plans for my life, and even the best birth control isn't 100%. And I never understood my friends when they said they 'got carried away.' I never felt that way. I doubt I ever will. I'm just not made like that."

Martin's eyes were filled with tears again. "You were 17," he said quietly. "Hardly more than a baby, in your first serious relationship. You can't know those things about yourself. You can't know if it would have been different with the right person. Not for sure." His voice cracked. "Give yourself a chance, Grace. You can't just decide not to love, not to live a normal life."

Something mean took her over then. "A 'normal' life? What the fuck does that even mean anymore, Dad? I was headed for college. Do you suppose that's going to work out for me now? I wanted to get my doctorate, pursue a career in academia. You think any of the Ivy League schools will re-open their doors in my lifetime? So, okay, scratch that plan. What's left? Hmm, let me think..." She tapped her chin and just let the ugliness seethe and roll. "Oh, I know! How about if I get married and have a kid! That's 'normal,' right? And lucky me! I already have a kid! And my dead boyfriend's brother is willing to marry me. He made that perfectly clear. Should we wait, do you think, until he's 18?" She waved a hand, sneering. "Nah. No biggie. How's that, huh? Is that fucking 'normal' enough for you, Dad?"

Martin stood up. Grace had never argued with him before, not like this, and in some distant corner or her mind she was cold with fear. They stared at each other across the rift. Then, he said words she had never heard before, the worst words she could imagine.

"I'm disappointed in you, Grace. You're better than this. You're a bigger person than this." He turned away. "I think we both need some time to cool off. We'll talk again when Naomi and I get back."

Grace's mouth opened and closed like a landed fish, but he didn't notice. Didn't look at her. Disappointed? She couldn't breathe. He was quiet for a moment, then went on.

"I've arranged for you and Persephone to stay with Anne at the library. Make sure you pack some things." He finally looked up at her, but his face was unreadable, his eyes impenetrable. "I'll let you know when I leave in the morning. It'll be early."

With that, he turned and walked to his bedroom, closing the door quietly behind him.

Still, Grace stood there. She was afraid to move, afraid she'd just blow apart. She had never even imagined a world without her parents' approval. It just didn't compute. Finally, she wobbled over to the couch and sat down. Her eyes burned, but she couldn't cry. Every breath she took ached, and her stomach was tight as a fist. Something was boiling in her chest, but she honestly wasn't sure what it was.

She had told him the truth about herself, and he had been disappointed. He thought she was too young to know herself, to understand her own nature. Grace shuddered, and bile rose in her throat. She swallowed down the burn. Given how he had reacted to her honesty, maybe it was better to just let him keep thinking that.

It was time to set her plans in motion. Better to rush things than to endure another confrontation like that. He was refusing to recognize the accuracy of her self-assessment. What would he think of her when he realized she'd been right?

Through the long hours of the night, she rearranged and recalculated her timeline. By the time the sky lightened with the approaching dawn, she had mentally outlined a course of action, and her misery had been replaced by cold determination. As soon as her father left, she would get moving. When she heard his bedroom door open, she turned her face to the back of the couch and shut her eyes, though she didn't really care whether he believed she was sleeping or not.

Little nails clicking on the hardwood floor surprised her; she had assumed Persephone was with Naomi. Her dad must have had her shut in his room so they could talk. Little Persephone got so anxious when conflicts arose, and it bothered both of them to see her distressed. Grace rolled to her back just as Persephone leaped, wriggling and licking her way up Grace's chest to her chin. Grace sputtered and turned her head, trying to escape the little dog's early morning enthusiasm. A giggle surprised her, and she heard her laughter echoed in her father's low chuckle.

He crouched down beside the couch, his eyes on Persephone. Grace could smell the fresh scent of soap and water on his skin. He was dressed for riding, layered against the chill of the early morning, and a sense of purpose vibrated around him. He stroked a calming hand down Persephone's back, then met Grace's eyes. "Like Naomi says. Little moments of joy. This little girl gives both of us that." He gazed at her for a few moments, then said, quietly, "I love you, Gracie."

He stood, then, and moved swiftly around the cabin, gathering the supplies he had set out the night before. He paused at the door, then lifted his hand in wordless farewell. Grace lifted her hand, too, and the door shut behind him.

Peace settled around her heart. It would help him in the future, she knew, to remember the last words he'd spoken to her had been of his love, not of his anger.

She let Persephone out, then fixed them both breakfast and packed her backpack with what little she wanted to take with her. She took a last look around the little cabin that had so briefly been her home, then slipped out and headed for the library. Her dad had found her a bicycle to make the back-and-forth trips easier, and they'd rigged up a basket for Persephone. The trip into town was almost all downhill, and she was parking her bike beside the library doors before the sun had even warmed the morning chill from the air.

In the open space around the library, people were stirring, setting up tables. She had forgotten today was what people had taken to calling "Market Friday" – the last Friday in the month, when everyone in both the Carroll Lakes group and Ignacio's people brought homemade goods or salvaged items to trade. Given the bumper crops of fruits and vegetables people were starting to harvest from their gardens, this place would be hopping today, and there would probably be festivities lasting well into the evening. Grace consulted her mental timeline and decided the event didn't alter her plans significantly. In fact, the hub-bub could work in her favor. Scooping Persephone out of her basket, she let herself into the library and headed straight for her work area.

Several hours later, Anne's hand landed on her shoulder, startling her. Grace pulled a piece of paper over what she'd been working on and smiled up at the older woman. She was truly going to miss this spirited lady, so wounded, and so creative in adapting around that wound.

"Good morning, Anne. Want to finalize our ideas for relocation this morning?"

Anne took a sip of her hot water – she still grieved coffee like a lost lover – and nodded. "Sure. I was going to work with the girls on the catalog, but I'm sure they won't mind being cut loose. It'll give 'em a chance to flirt their way around the gathering outside."

Grace and Anne shared mirror-image sneers, united in their disdain for the ever-wandering eyes of Karleigh and Viola, two of the teenagers from the Woodland Park community who were helping them with their card catalog project. The two of them whispered and giggled incessantly in the presence of any boy over thirteen or any man under thirty, both consumed by the agonies of teenage longing for love. Viewed in the context of the catastrophic changes that had swept the world, their adolescent flightiness offended Grace on every level. They were immature and frivolous. Then there was the kiss of death; Quinn was their current obsession. As if either one of them would ever, ever be good enough for him.

Anne went to tell the girls of the change in plans, then returned, murmuring softly into her steaming mug of water. Her eyes were a little vague this morning, and when Grace recognized the opening lines from the Victorian-era poem "The Lady of Shallot," she stifled a sigh. Anne "left the building," as her father put it, whenever the past rose up to haunt her, and it looked like this was one of those times. Grace bent her head back over the project she was working on, hoping Anne would come back to herself before the day was out so she could go over all of this with her. Just in case, though, she'd leave a detailed summary and instructions, along with the letter she'd written for her father weeks ago.

She took a break at lunchtime to eat a handful of nuts and an apple she'd brought from home, standing in the glass-fronted library and watching the activity outside. As she had predicted, the gathering was a hive of activity, tables piled high with fresh produce here, homemade tamales there, as well as the flotsam and jetsam people had salvaged from abandoned homes. Trading looked brisk, and children wove in and out of the crowd, their energy like bright ribbons among the adults. Grace spotted Ignacio, and with him, Ethan and Elise. As always, her heart started pounding heavily, then leapt and settled into a heavy thumping when her scanning eyes spotted Quinn.

He was sitting on a blanket spread out underneath a nearby tree, flanked by the twins, Sam and Beck. And there she was, triangulated between the three of them, chubby arms and legs churning and waving as she lay on her back. Almost four months old now, Grace thought. As she watched, one of the twins held a brightly colored rattle over the baby's head, trying to get her to reach for it.

"Too soon," Grace murmured. Maybe she'd looked up some information on developmental milestones for infants. You never knew when the information might come in handy. "Just put it in her hand."

As if he heard her, Quinn reached for the rattle, taking it gently from his friend and placing it in Lark's chubby hand. She beamed a gummy grin up at him, then brought the rattle to her mouth and began gnawing enthusiastically, her dark eyes locked on the young man who smiled down at her. Faintly, Grace saw light flicker between them, what looked like green and pink lines, and she gasped softly. Was this what Piper saw? The bond-lines she spoke of? They were beautiful.

Grace realized that she had both hands clenched in her shirt over her heart. If everything went as planned, this would be the last time she saw either one of them. Ever.

"Your daughter will live in interesting times."

Grace spun around. A tiny golden fairy of a woman stood right behind her, head tilted to the side, a gentle smile on her face. The expression was not reassuring. Grace swallowed hard. Other than Macy's memorial at Naomi's cabin, she had never spoken to Woodland Park's most eccentric and notorious resident.

"Hi, Verity."

"Hello, Grace." Verity glowed. Literally. "You remember me? I wasn't sure if you would."

Grace managed not to roll her eyes. "You're fairly unforgettable."

"Do you think so?" Verity preened for a moment, delighted by the praise. "Admiration is the best way for a friendship to start, I always say."

Grace's eyes narrowed. "You think we'll be friends?"

Verity dimmed. "Well, no, actually I don't. Social niceties and all that blah blah. I'm not very good at making friends, and when I do, they seem to die." She frowned thoughtfully. "Huh. Wonder if I'm the common denominator there?" Then she focused on Grace once more. "Anyway. As I was saying, Lark will live in interesting times. That's popularly thought to be a Chinese curse translated into English, but no Chinese attribution has ever been found. I looked that up a long time ago, and you're just the person to appreciate my thorough research."

Grace's squint became a frown. "Are you saying Lark is cursed?"

"Not at all." Verity looked past Grace's shoulder, and her face softened as she watched Quinn play with the baby. "But like mother like daughter. Her path will be anything but 'normal.'"

What to focus on first? The fact that Verity somehow seemed to know about the argument she'd had with her dad? Impossible. She went with the one thing she was sure of. "Lark isn't my daughter. She's Quinn's."

"Oh, yes, she truly is. They chose this in the time before time. They have loved each other through many lifetimes, and they are joyful to be together again in this one. You and Lark, on the other hand, are new to each other. Your path together will be complicated." Verity returned her eyes to Grace, somehow managing to look stern and mischievous simultaneously. "Hopefully, though, you'll both get your shit together and not have to go another round in your next incarnation."

Grace decided she had nothing to lose. "Have you ever been screened for clinical insanity? I don't mean any disrespect – I'm truly just curious."

Verity laughed, a sound that combined Christmas jingle bells and a happily babbling brook. "Shuh. Of course. Now." She checked a nonexistent watch. "I believe it's time for you to burn a few bridges, and say your goodbyes. We'll talk again, after."

Verity inclined her head towards the window, where Karleigh and Viola had taken up positions on the blanket beside Quinn, Lark and the twins. Karleigh's arm was resting casually against Quinn's thigh as she reclined beside him. He moved his leg, but she just shifted again, resting her hand on his knee as she made a show of cooing at Lark. A red haze dropped over Grace's vision, and her feet were in motion before she took her next breath.

Not until she was standing over all of them, glaring, did it occur to her to wonder what on Earth she planned to say. Her eyes locked onto Quinn's face. She saw his lips move, form her name, but she couldn't hear. It was as if all her senses were dulled, packed in cotton, except for the spot of white-hot rage burning in the center of her chest. Her eyes zeroed in on Karleigh, and she felt a snarl distort her mouth.

"Back off him. Now."

Karleigh was up in a flash. She was half a head taller than Grace, robust and curvy to Grace's boyish slightness, but she didn't step closer. She did, however, return Grace's snarl. "Or what?"

Grace had never looked for a fight in her life, but to her amazement, she wasn't the least bit afraid. Exhilaration joined the rage in her chest, and she stepped in, crowding the larger girl. "Or I kick your ass. Was that concept simple enough for you to grasp, or should I break it down a little farther?"

"Grace." Quinn's voice. "Stop. It's okay."

She cut her eyes to him. He was standing now, too, with Lark in his arms. She smiled at him, sharp and mean. "Actually, it's not. You've got a daughter to think about now. Gotta watch the company you keep." She kept talking to him but returned her eyes to Karleigh, who was standing there, chest heaving her outrage. "At the very least, you should set your sights higher than a trashy, shit-for-brains, bitch in heat."

Karleigh swung and Grace ducked. She planted her hands just above the other girls' ample boobs and shoved as hard as she could, sending Karleigh sprawling backwards. A wild ferocity surged in her blood, and she started forward, only to be brought up short by a hand fisted in her shirt at the scruff of her neck.

"Grace Ramirez!" Rowan let go of her shirt but took hold of her arm. "I saw that whole thing! You owe this young lady an apology!"

Grace pulled her arm free and straightened her shirt. Then, she shook her head slowly. "No. I don't apologize unless I'm wrong. And I wasn't. Everything I said was true."

Karleigh was up on her feet again, flanked by Andrea and Thomas, her face crimson with embarrassment and rage. "I wouldn't accept your apology on a silver platter, you freakin' bitch! I can't even believe you! You abandon Quinn and your own daughter –" Her gaze snapped around the gathering crowd. "Yeah, I said it out loud, and we all know! Lark is your daughter, and you dumped her like last week's garbage. Her and Quinn. You don't want them, but no one else can have them, is that it?"

Burning bridges. That's what Verity had said. So be it. Grace turned her cutting smile on Karleigh. "That's not it at all, Karleigh. I'd just rather see someone with a modicum of moral fiber and perhaps the intelligence of a kumquat step up. That means you don't make the cut."

"I'll kill you, you nasty little bitch!" Karleigh lunged, and Andrea and Paul struggled to hold her back. "I'll kill you with my bare hands!"

Grace watched until the bigger girl subsided, then smiled at her again, sweetly this time. Her voice, when she spoke, was light and conversational. "Have you ever seen two people fight to the death, Karleigh?"

Silence and stillness spread through the crowd at her words. She looked around, making eye contact with these people, these men and women who thought they had already survived the worst. Laughing and talking, enjoying their rustic little market, determined to stay here and "defend their homes and families." In a matter of hours, Hell on Earth could be in their midst. If not today, then tomorrow. It would come, and they were fools for refusing to see it.

"Have any of you? Seen an actual fight to the death?" Her eyes sought Quinn's. He was weeping quietly, unashamed, just as she'd known he would be. Dear Quinn, who always felt her pain. "I know one of you has," she said softly, then raised her voice again. "But the rest of you have no idea. It's nothing like the movies. It takes forever, most of the time. They cry, because they don't want to hurt each other – doesn't matter if it's men or women. Their clothes get torn, in awkward and embarrassing ways, and the crowd laughs. Then they get serious, and they stop being human."

She turned back to Karleigh, whose face had lost all color as she listened. Her dad had told her, once, that Karleigh could sense the feelings of others. Grace allowed herself to remember and stared at the other girl. "And you know who I always felt the most sorry for? The winner. The looks on their faces. The horror they felt, at learning what they could do. What was inside of them. It was terrible to see." Her eyes swept around again. "That's what will happen. Those of you that survive the initial attack will be kept for the arena. Except for the girls." Eyes back on Karleigh, Grace let her have all of it. The humiliation, the pain, the fear. "They keep the girls for a different kind of entertainment."

Karleigh's face crumpled, and she began to cry, great wracking sobs. She wasn't all bad, and, on some level, Grace had known that all along. She had been a tool, a means to this end. In the crowd around them, others were crying, battered by the horror Grace had stored in her heart and unleashed on them. She stepped away from Rowan, who seemed stunned, and walked to Quinn.

Lark was tucked under his chin, her head resting on his chest, but she was staring at Grace. Grace gazed back at her daughter, then reached to touch her willingly for the very first time, smoothing her palm over the warm, round curve of her little head. She looked up at Quinn, and cupped her other hand along his jaw, embracing them both.

"Make them understand," she said quietly. "You know what will happen if you stay. Take Lark, and go. Keep her safe. I'll do what I can to stop them, but you all need to go. Soon."

Quinn pressed his hand over hers. "Gracie, I love you. I know you don't love me like that, and I don't need you to. Come with us. Don't do whatever you're planning." His breath hitched in a sob. "Please don't leave us again."

Grace felt a hard tug in the center of her chest, and, for just a few seconds, her resolve faltered. She looked at Lark, and felt the tug again. She forced herself to take her hands away from both of them and stepped back, feeling Quinn's tears, cool and wet, in one empty palm, feeling the ghost curve of her daughter's soft head in the other.

"I can't think of any other way," she said shakily. "Someone has to start eroding their power base. Someone has to assess what's going on with those helicopters and see if there's a way to disable them. They're too organized. They have all the advantages." She looked at Lark, forced herself not to reach for her again, then looked back at Quinn. "It's all I can give her. The best I can give her. Don't you see? It's her only chance at a future."

She turned and walked away before he could answer, leaving unrest and fear seething in her wake, which was good and right. Back inside the library, she drifted back to the windows where Verity still stood. Together, they watched the crowd shift and clump, breaking apart and coming back together in new configurations as people discussed the bomb Grace had thrown into their midst. Neither one of them said a word.

Grace's eyes probed and analyzed, noting the resigned slump of Ignacio's shoulders and Andrea's dejection. The two strongest hold-outs were reconsidering. Now if only Naomi would see reason, this group might choose to survive. In spite of her resolve, Grace's eyes returned again and again to Quinn. He stood like an island in the chaos, his cheek resting on Lark's head as he swayed back and forth, his face written with the lines of his pain.

Karleigh had disappeared, but Viola still lurked about, and the twins were each hovering at one of his elbows, love and worry for their friend plain on their usually inscrutable features. Beside her, Verity lifted a graceful hand. Grace turned to look at her.

"May I?"

Grace nodded, and Verity moved to stand beside her, hands coming to rest like hummingbirds on Grace's shoulders. And even though Grace had been warned about the angels, there was no way she could have been prepared for their majesty, their beauty. She closed her eyes, and knew she was safe for the first time since her family had been stricken with the plague. The relief of it made her sob aloud. How could anything stop this woman, with such powerful beings surrounding her? She could do whatever she desired.

"Well, not exactly." Verity's wry voice sounded beside her ear. "Michael is a total stickler. One might even go so far as to say a killjoy. He totally refused to let me pull this practical joke I had in mind – seriously, it was pure genius and Raphael was all for it, but nooo – ow! Okay! Fine!"

Grace opened her eyes just as Verity lifted one of her hands to rub the back of her head, looking disgruntled. She sighed a long-suffering sigh, then returned her hand to Grace's shoulder and nodded towards the window. "Gabriel wanted you to have this. A gift, before you start your journey."

Grace followed the direction of Verity's gaze and once again found Quinn and Lark. As she watched, everything around them blurred and seemed to speed up. Her daughter grew, right before her very eyes, through toddling steps and messy pigtails, through gangly limbs and a sudden surge in height. Oh, she was so tall, much taller than Grace. She watched the years unfold for her daughter, Quinn a constant loving glow beside her, until a young woman stood where there had been a baby moments before. Lark smiled, but even with joy lighting up her face, those eyes were sad. And those eyes turned to lock on Grace's.

"You'll see her again," Verity said softly. "You agreed, in the time before time. It is written, and it will be."

Grace gasped, desperately wanting to believe, though her intellect kept searching for an explanation for what was happening. "And Quinn? Will I see him, too?"

"That's less clear," Verity answered. "Not all things are certain. His path is his own, but he won't be alone." Once again, she nodded at the window.

Grace turned, and this time, Quinn and the boy called Beck were centered in her vision. Except... "Jump back," Grace breathed. "Beck's a girl? Never saw that coming."

"Neither will Quinn." Verity's voice lilted with laughter. "It won't take them long to figure it out, though."

Grace watched as the scrawny boy became a lean, lovely woman, as pretty as her mother. That woman brought laughter and joy to Quinn's face, then something more. When their bodies curved together, Grace turned her face away. What she was feeling was too complicated to sort out. Quinn's strong arms would hold someone else. His great and golden heart would beat for another. She peeked again, and saw them surrounded by children, sweet-natured boys and fiery girls. She knew she should be glad that Quinn would find love, but her heart ached with loneliness.

Verity lifted her hands and stepped back. The world was once again hard and cold, and Grace shivered. She looked at Verity, who seemed so much smaller without her angelic posse.

"Why did you show me this? Am I going to die?"

Verity sighed, and shook her head. "You mental intuitives. So brilliant, and always in your own way." She lifted her hand and tucked a piece of Grace's hair behind her ear, just like her mother used to do. At her touch, Grace was once more cradled by the shimmer of angels' wings. "We did it to remind you that you're never alone. You've chosen a very difficult incarnation, Grace, one of the hardest I've ever seen. Terrible things have happened to you, and it must have seemed like you were all alone. You never were. None of us are ever alone. The angels won't interfere with a Soul Journey, but they never left you and they never will, not for even a single heartbeat."

Then, she stepped back and cracked her hands together, making Grace jump. She jumped again when Verity emitted a piercing whistle. From the depths of the library, Persephone barked. Grace heard the swift click of her nails on the foyer floor, and caught the little dog automatically when she leaped. Both of them stared at the suddenly purposeful fairy, who was gazing at them with her hands on her hips, tapping her foot impatiently.

"My bike's outside, parked next to yours. When do we leave?"

EIGHT
Piper: Limon, CO

In the chill, half-light before dawn, Piper and Ed huddled over a series of maps with Brian Weaver and a woman named Claire Valente, the leader of the group of survivors from the eastern states. Piper and her companions had been in Limon for three days, longer than they'd originally planned. Weather had delayed them, a series of fast-moving thunderstorms that had battered the area with wind and marble-sized hail. A rising barometer and clear skies this morning were signals to be on their way, and Piper found herself both eager to hit the road and reluctant to leave. These were good people, and even though she had spent every minute she could either interviewing people or writing down what she had learned, she still felt like there was so much information left to gather, especially from Claire's group.

Claire reached out and tapped the city of Grand Island, Nebraska. "Too big," she murmured. She had offered to share her advice and experience, both hard-earned on her nearly 1,500 mile journey here. "Swing to the north, west of Kearney, I think. You won't want to linger near interstates or major highways, or anywhere else traffic stacked up. Hustle through and don't look back, especially if you see a pile of supplies, like canned food or bottled water, just conveniently waiting to be picked up." Her mouth flattened into a grim line. "We lost two people learning that one."

For lack of a better plan, Piper had simply drawn an "as the crow flies" line on the pertinent maps between where they were and where they wanted to go. Loaded with gear as they were, with varying levels of riding experience and endurance among them, they might average 40 miles an hour, sometimes a little less. If they rode for six or seven hours a day, with no major detours or problems, they could make Pewaukee in five, maybe six days.

Ed was examining one of the maps Brian had supplied – different maps, they had discovered, could contain completely different information – and he made a noise of concern. "Piper, look at this." He, too, pointed. "The Prairie State Wolf Wildlife Management Area. Your plan has us going right through there tomorrow." He straightened and looked at her, eyebrows raised. "Do you suppose there are still wolves there?"

"What I wouldn't give for a Google search right about now," Piper muttered. She looked where Ed was pointing, then traced an alternate route with her finger. "I suppose we could swing even farther to the north..."

"Probably not worth the detour," Claire offered. "It's likely the wolves died in their enclosures soon after the plague went through. Ryan, one of the men traveling with us, lived near the zoo in Columbus, Ohio. Before he left, he said the elephants had made it out, and some of the primates, but he heard all the big predators starved. Too well contained. Even if the wolves escaped, there's no way to know if they're still in the area."

Piper swallowed hard, thinking of the animals she had grown up visiting in the Cheyenne Mountain Zoo. Had the pride of lions starved? What about that huge giraffe herd? What had happened to them? "Poor things," she murmured. "I'd rather they'd made it out, even if we did have to watch out for lions and tigers from now on. But I see your point. If I'm remembering my National Geographic channel right, wolves can have a range of hundreds of miles. They could be anywhere."

"There's no way to predict, and in my opinion, no need to alter your course because of it. We started out trying to avoid things like prison areas and such, and it didn't do us any good. We ran into our biggest problems in good old suburbia, U.S.A. The inner cities are safer, where there were businesses and high rise apartments before. People don't tend to live there now. No water, no place to grow food. If you can't avoid going through a major city, go right through the business district rather than the suburbs. Avoid big parks and natural recreational areas, especially if they include a water source, like a lake or river. Those seem to be magnets for people."

"There's so much to think about." Piper looked up at Claire and blew out a nervous breath. "Don't suppose you're up for another adventure? We could sure use your experience, and I wouldn't mind having another girl to share bathroom breaks with."

Claire smiled, but shook her head. "I'm all adventured out, I'm afraid. Most of my people are." She sobered and met Piper's eyes. "I wish you all weren't so set on going. It's terrible out there." She dropped her voice lower, enclosing them in a girls' only bubble. "Especially for women. Do not get separated from your group, you hear me? And don't think twice about stepping behind that giant, Owen. Gender equality is fantastic and all, but you've got to be alive and free to appreciate it. It's a damn shame what we've degenerated into."

Piper reached to rest her hand on Claire's forearm. She liked this practical, intelligent, determined woman. "I've already made it through some of the terrible, and it's worse than shameful. When all this settles down, you and I will have to knock some heads together." She started folding up the maps. "I guess we'll just have to work each problem as it shows up. There's no way to know where trouble will come from."

"That's mostly true. You can be pretty sure trouble will come from people, so avoid 'em. All things considered, I'd rather run into wolves. At least they're straightforward about their intentions. People are tricky and deceptive. They lie and justify, especially to themselves. Even with the new intuitive skills so many people have, it can be hard to assess the situation. You'll figure out how to think it all through and choose the best option." She looked grim again. "You'll also screw up, and learn the hard way. I just hope it doesn't cost you people, like it did us. You don't have as many to spare."

Ed whistled, calling Rosemary to his side. "Well, it seems like we're as ready as we'll ever be. Brian." He held out his hand, and the two men shook vigorously. "It's been a pleasure. If I'm ever back this way, my best girl and I would be happy to stay a while." He nodded with old-school politeness to Claire. "Thank you, for all your help."

"Go with God, Ed." She bent down and ruffled Rosemary's ears, then sketched the sign of the cross on the dog's forehead with her thumb. "You too, sweet girl. Stay safe. Gotta get me a dog now, thanks to you."

Ed headed for the motorcycles where Jack and Owen were completing preparations to leave. Bernice was with them, a shawl clutched around her thin shoulders against the early-morning chill. Murmuring her thanks, Piper hugged Claire, then stuck her hand out to Brian. He shook it, grinning at her.

"Now, Piper, don't embarrass yourself. I know how badly you want me to come along, but I'm needed here. Duty before beauty."

Piper grinned back. They had reached an understanding over the last several days, and she had grown to appreciate this charismatic man's combination of self-effacing humor and sensitivity. She schooled her face into sober lines, playing it straight as they walked together towards the bikes. "I have a confession to make." She paused, then went on solemnly. "If you were the absolute last man on Earth, I might maybe possibly *think* about giving you a chance."

His grin deepened into ridiculously attractive dimples, and he laughed. "No, don't beg. It's beneath you."

They were both laughing when they joined the others at the motorcycles. Jack looked up, his gaze flickering between them. He straightened, his face taking on the neutral expression Piper had come to think of as "shields up." Even his bond-lines dimmed when he did this. He held a hand out to Brian.

"Thank you for all you've done, your hospitality and your information."

Brian shook his hand. "You're more than welcome." He nodded to the guitar slung across Jack's back. "I see you and Traci worked out a trade?"

Jack self-consciously adjusted the strap. "Well, sort of. She wouldn't take anything for it – insisted on giving it as a gift, but I had to swear to stop in and visit if we come back through." He shot an embarrassed glance at Bernice when she cackled out a laugh, and rubbed the back of his neck. "Yeah, she's got a crush, I'm afraid. It weirds me out."

"She's nearly 19," Bernice pointed out, "And she doesn't like her options here." Then, she winked. "Plus you're the closest thing to a rock star she's seen in over a year."

Her words sent sniggers around the group, and Piper elbowed Owen. "Our very own one-man boy band. We are going to have some fun with this, you mark my words."

Jack smiled and shook his head good-naturedly, and looked at Brian again. "Please carry our love to our people."

"I'm looking forward to meeting them." Then, to Piper. "I've got the copy of your notes, safe and sound, ready to deliver to Anne and Grace when I go."

Bernice had suggested sending a copy of the information Piper had gathered back to the Woodland Park community, and Piper had readily agreed. Several people had helped with the transcription, and one of the older men in Limon had kept a copy for himself, expressing interest in expanding and adding to the project himself. In her notes, Piper had included information on the route they'd taken, identifying where they'd seen signs of habitation, where the road had been damaged, and where they'd sensed danger. She had also enclosed a personal note for her mother that read simply: "I got your message. And you used to say I got my stubbornness from Dad! I love you, too." She had signed her name, then thought to add a postscript: "Loki says 'Hi.' Totally creepy, Mom."

Piper inclined her head in thanks as she got on her bike. "I appreciate it. Let them know we're all safe and sound."

"Will do."

Owen reached to shake Brian's hand, and Piper took one last look over her shoulder. Pikes Peak was pink with the dawn, and she let her eyes linger on the familiar outline. Before the day was out, the mountains would be lost to view. Piper pressed a hand over her heart, where the bond-line connecting her to her mother was a steady, solid green. She sent love along that link, and the immediate, tender echo back made tears sting her eyes even as she smiled.

Jack was watching her when she turned her eyes away from home, his face warm with compassion. "Your mom?"

Piper nodded, not really trusting her voice, and he pressed a hand over his heart as well. He'd comforted her this way before, a show of sympathy, but this time was different. This time, the bond-line between them didn't crackle so much as warm and pulse, like a heartbeat. Sudden heat flushed up Piper's chest to her neck and cheeks, startling her. Jack, too, looked startled, and dropped his hand. For the first time since she'd met him, their eyes held just a few seconds too long. Then Jack looked down and started his motorcycle. "Let's get going."

They were off, roaring into the rising sun. From Limon, they zig-zagged to the north-east, following a route Piper had loosely plotted in her head. As agreed, she took the lead, though she checked in with the others often. They flew by tiny plains towns and deserted grain elevators, traveling under a sky so vast, it felt like they were standing still. Herds of antelope startled and fled from the sound of their motorcycles, and several times, they saw groups of placidly chewing cattle who ignored the humans and their noise. Here and there, an abandoned vehicle stood in silent testament to the changes in the world, but, otherwise, traveling across the plains was much as it had been before.

As morning climbed past noon, clouds built in the west, obscuring the mountains and stirring the prairie grass with swirls of wind. By the time they stopped for a break just before they crossed the Kansas state line, it was looking like they might not make it through the day without more rain. Piper stretched out muscles unaccustomed to riding, then jogged to the top of a nearby hill. Owen was already there, eyes crinkling at the corners as he scanned the western horizon. He wasn't as accurate as Jose back in Woodland Park, but his weather sense was the best among them.

"What do you think?" Piper asked. "Should we find shelter, or put on rain gear and tough it out?"

Owen scanned the horizon once more, then shrugged. "I think we should keep going. It seems to be slower moving than the storms we've been seeing, and it feels like it'll swing south."

"Feels like?"

He nodded. Piper examined his profile, and then glanced over her shoulder. Jack was rummaging in the bags on his bike, and Ed had disappeared from view. Rosemary was sitting patiently beside Ed's bike, so he'd probably stepped away to empty his "old man's bladder," as he liked to grouse. Piper looked back at Owen. No time like the present.

"You've never said, and if I'm prying, please say so. But have you changed?"

Owen glanced at her, then returned his eyes to the horizon. Again, he shrugged. "No, not really. I guess I'm kind of like Verity. I've always been different." He smiled a little, an expression of fond remembrance. "I'm just not as flamboyant about it as she is."

"What do you mean? You see the dead?"

"No." He looked down at the ground now, as if uncomfortable talking about this, but he did keep talking.

"I feel what's coming. I have all my life. My grandma always used to say I had 'the Sight,' that it was a 'gift.' The first time it happened was 9-11, and ever since, I've known that something was going to happen a few days before every major terrorist attack or natural disaster."

Piper was quiet for a minute, thinking about the implications. "But you don't know what's going to happen, or where?"

"No."

"What about the plague?"

Owen's jaw tightened. "Just like with all the rest, I knew something was going to happen, but not what. If I'd known that, I'd have taken my family somewhere safe, or at least away from other people." He looked at her, and a series of emotions struggled for control of his features. Guilt, anger, grief, remorse, more guilt. "And no, I didn't know they would die. I didn't know about Layla and the baby, either. I don't get warnings about stuff I could actually do something about."

"Oh, Owen." Piper reached out and slipped her hand into his big, warm, callused one. "I hope you're not offended, but I think your 'gift' sucks."

He laughed a little, as she had hoped he would. "So do I. As far as I can tell, it's worthless."

"You've never gotten information on a horse race or the Super Bowl or something? So you could place a bet?"

"Nah. I have been able to share information now and then, information that helped people." He nodded towards Jack, who was busily duct-taping a plastic tarp around his guitar. "We'll find Jack's sister. I know that."

Piper opened her mouth to ask if they'd all make it safely home again, then shut it. He'd share, if he knew. She squeezed his hand, then let it go. "I appreciate you telling me." Then she turned and headed down the hill. "And you may be able to sense the future, but I'm putting on my frog togs just the same. I don't think that storm's headed south, and I hate being wet and cold."

Owen laughed as he followed her down the hill, and they all shared a quick lunch. She caught Jack scrutinizing her and Owen a few times, but his eyes slid away every time hers swung his way. There was an odd new tension between them, something she hoped would just dissipate without a discussion. They rode on through the afternoon, stopping once to siphon and purify fuel from a cluster of abandoned vehicles, then rode on into the early evening. Finally, they stopped just outside of Cambridge, Nebraska, on what the map told them was Medicine Creek.

Owen's prediction had held; the storm had indeed swung to the south. The evening was beautiful, the light soft and pearly, with just enough of a breeze to keep the mosquitoes at bay. They set the tents up on a rise above the creek amid softly rustling cottonwoods, and Jack scrambled together some of the fresh eggs and vegetables they'd brought with them from Limon. After dinner, both Ed and Owen stretched out on their sleeping bags for a nap. Jack busied himself with the clean-up, while Piper took Rosemary with her for a walk along the streambank.

After the long day on the bikes, walking felt wonderful, though she could feel the pull of exhaustion in her shoulders and back. Hopefully, she'd sleep soundly tonight. They hadn't seen a single sign of life all day, no people, no smoke, nothing. The sensation of being alone in the world was deeply disturbing and brought with it an unease that Piper would bet originated in her brainstem. Like most primates, people functioned best when they were part of a social group. Humans weren't meant to be solitary.

Rosemary ranged far and wide as they walked, splashing in and out of the creek, giving a yip of excitement when she flushed some prairie chickens into flight. She seemed completely at ease until they rounded a bend in the creek where the cottonwoods opened up and gave way to prairie. A house sat on a hill amidst what had once been cultivated fields. The windows had been broken at some point, and dingy white curtains wafted in and out like ghosts.

Piper stopped walking, and Rosemary slid to her side, pressing against her leg as they stood together, looking. On the garage door, the words "God's Judgement" had been spray-painted in big, sloppy, black letters. Rosemary's ears were perked to full alert, her nose twitching as she analyzed the swirling wind for information. After a moment, her ears flattened, and a soft growl rumbled in her chest.

"Well, that's pretty much all I need to know." Piper did an about-face, and they headed back the way they'd come. She didn't know if Rosemary's agitation rose from the presence of the dead or the living, but even from where they'd stood, the combination of rage and despair that permeated the house was palpable. She hadn't seen or sensed anything which suggested they should abandon their campsite, but she'd be sure the others understood setting a watch wasn't merely a formality. She let her hand trail to Rosemary's head.

"You keep those ears awake tonight, okay? And your nose, while you're at it."

She returned to camp to find Owen and Ed still sleeping. Jack had settled down by the fire, leaning against his rolled-up sleeping bag, just staring into the low flames. He looked up at them and blinked owlishly. "I can't believe how tired I am. We basically just sat all day."

"A low-grade adrenalin crash, maybe. We've all been tense for hours, on the lookout, ready for anything." Piper sat down across the fire from him. "A walk might refresh you. If you decide to go, there's a house to the north that bothered Rosemary. Looked abandoned, but we didn't get close enough to confirm that."

"No bond-lines?"

"No, but that doesn't necessarily mean anything. A person alone might not have them. Or they might be able to suppress them, like you do."

Jack blinked again, looking surprised and a little more awake. "I can suppress mine?"

Piper shrugged. "You dim them, whenever you do that 'shields up' thing. Your face turns into a mask, like a poker face, when you don't want people to know what you're thinking. Your bond-lines get fainter when you do that." Her face warmed; it sounded like she'd been watching him, analyzing him. It came as a little shock to realize that she had been. She cleared her throat. "Anyway, we should all stay plenty alert on watch tonight. I'm glad Owen and Ed are getting some sleep now."

"Hmm." Jack made an affirmative sound. He paused, and she *felt* him make the decision to tackle the awkwardness between them. "It looked like you and Owen were sharing a moment earlier." Another pause. "Is something happening between the two of you?"

He was using The Voice on her again. It was subtle, just a smooth thread of *soothe* and *calm,* but Piper sensed it nonetheless. She felt a surge of annoyance. "If by 'something' you mean a friendship, then yes. Would it be a problem if it were something more? And stop with the voice thing. It's doing the opposite of what you intended."

"Okay." Jack didn't flinch at her irritable tone, but she could *feel* his internal debate over whether to be honest or evasive. Honesty won...sort of. "As for you and Owen, I think it would complicate things. He isn't over Layla's death yet."

Piper narrowed her eyes at him. Did he really think he could hide the fact that he was only telling part of the truth? "And?"

Now, he looked away. "Aren't those good reasons to avoid an entanglement, at least for now?"

She'd show him how this "honesty" thing was done. "Jack, the last thing I have on my mind these days is hooking up with someone. I've got some shit of my own to sort out, in case you hadn't noticed. But all that aside, you're not my big brother, and it's none of your business what I do."

He was quiet for a few moments. Then, he sighed, and gave her a peace-offering smile. "You're about Cara's age. So though I could be your big brother, I thank the good Lord I'm not. I'd have spent all my time breaking up the neighborhood brawls you started."

Piper held on to her disgruntlement for a moment, then let it go and laughed. "That Ed. He's been telling tales, I see. So you think riding herd on the neighborhood hot-head would have been worse than living with a fledgling Verity?"

Jack made a comical face. "Geez, when you put it that way..." His face grew serious. "We had no idea what was really happening with Cara – not my parents, and not me. I let her down so badly, Piper. Sometimes, it eats me alive, the need to tell her that. She was my baby sister, and it was my job to look out for her."

Piper looked down, thinking of Macy, missing her sweet smile so much her chest felt caved-in, hollow. "It was my job to look out for mine, too. Didn't work out great for either one of us, did it?" She sighed. "Well, Verity would spout some mumbo-jumbo about the Path and all that. And she'd be right. We can't go back and change things. We can only go forward."

Jack shook his head. "I can't tell you how hard it was for me to accept that Verity was always right. And I mean 'always' literally. I wanted to dismiss her as a nut-job, but God's hand is on her head. Now that I've seen what that can mean, I do not envy her."

"She's spent most of her life isolated by it," Piper said, remembering her earlier thoughts. "Walking with angels is one thing, but didn't your God create an Adam and an Eve, together? Humans are meant to be connected, one to another. The bond-lines that I see – I feel like I barely understand them, but I can *feel* how ancient they are, and how massive, too. There's so much more beyond what I can see."

Her eyes went unfocused, and she groped for words to express what she was just barely beginning to grasp. "We're all one. When one of us suffers, we all suffer. When we love, when we lift each other up, we are all lifted. It sounds so simplistic, but it's the most profound truth I've ever realized. I wish I had better words to describe it."

Jack smiled. "It's a lot like the Golden Rule. Do unto others as you would have done unto you." He tilted his chin at her backpack, which was resting beside her. "Simple or not, you should write that down in your notes." Then, he stood, and whistled for Rosemary. "I think I'll take that walk you recommended."

He headed south along the creek with Rosemary trotting right beside him. Piper pulled out her notes as he'd suggested but ended up just staring at the fire. Now that the moment was gone, she felt self-conscious about writing something down that seemed so un-scientific and un-supportable. What evidence did she have, other than what she'd observed when she had ended Josh's life? His complete separation from the group had been terrible to see, her bullet a mercy, releasing him from his aloneness. Piper contemplated that thought for a moment, trying to decide if she was justifying or if she was brushing another layer of truth about the bond-lines. She also wondered how

Jack would respond, if she told him the truth about the event her theory arose from.

On the rise, Ed stirred, stretching on his sleeping bag and yawning. He sat up, obviously looking around for Rosemary.

"She went for a walk with Jack," Piper called.

Ed nodded, then disappeared into his tent, emerging a moment later with a small duffel bag. He lifted his hand to Piper as he headed for the creek. "I'm going to go take a bath, get freshened up for the mosquitoes." He pointed his finger at her. "You keep clear, you hear? What's been seen can't be unseen."

Piper laughed and waved him off. A few minutes later, Owen followed suit, yawning and stretching, then following Ed down to the river. Piper added a few small pieces of wood to the fire and sighed deeply, feeling relaxed and content. A soft rustle and a croak in a nearby cottonwood made her smile before she even spotted the big raven.

Loki was gazing down at her when she tilted her head back. His black eyes sparkled with uncanny intelligence and curiosity. He ruffled his glossy feathers and shifted on his branch, as if presenting his best side. He croaked again, cocked his head, then let out a low, throaty rattle.

"You again. What I wouldn't give to understand how she does this." Piper shook her head and laughed softly, taking a moment to warm the bond-line between her heart and her mother's. As before, the answer back was immediate and enthusiastic. She grinned at Loki. "Do you have any idea how awful this would have been during high school? Man, I dodged a bullet there."

Rosemary chose that moment to rush back into the clearing, startling Loki into flight. A few seconds later, Jack followed, his eyes fixed on the raven's retreat to a cottonwood across the creek. He turned to Piper. "Is that who I think it is?"

"Yep."

Jack laughed in delight. "How totally cool is that?"

"Easy for you to say. You're not the one with a living nanny-cam reporting your every move." But she grinned back. "It is pretty damn cool. Do you suppose he flies all the way back home and reports to her? It's been a few days since we saw him. He probably could have made it there and back to us."

Jack shrugged. "Who can say? Maybe he just gives her the information telepathically. Or maybe she can sense through his senses, like she does with the dogs. What I really wonder is how he knows where you are. I'm pretty sure he didn't follow us from Limon. Does he have some kind of homing instinct that's fixed on you?" He laughed again. "And you should see the look on your face."

Piper shuddered. "I'm trying not to let this freak me out completely, okay? How *does* he know where I am?" She got up and put her notes away. "This is just too creepy."

Ed and Owen returned, and Piper headed down to the creek to hustle through a chilly wash. Owen had already gone to bed when she returned, and the sun was nearing the horizon. Jack jogged towards the creek with Rosemary on his heels. Ed was sitting with his back to the fire, his shotgun across his lap, sipping a cup of what her nose told her was some of Verity's herbal tea. He held the mug up thoughtfully.

"I can't even imagine the price a cup of real coffee would demand these days. I'd trade everything I own – except for Rosemary – for just one cup."

Piper smiled. "I know a lot of people who feel the same way. Maybe we should think about cultivating it, if it'll grow in Colorado." Then she grew serious. "Did Jack tell you about the house downstream, how Rosemary didn't like it?"

"He did. I'll have my eyes peeled, don't you worry." He sighed. "It was lonely out there today, but I was glad we didn't see anyone. I've never been afraid to meet strangers, but I sure feel that way now."

Piper just rested her hand on his shoulder for a moment. What could she say that offered reassurance or comfort? She felt the same way. She headed for her tent, eager now for the warmth and softness of her sleeping bag. They'd opted for single-person hiking tents, and as long as she focused on the mesh beside her face and not the proximity of the domed nylon roof over her head, it didn't feel too much like a coffin. From a few feet away, she could hear the rumble of Owen's soft snores, and she fell asleep between one breath and the next.

She slept deeply until Owen woke her for her watch shift at 2:00 am. Keeping her eyes turned away from the fire, she, too, set a cup of tea to steep. Then she stepped carefully around the perimeter of their camp, pausing to listen every few feet, rifle cradled in the crook of her arm.

She walked to a spot clear of the cottonwoods and surveyed the nighttime prairie. The stars were a breathtaking canopy overhead, and the moon was fuller than it had been on the way to Limon.

"Waxing gibbous," she murmured, remembering the old elementary school lessons. The constellations she'd been teaching herself during her time with Brody came back, and she located the summer triangle, the stars Deneb, Vega and Altair. From there, it was easy to spot the constellations that went with them, and she murmured their names as well. "Cygnus the Swan, Lyra the Harp, and Aquila the Eagle."

She indulged in a few more minutes under the stars before circling back to the fire the long way, listening, always listening. Once again, she was careful to keep her eyes averted from the fire when she picked up her mug of tea, preserving her night vision. She thought of some more ideas she wanted to add to her notes, but couldn't risk adequate illumination to write, so she memorized them. It made her think of writing papers in her head while she waited tables in college, and the memory made her feel nostalgic in a way she struggled to define. The things she'd thought of as difficult back then – unreasonable paper deadlines, double shifts at work, moody roommates, unreliable project partners – seemed like problems from another planet now.

When 4:00 am rolled around, she was tempted to just let Jack sleep. He, too, appeared to be sleeping dreamlessly, and she was wired. It seemed a shame to disturb him, but Martin's voice sounded in her ear as if he was standing right next to her. "Don't be an idiot. If you can't sleep, rest. Lack of sleep makes you stupid, and stupid kills." Piper sighed and listened to a man who was hundreds of miles away.

Jack opened his eyes immediately when she spoke his name, then zipped himself out of his tent and stretched. Owen and Ed slept on, with Rosemary curled on a blanket at the foot of Ed's tent. Jack's eyes met hers, alert and clear. "Four o'clock and all's well?"

"Quiet as can be," Piper confirmed. "Look, if you're still tired, I'm wide awake and –"

Jack held up a hand, stopping her. "If you can't sleep, rest. Lack of sleep –"

"Yeah, yeah." Piper waved him off and headed towards her tent. "Martin and I have already been through all that. Goodnight."

She did sleep, to her surprise, and awoke shortly after dawn. The others had already broken down their tents and loaded their bikes, and she scrambled to catch up. While she completed her morning necessities, the men pored over the maps she'd marked, discussing how fast they could get to the day's target destination if they avoided this city, took that route, turned here or turned there. Piper smirked to herself as she hurried down a cold breakfast. Men and road trips always boiled down to the holy grail of "making good time." Some things would never change.

They left while the eastern sky was still warm and rosy, and in just under two hours, paused to survey I-80 from the top of a hill. They shut the bikes down and removed their helmets, and in the sudden quiet, the only sound was the tick of rapidly cooling metal. On the interstate, traffic stretched in both directions as far as the eye could see. Here and there, piles of what might once have been people littered the road. Many of the vehicles appeared to have been ransacked, and some of them had been burned.

"Where were they all going?" Jack asked, his voice barely above a whisper. "And what happened when they couldn't get there? So many people. Where are they all now?"

Piper hunched her shoulders and hugged her elbows, shaken by the stillness, the absolute silence. Ed reached to rest his hand on her shoulder, as she had done for him the night before, and she covered his hand with hers. Gratitude for the people she was traveling with overwhelmed her for a moment, made her blink back tears. She was so glad these good men were alive, and safe, and here beside her, instead of rotting in a car somewhere.

They started the bikes and crept past the gauntlet. Piper concentrated on finding a path through the vehicles and tried not to look too closely at what they were passing, but images leapt out at her just the same: A woman's still-bright blonde hair, draped over a steering wheel; a fading infant mobile, jiggling softly in the wind from atop a haphazardly loaded trailer. And worst of all, the teeth. Bright white, shining from the shadowy interiors of vehicles, or gleaming from a disintegrating human face on the tarmac. Her stomach was quivering by the time they were clear, her throat tight with the need to cry. They rode on for another hour, and she was back in control of herself by the time they stopped to siphon more gas, but she doubted any of them would make it through the coming night without troubling dreams.

By noon, they were seeing signs of human habitation. They passed little towns that were completely burned out, and twice they passed barricades that had been erected across roads, with signs warning outsiders to "Stay Out." Here and there, smoke rose from single homes or small towns. The towns got bigger the farther east they traveled, and in the mid-afternoon, they saw their first people.

A woman and several children were working in a garden patch alongside a dusty country road. They straightened to stare at the approaching travelers, and one of the children, a boy of about ten, rushed to pick up a shotgun. He didn't point it at them, but held it at his hip with the ease of long practice. Piper was trying to decide if they should stop when a man broke from the cover at the back of the field. He was also carrying a shotgun, and he half-ran to stand between his family and the road.

"Move along!" he shouted, waving his arm to emphasize his words. "There's nothing for you here! Just keep moving!"

Piper nodded at the woman as they rode by and had to resist the urge to turn to check behind them. She felt like she had a target pinned between her shoulder blades. When they were well past, she stopped, sitting on her idling bike until the others joined her. Jack and Owen looked grim, but Ed just looked tired.

"Guess that was the Nebraska welcoming committee," he said. Rosemary, who rode between his legs with remarkable agility, chose that moment to bark sassily. It made them all smile. Ed ruffled her ears and kissed the top of her head. "Now that's more like it. We appreciate it, girl."

They were only 20 miles from the Iowa state line when they stopped for the night, once again finding a small stream to camp along. This one didn't have a name according to Piper's maps, but it was a bright and bubbly little creek, and the soft music of the water was soothing. They had made good time and probably could have ridden on, but they would be crossing the Missouri River when they crossed into Iowa, and Piper wanted to get another look at her maps. Rivers, especially in this part of the country, would draw people.

Ed was on KP this evening, and while he cooked up more eggs and vegetables, they all took turns washing up in the creek. It had been a long day, but Piper was nowhere near as tired as she'd been the day before. She added to her notes extensively while they ate, getting impressions and information from the others, describing what they'd seen and *sensed* in as much detail as she could remember.

After Ed had washed up, they settled around the campfire, each occupied with the task of their choice. Ed brushed Rosemary's scruffy coat, looking for ticks and burrs, then examined the pads of her paws. She sprawled happily on her back and basked under his ministrations, especially when they concluded with a tummy rub. Owen stretched out on the sleeping bag he'd dragged out of the tent, dozing before his watch shift, huge arms neatly folded on his barrel chest. Piper continued working on her notes, absent-mindedly humming along whenever Jack played a song she recognized on his guitar. She looked up when he strummed the opening chords of one of her favorite '80's power ballads.

"'Every Rose Has Its Thorn?'" She grinned. "I would not have pegged you for a Poison fan, Pastor Jack."

He kept playing, but shot a look at her out of the corner of his eyes. "I wasn't always a pastor."

He went on to play and sing a more-than respectable version of the song, then segued into music by Whitesnake and Night Ranger. By the time he played Mr. Big's "To Be With You," Owen was sitting up on his sleeping bag, grinning and nodding his head along. Both he and Piper joined in on the irresistible chorus, making Jack grin broadly as he sang. Ed clapped and whistled when they were finished, and Rosemary joined in with excited barks, which made all of them laugh.

Piper's notes lay forgotten on her lap. "Jack, I had no idea you were such a talented musician. Why were you hiding it? Ah!" She pointed her finger at him. "You were in an '80's hair band, weren't you? C'mon, confess!"

Jack rolled his eyes. "Piper, look at me and imagine me with long hair."

She cocked her head to the side and did so. "I can see it. Like, totally."

"Ha. Very funny. Now add a beard to that long hair, and who do I look like?"

Piper squinted at him, not sure where he was going, and a loud guffaw from Owen startled all of them. "You'd look just like Jesus." He grinned at Jack, and the humor on his face made him look years younger. "That's it, isn't it? You would look just like the picture of Jesus my grandma had hanging up in her dining room."

Jack pointed at him. "Got it in one. Not the image an aspiring rock-n-roll artist wants to project." He looked at Piper. "So, yes. I was in a band. But I did not have the hair."

Chuckles rolled around the campfire, and Jack started playing again. Piper settled back happily as he played Aerosmith and Kix, then strummed into her all-time favorite, Extreme's "More Than Words." When he hit the chorus, she impulsively picked up the harmony. Jack nodded encouragingly at her, then stopped playing before the next refrain.

"Hold on – let's do it again. You take the melody line on the chorus, and I'll take the harmony. Ready?"

Piper's face flashed hot. "Oh, my gosh, no. I don't sing."

"Yes, you do." Owen was looking at her, eyebrows raised. "You just did. It sounded really nice."

"I was just playing around," Piper sputtered. "I don't sing for real."

"You don't have to do anything but carry the tune," Ed offered his opinion. "Let Jack's voice do the work. My wife and her sister used to sing together at family gatherings. My wife had a pleasant enough singing voice, but my sister-in-law could make anyone sound amazing. Just give it a try."

"It's just us here," Owen chimed in. "What happens at the campfire stays at the campfire."

"Okay." She peeked at Jack, suddenly shy. "So just take the melody at the chorus?"

He nodded and started playing again before she could scramble for another excuse. At the chorus, she sang the melody, softly at first, then with growing confidence as she heard how beautiful it sounded. Jack's voice wove under hers, complementing it perfectly. They sang on, voices blending at first, then somehow fusing.

Jack's eyes were locked on hers, and the bond-line between them flared to a blinding rainbow of solid light. Piper felt something lift free in her throat and chest, and her voice rose to match that feeling. Tingles raced along her scalp and down the nape of her neck, then down her arms and legs. She felt like she was flying. She couldn't remember, ever in her life, feeling so connected to another person. Or so aroused.

Jack stopped playing, and total silence fell around the campfire. Then Ed burst into applause, whistling and stomping his feet, and Piper blessed his dear, oblivious heart. She couldn't have spoken a single word if she'd tried.

"Woo!" Ed hooted. "That was amazing! Heck, we'll be able to sing our way across the country – forget trading that marijuana! Hey, do you know 'Dust in the Wind?' I love that song, though it is pretty sad, now that I think on it..."

Jack stood up abruptly. "I, ah." He gestured with his hand vaguely, looking anywhere but at Piper. "I have to..."

Then he just turned and walked away from the campfire, still carrying his guitar. Piper didn't watch him go. She kept her eyes glued to the fire, struggling to calm her breathing, her racing heart. She was mortified. And exhilarated. A part of her she'd thought was dead was most certainly not.

She looked up to find both Ed and Owen watching her, Ed frowning in confusion, Owen's expression more difficult to analyze. "Well," she croaked, and cleared her throat. "I've sure never sounded that good outside of my own bathroom before."

Ed laughed, and chatted on, clearly excited. "I've never heard anything like it! It stands to reason, when you think about it. Jack can – for lack of a better word – manipulate people with his voice. No offense, Piper, but I've heard you sing. You're solid enough, but he made you sound like a million bucks." He craned around. "Did he run to the john? I wonder if he knows any John Denver..."

Piper was finally able to draw a deep breath. She peeked again at Owen, and this time, it was easy to see what he was thinking. He looked sad and happy at the same time when he nodded his head at her.

"It's going to happen, Piper. Get used to the idea."

NINE
Jack: Nebraska

Jack stalked along the streambank, clutching his guitar to his chest with both sweaty hands. When he was well out of sight of the fire, he stopped, and tipped his head back. He was sucking wind like he'd just run a half-marathon, and he could feel his heartbeat on every single inch of his skin. Ten long minutes later, he had finally idled down to where he could think.

What the hell had happened back there?

He closed his eyes and groaned softly in the dark, feeling a combination of embarrassment and lust he could say with absolute certainty he'd never felt before. He'd sung with hundreds of people in his life, in church when he was a kid, during his garage-band days and beyond, in his ministry. And never, not once, had he experienced something like the connection he'd just experienced with Piper.

"God?" He pleaded to the stars. "Could you, I don't know, just give them all amnesia? Especially her? How am I supposed to go back there and face them?" He groaned again, this time in disgust. "For pity's sake, Jack, what are you? Twelve? Get a grip."

A rustle in the brush along the streambank startled him, and a moment later, Rosemary trotted to his side, tongue lolling in the moonlight. Ed called out a few seconds later. "Jack? Everything all right?"

"Fine." Oh, Lord, his voice had cracked. He really was revisiting his adolescence. He cleared his throat. "I'm fine. Just needed to, you know." He decided to leave it at that.

Ed stepped into view, placing his feet carefully in the near-dark. "We're circling the wagons for the night. Owen and Piper have already turned in." He shook his head, and Jack could hear his grin even if he couldn't see it. "Sure enjoyed your music. You have a real gift."

"Thank you," Jack said tightly. "I guess I'll head back, then. We'll probably want to get an early start tomorrow, get across the river with our wits about us." Though he seriously doubted he'd ever collect all his wits, ever again, not the way they were scattered now. "You, ah, said the others had already gone to bed?"

"Yep. You go on ahead. I've got to see the same man about that horse. I'll be right behind you."

Jack left Ed and Rosemary and headed back to camp, forcing his feet to move briskly in spite of his reluctance. What if Ed had been wrong? What if she was still up? He stopped for a moment and closed his eyes. And if she wasn't, how was he going to face her in the morning? It took a considerable amount of willpower to get his feet moving again.

Owen and Piper had indeed gone to bed, and Jack quickly followed suit, settling into his tent and releasing a pent up breath as slowly and quietly as he could. He lay there, tense from head to toe, and tried to think it through.

Maybe she hadn't experienced what he had. Ed hadn't noticed anything – either that, or he was the greatest actor of all time. Jack hadn't made eye contact with Owen, but even if he had sensed Jack's emotions, he wouldn't talk out of turn. Jack smiled grimly in the dark. No, if there was one thing he could say about Owen, it was that he didn't run on at the mouth. Maybe it had just been him.

He thought back, remembering the way his voice had wrapped around Piper's like a lover, the sudden lock of energy between them, the way her eyes had glowed, green as grass in the firelight, the way her cheeks had flushed soft and rosy and her lips had seemed to caress each word she sang, looking so damn soft and kissable...

Jack barely stifled another groan. No. It hadn't been just him.

Through the long night, he dozed fitfully, imagining and dismissing a dozen different things he could say to her. He heard Owen take over the watch from Ed, then Piper take it over from Owen. When her low voice called his name two hours later, it was a relief. He unzipped from his tent and rose to face her, but before he could speak, she did.

"I don't want to talk about it," she said in a rush. "I meant what I said before, about not, you know, hooking up. With anyone." She set her jaw belligerently. "I know I'm not who you want. I'm not Layla. Let's just chalk it up to a bizarre alignment of the planets and move on."

He was speechless. He waited for words to rise up, but nothing came. Finally, he just nodded. She nodded as well, and said, "Good. Everything's been quiet. Goodnight."

Well, then. In under two minutes, it was over. Jack slid into his boots and retrieved his shotgun, then went to walk around the camp. As Piper had reported, the night was quiet, and he was left with all kinds of time to go back over what she'd said, brief though it had been.

He wasn't inexperienced. He'd dated his share of women and had been sexually involved with a few of them. But the whole "hooking up" phenomenon had come after his high school and college years, and it just served to highlight the difference in their ages. He felt suddenly old, washed up and humiliated. Why would a beautiful young woman even look twice at a pastor who was as close in age to her parents as he was to her?

Nor was he a stranger to sexual longing. He'd been lathered up over a woman before, had felt burned up by desire. After his ordination, he had still dated occasionally, though he had not sought to have sex with any of those women. His personal beliefs might accept sex before marriage, but the teachings of the church were clear, and he had an example to set for the kids in his ministry.

Then Layla had happened.

He paused in his circuit where the cottonwoods gave way to prairie, and looked up at the blaze of stars. "You're laughing at me," he said to her. He could feel her presence all around him, a tingle on his skin, a barely-there scent that stirred memories, some good, some bad. "Don't even try to deny it."

As if in agreement, a sudden gust of wind stirred grit and pollen into his face, and he sneezed. He swiped at his nose, then sighed. "I miss you," he said softly. "I think I always will. But what I felt for you was...dark. You were forbidden. What I felt for you was wrong. Not wrong because of you, but wrong because of what was in my heart."

Another swirl of wind, gentler this time, and he *felt* her sorrow as if she were standing right beside him, shields down, wide-open. His throat was tight. "I'm sorry for that. For how I treated you. You deserved so much better, and I'm glad you found it. But I'll bet you already know all that, don't you?" He was quiet for a few moments. "What I feel for Piper is different. Not easier, but different. I like her, so much. She's my friend. Until tonight, that was all."

He would have sworn, then, that he heard her laugh, the sound blending with the distant chuckle of the stream. It made him smile, if crookedly. "Yeah, yuck it up. Criminy, I've never felt anything like that. I thought my skin was going to catch on fire. And now we get to pretend it never happened. How well is that going to work?"

Frustration set him in motion again. He prowled several circuits around the camp before he felt a measure of calm, returning to the same spot he'd stood before and picking up the conversation where he'd left off. "She's not what I had in mind, Layla, not at all." He laughed wryly. "But then, neither were you. She's wounded, but she is as tough as they come. I can't think of anyone I'd rather have at my back or by my side, the way the world is now. Well, okay, I'd take Martin, too, but he's nowhere near as pretty as she is." He sighed. "I guess I forgot for a while that it's in God's hands. Everything is."

Dawn was an hour away, but a meadowlark burst into song just a few yards away, the sound lifting from an old fence line that was barely visible in the moonlight. Jack's eyes stung with tears. He could *feel* her fading. "Thank you," he said softly. "What a beautiful gift. Rest well, Layla."

Her presence dissipated on a soft, westerly breeze. He stood for a moment, until she'd faded completely, then returned to camp. Though it wasn't yet 5:00 am, Owen was already up, moving quietly around the fire, prepping for breakfast and sipping a mug of tea. He looked up at Jack, but didn't quite meet his eyes. "Couldn't sleep. Figured I'd get a jump on it, make some fresh biscuits."

"Piper will be happy. She loves her mom's biscuits. No pressure, though." Jack turned his back to the fire, and scanned the night around them, relieved that he could mention her name naturally. For the moment, anyway, he felt peaceful all the way to his bones. "Did you have bad dreams? It wouldn't be a surprise, given what we saw yesterday."

"No." Owen glanced up at him again. A few days ago, he would have left it at that. It pleased Jack that he chose to explain. "Good dreams. They're worse than the bad ones. For a few seconds after I wake up, I think she's still alive. Then I remember."

So Layla had visited Owen as well. How that would have bothered him, once upon a time. He gazed at the other man with genuine compassion, trying to figure out how to offer comfort. They may have reached a place of ease between them, but he doubted Owen would appreciate hearing Layla had stopped in to see him, too. "Verity says our loved ones can visit in dreams, that it's one way they let us know they aren't really gone, they're just with us in another form. I don't know if that helps, or hurts."

Owen looked to the side. "A little of both, I guess." He smiled a sad but very male smile, one Jack recognized from a long, long time ago. "I liked the form she was in." He stood up abruptly, grabbing their water bottles and a flashlight and heading towards the stream. "I'll fill these up and get them purified. I know Piper's anxious about getting across the Missouri, and the sooner we can get that behind us, the better."

Not long after Owen returned from the stream, Ed was up, and Piper was right behind him. She murmured a good morning to both Ed and Owen and nodded at Jack, meeting his eyes with a determined lift of her chin. He nodded back and smiled, though he kept it brief. Whatever was between them would have to wait.

Jack and Owen had already broken down their tents and loaded their bikes. Owen served breakfast, and they ate in almost total silence, all of them radiating tension in their own way. Owen's face was a stoic mask; Ed muttered constantly to Rosemary under his breath and jiggled his legs; and Piper was in full, magnificent Valkyrie mode, her face fierce with battle-readiness. Jack and Owen cleaned up while Ed and Piper broke down their tents. They were loaded up and on the road before the sun had completely cleared the horizon.

They were planning to make the crossing in Decatur, Nebraska, a tiny town roughly halfway between Omaha and Sioux City. If that bridge wasn't viable, they would head south to Blair, a larger town not far north of Omaha. After that, their choices got slim. Either they would have to chance the larger city bridges, or find a way to portage.

Long before they entered the town proper on Highway 51, they were sure there were people living there. Smoke rose here and there in the early morning light, and there was a subtle sense of activity about the little village. They paused where Highway 51 intersected with 4th Avenue to check in with each other. Jack looked at Piper.

"Bond-lines?"

"Not yet. I don't think anyone is in our immediate vicinity. But I *feel* people."

"I do, too." He looked at Ed and Owen. "Any input?"

Ed inclined his head down at Rosemary. The dog's scruffy ears were at maximum perk, and she was quivering. "She's nervous as a cat in a room full of rocking chairs, but she's not growling." He glanced at Piper. "Wish your mom was here. Sure would be nice to know what Rosemary's sensing."

Piper's face tightened; Jack would bet she was doing her best not to think of her mother right now. Swinging her rifle from her shoulder and placing it across her lap, she looked around, then lifted her chin to the east. "River's that way. Stands to reason the bridge is, too."

They wound their way through quiet residential streets. When they had gone several blocks, curtains started to flicker in windows, and Jack smelled, of all things, bacon. Rich, smoky, bacon. Piper, who was still in the lead, turned to look at him. "They know we're here now." Her eyes flickered to the other men. "Can you all smell that?"

Jack nodded, swallowing a mouth full of saliva. He glanced at Rosemary, who was whining softly now, two delicate strands of drool dripping from the sides of her muzzle. "If it's a trap, it's a darn good one."

They started to catch glimpses of the wide, brown river through the trees, and to the north, Jack spotted the white crisscross pattern of a large bridge. He pulled up beside Piper and pointed. "There – see it? Do you think they're just going to let us cross?"

She shrugged, but when they rounded a bend in the road and spotted the entrance to the bridge, he got his answer. Two people, both holding shotguns, were standing in front of the bridge, silhouetted against the morning sky. A man and a woman, Jack saw as they crept closer, both of them breathing heavily, as if they'd run to beat the travelers here. When they were about 20 feet away, the man held up his hand.

"That's far enough, for now." He paused to wipe his hand quickly on the leg of his jeans, then returned it to the stock of his shotgun. Beside him, the woman was discreetly wiping her mouth on her shoulder. The scent of bacon was thick as smoke. The man spoke again. "There's a toll to cross the bridge. We don't take money, but we'll take food, medicine, or gold jewelry. If you don't have anything you can spare, you can work the toll off in advance, but it'll be hard work. And if none of that's acceptable," his hands tightened on the shotgun, and his jaw jutted forward, "There are other bridges south of here, in Blair or Omaha, or north in Sioux City."

Jack looked at Piper. She spoke low, and out of the corner of her mouth. "Strong bond-lines stretching behind us, into the village. Not many. Maybe a dozen." Jack nodded, then raised his eyebrows and tilted his head at the pair, asking what she thought without voicing the words. She caught on immediately, and shrugged. "Seems fair, as long as they don't try to take us for everything we've got."

Jack turned back to the man, who was actually more of a boy, no more than 19 or 20. The girl looked younger yet, and there was a similar cast to their features. Siblings, maybe, related, surely. "We'll agree to trading our way across, if the rates are reasonable," he said. "Do you have any information about what's on the other side? What we'll be headed into?"

The pair exchanged glances. The girl nodded, and the boy's shoulders relaxed. He turned back to Jack, visibly more at ease. "Michaela says you're alright. My name's Christopher. We'll tell you what we know at no extra charge. We don't get many travelers through here, so we'd like to know where you've come from and what you've seen." His face reddened slightly. "I'm sorry we need to charge you for the bridge and all, but we need to survive. We have people depending on us."

Jack glanced at his companions and got nods all around. They shut their bikes down, but stayed on them, just in case. Owen backed his bike up and to the side so he could watch behind them. Ed let Rosemary down but kept her close with a low command. Piper scooted up beside Jack on her bike before she shut hers down and kept her rifle across her lap.

Jack performed the introductions and gave them the information Christopher had requested. Both of them nodded as Jack spoke, absorbing his words like water on parched ground. When he'd finished outlining where they'd been and what they'd seen, Michaela spoke.

"Have you heard from anyone from Phoenix? We have friends who were going to college there, and I just hoped..." She trailed off with a sad shrug.

"No, we haven't. I'm sorry." He paused a beat. "Now – two things: What can we expect ahead? And for pity's sake, is that bacon we're smelling?"

Michaela and Christopher both grinned, and Christopher spoke. "Only thing we've got an abundance of. A semi-truck carrying cold cuts and such stopped here just as the plague came through – the driver was already sick – and we ran generators to keep it all cold. Some of it we just couldn't eat in time, but the bacon is still good. We could work out a trade there, too."

He wiggled his eyebrows in what he probably thought was a shrewd and worldly manner, and Jack's heart broke at his youth, at the air of innocence he had somehow managed to hang onto. He reminded Jack of the kids they'd left behind in Woodland Park, and he missed their bright energy with a suddenness and intensity that surprised him. James, and Chloe, and little Rainbow Dash.

"A trade would be great." His voice was husky when he replied, and he felt Piper look at him curiously. He cleared his throat. "Now, Piper, if you'll get out your map and your notes, we'll find out what these young people know."

Christopher and Michaela both scooted around to flank Piper when she unfolded her map. Christopher traced a slightly grubby finger across the bridge and along Highway 175 where it ran into Iowa. "You can't see it from here, but around this curve, the road is impassable. Cars stacked up clear into Onawa, which is about seven miles past the bridge." He traced another line. "Same thing on I29. I have no idea where people were trying to go, but it seems like the whole world died in their cars." He swallowed hard and squinted a little. "We've been back and forth with Onawa quite a bit. Lots of folks from here worked there before the plague, and they're trying to clear Highway 175. They're also working their way north and south on I29, salvaging stuff from the vehicles. People packed up their valuables, and what food and water they had left, and there it sits." He shrugged, trying to be casual, but Jack could feel the horror the young man felt, even through his shields. "They're not using it anymore."

Piper touched the tiny dot on the map. "So the people in Onawa are friendly?" She looked up at Christopher and raised an eyebrow. "They won't charge us a toll to go through?"

Christopher's face reddened again. "No, I, ah...well...I don't think..."

Michaela rolled her eyes. "What my idiot cousin is trying to say is it's all good. Tell them we let you across, and it'll be fine."

Jack nudged Piper with his elbow. "Play nice," he murmured. He checked over his shoulder. Ed was walking a slow circle around the area they were in, letting Rosemary sniff, but keeping her at his heel. Owen was still scanning the town behind them, but his huge hand was splayed on his chest, and when Jack reached out for what the other man was feeling, he got an almost overwhelming wave of *sorrow*. What was that all about? With an effort, he returned his attention to Piper's map.

Michaela reached out to run her considerably cleaner finger in an arc representing a 50 mile radius around Decatur. "We've seen people from nearby towns, but only a handful from farther away. A man from Des Moines came through this spring. He was there on business and got stranded, and he was going to look for his family in Oregon. He said conditions there were pretty bad. And only about a month ago, a group came through from Madison, Wisconsin. They were headed for Montana – said they were going to hide out in the mountains like old-time trappers and live off the land." She glanced at Christopher and shuddered. "They bothered me. It was four men and two women, and the whole thing just felt...off."

Christopher looked grim and picked up the narrative. "Yeah, we didn't offer them any bacon. Anyway, they said they heard Chicago was a death trap. We've seen folks from a little further out traveling up and down the river. Only one from Omaha, but five or six from Sioux City, is that right, Michaela?"

"Six," she said. "Two just a few days ago." She looked at Christopher again. "That's about all I can think of."

"Me, too. Sorry it's not more."

Jack looked at Piper. She nodded and folded up her map, while Jack looked back at Christopher. "What do we owe you?"

Christopher wiggled his eyebrows again. "Whatcha got?"

Now that it came down to it, Jack was surprised at how uncomfortable he was offering marijuana in trade, especially to a couple of kids – he felt like a drug pusher. Never mind they'd brought it for this express purpose.

"Well, we've got some fresh vegetables and some eggs. And, ah, we've got some dried venison and some navy beans, too. Maybe we could spare one of our fuel filters…"

"Uh, Jack?" Piper was frowning at him. "What are you doing?"

He cut his eyes at Christopher and Michaela. "They're kids."

"Yeah? And?" She huffed out a breath and turned to the pair. "We've got pot. How much for the four of us to cross and some of that bacon?"

"Medicinal marijuana," Jack clarified, then rubbed a hand across his forehead, speaking low to Piper. "I just turned into a prissy, fuddy-duddy preacher, didn't I?"

"Totally." There was laughter in her voice. "You're a rock star, remember?" Then, to the kids, "Well? How much?"

Michaela and Christopher exchanged glances. "For grandpa," Michaela said. She looked at Piper. "It's good for pain, right? Arthritis?"

"Yes, it is."

"But will he smoke it?" Christopher looked doubtful. "You know how he is, Mikey."

"Don't call me Mikey, and he will smoke it, if I have to hog-tie him and stuff a joint in his mouth."

Jack could tell that Piper was biting the inside of her cheek to keep from smiling – there was no doubt that Michaela would do just as she threatened. Again, there was laughter in her voice when she spoke. "He doesn't have to smoke it. You can give it to him in an oil or fat base. Heck, you can even bake it into something and not tell him."

Piper pulled a blank page from her notebook and glanced at Jack. "Let me write down instructions for them." She looked at both Michaela and Christopher. "I'll give you enough for several months of pain relief, but you should see if you can find some locally. I guarantee you someone around here was growing, and if you think about it, you'll have a good idea where to look."

Michaela and Christopher looked at each other. "The Stedman brothers," they said in unison. Michaela turned back to Piper. "We know where to look. Now tell me what to do."

They bent their heads together over Piper's notes, and Jack took the opportunity to check in with Ed and

Owen. Ed gave him a thumbs-up, but Owen wouldn't meet his eyes when Jack walked to stand beside him. Jack cut right to it. "What is it?"

"They need to get out of here," Owen said quietly. "They need to leave. Something terrible is going to happen." He did look at Jack then, and his eyes were bleak. "I saw it. For the first time, I caught a glimpse ahead of time. I think this whole town is going to burn. They need to leave. Soon."

Jack didn't ask if he was sure. He nodded, and returned to Piper and the kids. When they finished, he cleared his throat, and decided the direct approach was best. "Look, I don't know if you all will believe me, but here goes. We have intuitive skills, you might call them psychic skills, that we didn't have before. One of my friends is getting a warning. He says your town is going to burn, and you need to leave."

Michaela and Christopher exchanged a long look. Michaela spoke. "We've got them, too. Me, most of all. Did he say when this was going to happen?"

Jack glanced back at Owen. "Not exactly. But soon."

"Okay." She straightened, and handed her shotgun to Christopher. "You go get grandpa and the kids and have them start packing up, then warn the others. I'll finish here."

Christopher nodded at Jack and Piper. "Good luck on your journey." Then he took off at a jog, nodding at Ed and Owen on his way past. Piper got out the marijuana, loading a generous amount into a plastic bag and scribbling additional instructions on the paper while Michaela ran, swift and graceful, to a nearby house. She came back with four familiar yellow and red packages, and Jack's mouth started watering again. She handed them to Piper, then impulsively hugged her.

"I wish you could stay," Jack heard her say. "If you come back through, will you stay for a while?"

Piper swallowed hard, but smiled. "You bet. Thanks for the bacon, and good luck getting that grandpa of yours high."

Michaela laughed, and lifted her hand in farewell. They fired up their bikes and rumbled across the bridge. When Jack turned for a look back, Michaela had already disappeared from view. He hoped Owen's warning was enough. In Onawa, they barely stopped rolling, pausing just long enough to identify themselves to a sentry and drop Christopher and Michaela's names. A strange urgency seemed to have seized all of them, and once they were past the town, they pushed the bikes faster than usual, hardly slowing as they passed through a series of tiny towns: Turin, Soldier, Ute, Charter Oak.

Denison was a little larger, so they scooted around it on unmarked country roads, eventually weaving their way back to Highway 30. Just east of Arcadia, Ed signaled that Rosemary needed to stop, and they pulled into a picnic area. While Rosemary took care of her business, Piper pulled out her map and they all bent over it. Piper traced the line she had marked, then straightened abruptly, wrapping her arms around her elbows.

"Okay, I'll just say it. Anyone else got the heebie-jeebies?"

Jack rubbed the back of his neck. "I've had them since Owen talked about Decatur burning. I thought it was just being there, but it keeps getting worse, not better."

Owen didn't say anything, but the miserable expression on his face spoke for him. Ed looked at Rosemary. "Well, you know I don't feel a darn thing, but Rosemary is sure keyed up." He looked around at all of them. "Question is, what do we do about it? Do we change course? Or do we keep on as we've been, and just stay ready?"

They were all silent for a while, each thinking their own thoughts. Then Jack made the call. It was something he would always remember – that he'd been the one to make the call, sending them all forward into something they had all seen coming. "Okay, we don't even know why we're feeling uneasy. It could be a lot of things, but here's what I know for sure: If we stop every time we get nervous, we'll never get there. I say we push through."

Ed nodded. A moment later, Owen nodded, too, though more reluctantly. Piper looked troubled. She opened her mouth to say something, then closed it and headed for her bike. "Let's get going, then."

They didn't even make it another mile down the road. As they were approaching a sprawling farm property on the south side of the road, they saw, just ahead, a trio of pickup trucks pull across the road, completely blocking it. Six armed men got out of the pickups as they approached and stood, not yet aiming their weapons, but clearly ready to. Piper looked over her shoulder at Jack as they slowed.

"Turn around," she yelled over the noise of the bikes. "We need to turn around!" Then her eyes locked on something behind him. "Fuck!"

Jack's head snapped around. A similar trio of trucks now blocked their retreat. He and Piper braked, Ed and Owen pulling in tight behind them. Jack scrutinized the open farmland to the north and south. "We don't need roads." He started to swing to the north. "Let's –"

"Jack, stop." Owen nodded at the deep drainage ditches on either side of the road; they were spiked with everything from farm tools to hefty sharpened sticks. "Looks like we're going to have to talk our way out."

Jack ran his eyes thoroughly over the ditches, looking for a gap, and once again looked behind them. Then, he looked ahead and smiled grimly. "Good thing one of us is such a smooth talker."

He looked at each of them in turn, nodding his encouragement. When he met Piper's gaze, there was something hectic in her eyes. "What?"

"Their bond lines," she said hoarsely. "They're all red, every single one of them, and they converge on a point just to the northeast of this group." She nodded her head towards the pickups to the east, and Jack saw that her whole body was shaking. "They've got a Brody back there somewhere, running the show."

Jack reached to cup her pale cheek in his palm, pitching his voice to wrap *comfort* and *strength* around her. "Then you'll know just how to handle him, won't you?"

She clung to him for a moment with her eyes. Then her spine drew up straight and tall, and she unslung her rifle. She tucked it against her body, under her arm. Her ferocious smile sizzled along his already humming nerves. His Valkyrie. "If it comes to it, hit the dirt when I say." She looked around at all of them. "I won't shoot to kill unless there's no other way. Please don't ask me to explain right now. I can still scare the shit out of them, and that may be enough."

Ed reached to rest his hand on her shoulder. "We're all in this with you, honey. It's not just on you. Besides, Jack here is going to hocus-pocus us right on through."

"That's right." Jack revved his bike and started rolling forward. "Let's get this over with. I want bacon for dinner."

They rode forward slowly, then stopped about 50 feet from the eastern pickups. Owen angled his bike to watch behind them, while Piper and Ed shifted to the north and south. Jack called out over the noise of the idling bikes.

"If there's a toll, we can trade for safe passage."

"Not interested in trading. We take what we need." One of the men stepped forward, a man who might have been handsome if not for the aggression twisting his features. He wore a battered Oakland Raiders baseball cap pulled low on his forehead, but his eyes glittered with excitement underneath. He was enjoying this, Jack realized. The Raider spoke over his shoulder, "Get the kid up here."

Another man stepped over to one of the pickups and reached into the bed. He hauled up a little boy maybe 8 or 9 years old, lifting him out and setting him on the ground. When he gave the boy a shake, Jack heard both Rosemary and Piper snarl, low and angry.

"Tell us, and be quick about it."

Even from this distance, Jack could see the boy's eyes, and he knew he would never forget them. Wide and round, blue as a Rocky Mountain summer sky and just as endless. The boy gazed at each of them in turn. When his eyes rested on Jack, every hair on Jack's body stood on end. The sensation was strangely pleasant, in spite of the tension of the situation. Finally, the boy pointed right at him.

"Him," the boy said in a resonant, musical voice. "He's the most dangerous. The man in front. Don't let him talk." Then, he pointed at Owen. "The big man sees, and has for a long time." His little arm moved again. "She's tapped into the grid. She sees, too, but in a different way." Then he hesitated, and his little face fell into sad lines. He tried to pull away, but the man shook him again.

"Finish! What about the last man?"

The boy shook his head, staring down at the ground, and muttered something. The man laughed, not pleasantly, and looked up at the others. "Nothing, he says."

The Raider pointed at Ed. "You. Get on out of here. We don't take Squibs, and we sure as hell don't take animals we can't eat." He gestured back the way they'd come and smiled a completely unconvincing smile. "Go on, you're free to go. If you leave quietly, no harm will come to you."

"He's lying," Jack said in a low voice, and out of the corner of his eye, he saw Piper nodding her agreement. "I think I've got this. Let me try." He turned back to the man. "Look, you need to –"

As one, all six men snapped their weapons to the ready, pointing them straight at Jack.

"Shut up!" The leader shouted. "Shut your fucking mouth now, and don't you say another word, or every last one of you will die in the dirt where you stand!"

Jack stopped talking and held his hands up, nodding his acquiescence. Behind him, he heard Owen speak low to Ed. "Listen to me, Ed. You need to get to Onawa. Get back there and wait for us – we'll come back for you. I saw it, when I saw Decatur burning, in my vision."

"I'm not leaving you," Ed said grimly.

Jack looked at Piper. She nodded and looked at Ed, reaching to clutch his hand. "Owen's right. If they wanted us dead, we'd be dead already. They want something else. You can't help us if they shoot you. Take Rosemary and go. Go!"

She looked back at the Raider. "We'll cooperate, but only if you let Ed go safely, like you promised."

The man smiled an oily smile at her down the barrel of his rifle. "Sure thing, sweetheart." He gestured with his rifle at Ed. "Go."

Ed's face was rigid when he turned his motorcycle around, and Rosemary was crying, a low, sobbing sound. Ed looked at each of them in turn. "I'll get you help," he vowed. "No matter what, I'll find a way. Don't lose heart." Then he looked at Piper, and tears started into his eyes. "Especially you, honey. No matter what happens, you'll be okay. I'll get help."

He rode towards the western pickups, picking up speed when they parted to let him through. When he had passed, the Raider let out a shrill whistle. One of the men in the western group lifted his rifle to his shoulder and sighted in on Ed's retreating figure.

It happened so fast, Jack could hardly process it. Piper's rifle snapped to her shoulder. She shot once, and the man aiming at Ed yelled and dropped his weapon. Piper pirouetted like a dancer, the move eerily graceful, and sighted in between the Raider's eyes. "Next one kills you," she said in a clear, carrying voice. "Call them off, or you're done."

They stayed frozen like that for the longest heartbeats of Jack's life. Behind them, the man Piper had shot at yelled to the leader. "Fuck it, Reggie! Kid called that one wrong – she split my god-damned stock and destroyed the firing mechanism! Either that was damn lucky, or she's a hell of a shot."

"Stand down. Let him go." The Raider had shifted his weapon to Piper, and they stared each other down over steel barrels. Slowly, he smiled. "I am really looking forward to hearing you apologize for this, sweetheart." He nodded. "Oh, yeah, you will apologize. You will beg for forgiveness before we're done."

The lust that darkened his face made violence boil and roll in Jack's gut. He clenched his hands into fists, and his mind raced for words he could say fast enough, words with enough power to stop the men before they could gun him and his companions down. Before he could come up with anything, Piper made a hissing sound.

"Jack, their Brody is headed this way. The bond-lines are shifting." Her voice hardened. "When he comes into view, I'm going to take him out. Then I'll wound as many as I can. We want them to panic. When they do, we ride like hell after Ed. Unless one of you can come up with an alternative plan really, really fast."

Her plan was suicidal – there was no way he could let her risk it. He tilted his head and spoke as quickly as he could out of the corner of his mouth. "Piper, no, we will get out of this without –"

A rifle cracked the air, and a split second later, a hot buzz stung Jack's right ear. His head snapped around, and the Raider called out. "That is the last warning you'll get! Now shut up!" He smirked at Piper. "Some of us can shoot too, sweetheart."

A commotion behind the pickups sent sudden tension bristling through Piper. Jack felt it as if it were his own body. He turned his head again so he could see her, while a trickle of what must have been blood slid down the right side of his neck.

"He's here," she said. Her voice had gone stone cold, and her eyes were dead and flat. "I'm taking the shot. Get ready to..." Her voice trailed away. "What the hell? It can't be." Her voice wobbled wildly. "Jack, it's a kid. It's just a kid."

Jack turned his head as much as he dared, and saw her narrowed eyes frantically searching. "This can't be right," she muttered. "It can't be him. It's not possible."

Jack looked back at the men. There was, indeed, a kid standing among them now, a beautiful boy, brand new to adolescence. He had a shock of white-blonde hair that was badly in need of a trim, and it stood out around his head like a halo. Only when his eyes met Jack's did Jack understand how very wrong that image was.

The boy was camouflaged under layer after layer after layer of deception. A glowing angel on the surface, underneath seethed every dark emotion Jack could name: Bitterness, rage, disappointment, jealousy, and at the very base, a bottomless pit of fear.

This child could kill them. He had killed before, and he was developing a taste for it.

They had to get out of here. Jack flicked a hand to signal Piper and sucked in a lungful of air through his nose. He opened his mouth, and the voice that left him sounded like thunder, booming with power.

"Drop your –"

A rifle cracked again, and a sledgehammer blow to Jack's right temple spun him around and sent him plunging to the ground. His face bounced on the tarmac, but curiously, it didn't hurt. Nothing hurt. He blinked. Then, he heard Piper scream, a rising crescendo of grief.

"Jack! No!"

She dropped her rifle with a clatter and scrambled towards him on her hands and knees. Her hands were shaking so violently, they looked like birds' wings fluttering. Jack blinked again, and tried to speak, to comfort her. But he couldn't move his lips. He was so tired, suddenly, so very sleepy. Piper brought her face close to his just before he shut his eyes, and his last conscious thought was, "Such pretty eyes."

Then, there was nothing.

TEN
Cass: Beaver Island, Michigan

"Cass, my darlin' girl, I swear by all I hold holy on Earth and under Sky, if you don't stop pacing, I will knock you upside the head with this here pot, stake you out in my herb patch like Gulliver, and let the ants pick your bones clean."

Cass stopped pacing. Veda's voice had never risen above a serene, conversational tone, and her stirring hand had kept right on gently stirring the pot she'd made reference to, but as threats went, it was top-notch. Cass plopped down at the kitchen table and cupped her face in her hands, scrubbing at her forehead with her fingertips.

"I'm sorry. I just can't settle." She thumped back in her chair and crossed her arms over her chest. "I woke up off-kilter, and it's just gotten worse as the day's gone on."

"Mmm. A disturbance in the Force you sense." Veda's imitation of Yoda was spot-on. She paused in her stirring to look over her shoulder at Cass. "Fear and doubt stifle the third eye. If you settle yourself down, whatever it is will come clear. You know that."

"I do know that," Cass muttered. She met Veda's calm gaze with a troubled frown. "I'm afraid to know. It's Jack. Something's wrong."

Veda turned back to the stove. "I figured as much. A few more minutes here, then this'll be ready to steep. If you want, I'll read for you."

Cass blew out a huge breath, relief softening the rigidity in her shoulders. She had wanted to ask, but had been afraid to do even that. "I'd appreciate it. Can I do anything to help, in the meantime?"

"You can bring in some more wood for this stove," Veda answered. "While the weather holds cool I want to get some of that ginger syrup put up for Emma. It's the only thing helping with her morning sickness, and she's just about out."

Cass stood up and kissed the top of Veda's head before she headed outside. After the plague had done its bitter work on the island, most of the survivors had settled together in a cluster of smaller homes on the northwest end of the island. While the mansions on the lakeshore stood deserted, they were building a thriving little community here, working together, sharing resources and knowledge and life. Cass and Veda's back yard butted right up to the newly pregnant Emma's, and the communal garden they shared sprawled into Charlotte and Paul's yard as well.

Speculation over who the father of Emma's baby was had run like wildfire through the community, but Cass and Veda's money was on Paul, Emma's much older and unhappily married neighbor. Neither Charlotte nor Paul had made any secret of the fact they'd both wished the other dead in the plague, and for the life of her, Cass couldn't figure out why they kept on keepin' on. She was hoping the resolution of the situation didn't cause too big an upheaval. When you lived in a group of less than thirty people, privacy did not exist.

The rest of the survivors lived nearby in two's and threes. There were only a couple of exceptions. Mr. "Smith," who always introduced himself with air quotes and never, ever revealed even a scrap of personal information, still lived on his off-grid property at the southern end of the island. Another group, a family of four, also maintained their off-grid homestead from before the plague. The Nolettes, however, were considerably more interactive than Mr. "Smith." Gavin and his wife Maddie were both in their mid-forties and had lived together on Beaver Island for years. Gavin built custom boats entirely by hand, and Maddie was an artist. Their sons, Luc and Bastian, were 17 and 15 respectively, and as independent-minded as their parents. The boys had been invaluable during the winter just past, sharing wild game and showing people who had never touched meat not purchased in a supermarket how to skin and prepare wild game for consumption.

The boys were emulating their parents, who had also assumed "teaching" positions in the community in the wake of the plague. In nearly thirty years of living without modern amenities, Gavin, especially, had become a master at improvisation and adaptation. All things considered, and especially compared to the mainland, they were thriving, in large part thanks to the Nolette family and their tutelage.

Cass didn't dare say it out loud to people who had lost so much, but to her, there was a touch of Nirvana about their current situation. This was life as she'd always sensed it should be, lived in intimate contact with the land and swaying in time with the passing seasons. She resonated with this way of life much more than the techno-saturated, social-media-ruled world of before. She knew they'd been lucky, and also knew hardships would come that would make her long for the old days. But for now, if she could just figure out how to get a horse or two to the island, a childhood dream could be realized, and life, as far as she was concerned, would be complete.

Cass hopped off their back stoop and filled her arms from the woodpile just outside their back door. She took three loads in, filling the wood box beside the stove to bursting, then returned to the back stoop to enjoy the summer day while she waited for Veda.

On the opposite side of the stoop, a weathered string of jazz cd's hung from bright pieces of yarn strung between two sturdy sticks, spinning and glinting dully in the breeze. The cd's marked the graves of the couple who had died in this house – Brent and Amelia Walker, their driver's licenses had said. Both souls had long since crossed to rest permanently in the spirit world, thanks in part to Cass. Brent, especially, had struggled with the passage. His big, booming personality had been nearly as bombastic in death as it had been in life, and Cass had been plenty relieved when he had at last accepted his death and transitioned.

So many had died so quickly, their remains as yet unburied, and the resulting abundance of lost souls could be overwhelming. Most of the homes the survivors now occupied were quiet, the bodies of the previous owners respectfully buried, and their graves marked, their souls safely crossed over. Cass had helped with that process whenever necessary, though it hadn't been her preference in the time before to work with the restless dead. She had left "ghost-whispering" to others, but in these times, one did as one must. When she needed a break from it all, she went to the island's cemetery, a habit she'd carried over from childhood. It had always amused her that people considered cemeteries frightening. In her experience, they were the least-haunted places she knew.

She lifted her face to the soft sun, and deliberately steered her mind away from her worry about Jack. As Veda had said, her fretting was getting her no closer to understanding. What she needed was some activity, something to take her mind off it. Maybe later this afternoon she'd head to the marina, see if she could get in some sailing practice. Veda had grown up on the water and had been sailing as long as she could remember, but her age and poor health made Cass reluctant to take her out now that she'd learned the basics. She was diligent about studying the how-to books she'd found, but she learned best by doing. She needed another teacher, and that was that.

"Hey, Cass."

She opened her eyes, and lo and behold, there was the teacher she'd called for. Crazy how often that worked.

"Hey, Luc." She returned the greeting, then tilted her head to the side, scrutinizing him. "So, I'm betting the son of a boat builder would know just about all there was to know about sailing."

Luc scuffed a foot in the dirt and shrugged. Dark-haired and dark-eyed like his French-Canadian father, he had already matched his dad's lanky six feet and would probably surpass him in another year. Right now, though, he was all shy boy. "I guess I know a fair bit. I've been sailing all my life."

Cass hopped up, ready to bargain. "What would you need in trade, to give me lessons? I know you and your folks are awfully self-sufficient, but surely we could come up with something? I need to learn, and –" She glanced conspiratorially over her shoulder at the door to the cottage. "I don't want Veda taking me out anymore. Her hips give her so much pain, and she just can't move fast if we were to get into trouble."

"I understand." His face took on a rosy hue, and his dark eyes dropped back to the ground. "I'd just teach you. For free, I mean." Again with the shrugging and the scuffing. "It wouldn't be any trouble. None at all." He glanced up, and his eyes were filled with a longing he was trying – and failing – to hide. "I'd like to help you, Cass."

Uh-oh. Cass didn't need to be psychic to see what was going on here. Luc was sweet 17, and clearly thinking about being kissed. Unfortunately, his prospects on the island had diminished considerably. At 22, she was the closest to his age, if you didn't count Emma's little half-sister, who was nine. So unless he wanted to wait for Tiana to grow up, Cass was his best bet. Cass felt a flood of sorrow for him. How much would it suck to have your dating years stunted by a pandemic? His crush would fade in time, and in the interim, she would be sure to be careful of his feelings.

"Thank you for the offer, Luc, but I would have to insist on a trade. You've already done so much for the rest of us, and I believe in an energetic exchange. Like for like. Would one of Veda's herbal preparations come in handy?" She hesitated, not wanting to weird him out. "Or one of us could do a reading for you. Veda reads palms and does Tarot, which can help you understand your path and the circumstances going on around you. I communicate with those in the spirit world."

"I know what you do." His rosy hue got even deeper. "I think it's really cool. And now that everyone is different, they all believe you, too."

Cass laughed. Out of the mouths of babes. "Well, that's nice to hear, because they sure didn't before. Well? Do you want to think about it?"

"No, I don't need to think." His rosy flush dissipated, and his eyes went liquid with sorrow. "My best friend, Zeb, died in the plague. Would you…could you check in with him, to see if he's okay?"

"Sure. He may or may not come through, but we can try. I can ask right now, if you're comfortable."

At his nod, Cass sat down on the stoop. Luc shuffled around awkwardly for a moment, then sat down beside her. Cass shut her eyes and cleared her mind, centering herself, asking for her spirit guides to support her and praying for protection for all involved. She took several deep breaths, and enclosed both herself and Luc in white light, through which evil could not penetrate.

She opened her eyes and smiled at Luc. "May I hold something of yours?"

Luc fumbled around, patting his pockets, then pulled a ratty paperback book out of his back pocket. *1984* by George Orwell. He held it up. "Like this?"

"Yes." She took it from him, then raised her eyebrows questioningly. "What, the world isn't dystopic enough for you these days?"

Luc shrugged. "It's the book my mom and I are currently studying. I'm supposed to be drawing comparisons between Orwell's vision and what we know about our current situation."

Cass was intrigued. "I may have to jump in on that, if you guys are open to a book club. I love book clubs, but we never stayed anywhere long enough for me to join one. Anyway." She held the book in her hands and closed her eyes. "Time enough for that later. Let's see if spirit wants to talk."

For a moment, the world around her shifted. Then she felt the familiar tingle that signaled an arrival from the spirit world. "Someone is coming through for you. He says he's above you? Above and to the side – an uncle? Do you have an uncle who has passed?"

"We don't know. My dad's brother lives in Big Rapids, but we couldn't reach him or his family. My mom has a brother, too, but they weren't close. I haven't seen him since my grandpa's funeral when I was little."

"He's one insistent guy," Cass murmured. "His name starts with an S. Steven? No, it's more unusual. Sebastian? Was that his name?"

Luc's voice was excited. "Yes! My little brother Bastian is named after him!"

"Okay, well, he's telling me to tell you to tell your dad that he's..." She frowned, and addressed the spirit she was interacting with. "I'm sorry, can you show me in a different way? I'm not getting it. Oh! He's saying to tell your dad that he was right and your dad was wrong – there *is* an afterlife, and it's beautiful, and he's in it. Okay." She grinned at Luc. "He's doing that 'nanner-nanner-boo-boo' thing, and he wants you to say that to your dad. Does that make sense?"

Luc's jaw went slack with shock. "Holy shit!" He reddened again. "Sorry," he muttered. "That's what they always said to each other. They were really competitive, especially when they were growing up. Grandma was super strict about trash-talking, so that's what they came up with. Wow." He was quiet for a moment. "Wait. That means he died, doesn't it?"

"Yes," Cass said quietly. "He's in the spirit world with your aunt and your cousins. He said your grandparents were there to meet him, and other friends and relatives as well." She reached to rest her hand for a moment on his strong, young forearm. "He's okay, Luc. They're all okay, and at peace."

Luc looked down at her hand, and, as casually as she could, she removed it. She usually didn't hesitate to touch a client, but she didn't want to lead this poor kid on. Luc swallowed hard a few times, then looked up, his black eyes glossy with tears he didn't want to shed in front of her. "Is there more?"

Cass focused once more. "Not from your uncle. He's pulling back. He said what he came through to say."

"Can you ask for Zeb, please?"

His politeness made her smile. "I wish it worked that way, but it doesn't. Spirit comes through according to its own rhyme and reason. Zeb knows you're wondering about him. Let's just give it a minute."

"Okay."

They waited together under a pure blue July sky while a breeze stirred the leaves of the huge Elder tree that sheltered their yard from northern winds. Veda had chosen this cottage specifically because of that tree, and though she wouldn't sit underneath it for love nor money, she had a use for all of its parts, from flowers, to leaves, to berries, to wood. Cass didn't know if her fear of getting whisked away to the world of Faerie was real, or if it was a fantasy Veda had created for her eccentric, tarot-reading public persona. The line between those distinctions was starting to blur as Veda aged.

Cass closed her eyes again and let her mind shift into a neutral, receiving space. She tucked Luc's paperback into the crook of her lap, and opened her hands on her legs, palms up, signifying that she was willing to convey a message from spirit to Luc. No sooner did she issue the invitation than it was accepted, and another energy made itself known. Youthful, shy, masculine. Without opening her eyes, she started talking.

"There's another person coming through for you, a boy. But he's saying his name starts with an 'M,' not a 'Z.' Wait, hold the phone. He's going really fast, showing me a lot of images," she explained to Luc. "A Bible, specifically the gospels. Let me see if I've got this straight. He says his name starts with an 'M.' It's something biblical, Matthew or Mark. Is any of this making sense?"

Luc nodded. "His name was 'Matthew,' and he hated it. He said it was the most generic name of all time. When we were ten, I told him I'd call him 'Zebulon' instead, 'Zeb' for short, and it stuck. Even his mom called him 'Zeb.'" He drew in a long breath that shuddered, and wiped at his eyes, too overcome to hide his tears. "It's him."

"Okay." Cass was quiet for a few seconds. "He's showing me an overturned fishing creel, and..." Now it was time for her face to heat up. "And, ah, a Playboy magazine. Open to the centerfold. He's saying that those were both him, that he was just saying 'Hi.'"

"Oh my God, Zeb – my mom found that magazine and she is still ripping on me about how 'porn warps and pollutes a young man's mind.' She made me write a 1,500 word persuasive essay – dude, I am so going to get you back for that!" Then it hit him, and his face crumpled. "But I can't, can I? God, I miss him. He was such a practical joker, always getting us into trouble. This spring, I kept finding my fishing creel turned over and emptied out, no matter where I stored it or how carefully I locked it up. And the magazine, well, yeah." His face didn't color now; it flamed. "I gave Bastian hell for that – I figured he was paying me back for, well, never mind. And it was Zeb, all along." He shook his head in wonder. "So he's, what? Still alive somehow? Or is he a ghost?"

"He's spirit," Cass explained. "We're made of energy – all of us, everything is energy – and energy cannot die. Here's how I understand it, from the glimpses I've caught. As spirit, we inhabit a human form, and we live out a human lifetime according to a soul journey which was planned in the spirit world. When the human body we're currently inhabiting dies, we return to the spirit world to be with the Divine, to rest, to be with loved ones, perhaps to plan another incarnation. So in that sense, yes, Zeb is still alive, because his spirit will never die."

"So he's not a ghost?"

"If by 'ghost' you mean a lost soul, then no. I use the words ghost and spirit and a few others interchangeably. But a lost soul is someone who either doesn't realize they're dead or is angry or conflicted about passing. That's what that 'Ghost Whisperer' show was based on, and Zeb is not lost. He is telling me to tell you that he's okay, that his mom was there to meet him, and they're both happy." She listened for a moment. "He's fading now. Is there anything else you want to ask?"

"Will he come back again? Just to visit?"

Cass asked, but Zeb had gone. "He didn't answer." At the crestfallen look on Luc's face, she started to reach for his arm again, then pulled her hand back and hid the gesture by returning his paperback. "That doesn't mean he won't. It just means he felt it was in your best interest to pull back right then. That's what our loved ones in spirit form want most – what's best for us. Many of them do pop in now and again to visit, to check on our lives. So if you find more scattered fishing supplies or incriminating porn, you can bet it was him."

"Wow. Wow." Luc was staring into space, exhibiting what Cass called "First-Time-Shock-and-Awe." His face was slack and blank while his mind circled over and over what she'd said, trying to come up with some way she could have known all that and failing to produce a logical explanation. She left him to it and stood, opening the door to the cottage just as Veda was reaching for the handle on the other side.

"I thought I heard voices," Veda said. "Hi, Luc. I've got the tincture your mom asked for ready to go."

Cass looked at him and raised an eyebrow. "So you two are already trading? You could have let me know."

Luc fell back on his all-purpose shrug. "That was between my mom and Miss Veda. And now I owe you, so when do you want to start?"

Cass looked up at the sky. "Weather looks like it's going to hold clear, so how about this afternoon? Maybe in a couple hours?"

Luc nodded. Then, he looked past her and frowned. "Miss Veda, you don't look so good. Maybe you should sit down?"

Veda was staring, as slack-faced as Luc had been moments before, and Cass knew what that meant. As Veda would put it, the "sight was upon her," and she'd snap out of it when she was good and ready. Cass steered her towards one of the kitchen chairs and eased her round body into it, then spoke over her shoulder to Luc. "She's okay. She's having a vision." She made a wry face at him. "Welcome to our world."

"Dang," he breathed. He moved to stand on the other side of Veda, taking her hand and patting it gently. "Must be weird, living with you. I mean," another blush, "Visions and ghosts and such. You sure she's not having a seizure or something? Zeb's little sister used to have those what-ever-you-call-'ems – petit mal seizures. They looked just like this."

"Huh. I never thought to ask her if she'd been checked out by a doctor. I suppose if you hooked her up to a machine, there would be some abnormal neurological activity, but this is a vision. She says she's had them her whole life, and she always comes out with information to share, though it doesn't always make sense."

Just then, Veda shuddered and sucked in a huge breath of air. She swayed in the chair, and Cass steadied her with an arm around her plump, soft shoulders. Luc picked up the speed on his hand-patting. After a few moments, Veda lifted a hand to rub at her forehead, and Cass hurried to get her a drink of water. Veda sipped, sighed again, then looked up.

"Well, then."

Cass waited, but in vain. "That's it? You usually talk my ear off about what you see. Did you not see something this time?"

"I saw." Veda sipped again. She looked up at Cass, then looked at Luc, then back at Cass. "No need to share everything, now is there? Luc, dearest boy, your mom's tinctures are right here on the table in this box. Mind you don't break them – they're in glass bottles. I'm sure we've kept you long enough."

Luc picked up the box, then stood uncertainly, holding it. "You sure you're all right? You don't need to go lay down or anything? I feel bad, leaving."

Veda gave him a very warm, very fond smile, but shooed him off. "You've done enough, sweetheart. Give your mama and daddy my regards."

He nodded, then nodded at Cass. "I'll see you this afternoon at the marina, right?"

"That'll be great. See you then."

She shut the door behind him, then wheeled on Veda, eyes narrowed. "'Dearest boy?' 'Sweetheart?' Just what are you up to?"

"What? He is dear and sweet, and it doesn't hurt to let him know that others appreciate him."

Her innocent expression would have fooled anyone but Cass, who was playing with an unfair advantage. She checked in briefly with her guides, and sure enough. "You are so lying to me."

Veda sighed. "'Lying' is such an ugly word."

"If the shoe fits, Veda."

Veda took another leisurely sip of her water. "For right now, what I saw is none of your business. Now." She leaned forward, all business, and picked up the silk bag that held her Tarot cards. "Did you want a reading or not?"

Time enough to weasel it out of her, Cass decided. "Yes," she answered. "But I want you to read for Jack, not for me. I can check in with my guides when I choose a course of action. I want as much information as possible on what's happening with Jack, and what his mindset is, so I can try to figure out what he'll do."

Veda folded her lips, but nodded. "Very well," she said. "I don't usually hold with absent readings, but I do see your point. If the spirits cooperate, we'll read for him." She handed Cass the deck. "Choose a significator for him, then."

Cass shuffled through the familiar cards, looking for one in particular. When she found it, she handed it to Veda, who raised her eyebrows. "The Knight of Wands? Usually the Knight of Cups represents a brother."

Cass shook her head and tapped the card. "This fits. I'm sure."

Veda put the significator card in the center of the table, then took the rest of the deck from Cass. As she shuffled, she began the mantra that Cass had heard thousands of times, the words Veda started every reading with. "Tarot cards are not all-powerful, nor are they evil. They can offer insight into the events in your life and guidance when we need to make decisions, but they do not have all the answers. Tarot is a method of using your own intuition to better understand your past, present or future, as well as the lives of the people dear to you. They can be a light in the darkness, but only if you're willing to see." She paused, then asked, "What is your question?"

Cass had thought about this; questions were very important. "What do I need to know about Jack?"

Veda nodded her approval, then shuffled three more times and set the cards in front of Cass. Cass cut the cards, then sat back and watched while Veda dealt. As always, she dealt out all ten cards in the Celtic Cross spread, then paused once more with her hand resting over the cards. "The future is mutable. What is portrayed here represents only one possible future, the likely outcome given the events currently in motion. Nothing is written in stone. Do you understand?"

Cass nodded. Then, she watched with growing dismay as Veda flipped the cards over one by one. By the time she reached the tenth card, Cass was nearly hyperventilating.

"Never mind," she said, reaching to push the cards away, to negate the reading, to un-see what she'd already seen. "This was a terrible idea –"

Quick as a snake, Veda swatted her hand. "Don't touch them. What do I always tell you about Tarot? What do I always tell *everybody* about Tarot?"

"'The future can be changed by anyone willing to make the effort, but only if they have the facts,'" Cass quoted meekly. She stared at the cards, then spoke again, her voice barely above a whisper. "Have you ever seen a reading that was completely Major Arcana?"

"Not completely." Veda reached to tap the Ten of Swords, and Cass blanched.

"Jesus, Veda, that's only the worst card in the Tarot!" She flinched when Veda reached to snap her on the top of the head with her deceptively soft fingers, a gesture she hadn't employed since Cass had been a belligerent teenager.

"You settle yourself down, now. This is not a terrible reading. I know there are a lot of big-hitters here, but it's all about context." She touched Cass's hand, her voice gentler. "Honey, he's in trouble. You already knew that. Let's see what we can learn about it."

Cass nodded, gulping back the huge, childish sobs that wanted to rise out of her chest. Veda was right. If she wanted to help Jack, she had to get calm, and get clear. "I'm sorry. I'm just scared I'll lose him again, and I haven't even found him yet."

"I know, honey. Let's find out what we can do to help." She touched two cards: The Hanged Man, and The Fool. "Whatever the situation is that he's in, he's a willing sacrifice, in a sense. He's willing to endure pain and personal hardship to achieve his goal." Her eyes narrowed, and focused on something far-away. "And to protect his friends. He would do anything to keep them safe."

She shook her head a little, then tapped The Fool again. "A traveler that didn't watch where he was going," she said, then shot Cass a stern look. "Sounds like someone else I know, haring off into God knows what. One might think you two were related." Her fingers lingered on The Fool. "He's determined to travel down a certain path, and right now, he's ignoring all the warning signs. This speaks to his soul journey, Cass. He needs to learn to listen to Wisdom."

Her fingers touched another card: The Devil. "This card represents what stands in Jack's way, and I'm reading two different meanings. Very rarely is The Devil read literally, but in this case, he's dealing with someone who is the antithesis of good, someone who wants to upset the harmony of nature, just because he can. Young," she said, frowning. "I'm getting the words, 'Rotten little shit,' though that doesn't really convey the depth of this young man's nastiness. He's completely controlled by fear, and he's desperate to recreate the world as he knew it before. He wants to feel safe and in control, and he'll do anything to achieve that end."

She was quiet for a moment, thinking, then went on. "On another level, this card also speaks to Jack's soul journey. He needs to watch out for the quick fix he'll be offered to his problems, the way of violence and destruction. It might get him what he wants in the short term, but at a terrible price."

She straightened with determined cheer, and reached to touch another card: The Lovers. "As you know, this card isn't limited to romantic love. It can also refer to a union of opposites, a close bond between people, especially when there's been a barrier or obstacle between the two souls involved. This is his goal, the reason all of this is in motion." She smiled at Cass. "In short, he's looking for you."

Cass pressed her hands over her heart, where the ancient adoration for a big brother still resided. When she was little, before her "imaginary friend problem" had revealed itself, she had thought he hung the moon and the stars in the sky. Even after the trouble began, he'd been her longest-lasting ally. The day he had drawn back from her, a frown on his face and disappointment in his eyes, had been the loneliest day of her life.

Veda rested her finger next on the Death card and looked up at Cass. "You know better than to be afraid of this. Almost everyone I read these days has this card come up."

Cass nodded. "Profound change. An end to the way things once were."

Veda nodded back. "Yes. Very rarely does it signify physical death, though I've seen exceptions to that lately. Now tell me what the position of this card tells us."

Cass frowned down at the spread. She didn't read the cards, though Veda had tried to teach her. For the way Cass worked, they just got in the way. Nevertheless, she'd picked up a lot over the years. She reached out and touched Death, too. "This lies beneath the significator. It describes the foundation for the current situation."

"Exactly. Your brother went through a profound change, and it set him on this path." Veda touched the next card, the dread Ten of Swords. "And this?"

Cass's heart began to pound again, but this time in excitement. Now that she was looking at the cards in context, she was seeing what Veda meant. "What is behind him. Events in the recent past that are in the process of being completed."

Veda tapped the Ten of Swords again, which didn't seem so dread now. "Cass, honey, whatever he's going through right now doesn't compare to what he has already survived. He hit rock bottom, but he's on his way out of it." She puffed out a breath of air. "That doesn't mean he's not in danger now, but according to the cards, he's been through worse."

She touched two more cards, both of them upside-down. "The Magician, reversed," she murmured. "Again,

I'm getting two layers of meaning from this. Jack is dealing with someone who is willing to exploit everyone around him for gain. He's also facing that same tendency in himself. He can be a bit manipulative, I see."

Cass rolled her eyes. "You don't know the half of it." She reached out to touch the next upside-down card herself. "The Tower. I know enough to be glad this is reversed."

"Yes. Upright, it foretells catastrophe. In this position, and from where it lies in the spread, he's still facing adversity and disruption of his plans, but to a lesser degree."

She touched the second-to-the-last card, and for the first time since she had started the reading, she beamed her beautiful, joyous smile. "Strength. He has everything he needs to prevail, both over himself and over the adversary he's facing: courage, determination, defiance, and most importantly, moral strength. Whether or not he'll make the right choices remains to be seen. But this bodes well."

Veda rested her hand on the last card in the spread. "And so. This card reveals what will happen, based on all the influences currently in motion. Justice." She looked at Cass. "This is Divine Justice, as opposed to human justice. What should be, will be. If your brother stays true to his moral compass, if he chooses the side of creation and love, even if destruction and fear would get him what he wants in the short term, he will triumph."

Cass leaned forward on her elbows and took it all in, absorbing, thinking. Then, to Veda. "Okay. One card, one question."

Veda's chin jutted out, but she nodded and started shuffling. "Ask."

"What's my role in all this?"

Veda pulled the top card off the deck and put it right in front of Cass. She stared down at it. "Temperance? I'm supposed to just be patient? You've got to be kidding me!"

The look on Veda's face told her, even before her guides gave her a nudge. "Veda. You palmed that card." She pointed at the pile of cards, still in Veda's hand. "Show me the real answer."

Veda flipped the card over on top of Temperance, but didn't look at it. Her chin was wobbling, and tears sheened her eyes. "I worry so for you, when you go."

Cass looked down at the Six of Swords, the image of a woman paddling a boat under cover of darkness. A journey of uncertain outcome. She reached across the table, pushing the cards to the side to take Veda's hands.

"I have to go. If he gets clear of whatever's happening, he'll head to Pewaukee, to our parents' house. It's the only place he would know to look for me. If nothing else, I have to leave a message there for him, telling him where I am now." Tears spilled from Veda's filled eyes, and Cass squeezed her hands tighter. "Tell me how to make this easier for you, and I will. But I have to go."

"I know that, dearest girl." She straightened up and wiped at her eyes, then pointed a finger at Cass's nose. "You promise to be back by Lammas. Swear it."

Just under a month away. "I promise. Anything else?"

Now something like cunning sparkled in Veda's smile. "And you don't go alone. You didn't ask anyone to go with you before, and that was pure foolishness."

Cass groaned. They'd been over this ground before, way too many times. "Veda, I didn't ask anyone because I didn't think it was right to take someone else into an unknown situation. I still don't think it is. We needed to know what was going on out there, and I was the logical person to go. The same thing is true of this trip. It's my brother. It's my task."

"Luc will go with you." Veda was once again sipping water, serene and sure of herself.

Cass blinked, startled, then shook her head. "Not a good idea. For starters, he's just a kid. Secondly, he's got a crush on me, so it wouldn't even be fair to ask. Third —"

"I saw it." Veda interrupted. "My vision. Luc will go with you. And he'll save your life."

ELEVEN
Naomi: Colorado Springs, CO

Naomi swiveled in the saddle for the third time – she had kept track – to stare at Martin over her shoulder. And as he had previously, he held up a hand before she could speak.

"Was I doing it again? Sorry. I'll stop."

This time, Naomi didn't turn around right away. Instead, she glared. "You're trying to pick a fight."

"Nope."

"You are! Admit it!"

Martin just shrugged by way of an answer. His body shifted lazily from side to side with Shakti's gait as they rode along. His eyes were hidden in the deep shade under his hat, but was that a smile? Was he actually smiling at her? Naomi's mouth tightened with outrage and indignation, and she huffed back around to face front. The nerve of him!

The morning sun was soft and warm on her shoulders, and a tender little breeze stirred the leaves of the scrub oaks that bordered the trail. Wildflowers were rioting all around them, cheerful and vibrating with life under the true-blue sky. As summer days went, it couldn't have been more perfect.

Naomi hated it. All of it. The beauty, the breeze, the sky, and Martin most of all.

For the last week, her spirits had death-spiraled. The trip over Rampart Range Road had taken three times as long as they'd planned. Violent afternoon storms had delayed them every single day, bringing dangerous hail and torrential rains, both of which did further damage to the already degraded road. Every time they hit a section of road that had been completely washed out, every time they had to backtrack and ride cross-country for miles and miles, Naomi got angrier.

On the third day, Martin had asked what was bothering her. She couldn't actually remember what all she'd said to him. She did recall snarling – she seemed to be doing that a lot these days – and she remembered as well the way his jaw had tightened, clamping down on words he didn't say. The memory made her face heat in embarrassment now, but she couldn't bring herself to apologize. Not yet. Apologizing would mean thinking. It would mean analyzing and admitting to herself what was driving her dark mood. That, she was simply not prepared to do.

It came again – the grating, tuneless, muttering drone that Martin called "singing." Naomi spun around so fast, it made Ben snort and shy. "Would you STOP it?"

Her shout echoed and bounced down the long, sloping valley. This time, Martin didn't smile. He grinned.

He rode up beside her and reined Shakti in. "That's more like it." He dismounted, and looped an arm around Shakti's neck, stroking her nose. "Let's get this over with, then have a snack. I'm starving."

Naomi dismounted as well, and both horses shifted and sidled, tossing their heads fractiously. A few feet behind Shakti, Pasha got in on the action as well, tugging on the lead rope that connected her to Shakti's saddle. Naomi grimly hung on to Ben's reins and felt her lower lip begin to quiver. Even the horses were against her.

Martin led Shakti and Pasha off the road and into the shade of a huge, shaggy Juniper. He ground-tethered them both, then moved out of range of their ever-swishing tails and sat down on the sandy ground. Removing his hat, he ran his maddeningly clean handkerchief over his face, watching her all the while. Not knowing what else to do, she joined him in the shade, tethering Ben next to the other horses. She, too, moved out of tail range but didn't sit. Instead, she folded her arms across her chest.

"What, exactly, are we 'getting over?'"

Martin leaned back on his hands, stretching his legs out and crossing them at the ankles. "You tell me."

Hades, who had been ranging ahead, picked that moment to trot into the shade. He sat down beside Naomi, pressing close in spite of the warmth of the day, and lifted his head to gaze at her with sad, confused eyes. She *felt* his soft whine, and caught a glimpse of herself through his perception: *Sad, angry, sad, scared, sad sad sad.* Naomi's lip quiver turned into a full blown chin wobble.

Martin's voice was soft but insistent. "I will be the first person to admit I don't have a great track record with women. I may not have made the smartest choices, but I sure as hell learned a few things. I know when a woman needs to cry, and you need to cry. So let 'er rip, and let's have done with it."

Well. Well, then.

Stooping, Naomi scooped up a clod of dirt and threw it at him. Then another. And another. Martin fended off all three, his eyebrows climbing steadily higher with each pitch. And once again, she found herself snarling.

"You think you know what I need? You think you can tell me what to do?" A fourth clod of dirt exploded in the center of his chest, and it was all she could do not to throw her fists in the air and scream her victory. "I've got two words for you, Martin. 'Fuck,' and 'you!'"

His jaw dropped open, and he goggled. Naomi had never actually seen someone goggle before. The next thing she knew, she had both hands clamped over her mouth, making sounds that fell halfway between sobs and whoops. Martin dusted his chest clean with great deliberation, his expression now wary, worried and pissed.

"Are you laughing? Or crying?"

Naomi took her hands away long enough to half-shriek, "I'm not really sure!" Then she was back at it again, tears streaming, nose running, an enormous sense of release blowing her chest wide open. She plopped down on the ground beside Martin and rocked with her arms clamped around her middle. When the sounds she was making diminished to occasional hiccups, she spoke.

"I heard Piper say that to one of her boyfriends once, and God help me, I was so proud of her! He was such an arrogant prick." She accepted the handkerchief he handed her and swiped it over her face, taking one deep, shuddering breath after another.

"So...you're calling me an arrogant prick?"

Naomi snorted. "Maybe." She put her head to the side and considered him. "Yes. I am." His eyes went storm-dark at that, but she didn't backpedal. "I appreciate your concern, Martin, and I do owe you an apology. I've been a foul-tempered traveling companion, but I'm not ready to talk about it yet. I just need to deal with...what's eating at me in my own time, in my own way."

"Okay." His voice was gruff, but the storm had blown over. "Will you at least tell me what the dreams are about?"

Naomi wrapped her arms around her bent knees. "I think it's Piper," she said. "I've been getting these flashes of her in unfamiliar places since a few days after they left. Really vivid, really weird flashes. The colors are almost fake, they're so bright. They're not like any dreams I've ever had before. A few days ago, they changed." She started rocking again, just a little, soothing herself with the gentle motion. "I'm still getting flashes, but Piper isn't in them. I see a town and a boy I don't know, other strangers. And Piper hasn't checked in since this started." She pressed a hand over her heart. "I've sent her so many messages. She's not responding."

Martin's gaze didn't waiver. "Is she alive?"

"Yes."

"You're sure?"

Naomi shut her eyes for a moment, then opened them. "Absolutely. I know what it felt like when Scott and Macy died. I wasn't that close to Layla, but I felt that change, too. Piper's alive." She clenched the hand that had been pressed to her chest into a fist. "Either that, or she's taken a part of me to wherever it is they go, because she's right here."

"Okay." Martin nodded. "I was picking a fight, and I'm not sorry. You've been shut up tight as a tick. I had to get in your head somehow. Unless we run into the mother of all mudslides or some other catastrophe, we should be in the Springs by this afternoon. We need to be on the same page."

Naomi made a face at him. "You mean I need to stop acting like a tired toddler."

Anger flared in his eyes. "No," he said, and she could *feel* how much effort he put into the level tone. "What I said was, we need to be on the same page. Communicating. You've been distracted and oblivious to what's going on around you. You've alienated not just me but the horses, and you need to reconnect with them, too. The only one who's not pissed is Hades, and you've got him so worried about you, he's tied in knots. We're riding into a dangerous, unknown situation. Connect the dots." He stood. "Now, if you're done putting words into my mouth and twisting them into some kind of criticism I didn't intend, I'm going to get something to eat."

It was Naomi's turn to goggle. Martin stood up and moved to Shakti's side, rummaging in the saddle bags.

They'd packed plenty of food for the two or three day journey they'd expected, and the delays meant they'd been on light rations for days. It was tempting, to attribute Martin's sharp words to hunger, but she knew better.

She stood, and moved to Ben's side. From the depths of the saddlebag, she unearthed the very last crumbly ginger snap cookies. She handed them to Martin without a word, then returned to Ben. He shifted uneasily at her approach and she paused, feeling sorrow, along with an echo of the fear she'd felt the day she'd first met him. She went back to that day in her mind, and heard Ignacio's patient voice in her head. *Ben can handle all the grief you or I have to dish out. It's the conflict that confuses him.*

And that, as Ignacio had said, was the crux of it. It wasn't the depth of what she was feeling. It was that she was feeling everything at once, too much to sort out, every feeling a paradox or contradiction for another. Naomi closed her eyes and Ben's familiar energy was there, a little ticked, like Martin had said, but still her gentle, giant-hearted boy. She leaned into his side and felt his head curve around her. His forgiveness was instant and generous, releasing a burden on her heart she'd been unaware of carrying. Without opening her eyes, Naomi started talking, trying to unravel the knots around her.

"I'm angry, Martin. So god-damned angry. You talk about 'deciding' whether to stay in Woodland Park or to leave. You talk about that as if it's a choice." She opened her eyes and felt her face fall into the bitter lines it had been wearing since they'd ridden away from her cabin. She hated the way the expression felt. She was becoming a stranger to herself. "It doesn't matter what I want. I can't even remember the last time I had a choice about something. I just keep doing what I have to do, whether I like it or not. So don't talk to me about 'choosing' like that's something I can do. Frankly, it pisses me off."

Martin listened, and after a moment, nodded. He dusted cookie dust from his fingers, then moved to stand on the other side of Ben. He crossed his arms on Ben's saddle and leaned his chin on his forearms. "The people who killed themselves after the plague," he said. "Was that a choice?"

Naomi's frown deepened. "Of course it was."

"Try to imagine what they were thinking. What was in their minds?"

"Pain. Loss and grief and loneliness. Some of them felt like they didn't have anything left to live for." She remembered the couple they'd found, corpses holding hands. "Some of them didn't want to live in a world that had changed so much. They were too scared to try. What are you getting at?"

Martin shook his head, his expression gentle. "It's so easy for you to understand and forgive the feelings of others, and so hard for you to show yourself that same compassion. Naomi, people will choose to stay in Woodland Park to defend their homes. You can choose to do that, too. No one is forcing you to do anything. Stay or leave. It's your decision."

Naomi's eyes filled with tears again. "You and I both know Grace is right. They'll come. I *felt* it, the moment she said the words. Staying is suicide."

"I think so, yes." He reached to gather one of her hands in both of his and brought her fingers to his lips. "But it is still a choice. You don't have to like it, you can be pissed as all hell about it, but don't give away your own power like that." His warm breath feathered across her knuckles, and the nape of her neck tingled. "You're not just a helpless victim of circumstances, even when you hate those circumstances. If you need to stay, I'll help you prepare, help you supply a bolt hole."

"But you won't stay with me."

"No. My choice is Grace and Lark, and I intend to get them as far away as possible." He pressed her fingers against his mouth again, hard this time. "But I won't promise not to try to change your mind."

"You make it seem so simple." She narrowed her eyes. "That kind of pisses me off, too."

"It is simple. That doesn't mean it's easy." A teasing smile touched his mouth. "You know, it would help a lot if you didn't bottle this shit up and force me to pry it out of you. Are we good now? Did you get it all out?"

Something huge shifted inside her chest, something that wouldn't wait much longer to be dealt with. She leaned her cheek against his hands where they still cradled her fingers. "No. But the rest of it has to wait. I don't have words for it yet."

"Fair enough." He freed one of his hands, and smoothed his palm over the strands of hair that had come free of her braid. The gesture was unpracticed and a little rough and swamped Naomi with tenderness. "You just let me know if I need to start singing again. Let's get going."

They rode into the Garden of the Gods in the high heat of the afternoon, then slid south out of the park into quiet, disintegrating neighborhoods. Here and there, groups of homes were burned to blackened husks, and evidence of looting was everywhere. When they reached Highway 24, the changes were even more ominous. Vehicles had been removed from the road, rolled into adjacent parking lots or ditches, both to the east and west of where they sat. Naomi reached out with both hers and Hades' senses, and the danger she sensed on this stretch of road smoldered along her nerve endings like an electrical fire. She wondered how to ask Hades if there was anyone nearby, but even as the thought formed, he was scanning with eyes, ears and nose. She met Martin's questioning gaze.

"There's no one in the immediate vicinity, but this doesn't look good." She inclined her head at the highway. "Plenty wide enough for vehicles to pass through."

"Or tanks." At her look, he nodded grimly. "Yeah, they've got those on Fort Carson, too."

They rode east until they hit 31st Street, then headed south and climbed the steep switchbacks, finally arriving at the intersection that looked down on the old Bear Creek Nature Center. The sentry flags which had been prominently displayed on nearby buildings and rock formations were gone. Again, Naomi reached out through Hades, *feeling* for what was going on. This time, she picked up a buzz of activity driven by unsettled emotions: Anxiety, worry, dread and loss, all united by a steady beat of *hurry, hurry, hurry*.

"There are still people here, but something has them rushing around," she said. "They're almost frantic, and they're scared."

Martin's eyes swept ceaselessly around them as he answered. "Should we ride on or get out of here? Is there danger?"

"I don't think so - not immediate danger, anyway. I think we should find out what's happening."

Martin nodded, and they continued on, groping forward cautiously, guided by Naomi's Hades-enhanced instincts. When they turned into the parking lot by the old nature center, the cry went up from sentries at last. One of the men standing watch had met them on their previous visit, and he hurried forward to greet them, armed with a rifle tucked in the crook of his arm. He shook hands with Martin and nodded at Naomi.

"You've caught us at a bad time," he said, his words as hurried as his movements. "We're getting out of Dodge. I'll take you to Isaiah."

They secured the horses and left Hades on watch beside them, then followed the sentry into the cool, dark interior of the nature center. Isaiah was in one of the rooms behind the long counter, packing books into boxes. He looked up when they entered, and as before, the *power* this mild-looking man radiated was palpable. He nodded at them both, but kept right on packing.

"Martin and Naomi. Welcome. One of our women said we'd have friendly visitors today. I'm glad it's you." He stared at a book spine in an agony of indecision Naomi remembered all too well, then set the book aside with obvious regret and reached for another. "You'll have to forgive our lack of hospitality. We're preparing to leave."

"So we were told." Martin took off his hat and wiped sweat off his forehead. "Can we ask where you're going, and why you're leaving now?"

Isaiah paused to scrutinize them both, his eyes traveling between Martin and Naomi several times before he reached for another book. "I don't know if you're aware, but the gang has managed to get some helicopters in the air."

Naomi spoke. "That's why we're here. We saw one in Woodland Park over a week ago. Just the one, and just that one time. We were hoping you'd have some information about what's going on."

"Precious little, I'm afraid, and what we have came at great cost. We've seen one every day for the past ten days – usually a Blackhawk, but once we saw a Chinook, and yesterday, my people tell me it was a pair of Apaches. Short training flights, it appears, and we're guessing they're learning via written instruction manuals. If they had an experienced pilot, we think they'd have been in the air long before now, and in greater numbers. Other than one fly-over, they haven't approached our settlement, so we were planning to just watch and see what happened."

He paused in his packing, straightening to gaze at them. "I need to back up a bit to tell this properly. About six weeks ago, we lost four of our outlying sentries – two men and two women. They just disappeared. At the same time, we heard the gang had closed its borders down tight. They were no longer letting people come and go, as they had been before. We didn't know exactly what was happening until a couple of days ago. One of the sentries we'd lost literally crawled back to us."

Isaiah paused, drawing a deep breath in through his nose and holding it. A muscle flexed in his jaw. He closed his eyes and slowly released his breath, and Naomi *felt* him force himself back to calmness. His self-control was formidable. "Jana had been raped, beaten, and left for dead," he said flatly. "She overheard bits and pieces of information during her captivity, and she used the last of her strength to bring us a warning. We had noticed that the raids on some of the smaller groups in the area had stopped, and we weren't sure why. The more optimistic among us hoped it meant those criminals were finally developing their own food sources. Now, thanks to Jana, we know what's really going on."

"They're letting you grow and harvest," Martin said. "They're letting you do the work and lulling you into a false sense of security at the same time. When your crops are harvested and preserved, they'll come with overwhelming numbers, take everything they want, and kill everyone they don't take captive."

Isaiah nodded slowly, his eyes locked on Martin's. "Jana gave her life to bring us that information. How did you get it?"

Martin looked down at his feet. "My daughter escaped the gang, too. She paid our price," he said quietly. He looked back up at Isaiah, his expression one of mingled pride and agony. "She's brilliant. She predicted this would be their plan."

Isaiah went back to packing his books, and only the most careful listener would hear the thread of grief in his otherwise controlled voice. "Jana shouldn't have lived long enough to get to us, but she did. She said angels carried her the last few miles, and I do not doubt her. God brought her home to us, so she could die among the friends she came to warn. Because of her, we know what we need to do, and I will not allow her sacrifice to be in vain. We're leaving tomorrow at first light, before they can get wind of our plans."

"Where are you going?"

"South, near Monte Vista, on the Rio Grande River. It's not as far away as I would like, but one of our people has family there. She knows the area and the people. It would be best, obviously, if we could send scouts ahead, but we won't risk the delay."

"We're considering the same course of action." Martin's eyes touched Naomi, then returned to Isaiah. "The San Luis Valley is a good spot for agriculture, even though it's dry. We're looking at Pagosa Springs. If we decide to leave, that's probably where we'll head."

Isaiah nodded again. "If we didn't have the connection in Monte Vista, Pagosa Springs was an option I liked. Protected by the mountains, surrounded by all that undeveloped land. A good choice. If Monte Vista doesn't work out for us, maybe we'll join you there." He straightened from the box he had just finished filling. "But what do you mean 'If you decide to leave?' What's stopping you?"

There was a beat of silence. Then Naomi lifted her chin and answered. "Me." Her eyes flickered to Martin. "Me, and a few others. We're not sure yet what course we'll choose."

But even as she said the words, she knew the choice – at least on her part – had already been made. The pain of a leave-taking that hadn't even occurred yet tightened her throat, made her squint through tears of both anger and grief.

Behind his thick glasses, Isaiah's eyes seemed to glow. As he gazed at her, she felt the *pull* of his persuasive gift, so like Jack's, before he even said a word. Then, with no warning at all, he slid a dagger right into the heart of her.

"Being a leader is like being a mother, Naomi." His eyes really did glow, like Verity's skin. "You don't have the luxury of putting yourself first. You have to consider the ramifications of your actions and decisions on others, those that look to you for guidance, direction, and love." His eyes went unfocused, the pupils dilating until they eclipsed the light blue of his irises. "Your daughters prepared you for the tasks that lie ahead. Whether you're ready to admit it or not, you are the mother of your community. The path you're being called to will challenge you to your very core, and if you take it, you'll be forever changed. The choice to stay or go is yours, but remember that a life lived to the fullest isn't lived only in comfort and safety."

Isaiah fell silent, his head dropping forward, his fingers rising to rub at his temple. Naomi's mouth opened, but words failed her. She'd been wrong. Isaiah wasn't like Jack. He was something else altogether. He hardly knew her, but he had zeroed in on the one thing she could never deny or turn away from: her mother's heart, and the responsibilities that came with it.

Naomi fell back on the conventions of a dead time and nodded with polite formality. "Thank you for your thoughts, Isaiah. Good luck on your journey and in your new home." Then, she walked towards the door. "Martin, I'll meet you outside."

She ignored the people she passed and headed straight for the animals. Ben tossed his head in welcome, and Naomi immersed herself in all of them, loving on each of the horses in turn and making up with Hades, who wiggled and wagged his delight at the attention. Then she returned to Ben, gazing into his eyes for long moments, humming a wordless, soothing sound that comforted them both. She tucked herself under his chin and leaned on his shoulder, pressing her cheek to his warm, dusty neck, filling her lungs with his scent. Shakti pressed close on the other side, and Naomi looped an arm around her neck as well, using their big bodies to block out the activity around them, where people hurried to and fro, trailing urgency and worry like unpleasant perfumes. Finally, Martin walked out the doors she had exited.

Naomi slid back under Ben's chin and walked to meet him. "Staying here isn't an option if they're leaving first thing in the morning."

"No, it's not. We've got the information we came for and good reasons to head home sooner rather than later. We can't take 24. Isaiah's people confirmed the gang's behind the activity there. We could take the hiking trails out of Manitou, but I don't know if I'm comfortable with that. Still too close to the highway." He judged the position of the sun, then frowned at the dark clouds massing, once again, over the mountains. "Doesn't really matter at this point. We need to find shelter and hunker down. This weather pattern is killing us."

"I want to go home." Naomi spoke the words before she thought them, and oh, the layers of meaning there. "To my house," she clarified.

"I knew what you meant." Martin moved to mount Shakti. "Let's go, then."

They rode south out of Bear Creek, the quiet of the afternoon broken only by the creaking of their saddles, the rhythmic thump of the horses' hooves, and the wind rising ahead of the storm. Naomi's old neighborhood was even more run-down than before, and it looked like another round of looters had gone through. Windows were broken in every house and front doors hung crookedly off hinges.

Naomi's house had not escaped the vandalism. Her living room picture window lay in pieces on the front lawn, along with the dining room chair that had been used to shatter it, and obscenities had joined the message she'd spray-painted for Piper on the garage door. Naomi waited with the animals while Martin checked out the interior. When he had cleared it, they settled the animals in the backyard and entered the house through the ruined sliding glass door, their boots crunching on still more broken glass.

"Let's get this over with." Naomi headed straight for the basement door, not even taking the time for a deep breath, hurrying down the stairs. Chaos met her at the bottom, even more boxes than before overturned and their contents dumped, but the door to the hidden room remained closed behind the wreckage. Automatically, Naomi reached to flip on the light switch, then sighed and hung her head for a moment. She looked over her shoulder at Martin. "Do you think I'll ever stop doing that?" Then she pushed the piles aside with her feet and opened the door.

Just as she'd left it. Here, where vandals and the elements hadn't intruded, she could still make out the faint scents of her old life: The black cherry candles she had loved, the herbs from her garden she'd dried for cooking and homemade potpourris, that alchemy of smells from favorite foods, soap and shampoo, laundry detergent and cleanser every house took on over time. It made her legs wobble as memories rushed up. A lifetime in this house, a life she had loved so much. Her lost ones were so close here. If she just closed her eyes and stayed in this room...

Martin stepped in behind her and looked around. "You should take everything you want this time. Just in case."

Naomi shook herself, then nodded, grateful for the distraction. "I know." Time enough to square up with the past after the necessities of living had been dealt with. She gestured to the shelves containing food and bottled water. "I'll grab a case of water for the animals. Why don't you find something that looks good, and we'll eat before we do anything else."

"Sounds good. I'm still starving."

She hauled the water up, found a bucket in the garage, then emptied the plastic bottles, leaving the horses to take their turns. Then she returned to the kitchen where Martin had arranged his supplies on the counter: two more cases of water, several cans of dog food, a half-dozen cans of soup, vegetables and fruit. He scrutinized the stove, which was electric, then shook his head. "Too risky. It looks undamaged, but I'd rather not fire up the generator and have something else in the house spark a fire. We'll have to eat it cold."

"I've got a fire pit table out back that has a little metal grill. That could work to heat the soup, couldn't it?"

He shook his head. "Of course you have a fire pit table. What about fixin's for s'mores? Do you have those?"

She rolled her eyes at him, then moved to dig under the counter, coming up with a small sauce pan. The utensils drawer had been dumped, so she had to hunt around until she found the can opener wedged beside the refrigerator. When he went outside with his supplies, she hauled a chair over by the refrigerator and strained to reach the highest, most inaccessible cupboard. A few minutes later, she joined him outside, carrying a pretty tray on which she had arranged stale graham crackers, rock-hard marshmallows, and perfectly edible chocolate bars. He took one look and shook with laughter.

She smiled serenely. "Do I have fixin's for s'mores? Please."

They heated the soup over a tiny fire, and Naomi opened one of the cans of dog food for Hades. He ate it in a single, ecstatic slurp, then sat staring at the other can with strings of drool hanging from the corners of his mouth until she gave in. He had been running on the lean side lately, missing Persephone's superior hunting skills. Other than Ed and one other woman in Woodland Park, Naomi hadn't observed people keeping pets; she knew the practice was outlawed in the Bear Creek group. They'd seen some dog packs from a distance, all of them mid-sized dogs, no more than 30 or 40 pounds. Large dogs required too much fuel and had trouble getting enough to eat, while small dogs made easy prey, making both Hades and Persephone oddities. Naomi had always been a proponent of allowing dog breeds to mingle for the health of the species, but she had never imagined it coming about like this.

As they ate, they discussed options, agreeing it would be best to travel back the way they'd just come, via Rampart Range Road, also agreeing they'd stay tomorrow to give the horses a rest, then leave the following morning at first light. Those decisions made, silence fell between them. The space was filled with the steady crop and crunch of the horses grazing, and the pressure of the words she was waiting for Martin to say. Finally, he took a deep breath and started pushing out halting phrases.

"I need to go. Out. Tonight. Late." He shook his head and made a disgusted sound, then went on in a rush. "I need to go check on the gang."

Naomi nodded. "I figured." She remembered the smell of blood and smoke, enhanced through Persephone's senses, and made herself make the offer. "Do you want me to go with you?"

"No." He wasn't meeting her eyes. "No motorcycles this time, so I'll be on foot. I just need to... I just need to see."

Would he take a pound of flesh for Grace, if the opportunity presented itself? She knew he'd be honest with her, if she asked. She chose not to. Martin had his demons to deal with, and she had hers. In this, they were both on their own.

Martin stood. "I'm going to check out the nearby houses, see if there's anything useful. Do you mind if I take Hades with me?"

"Not at all. The horses will warn me if any strangers show up." Naomi clicked her fingers, and Hades joined her instantly. She rubbed along his side when he pressed against her, and she showed him what she wanted with her mind. *Go with Martin. Keep him safe.* Hades' tongue lolled and he grinned his Rottie grin in anticipation of the adventure, but Naomi knew he'd take his duties very seriously the minute they set foot outside the fence.

After they left, Naomi sorted through what was left in the kitchen, stacking useful items in a pile on the ruined butcher block island. She went through the bathrooms and did the same, then scanned what was left in the thoroughly looted garage. Those tasks complete, she headed back outside to empty more water bottles for the horses, and reached out to Hades to see if she could get a feeling for where he and Martin were.

Faintly at first, then stronger, she began to catch glimpses of the neighborhood from a much lower perspective than she was used to, the colors flat and nondescript. By contrast, scents bloomed in her nose like overblown, strange flowers: old death and rot; mule deer, rabbits and squirrels everywhere; despised coyotes; innumerable types of vegetation, some edible, some poisonous; and Martin. Naomi put a hand out to steady herself on the deck railing, disoriented and a little dizzy. She was suddenly hyper-alive with awareness. Sounds felt like physical touches in her ears: wind, small skitters and stirrings of animals, and the crunch of Martin's boots on the gravel at the side of the pavement. She laughed softly in wonder. She'd lost so much, sometimes she forgot to marvel at what she'd gained.

Reassured that they were safe at least for now, Naomi let the connection with Hades fade and headed back down to the basement. She ferried up load after load of the preserved food and other practical supplies that remained. She didn't know if they would be able to take all of it with them, but it shouldn't be hidden away any longer. If they couldn't use it, someone else could. When she had finished, she returned to the hidden room again and just stood there, gazing at the treasures that remained on the shelves.

The Finnish crystal bowl her grandmother had given her for her wedding. Her jewelry box, filled with gifts Scott and the girls had given her over the years. Stacks of home movies on VHS tapes she'd always meant to convert to DVDs. The ceramic candlesticks Piper had made for her in art class. Macy's little box of quilt pieces. She opened this last and touched the bright squares of rainbow gingham, remembering that evening, just before. An evening like any other, skyping with Piper, making plans for

Easter, but the shadow of the plague had fallen over them even then. She remembered standing in her sunny kitchen the next morning, hearing news of the quarantine, and knew those had been the last moments she had believed in "forever," or failed to count the cost of such a belief.

She touched each treasure, remembered, lingered. Precious as these things were, none of them could heal the brokenness inside her. Only time and living could do that. Naomi took one last deep breath, drew in the faint traces of a life gone by, then stepped out and shut the door behind her. She leaned against the door and shut her eyes.

She could feel the outline of herself shifting and changing to accommodate something new, something that had been growing in her since the first time she stepped out her front door in flimsy, impractical sandals to confront an awful new world. She had been a sheltered and protected woman, and she could have chosen to die here in this house, cowering, with her pretty things and her memories of safety and happiness.

But she hadn't. She'd gotten her plump, wimpy keister moving. She had gotten her daughter safely to the cabin, and though Macy's death would send "what if" whispers through her mind always, always, she had survived. She had gone on. She was a vital, valued part of her new community, and not just because she could still, by thee gods, bake a mean cookie. Naomi opened her eyes, straightened her spine, and smiled to herself.

"One might," she said softly, "Even call me bad-ass."

That thought brought Piper to her mind, and she warmed the connection between them, though she didn't wait for a reply. There was still one thing left she needed to do.

The western-most garden bed was filled with weeds. She cleared it, and when the weeds were gone, the loosened ground was soft enough to dig. She retrieved a shovel from the garden shed and set to work, digging until she hit the hard clay a few inches under the bed. In just over an hour, she'd cleared all the dirt she could manage. It wasn't all that deep, but it would have to do. She rested, leaning on the handle of the shovel, gazing up the familiar outline of Cheyenne Mountain while sweat dried on her forehead and cooled her spine. Then she went to get Scott.

Their room had been ransacked again, but this time, the looters had left the bed and its occupants alone. Scott and Zeus lay just as she'd left them, the tattered plastic tarp covered with the beautiful quilt. Death was old here, so faint, she would have missed it if not for her connection to Hades and the constant low-grade enhancement of her senses that connection provided.

"Hi, honey." She sat down beside him on the bed, and rested her hand over the bones of his chest. Scott had always seemed so strong and invincible to her, rarely ill, quickly recovered. Surreal, still, that such a robust and healthy man had been struck down so quickly. She patted the quilt and felt his bones shift under her palm. "I think it's time we did this properly, don't you? I tucked Macy into the warm, springtime Earth so her body could help things grow – that's how I think of it, anyway. How I have to think of it. I want to do the same for you."

She rose, and carefully pulled the quilt away from the tarp. Through the broken seals in the plastic, she could see dark bones. Zeus' remains had been tucked by Scott's side, and she gently gathered up what was left, the bones and tufts of black fur, and slid them in the tarp with Scott. His book, bookmark still in place, went in too, and a picture of their family taken at Piper's high school graduation, which she'd had enlarged and framed for him for Father's Day one year. Then she realigned the seams in the tarp and resealed them with the silver duct tape she'd brought upstairs with her. She smiled, perfectly recalling the sound of Scott's warm chuckle, certain she'd be hearing it now if she only knew how to listen.

She stepped back to consider the practicalities of getting him downstairs and *felt* Hades return to the house. He found her moments later, lifting his head and searching the room with his nose even as he crowded close to her legs. Martin was just a few seconds behind him, his eyes going first to Scott's corpse, then meeting her gaze.

"I saw the grave." A pause. "I would have helped you."

Naomi shrugged. "It was mine to do. Compared to splitting wood, it was easy."

Martin glanced at Scott again. His face was inscrutable, his voice level. "Do you want help getting him downstairs? Or do you need to do that yourself, too?"

Naomi smiled gently. "Now that I could use some help with. I was picturing dragging him." She huffed out a soft laugh as she moved to lift Scott's head. "Not very dignified, thumping down the stairs."

Martin lifted Scott's feet, and together, they maneuvered him out of the bedroom and down the stairs. Scott's remains were heavier than Naomi thought they'd be, and by the time they reached the garden bed, she was red-faced and sweating again. They lowered him into the grave, and Martin stepped back, waiting for her to give further direction.

Naomi knelt beside Scott and reached for the tarp where it covered his skull. She closed her eyes and just rested her hand on that curve, the plastic crinkling softly under her touch. "Thank you for a beautiful life, love. Keep him good company, Zeus. I'll see you both in the sweet by and by."

She stood, expecting the tears to come, surprised when they didn't. Grief would circle back, that she knew. It was a part of her now, the ache where Scott and Macy should be, and it would be a part of her to her own dying breath. Grief wasn't something you finished with. It was something that changed you, something that remained lodged in you, something you grew around. She pressed a hand over her heart, over the healing scar-tissue that marked a once-living love, and sent her beloveds on their way.

Martin helped her cover their bodies with soil, and together, they dismantled part of the retaining wall that circled the yard, covering the grave with the heavy stones to discourage predation. Naomi found her garden trowel in the shed, and as the sun approached the top of the mountains and the birds began to sing their evening songs, she walked around the yard, selecting plants to move to Scott's grave.

When she was finished, she and Martin settled the animals for the night. Neither spoke more than was necessary, both lost in their own thoughts. Twilight shifted towards full dark, and Naomi unfurled her sleeping bag, spreading it out on one of the chaise lounges. She looked up to find Martin watching her.

"I figured you'd want to sleep inside, under your own roof."

"No." Naomi didn't know how to explain. She didn't fit under that roof, in that life, not anymore. So she defaulted to the practical. "I sleep better near the horses."

"Okay." Martin retrieved his sleeping bag and set it up on the other lounger. Unlike Naomi, though, he didn't remove his boots and start to settle in. Instead, he prowled the perimeter of the yard, then stood staring at the moon, which was slowly rising in the east above the roof of the house.

Naomi crawled into her sleeping bag, and watched as he began to methodically prepare himself for his nighttime excursion. He removed the shirt he'd worn all day and replaced it with a long-sleeved black t-shirt. Then he un-self-consciously shucked off his jeans and slid into black, multi-pocketed cargo pants. He double-checked his pistol, clipped extra ammunition to his belt, and began smearing his face with a blacking agent he took from his backpack.

Long before he actually left, she *felt* his energy withdraw from her. He stood there on her deck, a lethal shadow, both familiar and strange to her. "I'll be back by dawn, maybe sooner, depending on what I find." His eyes met hers, cold, flat, focused. "If I'm not back by noon, I'm not coming back. Don't load Shakti up with supplies if that happens. Just get out of here as fast as you can, by the route that feels safest."

She could not speak. What could she possibly say? To speak so dispassionately of your own death and the practical matters in the aftermath was beyond her ability to understand. What had his wife said when he had deployed to active duty? Be careful? I love you? Watch your six?

So instead of speaking, she just nodded, and sent a pulse of all she had to give from her heart to his: warmth, protection, safety, luck, love. She closed her eyes and reinforced that last, let him *feel* what was in her heart for him, and heard him catch his breath. A moment later, she felt his fingers touch her cheekbone, but she didn't open her eyes.

"Christ on a crutch, Naomi, you sure know how to distract a guy."

Then he was gone, without even a whisper of sound. Hades whined low in his throat and crowded up on the chaise lounge with her, lying with his head at her feet, his rump pressed into her stomach. Naomi lay back and curled around him, staring up at the glittering stars. She let her mind drift and rest while her body relaxed completely, a trick she'd learned watching over sick babies. The moon slid through the night sky, so bright she could have read by its light. Sometime around midnight, she dropped into a light sleep, lulled by the total relaxation of the animals.

Hades woke her when Martin returned just before dawn. His big head was a darker shadow as he stared towards the house, and his senses told her that Martin was unharmed, as well as some of what he'd seen. The faintest miasma of smoke clung to him, and when Naomi reached out for his feelings, she touched *despair* and *helplessness*, and a storm of other emotions she couldn't begin to sort out. She put Hades on a stay and went to find him.

Martin was in the living room, standing in front of the fireplace, staring up at the family portrait still hanging over it. Moonlight streamed in the windows, illuminating both the picture and the tension in his posture as he rested both hands on the mantle, looking up at her family as it had once been, her as she'd once been. He spoke then, but not of the depravity and death he'd surely seen.

"I'm not Scott. Best I can tell, I'm nothing like he was." Martin's still-blacked face was in shadow, but she could *feel* how his emotions rolled and boiled.

Naomi shook her head slowly, and moved to stand beside him. "No, you're not. Did you think I expected you to be?"

He dropped his hands from the mantle and shrugged, but the nonchalant gesture did nothing to alleviate his tension. Her answer mattered to him, a great deal. She gazed at his profile for a moment, then returned her eyes to the portrait.

"I can see how you'd think that, that I'd want to just slide you into his place. You, and Grace, and little Lark – I could just plug you all into the empty places my family left. But I wouldn't, even if I could. I wouldn't diminish my memories of them that way, and you deserve your own place."

Finally, he looked away from the portrait, touching his fingers to his chest. "Did you mean it?" he whispered. "What you made me *feel* before I left?"

She stepped in close to his strong body, and there, surrounded by the wreckage of her old life, she lifted her mouth and kissed him. *So different from Scott*, her mind whispered, then Scott was gone. She let her lips linger, then drew back. Martin hadn't moved to touch her, but when he opened his eyes, what she saw there made heat lightning dance down her spine and left her breathless. She smiled, and gave him the words they both needed to hear.

"The woman who loved Scott doesn't live here anymore. This woman, this one right here, loves you."

TWELVE
Grace: Rock Ledge Ranch, Colorado Springs, CO

"...ninety-nine, one hundred." Grace finished her count and rose from where she'd been crouched, in the back yard behind one of the houses that bordered Rock Ledge Ranch to the south. She slipped through a gap in the fence and moved to stand in the middle of the deserted street, scanning in a slow circle, letting her eyes float and probe, her ears tuned to every stray sound: the brush of the late afternoon breeze through the nearby cottonwoods, the rustle of overgrown bushes against empty houses, the occasional chirp of a nearby robin, warning of the coming rain.

By now, she'd learned to trust her senses; she'd know if something was off. When nothing triggered her inner alarms, she turned and ran swiftly down the path to the Chambers House, her footfalls only soft crunches on the gravel. She circled the house when she arrived, once again opening her senses to feel for danger, perceiving none. The house was safe. And deserted. She knew before she even opened the door and stepped into the kitchen that Verity was gone.

Again.

Grace opened the door to the modern bathroom off the back side of the kitchen, and Persephone greeted her with dancing feet, nails clicking a joyous rhythm on the floor. Verity had left the little dog with fresh water and a blanket for a bed, just as she'd done the previous five days. Grace sighed heavily and scooped Persephone up for a cuddle as she carried her outside. Nothing to do now but hang out on the front porch and wait for Verity to bring Death back to the ranch with her.

"Because that's what she's going to do, you mark my words." She set Persephone down on the grass, watching for a moment as she sniffed around before taking care of business. When the dog was finished, she trotted off to sniff around the old animal barns which were empty now. Grace headed for the porch. She settled onto one of the benches and hunched forward, elbows resting on her knees, eyes alternating between Persephone and the trail on which Verity was likely to return. "She's going to lead them right back here, like some kind of Pied Piper. Like Hansel and Gretel, dropping white pebbles."

Grace had fallen back into the habit of talking to herself, in part because she was the only person she could rely on to make sense. Verity was prone to announcements such as, "Figs are quite nutritious when they're not in Newton form," or, "According to my sources, Channing Tatum didn't cross over in the plague, but his wife did. I think my chances are good there, even if Raphael says it's not meant to be..." Grace just nodded. A lot.

By now, she could see the writing on the wall: She was in a race against luck. While she scuttled around on the outskirts of the gang in her corpse-scented clothing, with her pepper-induced hives and streaming nose, Verity did God-knew-what, God-knew-where. Grace had begged her to go back home. Failing that, she'd begged her to just stay at the Chambers House and keep Persephone safe. But no. Oh, no. Verity wouldn't say where she'd been or what her objective in leaving was, and the more Grace pressed the issue, the more nonsensical Verity became.

When begging hadn't worked, Grace had tried to talk herself into just leaving the eccentric woman behind, but she had Persephone to consider. She had never intended to bring the little dog, had planned to leave her with Anne, but nothing on this journey was going according to her carefully thought-out plan. For a few hours at a time, Persephone was fine when shut in the bathroom. But what if something happened to Grace? What if she was discovered and re-captured? She wouldn't escape a second time, of that she was certain. The thought of dooming Persephone to a slow death by starvation and dehydration was not to be borne. Left free to roam, the little dog would follow her, endangering them both. Grace felt responsible for Persephone, of course, and inexplicably, for Verity as well. As badly as they were mucking up her plans, she couldn't just abandon them.

To compound her frustration, she hadn't learned much so far. As she had expected, the gang had closed their perimeter, and rumors buzzed of plans to blitz outlying communities later in the summer, but she had yet to talk to someone who had hard facts. Grace had slipped back into her fringe position in the group by virtue of a full bottle of vodka she'd "borrowed" from Rowan's supply months ago. Loudmouth himself had remembered and cleared her at the checkpoint with a bark of laughter and a sneer.

"Where ya been, Stinky?" he'd asked as he'd waved her through. Grace had been ready with a cover story, but he hadn't asked. She had swiped a greasy hand under her nose to hide a smirk as she'd sauntered right past one of the men who had brutalized her. Right past one of the men who might be Lark's father. Right past one of the men on her short list to see dead. She kept that irony in her mind like a pampered pet, stroking it whenever what she was seeing became too much.

As hard as it was to believe, conditions had deteriorated even further. The majority of people still living under the protection of the gang had become nothing more than slave labor. For the life of her, Grace couldn't imagine why they stayed. Fear was one thing, but had all these people lost their memories? Did they really think their only option was to endure terror and abuse in exchange for getting their basic survival needs met? Sometimes, it was all Grace could do not to stop the next person scurrying by and whisper to them: *Do you know how valuable you are? Do you understand how precious your life is? You're a survivor!* She refrained, of course, but the effort of doing so was starting to wear on her. They were like sleepwalkers, stumbling around in an endless nightmare, just waiting for someone to wake them up.

In the past few days, Grace hadn't seen a single child and very few women. The "nightly show" was still going on and still involved rape as well as gladiator-style combat between unwilling participants. But from what Grace had gathered, they'd run out of women to keep as disposable victims. Instead, women were chosen from among the survivors to service the gang leaders and were allowed to return to the general populace, humiliated and bleeding, but alive. No less sickening or terrifying, just conservation of resources. Grace had forced herself to watch for three nights running, until she'd figured out the lay of the land. Now, she just kept her ear to the ground for whispers and rumors during the day and cleared out before they fired up the lights and the music each night.

As far as the helicopters were concerned, she'd learned almost nothing beyond what she'd already guessed – gang-affiliated group on Fort Carson was in possession of the aircraft, and in this populace, that was all anybody knew. Grace was frustrated by the all-around lack of information and knowledge. She needed to know numbers. How many helicopters did they have? Was aviation fuel more stable than regular gasoline? If so, how long was that fuel good for, and how much did they have? How many pilots had they managed to train? Answering those questions had become her top priority. She planned to skulk around this encampment for one more day. After that, she had to ditch Verity and Persephone – somehow – and find a way to infiltrate the Fort Carson group. She didn't have the same "in" there as she had here, and given how tight security was likely to be, she had no idea how she was going to pull that off.

Just the thought made her stomach clench violently. Attuned as always to the needs of the people around her, Persephone chose that moment to abandon her sniffing. She trotted up to the porch, butterfly ears bouncing perkily, and leaped onto Grace's lap, curling into a little, comforting ball. Grace leaned back, feeling her tight muscles and tense shoulders ease, pulling Persephone's small, sturdy body onto her chest. She may not have intended to bring the little dog with her, but she was sure glad she was here, especially when the reality of what she planned to do loomed so dark and large.

Grace may not have learned much since she'd arrived back in the Springs, but she'd reached an important conclusion: It wouldn't be possible to achieve both of her objectives. She could either focus on taking out the gang leadership, or she could focus on disabling the helicopters. Not both. The likelihood that she would survive the execution of either objective was too slim. Once she got a look at the situation on Fort Carson, she'd make her choice, but the question to be answered was simple: Which path would give Lark the greatest chance at a future? She couldn't be a mother to her daughter, but she could stand between the baby girl and danger. Grace's own survival was secondary. And unlikely. And that was okay.

She rubbed her hand over and over the small, soft curve of Persephone's back as she thought about this. She didn't consider herself suicidal. She wasn't feeling despair or suffering from depression. She didn't want to die. She had a job to do, and logic and analysis told her she probably wouldn't be able to do that job from a safe distance. Whichever course she chose, she was going to have to walk into the very heart of danger. Walking out unharmed was improbable. She knew cognitively that the prospect of her own death should frighten her, or at the very least make her sad, but all she felt was a curious, calm determination.

This was all Verity's fault.

It was the strangest thing, but it was nearly impossible to feel fear when Verity was around. It had nothing to do with physical prowess of any kind. Grace had never seen Verity so much as swat a fly. Nor did it have anything to do with trust. As nearly as Grace could figure, Verity served a Divine agenda that had little to do with human hopes, fears or goals. Grace didn't trust her, not even a little bit. Rather, it was what happened when you looked into her laughing, innocent, all-knowing eyes. Grace considered herself a practical and down-to-earth person, but she would swear you could glimpse the Cosmos in that pure blue. Fear just dissolved, sorrow softened, horror was filtered through an infinite perspective and given context.

The first few days back, when she'd been struggling to acclimate once again to the dark violence around the gang, the phenomenon had terrified her. Fear kept her alive, kept her instincts functioning at maximum sensitivity, kept her from getting careless and making a mistake. Fear helped her feel the gaze of eyes that were too interested, helped her know when to change course and take a different path. Without fear, she was as good as dead. Now, the best she could work up to was a healthy agitation.

It had nothing to do with complacency, and everything to do with the strange conviction that settled in her heart whenever she looked into Verity's eyes: Things were unfolding as they should, and no matter what happened, Grace would be okay.

At that thought, Grace snorted. When Verity wasn't around, it was much easier to apply logic to the paradox. Grade had been lucky. And she had to complete her tasks before the odds shifted.

"Hello!"

Grace looked up and had time for exactly one thought before her survival mechanism kicked in: "Too late."

She was off the porch of the Chambers House and running before she took her next breath. Persephone raced at her heels, easily keeping pace as they pounded down the gravel path towards the barn. As Grace ran, her brain registered what she'd seen: Verity, waving cheerfully, followed by two hulks carrying rifles at the ready across their chests. Her mind replayed the men's movements, the rolling prowl of their gaits, the way their heads swiveled in synchronized vigilance, the aura of menace that preceded them. Military. And in Colorado Springs, post-plague, that meant the gang.

Grace slid to a stop in front of the barn door and slapped the latch, reaching inside the cool dark to grab the go-bag she'd positioned right beside the door. She slung one strap over her shoulder and pivoted, her whole body coiling for a fresh sprint, when a sudden jerk made the world cartwheel. Her feet flew out from under her, and she landed on her back so hard the air was driven from her lungs. For precious seconds, she could neither move nor breathe.

A huge man stepped out of the barn, still hanging on to the other strap of her go-bag. Like the men behind Verity, he carried a rifle – an AR-15 like the one Piper used. Grace's brain was on overdrive, cataloguing and analyzing tiny details. His finger rested near the trigger of the rifle, but he didn't point it at her. His eyes were the coldest blue she'd ever seen, his face a blank, unreadable mask.

A scatter of gravel hit Grace in the face, making her flinch. Persephone had raced ahead, then doubled back. She slid to a stop between Grace and the man, barking wildly. She backed her little rump against Grace and shoved, trying with all her small might to urge Grace to safety while she snarled and snapped. The man stared down at the little dog, then met Grace's gaze.

"Call it off or I'll shoot it."

Grace struggled to sit up and scoot back in the same motion, mind racing, as the first puzzle piece dislodged from the picture she'd formed. That didn't make any sense. A member of the gang would have already shot Persephone with immediate plans to gut, skin and spit her over a fire for dinner. She hauled the little dog into her lap, scooting back again, then burst into action once more.

Tossing Persephone in one direction, she launched in the other. She was only a few feet away from the steps that led up to the Chambers Trail. Persephone would find her – they'd been playing hide-and-seek on these trails and the others that led away from the ranch for the last several days. If Grace could just make it to the top of the steps, he'd never catch her –

Once again, her feet flew out from under her when a hand fisted in her shirt between her shoulder blades. Grace had been half-expecting it this time, and instead of struggling, she went limp, flopping to the ground like a rag doll. The man held onto her this time, and Grace used every bit of willpower she possessed to keep her muscles lax, limp. Finally, he let her go, and the second his hand released her shirt, she was up again.

This time, though, she didn't run. She balanced on the balls of her feet and locked eyes with him. In her very depths, she'd gone still as stone. She hadn't been certain how she'd react if she was captured again. Now she knew.

"You'll have to kill me," she said quietly. The animal-like growling of a long-dead girl echoed in her ears, and Grace remembered the contempt she'd felt – why die fighting when you could submit and live another day, live to escape? She understood now, and sent an apology winging to that girl's soul, wherever it now resided. "Either kill me now, or I will find a way to kill myself. I won't go back. I won't be used again."

Persephone shot out of the underbrush and pressed against Grace's leg. The man glanced down at her tiny, snarling, up-turned face, then looked at Grace again. "You were just planning to run off and leave your friend to her fate?"

Grace's brows drew in. What kind of mind game was this? There was no logical reason for him to ask her such a question. She chose to not answer, lifting her chin and staring at him. Most people couldn't stand silence, and if he started filling it, she might learn what was going on here.

Unfortunately, he seemed to be familiar with the gambit. Patience settled around him, a cloak of watchful stillness. After the longest minute of Grace's life, a low whistle sounded from down by the barn. The man whistled back, and Grace heard the muffled thump of boots jogging up the trail. Her heart picked up, speeding with both fear and hope. All she needed was a moment, a single moment of distraction. She could run like the wind, and she knew every turn, rise and fall of these trails.

One of the hulks appeared at the top of the trail, a baby-faced man who might be in his mid-twenties at the most, at least a decade younger than the man who'd captured her. The younger man's eyes touched the fresh dirt and debris on Grace's filthy clothes, took in Persephone's tiny fierceness, then lifted to the other man. "Everything under control?"

His attitude was deferential. Her captor, then, was probably the leader of the trio. The older man nodded, his gaze never leaving Grace. "We were just discussing how to proceed."

"Ah. Okay." The younger man nodded as well. After 30 seconds of nothing but softly chirping birds and Persephone's constant, low snarl, he started talking, obviously not comfortable with the strategy of silence. "She went for the go-bag, just like Verity said she would."

The older man's face tightened ever-so-slightly, the barest hint of annoyance. Still, he didn't blink or look away. His gaze made Grace think of a snake mesmerizing its prey, of Kaa in *The Jungle Book*. He grunted a confirmation, and once more, silence reigned. Then, the words sank in. Grace surrendered the stare-down and turned to look at the younger man, eyes narrowing as she thought about what he'd just said.

In all the time she'd spent with the gang, she had never once heard one of the men call one of the girls by name. Dumb Bitch. The Sisters. Cowgirl. They all had their nicknames. Grace's eyes shifted back and forth between the men. The time for silence was over.

"You're not with the gang. Who are you?"

The older man's face gave nothing away. "How do you know we're not with the gang?"

"You didn't kill my dog. You didn't hurt me after I ran." She glanced at the younger man, then returned her gaze to the leader. "He knew Verity's name. And used it."

After a moment, the older man nodded. "Verity said you were intelligent, as well as knowledgeable about the gang. You escaped from them?"

The question was asked with such matter-of-factness, it allowed Grace to answer the same way. "Yes. How do you know Verity?"

Another careful measure of silence, and the older man replied. "We met her when we brought Piper home to Woodland Park."

Grace's eyes flew open wide. "You know Piper? You were part of her group?" Her mind raced through the few facts she knew. She hadn't been present at Piper's return and had only her father's bare-bones, carefully-edited account of the dramatic event to go by. Piper had never talked about it. Grace wasn't even sure how many people had continued on, after Piper, Ethan, Elise and her kids had been left behind. She could wish that she'd pumped her dad for more information, but all she really needed was the answer to one question: "Are you Brody?"

The younger man flinched. Later, Grace would remember that. Right now, though, she was focused on the older man, watching him for signs of deception or subterfuge. She didn't have her dad's radar for lies, but she'd learned a lot about reading body language. After another lengthy pause, the older man answered. His voice was completely level, neutral. His posture, his hands, his face, all said he was telling the truth. "No. We left him behind. You can call me Levi. This is Tyler."

Grace glanced at the younger man. "The mechanic. Ethan spoke well of you. He misses your cooking."

Tyler nodded, a brief smile flitting across his baby face, but didn't quite make eye contact. "Ethan is a good man. I hope he's hangin' in, him and Elise and the kids."

"They're all fine." Niceties done, Grace turned back to Levi. "What do you want?"

"Information. Whatever you're willing to share, about the area and the gang. Verity suggested you might be of assistance. She..." He grimaced slightly, "Found us this morning. We were camped on Monument Creek, south of the gang's territory."

Grace nodded. "No-man's land. Are the lions still in the area?"

"From what we could ascertain, just the male. The lionesses have moved east, onto the plains. The male has been sighted recently by some of the people settled further south on Monument Creek, but he appears to have been wounded, and it looks like he's starving. They don't think he'll make it much longer."

Grace felt a sharp stab of loss at the news. It had satisfied her, knowing they had survived, knowing they were roaming free. She brushed the sorrow aside. "You said Verity found you. Is that what she's been doing every day? Looking for you?"

For the first time, Levi looked less than sure of himself. "Yes. That's what she said, in any case." He gazed at Grace, his brow furrowed. "It's unclear what she's talking about much of the time. You're aware that she's unstable and frequently disconnected from reality?"

Grace snorted. "Yeah. I had noticed that, now that you mention it." She bent down and picked up Persephone, whose hostility had softened into a hard, watchful stare. Grace straightened and locked eyes with Levi. "I'll share what I know with you and your men, if you'll share what you've learned with me."

Levi nodded. "That's fair."

Grace didn't look away. "And if you give me your word that neither you nor your men will harm either Verity or I."

Another nod, no hesitation. "You have my word."

He slung his rifle over his shoulder and gestured for her to precede him back down the path. Wordlessly, Grace complied. Tyler fell into step behind them, though he didn't put his rifle away, moving instead with the same prowling watchfulness Grace had noted before. They walked in silence until they reached the path behind the barn and started towards the Chambers House. On the front porch, Verity was gesturing animatedly as she chattered to the other hulk. Even from this distance, the man looked baffled.

Grace looked up at Levi, who had moved to walk beside her. "You're all military. Did you serve together?"

"No." Like Tyler, Levi's arctic-blue eyes never stopped scanning, though he glanced at her briefly. "I was in the Marines. Tyler and Adam were both Army Rangers. They met in basic on Fort Carson. My father and an old friend of his put our group together. We were in Walden until we got burned out."

"Piper mentioned the fire." Grace was quiet for a few moments. She didn't want to probe too deeply, wasn't yet ready to find out if this man and his companions had been complicit in Piper's abuse at Brody's hands. She'd get their information first, and make decisions from there. She shifted gears. "So Verity told you she's been looking for you? Did she say why?"

"Not exactly."

"Well, it's more than she told me. I didn't plan for her to come along, or even ask her to. Now I can't get rid of her."

What might have been amusement lifted a corner of Levi's mouth, though it didn't warm his eyes. Grace doubted those eyes could warm, ever. Again, his scanning gaze touched her briefly before moving on. "You were relatively safe in Woodland Park, from what Verity told us. Why did you leave? Are you looking for revenge?"

Grace kept her face still. "That's private," she said calmly. She wasn't intimidated by stone-faced ex-Marines, being the daughter of one. She turned the question back on him. "What about you? Why are you three still in the area? You left Woodland Park months ago."

Levi didn't answer right away, which wasn't a surprise. Grace had already observed he parceled out every word he said, like the most valuable currency. As they neared the Chambers House, he stopped walking and turned to look at Tyler. He gestured with his head, and the young man slipped around them, joining Verity and a relieved-looking Adam on the porch. Then Levi turned to face her.

"The gang needs to end," he said bluntly. "The most expedient way to bring that about is to eliminate the leadership."

"On that, we agree." Grace paused. "Why is this your fight?"

Levi gazed at her, still and thoughtful, then shifted his gaze to a point beyond her shoulder. "I live by a code. There are rules. The men in the gang have broken that code." His eyes went slightly unfocused, and his voice took on a rhythmic cant, as if he were reciting a verse from memory. "Any man who rapes a child is lower than an animal and needs to be put down. No exceptions."

He met her eyes once more, and they stood there in the late afternoon sun, considering each other.

These men should terrify her. Why they didn't, Grace couldn't say. She didn't doubt they were as lethal as any member of the gang she'd known, and more deadly than some. Maybe it was Verity's presence, maybe it was some instinct she couldn't verbalize, but somehow she knew they would not harm her. Somehow, she knew they were part of the "rightness" that had settled around her heart. Since such knowings were exceedingly rare for Grace, she trusted them when they showed up. It would all be okay. She nodded. "That's reason enough for me."

They walked up on the porch, where Grace was introduced to Adam. Tyler volunteered to put together a meal from their combined provisions, and they all moved inside. Grace, Levi and Adam sat around the table while Tyler moved efficiently around the kitchen. Verity flittered around the room like a hyperactive pixie for a few minutes, then took Persephone back outside.

Conversation was stilted at first, but took off when Grace learned the three men had scouted the perimeter of Fort Carson. She left the table briefly and came back with the grubby, ragged map of the mountain post she'd found in the glove box of an abandoned vehicle. She spread it out on the table, her heart beating faster with excitement. "Show me where the helicopters are."

Adam glanced at Levi as if seeking permission, then reached out and touched a spot almost dead-center in the rough triangle that was Fort Carson. "Here." He traced another line, a rough rectangle, around the spot he'd indicated. "They've brought their borders in, redistributed their personnel and resources, but they've kept the airfield pretty much dead center."

Grace's heart sank. If he was right, the helicopters were miles from any perimeter. Just getting a look at them would almost certainly mean getting past layer upon layer of security. After a moment, Adam spoke.

"Why do you want to know about the helicopters?"

"Why do you think?" Grace snapped. She rubbed at her forehead, then sat back and folded her arms across her chest. "I'm sorry. Those aircraft pose an enormous threat to the outlying communities. Even if I'm able to eliminate the core of the gang's leadership, they're still a problem. They negate distance as a safety measure, and they're just too powerful to defend against."

Grace suddenly felt exhausted, then felt irritated with herself for feeling that way. Had she really thought the helicopters would be conveniently situated, conveniently unguarded, conveniently waiting to be sabotaged? While she was indulging in wishful thinking, she might as well hope they'd all have a big, red button labeled, "To blow up aircraft, press HERE." She stared at the map without seeing it for a few moments. Then she shook herself and pressed on. "Did you get an accurate count as to how many they had of each type? Or how much fuel they've got?"

Tyler appeared from around the corner in the kitchen. As he spoke, he dried his hands on a cheerful yellow dish towel. "No way to know about the fuel – too many variables. Under some circumstances, avgas is more stable than mogas, but we have no idea how that fuel has been stored over the last year, whether stabilizers were added, nothing. But there's this – whoever has them in the air feels like they have enough fuel to put up training flights."

He turned and tossed the dish towel onto the little wooden table he'd been working at, then leaned a shoulder against the door jamb. "As for a count, we've only got the roughest estimate. We could only see the airfield from one angle, long-distance. We had visual on fourteen Black Hawks, four Apaches, and two Chinooks, but I know Carson was scheduled to receive 24 of the new AH-64E Apaches before the plague." He shook his head, voice warming with enthusiasm in spite of the circumstances. "Man, those E-style machines are something else. Upgraded electronics and flight instruments, a new powertrain that's tons more effective at altitude, and each one can carry up to 16 Hellfire missiles. Whisper-quiet, too – you can't even hear them beyond a few hundred yards." Another head shake. "If we could get our hands on just one of them, we could take out all the rest."

And just like that, the roller-coaster swooped back up again. Tyler's words shifted and jostled her mental map, creating possibility where there had been impossibility moments before. Grace felt a prickle along her scalp as puzzle pieces started to click into place and a picture started to form. She stared at Tyler. "Could you fly one of them?"

Tyler shrugged. "Sure, given enough time to fart around and figure shit out."

Adam spoke again. "Doesn't matter if he could fly one or not. There's no way to get anywhere near them. We've been watching them on-again-off-again for weeks, and those birds are always under heavy guard. Security got even thicker after they started putting them in the air."

"I could get in."

All three men just stared at her. Then, Levi joined the conversation for the first time. He inclined his head to her clothes. "You move among them freely? Disguised like this?"

"Not quite like this." Grace took the sachet of black pepper out of her pocket and pressed it to her nose, then gave a mighty sneeze. She scratched her neck, and looked at them through reddened, watering eyes. She swiped at her streaming nose, and let her mouth drop open slackly. Last of all, she let her eyes drift, empty and dumb. "More like this."

Adam and Tyler exchanged amused grins, but Levi's face remained serious. "If they figure out you were once their captive, they'll kill you, and they won't make it quick. They'll make an example of you."

"I know that." The plan was coming together rapidly in her mind, the details, the logistics. And there was a role only she could play. "In fact, I'm counting on it."

Grace rose from the table and went to the antique wooden sideboard across the room, opening the doors underneath. Inside, she had stored every scrap of written information she had accumulated on the gang, both her original project, and everything she'd gathered since, including rough sketches of the original six leaders. She was no artist, but she'd done the best she could, accompanying each sketch with every physical detail she could recall. She brought the materials to the table and began to spread them out.

"This is everything I know. All of it." She touched a filthy stack of ragged papers filled with her tiny, meticulous hand-writing. "This original document contains every word I heard spoken during my nineteen days with them. They didn't worry about watching what they said around the girls – most of us were dead in under two weeks. As far as I know, I'm the only one who survived from those early days."

She set the six sketches out but kept her face turned away as she did so. Her emotions were not appropriate here. These men would respond best to an appeal to logic. "These six were the leaders then, but at least eight more men are now part of the inner circle. I haven't gotten close enough to the new men to learn anything or even to provide an accurate sketch. To be thorough, they should all be terminated, but there is only one man that needs to be killed at any cost. The Boss." She touched his sketch. "He did not participate in the rapes nor did he partake of the drugs or alcohol. He watched, and he planned. In my opinion, he must be eliminated. If he survives, even if all the others are killed, the gang will go on."

She began setting out another series of documents. "This is all the information I've gathered moving among them as a boy. It's not much. I've had direct contact with only Bean Counter – people call him Mr. Watts – and Loudmouth." She couldn't stop the curl of her lip when she touched his sketch. "Five of the original six leaders live on the old Colorado College campus. From what I've heard, the sixth is in charge on Fort Carson."

She touched the sketch of Sleeper, then straightened and gazed around at all three men. "He would recognize me. If you turn me in to him on Fort Carson, you're in. There was a reward for my return after I escaped. You could convince him you'd kept me for yourselves for a while, then decided to cash in when you got tired of me." She looked at Levi. "Like you said, they'll want to make an example of me. I'll be brought back to the CC campus, but you won't need to worry about that. You find a way to get Tyler into one of those Apaches, and he can get the job done." She fidgeted with her papers, thinking hard. "If I could find a way to keep a weapon on me, just a small knife, I might be able to get close enough to the Boss to end him. My dad was a Marine, too." She glanced at Levi. "He always said you could kill someone with a toothpick, if you used it right."

As she had talked, Tyler had abandoned the kitchen doorway and moved to stand beside the table, lifting her papers and examining them one by one. He looked up at her with an expression she couldn't quite define. "Let me get this straight: You left Woodland Park, and you came here planning to both assassinate the gang leaders *and* destroy all of the helicopters?"

Grace lifted her chin. "Yes."

"By yourself?"

Grace kept her chin high, though it took every bit of determination she had. "I know it sounds ridiculous. I had reached the conclusion that I couldn't achieve both objectives, and I was in the process of analyzing which course I should choose. Which task I was the most likely to succeed at. Until they got the helicopters in the air, my original plan was to disrupt the behavior patterns in their power base, to create alternative beliefs over time, person to person."

"You've studied Roszak," Levi said. His expression, too, was impossible to decipher. "Unfortunately, 'it is difficult to free fools from the chains they revere.'"

"Voltaire." Grace nodded. "People stay because they can't see an alternative. The gang's power is fear-derived, constructed on the mindless dependence of the masses. If I could have convinced those masses that they don't need to be either afraid or dependent, I could have dismantled the gang's power base without violence. But the helicopters changed everything. We're out of time."

Gently, she removed a notepad from Tyler's hands, flipping to show them the timeline she'd originally projected. It had been such an elegant plan, and talking about it was satisfying, even if it was moot. "I had established just about the perfect cover for it. If there were more kids around, I'd have been talking to them, every chance I got. Children are very sensitive about injustice and very powerful agents of change. There was this kids' movie, with ants and grasshoppers..."

She trailed off at the expressions on Adam's and Tyler's faces. Adam had laced his fingers on top of his head and was glaring at the ceiling like there was something there he wanted to kill. Tyler was staring at her, bumping his fist against his mouth as if trying to hide his expression, but his eyes said it all. Angry. And sad. Grace looked at Levi, but his face remained inscrutable. She looked back at Tyler.

"Did I say something wrong?"

Adam spoke. "How old are you, Grace?"

"Seventeen." She shook her head slightly. "Eighteen. I keep forgetting. What does that have to do with anything?"

Tyler spoke. "You talk about kids as if you're not one, but I've gotta tell you, we had you pegged at fourteen. Tops. Just-turned eighteen doesn't seem all that different. Not to us. We don't use children to fight our battles. Before this whole shit-storm of a plague went down, we saw enough of that on the other side of the world."

Grace started to interrupt, and Adam tagged in. "No. Just no. You're a tactician, we'll give you that. Your plan is brilliant." His eyes flicked to Levi. "But we won't send you to your death. And that's what your plan amounts to."

Grace didn't bother arguing. She turned to Levi. "Can I talk to you alone?"

Levi slid his eyes to both Adam and Tyler and tilted his head towards the door. They rose and left the house, both of them moving with graceful stealth that was automatic. Grace waiting until the door had clicked shut behind them, then met Levi's gaze.

"How have you all changed? Since the plague, I mean?"

His face gave nothing away. He considered her for a moment, then answered. "Both Adam and Tyler have increased intuition. I wouldn't advise playing cards against either one." A much longer pause this time. "I see...future possibilities. What the outcome of the current situation is likely to be."

Something about that nagged at Grace's memory, but she set it aside to be considered later. She leaned forward. "I haven't changed." She waved her hand at her stacks and notes and diagrams. "I could do all of this before. I didn't evolve, like the rest of you did. I don't subscribe to all of Verity's talk of a Divine Path, but I do believe in fulfilling a destiny."

She hesitated, then reached across the table and gripped his forearm. Without their help, she was dead in the water, and she knew it. Verity had brought them into this to help her. She was more sure of it than she'd ever been of anything. "I wasn't selected by nature, don't you see? This is the best thing I can do with my life. What higher purpose could I possibly aspire to? If I can use my brains to make something useful of the hell I survived, if I can take the circumstances they forced on me and use it to end them, then I'm good. I can call it a good life, and know that I did everything I could to leave a better world behind."

Levi leaned back in his chair, arms crossed over his huge chest. "Very altruistic. But you would have run and left Verity behind. That doesn't add up."

Grace rolled her eyes. "It will when you know her better. Ask her to touch you one of these days – just lay her hand on your arm or touch your shoulder. You'll see first-hand why I wasn't worried about leaving her."

Levi looked away, and for the first time, Grace sensed subterfuge in him. "I may know what you're talking about," he said in a low voice. Then, he sat up straight and leaned forward. He grabbed Grace's legal pad and flipped to a clean page. "The logistics shouldn't be complicated, but we should have at least two contingencies. It's just over ten miles to the northern border of Fort Carson. How fast do you travel overland?"

Grace swallowed. She swallowed again, and looked at the ceiling, trying to blink the tears away. They were going to help her. Just to be sure, she had to verbalize it. "You're going to help me. You're actually going to help. You're not just speculating or considering?"

Levi's hands stilled on the pad of paper. He stared at his hands, then stared at her. For the very first time, she saw something that looked like strong emotion move across his features. "We'll help you," he said hoarsely. "I've seen it. It's my destiny, too."

THIRTEEN
Piper: Maple River, Iowa

And so now she knew. At last. There was something Piper would not do to survive.

She had cut into her own flesh to keep her mind balanced. She had poisoned people. She had submitted to Brody's rape, night after night. She had played people who cared about her like chess pieces, and she had put a bullet in a man's brain. But she would not kill a child.

Not even when that child was giving serious consideration to killing her.

Death was there, in Trent Donnelly's summer-blue eyes, though it was not a heated, nor even an angry thing. It was a calculation, and the coldness of it made Piper's skin ripple with waves of fear. Only the year she'd spent under Brody's tutelage allowed her to hide what she was feeling and meet Trent's gaze head on.

"My terms are reasonable. Let me see my people, and I'll help yours."

Trent swung from side to side in his cushy office chair as he frowned at her. In the dim little man-cave behind him, an amalgam of gaming electronics slept under a thick layer of dust: the latest X-box and Playstation models, both hooked up to a huge-screen TV, stacks and stacks of games, and an Alienware laptop Piper would have given her eyeteeth for in the time before. The walls were lined with posters depicting characters from the fantasy games he appeared to favor, and Piper deliberately mimicked the stance of a warrior-woman with impossibly huge breasts and an itty-bitty waist. She forced herself not to wince when Trent's eyes snuck down her body. Until she figured out what his game was, she needed to use every weapon at her disposal.

Bright flags of color were flying on his cheekbones when his eyes returned to hers. "You're a medic. A healer," he snapped. He was flustered, and being flustered made him angry. He didn't like being off-balance or out-of-control. She flustered him every chance she got. "I can't believe you would just sit by and let people suffer when you could help them."

"You've left me no choice. You won't tell me why you're holding us, and you won't let me see my friends. Jack is injured. He needs treatment." After Jack had been shot, she had gotten a brief look at his wound before they'd been separated. The bullet appeared to have creased his skull just above his right ear. She was sure he was concussed, but with care and luck, he should make a full recovery. Problem was, she hadn't seen either him or Owen since they'd been brought here to the little town of Maple River, Iowa, five long days ago.

The first day, they had left her to pace and fret in a tiny, airless, second-floor bedroom, a little boy's room, once upon a time, judging by the Thomas the Tank Engine décor. First thing the next morning, she had been brought here to see Trent, and the parry and thrust of negotiations had begun. Trent wanted information and the use of her medical skills – no one here even knew how to do CPR, he'd told her. Piper wanted to see Jack and Owen, and she wanted all of them to be released. Stalemate, until this new crisis had occurred.

Piper leaned forward, bracing her hands on the table that separated her from Trent. He leaned back before he could catch himself, and she counted that as a victory. "Your people are dying. Many of them are already seriously dehydrated, and soon, they'll start having seizures. Without proper medical intervention, they're not going to make it."

Good old Sulfur Tuft mushrooms. She'd hidden the last of her supply in an empty tampon applicator, and thanks to good, old, reliable male squeamishness, she had been allowed to keep the plastic tube on her person. Two days ago, she'd finally gotten a chance to dump them in a communal soup pot. Now, she was under the gun. Without additional doses of the mushroom, the people she'd poisoned would begin to recover, and her leverage would disappear.

Trent folded his arms across his chest. "And you're trying to tell me this is some kind of follow-up to the plague. Some kind of – what did you call it?"

"A second-wave lethal infection." So lame, but it was all she'd been able to come up with under pressure. "We saw it in towns all across the plains as we traveled."

"If there was going to be another plague, I would have *seen* it, like I did the first one." One heartbeat. Two. "I think you're lying to me."

It was easy to forget this kid was only fourteen; he wielded *menace* like a machete. Piper kept her features still, and her shields at maximum. "Why would I lie?"

She was lying, of course. The trick in these times was to do so without hesitation or remorse. Like Brody and Owen, Trent claimed to be able to *see* future events, but he couldn't tell *truth* from *lie*. Piper had tested that hypothesis thoroughly. But Trent kept at least one of his inner circle around at all times, and it was safe to assume one of them was a truth-seer. She sent up a prayer that the man standing in the shadows behind her wouldn't cry foul, and went on.

"And it's not a plague. It's an infection caused by exposure to the plague pathogen. Even in people who didn't get sick, contact with the bacteria that caused the plague altered their immune function. Weakened it. A simple infection can kill." She could use loaded pauses as well as he could. "Unless they're treated."

Trent made a disgusted sound and spun away from her. When he whirled back a moment later, his youthful face was ugly with the rage he never had completely under control. "I've taken good care of you. I've given you food and shelter, and I haven't let any of the men touch you." His eyes flickered to the man behind her, and his expression shifted subtly, animated by the titillation of the thoughts she knew he was stroking. "They want to, you know. It's all they talk about. They think I don't know, but my ears are everywhere." Those ears turned pink. Trent might be one of the most terrifying individuals Piper had ever met, but he was still just a boy. It was as heart-breaking as it was disturbing. "They think you're hot, and they want to...to... You know what they want to do. I've protected you from that."

Only because you're saving me for something else, Piper thought, though she hadn't figured out what that something was. Nor did she have any illusions about her value to him. She was a commodity to be used. He wanted access to her skills and experience, and when he'd used her up, he would discard her. The question was, why? Somehow, she needed to ascertain what his objective was. If she could figure out what he wanted, she could figure out a way to leverage that information and bargain them out of here. She kept her face neutral and chose her next words with great care.

"I understand my situation." She would not thank him, by thee Gods, she would not. "I just want you to understand yours. Your defenses have already been compromised. If more people get sick, you won't be able to maintain your perimeter. If people start dying, other people will start leaving. Word will get out that you're vulnerable, and when that happens..."

Piper shrugged and let him walk that line of logic out to whatever conclusion he wanted to, then switched gears. "What could it hurt, to let me see them? A guard could stay with us the whole time."

Trent cocked his head to the side. Innocent. Curious. "How do you know they're not dead already?"

Little shit. She should have seen that coming. By some grace, she didn't flinch, though she couldn't speak for a few moments. She double-checked the bond-lines that still connected her with Jack, Owen and Ed, and trusted what they told her. "They're alive. I know."

Trent's gaze turned sharp. "Tell me exactly how you know, and I'll say yes."

"No."

She didn't know how her skills might be used against her, but she was sure he'd find a way. That, she was beginning to suspect, was Trent's real "gift." He manipulated the people around him into doing what he wanted. Logic and her own instincts suggested that he used their intuitive skills against them. She hadn't gathered enough data to confirm her hypothesis yet, but it explained how a teenage boy had come to be the leader here.

The red grid of bond-lines surrounding him had alerted her to his Brody-like influence in this community, but she hadn't been prepared for the bond-lines that went the other way, from Trent to these people. Like vines, they were, penetrating tendrils that pulsed with energy when people did what he wanted, and constricted when they defied him. Not that she'd seen much by way of defiance; the people here appeared to be both well trained and oblivious to what Trent was doing.

Piper wasn't sure Trent knew, on a conscious level, the nature of the power he wielded. He appeared to be some sort of energetic parasite; when people pleased him and did as he asked, he rewarded them with his approval, which Piper saw as surges of energy along the bond-line connecting them. She had only witnessed one instance of dissention, but it had been highly instructive.

A man named Paul had been here the day before yesterday when she arrived. He'd been petitioning for permission to leave the community, to head farther north in the state to see if any of his extended family had survived. Trent had stared at Paul as he spoke, his face cold. Paul's voice, so confident and sure when he started talking, had quickly wobbled into uncertainty. When he finally trailed off with a series of half-mumbled apologies, Trent was silent for long moments. What Piper saw in those moments, she was still trying to process.

The vines connecting Trent to Paul had writhed over the man like hot orange snakes, sliding up his spine to penetrate the base of his skull and locking around his lower back, glowing hot over Paul's kidneys. The physiological effect on Paul was immediate: his breathing quickened, a sheen of sweat appeared on his flushed face, and every muscle in his body tensed. He glanced at Piper, and she could see that his pupils were abnormally dilated, nearly eclipsing his iris.

Trent spoke. "I thought we could count on you, Paul."

As soon as the words were out of Trent's mouth, the orange vines constricted to a tight, cold, black. Paul gasped and leaned forward to brace a hand on the table, his limbs now tremoring and his sweat-slicked face grey as he gasped, open-mouthed, for air. Piper's own mouth dropped open.

If she was assessing the situation correctly, Trent had just fired Paul's adrenals, triggering a fight-or-flight response. Then, somehow, he'd induced an adrenalin crash.

Paul had excused himself then, and Trent had accompanied him to the door, pouring out hypnotic, soothing words as he held the stricken man's elbow. "You get some rest. When you're feeling better, I'm sure you'll see how valued your skills are here. No one is as attuned to danger as you are, Paul. We need you. We won't be safe without you. You're vital to this community…"

Trent had returned to his seat, and Piper hardly remembered stammering out her "second wave lethal infection" story, so busy had her brain been trying to analyze what she'd seen. Trent had listened politely. When she finished talking, he had sent multi-colored vines questing in her direction – as he had every time she'd met with him – red and orange predominantly, with traces of yellow. Before, Piper had thought he was trying to make a connection because he was attracted to her, and she'd toyed around with the idea of letting him succeed. "All the better to control you with, my dear," she'd thought. Now that she'd seen what he could actually do with those vines of his, she needed to rethink.

She had thrown everything she had behind her shields. When his vines failed yet again to find purchase, Trent had scowled and redoubled his efforts. The silence between them had stretched on and on. Finally, frustrated, he had snapped a denial at her and sent her back to her stuffy little train-themed prison.

The same little power struggle had occurred the next day, and here they were, again today. Piper stood in silence, watching him, watching his horrifying little vines attempt to penetrate her shields, and decided it was time to change it up. She turned, and headed for the door.

"I can help your people when you've let me help mine," she said over her shoulder. "Until then, you know where to find me."

"Wait!"

Piper turned. Trent looked incredulous. She'd lay odds that people didn't usually walk away from him without being excused. She felt an overwhelming urge to snap her fingers, give him the old head swerve and keep right on walking, but she made herself wait. Head high, spine straight, channeling the courageous warrior on his silly poster with all her might.

Trent had half-risen from his seat, and he sank back down, trying to recapture his "cool." His eyes slid down her body again, and this time, when his vines slid towards her, they were green and rosy pink with just a trace of lustful orange. She narrowed her eyes. What was this? Was he beginning to fancy himself in love with her?

Trent's eyes dropped shyly, and this time, in the silence that stretched between them, Piper found herself wrapped, head-to-toe, in a delicate tracery of green, enhanced here and there with blossoms of soft pink. From sinister to beautiful, just like that. It was hard to believe something so lovely could be dangerous.

"You're different," Trent finally blurted. "The others, they just do what I want. I like that you're different. I... I really hope we can become friends."

Piper's eyes narrowed. Was this a trick? If not...her mind raced with the implications. Lust was powerful, but the more tender the emotions, the more readily she could manipulate them. Piper *felt* her mother's disapproval as a buzz in her ear and a discordant tone in the bond connecting them but brushed both aside. Desperate times. She drew a deep breath, not sure what was about to happen, and lowered her shields enough to let Trent's shy green vines slip in.

The connection, on her part, was subtle. She felt a brief warmth in the center of her chest, then a soft tightening, and a tug. Then nothing. Trent's response was more dramatic. For a moment, his eyes flew wide, and bright color once again slashed his cheekbones. His lips parted as he stared at her. Then his eyes went soft with longing. Piper felt just a niggle of guilt, but brushed that aside, too. Whatever he suffered when she severed this connection, he had coming.

Trent dropped his eyes. Soft and shy. "What if..." he began, his voice cracking with youth and nerves. He swallowed, and tried again. "What if I could find a place for you here? A permanent place?"

As badly as she wanted to tell him what she thought of his offer, she had to play along. "I'm listening."

Trent spread his hands on the table in front of him, reasonable now, almost apologetic. The kid was an extraordinary chameleon. "Well, we have rules. Our resources are limited, so we only take people in who have changed. You have medical skills, so I might be able to argue for an exception, but it would be best if you would just tell me what your gift is."

Interesting. So the small bond she'd allowed hadn't given him total entrée. "I can shoot," she said. "I was a good shot before, but I don't miss now. Ever."

Trent's face glowed with pleasure at her apparent trust in him. "I thought that might be it. The men have all been talking about how well you can shoot. Reggie says you were just lucky, but he's my shooter, so he kind of has to say that. He has to, you know, whatever you call it."

"Save face." Reggie, Piper had learned, was the jackass in the Raider cap, and she really hated it when he was her escort. He hadn't touched her yet, but he stood way too close, breathing his foul breath on her while he muttered filthy things in a barely audible hiss.

"Yeah. That." Trent started swiveling in his chair again, cocky arrogance restored. "This is excellent. All you have to do is prove your skills, and you're in."

Piper kept her face still, even as her heart gave an awful lurch. She'd thought she was being so clever. "I've already proved I can shoot."

Trent's face dimmed. "Well, sure, you made a good shot. One good shot. But you still have to prove your skills in front of the whole community." Suspicion, just a whisper of it, darkened the blue of his eyes. "You can do that, can't you?"

No way out. "Of course."

His face brightened again. "Excellent." Inspiration made him beam. "I know! We'll have a skeet-shooting competition between you and Reggie. That'll be fun!"

Piper nodded, and smiled pleasantly. "Whatever you think." Shit. "I'd like to return to my room now, if you don't mind."

Trent tried and failed to mask his disappointment. "Oh, well, sure…"

Piper headed for the door.

"Wait!"

Piper turned back. Trent was on his feet, and his eyes were once again filled with longing. His slim chest rose and fell with his swift breathing for long moments, and the bond-line connecting them glowed with tensile, green strength.

"I want you to be happy," he blurted at last. "If you win, I'll let your friends go. After you've healed my people, of course."

Christ, Piper thought. No pressure. "And if I don't win?"

"Well, but, you never miss… Isn't that what you said?" Trent's voice trailed off and she hurried to reassure him in spite of the fact that she wanted to vomit.

"I'll win," she said, and walked to the door.

The man who had been waiting opened it for her, and they left together, walking through the quiet streets to the old two-story farmhouse where they had been keeping her. Not until Piper was alone in the tiny upstairs bedroom did she drop the warrior façade. Her whole body wilted with exhaustion, and she dropped onto the bed, covering her eyes with her arm.

"Holy hell," she muttered. "I am well-and-truly screwed."

A soft rustle from the closet made her sit bolt upright. The door creaked open, and a tuft of matted blonde hair appeared, followed by a pair of unforgettable, summer-sky blue eyes. When those eyes connected with hers, every hair on her body prickled and rose to attention. She wanted to hold her breath, feeling as if a wild bird had just landed on her shoulder to regard her.

"Hi there," she said in the tender voice her mother always used with little kids. "We haven't met. I'm Piper. Is this your room?"

"No. Thomas is for babies." A dirty nose and solemn mouth emerged from behind the door. "I know who you are. You're Jack's Valkyrie."

Piper lurched forward. "You've seen Jack? And Owen? Are they okay? Where are they?"

The little boy vanished. Piper heard a series of soft scuffling noises and hurried across the room to pull the closet door open. A narrow rope hung from an attic opening in the ceiling above, and the little boy dangled half-way up it, frozen, staring at her with huge eyes. Piper held her hand out, palm up, and spoke with Naomi's soft voice again.

"It's okay, honey – I'm sorry if I startled you. Will you come back down and talk with me a while?" She smiled her mother's warm smile. "I could sure use the company."

The terror receded from his eyes, and he dropped to the ground with the grace and assurance particular to active little boys. Piper backed away from the closet to sit on the bed, and he followed. He stared at her for a few more moments, then moved to the table at the foot of the bed where a wooden train set had been set up. In spite of his earlier assertion, his face lit with quiet joy as he busily started rearranging tracks. Piper willed her voice to be soft and casual.

"So Jack and Owen, they're okay?"

"Yeah." He glanced at her, and just that brief contact with his eyes made her scalp tingle. "They gave Owen stuff to clean the blood off Jack's head. Jack slept the whole first day. Then he woke up and puked like eighty times." He sighed. "Maybe more like ten. But he's better now. He still gets headaches, he says, but he's not as dizzy."

"And Owen's okay? When did you see them last?"

"Last night. Owen's fine." A shadow flitted across his face. "Well, sort of. He's so sad."

Interesting, that such a little boy could see Owen's core of sorrow. She thought back to the ambush on the road, remembering the things he'd said, but decided she'd better put first things first. "What's your name?"

"Gideon." He scooted a train along the tracks, making little chugging sounds. "Trent is my brother."

Piper nodded, hiding the spike of excitement she felt. An opportunity was blooming here. "I thought maybe you two were related. You look a lot alike. I haven't seen you around, though. Not since that first day."

"Trent doesn't let me out much." Gideon's lower lip crept into a plump pout. "He says he's keeping me safe. He says he's the only one who can understand me and that other people would hurt me."

"Hmm." Piper's eyes cataloged the signs of neglect, the dirt caked in the creases of his little arms, the too-small clothes. She remembered how her mother wouldn't allow either of her girls to leave the house unless their hair and clothes were neat and clean. "Your appearance is your shield," Naomi always said. "It tells people that someone loves you and is watching out for you." No one was watching out for little Gideon, that was obvious. "So he doesn't know you're here right now."

"No. I sneak out whenever I *know* he won't catch me. It's easy, if you can climb ropes. And if you can *see*."

Slowly, slowly, Piper cautioned herself. "I'd hate for you to get in trouble. Your brother sees the future, right? Seems like he'd catch you, easy."

Gideon huffed and shot her a disgruntled look. "Trent doesn't see the future." He frowned in concentration as his little hands fumbled to construct a bridge, then met her gaze again. "I do. I see all kinds of stuff."

Piper's breath left her on a long exhale. Grace used to talk about the big picture coming together like pieces of a puzzle, and Piper felt that happening now. She had sensed something off when Trent spoke of his ability, and now she knew why. He was passing his little brother's ability off as his own. "Will you tell me what Trent can do?"

Gideon's face fell into troubled lines. "He knows how to hurt people if they won't do what he wants. He gets them to let him in, then he *knows* how to make them do stuff, or how to make them sick." He looked up at Piper, and his eyes went unfocused for a moment. Then he shook his head sadly. "You shouldn't have let him in."

"I'll be okay. I'm pretty tough." But a chill tightened the pit of her stomach. It was possible she'd miscalculated. "What does he want, Gideon? Why is he keeping us here? Do you know?"

"He wants it to be like it was before, when he could play his games all the time." Gideon scratched his nose, his expression thoughtful. "His games made him happy. I think they made him feel safe. But there's no more internet, so he wants Maple River to be like his games, I guess."

More puzzle pieces were clicking into place, faster and faster. "But why does he need us?"

Gideon hooted a soft train whistle sound before he answered. "People with strong gifts make the best avatars, he says. If someone doesn't have a gift, or if he can't figure out how to control them, he doesn't want them here."

"What happens to those people?" She remembered the men on the road aiming their weapons at Ed's retreating back, and thought she might already know the answer. "What happens to people he can't control?"

Gideon wouldn't look at her, and for long moments, he didn't answer. Finally, he whispered, "Reggie. Reggie happens to them."

Piper smiled a reassurance she didn't feel, and stood. "Thanks for telling me, Gideon. You go ahead and play – I'll be right over here." She left Gideon to his trains and moved to stare out the window as her brain raced to process what she'd learned.

Of course. In his quest to recreate the comfort and security of his gaming world, Trent had weaponized his intuitive talent. His vines were puppet strings. Or maybe more like video game controllers, she corrected herself. Her mouth, she discovered, was suddenly dry, and she was shivering in spite of the stuffy warmth of the room. In all the discussions she and Jack had shared about the changes humanity had experienced, neither one of them had ever considered this.

Piper thought about the various manifestations of intuition she'd seen or heard of, and a deep chill settled in her core. How lethal would Naomi be with a pack of dogs at her command? And what about Jack? He'd admitted to hurting others with his voice, but did he have more power than he'd even realized? Could he maim? Or kill? That people would learn to use their new skills to their best advantage was a given; that they would use their gifts to make weapons of themselves was terrifying on a new level.

Piper leaned her forehead against the glass, watching people move around in the street below, wondering what their talents were, wondering what they might be capable of. She had been totally unprepared for this, and she, of all people, shouldn't have been. Brody's cold-blooded orchestration of the people and events around him should have taught her to look for the dark side of humanity first. She was a fool, wishing for the light.

"That's not right."

Piper looked over her shoulder. Gideon was gazing at her, a sad frown on his small face. "That's not what that man was supposed to teach you. I'm sorry he hurt you. He'll be sorry, too, in the time after this time. But he taught you things you needed to know, especially about yourself."

Piper felt a chill of an entirely different sort envelop her. "How do you know that?" she whispered. "How do you know those things, Gideon?"

He scrambled to his feet and walked to stand beside her, then reached to tuck his grubby little hand in hers, touching her for the first time. Piper's air left her on a rush as she gazed around in wonder. Power and beauty surrounded them, a circle of strength and peace and grace. "You're like Verity," she breathed. "You speak with angels."

"Yup." Gideon dropped her hand and gave her a cheeky grin. "So you better be nice to me."

His eyes went unfocused again; then he looked at her with regret. "I have to go. They're coming now, so you can shoot with Reggie." He headed to the closet, then turned back. "You can beat him. But you shouldn't. You should lose."

Piper followed, mind scrambling with unanswered questions, heart pounding with fresh anxiety. She watched as he slithered up the rope, and seriously considered climbing right up after him. He pulled himself into the square of darkness, little legs churning, but his flushed face re-appeared just seconds later.

"You can't come with me," he said. "That would make everything go wrong. Go shoot with Reggie, but you have to lose. Tell Trent you won't make the sick people better. He'll be so mad." Gideon grinned. "And everything will go just right."

"Wait!" She held a hand up to him. "If it doesn't go right, can you get Jack and Owen out? They're good men, Gideon. They'll take you with them, if you want them to."

"I can get them out."

Relief flooded her. She heard footsteps in the hallway outside and made a shooing motion with the hand she still held outstretched. "Go, quick. Tell them I love them both. Will you do that, too?"

Gideon grinned and reached to brush her fingertips with his. "Nah, that's mushy stuff. You can tell them yourself. You'll see them in just a little bit."

Piper blinked, stepping clear of the closet just as a key rattled in the door. Reggie stepped in, with his oily smirk and bad breath, but neither could penetrate the golden glow that still held Piper like warm arms. She smiled at him, feeling both far away and absolutely present in the moment.

"I'm ready whenever you are."

She followed him outside. People were already gathering in the street as he led her into an old barn set just off the main drag. In the cool dimness, he unhooked a ring of keys from his belt, dangling them tauntingly in the air. "I might just let you use your own weapon if you ask me real nice."

His juvenile flirtation would have annoyed her before. Now, she just felt still. Calm. "I'd prefer to use the weapon you took from my friend," she said. "The shotgun Jack was carrying."

Reggie just kept jingling the keys as he stared at her, sniggering softly. Under his leer, though, she could see his nerves. Both his reputation and his place in the community were on the line. She just waited in her golden stillness until he finally gave up. "Fine."

He unlocked a storage room door and reached up to pull a string, illuminating the interior with a bare light bulb. The room was ringed with shelves, and on those shelves were stacked all manner of firearms. Reggie stepped out of sight, reappearing a moment later with Jack's shotgun. He broke it open and handed it to her, all without taking his eyes off her. "Let's go powder some, sweetheart."

She preceded him out of the barn with the shotgun draped over her forearm, squinting in the bright sunlight. In silence, they walked to the north side of the barn where a group of men were lounging in the shade, many of whom Piper recognized from the confrontation on the road. They stood as Reggie and Piper approached, and one of them called out. "You two gonna put on a show?"

"You got that right, hoss." Reggie's words sent sly sniggers around the group. He looked at Piper and played at chivalry. "Would you prefer outgoing or incoming targets, honey?"

Piper shrugged. "Whatever you choose. Crossing and rabbits are fine, too."

Excited murmurs went around the group, and they scrambled to set up the launchers in various positions. Behind them, people were setting up lawn chairs and spreading blankets in the shade of the huge old Maple trees that had probably given the town its name. The mood was celebratory, the people buzzing with excitement at the prospect of entertainment.

Piper looked over at Reggie. "May I fire a few shots? I haven't used this shotgun lately."

"Mmm, such pretty manners. Just what a man likes." He rearranged himself in his pants, and probably thought he was being subtle about it. "Sure, honey, go right ahead."

He handed her two shells and nodded at her weapon. "A double-barrel 12 gauge is a lot of gun for a woman." His voice dropped lower. "But I'll bet you can handle a lot of gun, can't you sweetheart? I bet you like 'em big and hard to handle."

Piper slid the shells into the over-under barrels and wondered how many times she would have to not answer him before he got tired of talking. "I'll sight in on those trees."

She didn't wait for his nod, bringing the shotgun to her shoulder in a smooth motion and firing. She nearly wept at the familiar sensation, the reassurance and comfort of it, the explosion of memories that went with the sight, feel, and sound of this gun. This was the weapon Jack carried, true, but he did so because it was hers. Her father had given her this gun, and her mother had taught her to use it. As Jack freely pointed out, he would never be a marksman; he carried the shotgun as a backup weapon for Piper, and she sent a silent blessing to far-away Martin for suggesting it.

She fired another shot, ejected the spent shells, then held her hand out. "Two more, please."

Reggie deposited the shells in her palm, and she fired two more shots in quick succession. She turned to face him, and noticed that the shots had silenced the crowd. A quick count told her most of the town was accounted for, except for those who were ill. Trent had arrived, and was standing with Reggie's cronies. When his eyes met hers, a pink flush swept from his neck to his hairline. At his side, his fingers lifted in a shy little wave before he turned to Reggie. His expression was noticeably cooler as he nodded his permission for them to begin.

Reggie nodded in return, then looked at Piper. "Twenty five shots." He leaned close, bathing her face with his foul, moist breath. "Winner takes all."

She kept her expression bland. "And if we tie?"

"Well, then, we shoot another round. We shoot until somebody wins or we run out of skeet." He gestured her forward, all courtly-like. "Ladies first."

Piper stepped forward, and closed her eyes for a moment. She reminded herself that she was her mother's daughter, and for good measure, warmed the bond between her heart and Naomi's. "Sure wish you were shooting instead of me, mama," she whispered. "Help my eyes and hands do what I need to do."

Naomi's presence circled around her, warm with love, vibrating with worry. Piper sent back a reassurance, and Naomi's energy settled into a steady warmth in the center of her chest, joining the peaceful golden glow Gideon's touch had left her with.

Piper opened her eyes and smiled. "Pull."

They shot the first round to a tie. Then another. And another. After that, Piper lost track. From every angle, every possible configuration, even two at a time, and neither of them missed. They took a short break for water and a moment to cool themselves in the shade. Reggie's face was bright red from the sun, but the sweat that stained his armpits was all nerves; Piper could smell the sour tang of it. As they returned to the mark, one of the men held up two clay pigeons. "Last two, Reg."

Piper looked over at Reggie, and nodded. "After you."

He didn't argue – he'd left chivalry behind long ago. He stepped up to the mark and blew the clay to smithereens. He couldn't quite summon a smirk when he turned to face her, but his shoulders relaxed. She couldn't beat him now. At the very worst, this would end in a tie. Piper took his place and lifted her shotgun to the ready. "Pull."

It surprised her, how hard it was to ignore the clay spinning away from her, to let it go, but she did. Instead, she pirouetted to face Trent, settling her sights right between his beautiful blue eyes. All around her, she heard a collective intake of breath. Her peripheral vision registered weapons coming up all around her, and still she held her position, locked in a stare-down with this lethal young creature, allowing him time to process all the implications of her action. She hadn't just lost. She'd also made sure this group would never accept her. When at last she heard the distant, tinkling pop of the clay hitting the ground, she pointed the barrel of her shotgun over his head and fired her last shot. The men were on her before she could break her weapon open to eject the spent shells.

She did not fight their rough jostling; to do so would only invite more violence. She allowed them to take the shotgun from her and secure her arms behind her back with a quiet dignity that would have done her mother proud. Trent stared at her all the while, his face twisted with betrayal, and bitter, bitter disappointment.

"I made a place for you," he finally managed to say, his voice high and very young. "I made a place for you here, and this is how you repay me?"

"I don't hang with campers," Piper said calmly. Her gamer insult was lost on everyone but Trent, who went scarlet, then white, then back to scarlet. "If you still want to replace Reggie, you'll have to keep looking. I don't kill."

As soon as the words left her, she recognized the Truth of them. The jagged edges she'd been carrying around in her chest since that long-ago winter night, the heart she'd shattered herself when she had ended Josh, at last began to soften and mend. She closed her eyes, feeling the burn of grateful tears. No matter how this ended, her heart was eased.

"I don't kill," she repeated softly, opening her eyes, looking not at Trent but at the sky. She sent that Truth winging into the soft blue, hoping it would find Josh, hoping her regret and sorrow would somehow reach and console his spirit. "I do not kill."

Trent's chest heaved, and his eyes glittered with angry tears. He looked at Reggie, then gestured with wild hands at Piper.

"Kill her! Kill her now!"

Reggie, though, continued to stare at Trent. "You want to replace me? Is that what this was all about?"

Trent made an impatient sound. "Don't be stupid. That's just what I told her." But his face was tight with fear. "Now do your job!"

Before Reggie could respond, Piper spoke. "If you kill me, your people will die." She looked around at the crowd, making eye contact, giving them time to think about what she was saying. Then she returned her gaze to Trent and raised her eyebrows. "Pretty irresponsible, killing the one person who has the training to save a third of your community."

An unhappy murmur buzzed through the crowd, and Trent's eyes darted furtively around the same path Piper's eyes had taken. "Fine," he snapped. He raised his chin, trying to appear calm and in control, but the quiver of his lower lip belied him. The red grid of bond lines connecting his people to him were beginning to sputter and fade. Under different circumstances, Piper would have pitied him. "You can treat our people first, then I'll decide." Again, he gestured at Reggie. "Take her to the infirmary."

"No."

Piper and Reggie spoke in unison. Echoing his earlier courtliness, perhaps even meaning it this time, Reggie swept a hand towards Piper. "Ladies first."

She inclined her head. "Thank you. Good shooting, by the way." She turned to Trent. "I told you earlier. I won't treat your people until you let me treat mine."

"I'll have them killed," Trent hissed. "Or tortured. You have to do what I say!"

Her heart twisted horribly at his threat, but she didn't let him see. "No, I don't. Don't you get it?" Her eyes went to Reggie, and she shook her head. The Reggies of the world held little terror for her now. She returned her gaze to Trent. "There is nothing you can do to me that I haven't already survived. I won't help you. Your people will die, and this whole community will know you could have saved them, if you weren't a spoiled rotten little boy who had to have his way."

And that was it. The end of Trent's self-control. With an inarticulate cry of rage, he threw his arms wide. Piper raised her hands reflexively, momentarily blinded by the flare of Trent's bond lines. She felt a hard tug in the center of her chest, felt her heart stutter, and was suddenly lightheaded. She heard the men on either side of her gasp, and she was abruptly released. Somehow, she managed to brace her legs and stay upright, but all around her, people were dropping to their knees or collapsing in dead faints. She held a hand up to protect her eyes and looked back at Trent.

To Piper, he looked like something out of a horror movie, sprouting with writhing orange vines that punched through people before constricting to cold black. Reggie had managed to stay on his feet, but his complexion was a waxy grey, and he was clutching his head as if he feared it would split in two. Piper sucked in breath after breath as she tried to shore up her shields, tried to shove Trent out, but she understood Gideon's words now: She never should have let him in.

Trent held them all in thrall for long, long moments, then dropped his arms. He, too, was breathing heavily and was waxy pale, but his eyes glowed electric blue.

Piper felt her fluttering heart stabilize and begin to pound, steady and strong once more. Across from her, Reggie cautiously dropped his hands from the sides of his head. He straightened to stare at Trent with a combination of fear and loathing. All around them, people were starting to struggle to their feet, though some seemed to have been rendered unconscious.

Trent looked around, and a slow smile replaced his dazed expression. An occasional crackle of bond-energy rippled along his limbs, making him shudder with what looked like euphoria, or maybe pleasure. Piper thought she might vomit. He hadn't known he could do this. And she'd goaded him into it. He was still pasty pale, so the effort had cost him something, but what?

"Go home." His voice, so whiny and thin before, was deeper. Stronger. "Think about who's in charge here, and why." He looked at Piper, and his lips twisted in a sneer. "You want to see your friends so bad? Fine." He jerked his head at Reggie. "She can spend the night with them in their comfy cell. In the morning she can treat our people, or suffer the consequences."

Reggie's eyes narrowed, and he didn't immediately obey. When he finally did walk to take Piper's arm, his reluctance was obvious in the slow deliberation of his movements. He didn't speak to either Trent or Piper, just urged her away from the gathering and towards the northern edge of town. Around them, people were staggering and scurrying away, carrying those who had yet to regain consciousness, their terror glowing in the red-hot lines connecting them to Trent like wires.

Piper was stunned. What had she done? For a few moments there, it had looked like she'd brought Trent's little empire crashing down around him. Now, she feared all she'd managed to do was unleash him. She'd seen him disable the man named Paul; should she have anticipated this? She snorted, and felt Reggie look at her as he towed her along. Who the hell could have anticipated such a thing? He was more than an energetic parasite; he could manipulate bioelectrical systems in others. And now he knew it.

They arrived at an older home, a Victorian-era farmhouse that appeared to have been well loved, not too long ago. Reggie led her up the broad porch steps and inside. The afternoon had disappeared into evening as they had competed, and the sun was nearing the western horizon. Long, golden rays slid in through the front windows, momentarily giving the illusion of life, of warmth. Piper closed her eyes, and wondered if it was the adrenalin still pumping through her body that made her smell popcorn and spiced cider, made her hear laughter. Reggie led her through the house to the kitchen, where he released her long enough to unlock a door, which led down into darkness.

Still without speaking, he took a flashlight from a holder on the wall and snapped it on, then led her down the stairs into an old-fashioned fruit cellar. Dim light filtered in through high, dirty windows, illuminating another pad-locked door. Reggie stepped close to the door and pounded on it.

"Step back," he called. "And keep your mouths shut. You so much as sneeze, I shoot."

He drew a handgun from a holster in the small of his back, then unlocked the padlock, though he left the latch in place. Hesitating, he met Piper's eyes for the first time. He opened his mouth, shut it, frowned, then shook his head and opened the door. Aligning his handgun with the flashlight, he pointed both inside the dimly lit room and gestured for Piper to step forward with a jerk of his head.

"Go on, then."

Owen blinked in the sudden light, holding a hand up to shield his eyes. He was sitting on a straight-backed chair beside a cot, on which Jack lay. Still. Very, very still. Piper's throat closed so tight she could hardly speak. She stumbled forward, gazing at Owen in anguish. "Is he...? Is he...?"

Reggie shut the door behind her. Dimly, Piper heard the latch rattle and the padlock snap shut. Jack stirred then, finally, sitting up and scrubbing his face with both hands. He blinked at Piper blearily, then scowled. "If you let them eat my bacon, Piper, I swear I will never forgive you."

FOURTEEN
Jack: Maple River, Iowa

To Jack's consternation, Piper responded to his attempt at levity with tears. A lot of them. Owen stood, and she stumbled into his open arms, hiding her face against his chest while she sobbed. Owen looked at Jack over her bright hair and shook his head.

"You sure are stupid about women."

Jack hung his head for a moment, wished he could blame his gaff on his head injury or lack of sleep, but Owen did have a point. He rose to his feet, and when the room stopped spinning, simply went and wrapped his arms around both of them. As soon as he felt her against him, felt her familiar energy blend with his, the awful, grinding anxiety that had been cramping his stomach for the last five days eased. The three of them rocked gently from side to side for long moments. Then Piper lifted her head. She scrubbed a wrist under her streaming nose, swiped at her cheeks with both palms, then slugged Jack in the shoulder hard enough to rock him back a step.

"You scared the crap out of me!" she hissed. Then she hiccupped, and reached to cup first Owen's face in her hands, then Jack's. "I love you both," she choked. There was something different, something wide-open in her bright green eyes as she looked at each of them in turn. "I was so afraid I wouldn't get a chance to tell you that."

Owen's smile was bright in the nearly dark room, his words tender and warm. "We love you too, honey." His tone might have been easy, but his eyes were sharp as they searched her face. "We're as relieved to see you as you are to see us. We were pretty worried, but Gideon kept us filled in on what was happening – did you meet him? He said he was going to introduce himself."

Piper made a sound of wonder. "What an extraordinary kid – I can't imagine what would happen if we got him and Verity together. He said he'd been sneaking in to see you, and that you were both okay. My bond lines told me you were both still alive, but nothing more, and I was starting to wonder if I wasn't just deceiving myself."

Jack's eyes, too, had been probing and assessing. As long as he'd already stuck his foot in it once, he decided he had nothing to lose. Grasping Piper by the shoulders, he turned her to face him, ducking his head down to look her straight in the eyes. "Did they hurt you?

She understood what he was asking, what both he and Owen needed to know, and shook her head. "No." She reached up and wrapped her hands around his wrists, and he *felt* the truth of her words. "Not in any way."

Jack allowed his eyes to close for just a moment, swamped with a relief so intense it made his knees wobble.

"Thank God," he breathed. "I've been praying non-stop, and you have no idea, the dark scenarios we've been concocting in here, if they had hurt you." He opened his eyes, and tried once again for levity. "You know, just to pass the time." He gave up trying to play it cool and pulled her close, wrapping both arms around her and just holding on. She nestled into him, and he could feel her drawing as much comfort from him as he was drawing from her, a give-and-take that balanced everything inside him. "Piper. Thank God."

Owen's big hand landed on his shoulder a moment later. "I hate to break this up, but we may not have much time. We need to make plans."

Piper stepped back. "We do, but first things first. Have a seat, please."

She waved Jack towards the chair, then took his chin and turned his head towards the pittance of light still trickling into the room from the window. Her fingers pressed delicately along the edges of the wound over his ear. A dull ache bloomed from each point she touched, followed by a tingle that slid along his nape and down his spine. Interesting. It sure didn't feel like that when Owen touched him.

She turned his chin again and touched the scuffs on the side of his face where he'd hit the tarmac. "Tell me about your symptoms. Still nauseated?"

"No, not for a few days."

"How about dizziness?"

"Only when I stand up. Or bend over. Or move fast." He made a wry face at her. "So, yes. Still dealing with dizziness."

She bent, bringing her face close to his, looking at his eyes. "Wish I had a flashlight," she murmured, and her breath feathered his cheeks, soft and warm. "Owen, did you notice any difference in the size of his pupils? One bigger than the other?"

"That first day, yes." Owen moved to stand beside her. "I can't remember which was bigger, though. And I haven't seen it since then."

"Hmm. Good." She looked into his eyes then, instead of at them, and again he was struck by how wide-open her gaze was. "You are one lucky preacher man. I just shot it out with the man who did this to you, and if he had wanted you dead, you would be dead. He might even be as good as my mom."

Jack's eyebrows rose. "Shot it out? Sounds like you've been busy. Did you win?"

"No, but Gideon told me not to." She took a deep breath. "Owen, you might want to get comfortable. This could take a while. I don't know what Gideon has told you about his brother, but I'm afraid it just went from bad to worse."

They ended up ranged around the tiny, dank room: Piper seated on the cot, Owen sprawled on a thin, ratty mattress in front of the door, Jack still seated in the straight-backed chair. She talked them through everything she'd seen and experienced since they'd been separated, culminating with a detailed description of the afternoon's events. "It's hard to say how much power Trent has or how much harm he could do, if any, to someone he's not connected to. Everyone here has let him in, to some degree." She grimaced, shaking her head. "Including me. Don't ask me what I was thinking, because obviously it didn't work out the way I intended. If you end up face to face with him, don't drop your guard for even an instant."

Jack nodded. "What about Ed? Have you heard anything? What about your bond line?"

"Our bond line is still strong, but I haven't heard a thing. They've kept me locked down pretty tight." She looked at Owen. "On the road when they captured us, you told Ed you *saw* him in Onawa, when you *saw* Decatur burning. Did you really?"

"No." Owen hunched his shoulders. "That was a lie. I just wanted to get him out of there. He wasn't going to leave us. I could see that in his face."

"Hmm. Might turn into a self-fulfilling prophecy, if we're lucky. Maybe Ed can convince the people in Onawa to help." She pulled her knees up and wrapped her arms around them. "In the meantime, do we have any other plans for getting out of here?"

"Nothing solid," Jack answered. "Some desperate hail Mary's. Now that we're together, some of them would be less risky."

They talked through some of the ideas he and Owen had come up with, then started creating a new plan based on a series of if-then scenarios. How many men would show up in the morning to take Piper to the infirmary? Could any of them be persuaded to change allegiance? Prior to

Reggie's arrival with Piper yesterday, they had never interacted with less than two of their captors at a time. Jack had disabled multiple armed men with his voice before, but these people were forewarned. If he tried and failed, it might escalate an already perilous situation. Finally, after what felt like hours of troubleshooting and worst-case contingencies, they had a plan.

Full dark had fallen as they talked, the room illuminated only by the faint glow of the moon through the tiny, grubby window. Piper was no more than a shadow curled within the shadows on the cot, and Owen was a disembodied voice from near the floor. Jack shifted on his uncomfortable, rickety chair, then stood and gave a mighty stretch.

"I think we have a little water left. My mouth feels like glue. Do either of you need a swallow?" He patted his way to the corner where they kept the plastic jug of water, then shared sips with Owen and Piper. It was lukewarm and brackish, but it soothed his throat.

"Have they been taking decent care of you?" Piper asked. "Feeding you enough?"

Jack made a so-so gesture with his hand, then remembered she couldn't see him. "Sort of. They take us out a couple of times a day to use the facilities, such as they are, though they haven't let us wash up. I imagine we're both pretty aromatic."

Piper's voice had laughter in it now. "It's okay. My eyes stopped watering after the first ten minutes or so. And I see what you meant by the beard – you are rockin' that Jesus look, there."

Jack winced, then continued. "The food has been a little scarce, and we could use twice the water they've been giving us, but we're not desperate yet."

"I wonder if they're deliberately trying to weaken you? Or if they don't want to waste food on prisoners? Maybe both? Trent said their resources were limited. That's why they turned Ed away. Trent's not interested in supporting people who don't have some kind of gift he can exploit." She told him what Gideon had told her about Trent's video games, then shared her theories, based on what she'd observed. "The people here seem unaware that they're being manipulated. Or they did, before that little exhibition this afternoon. Pretty sure they're aware now. And you know what I just realized? Other than Gideon and Trent, I haven't seen any other children. None at all."

"Too powerful, maybe? Or maybe too hard to control? Our little ones all had strong intuitive skills, but they were unpredictable, to say the least. Remind me to tell you the Viagra story someday." Jack was quiet for a moment. "Do you think Trent was literally addicted to gaming? I saw that, a lot actually – kids needed their electronics, just like any junkie needs a fix."

"Absolutely. We talked about this in my aberrant psychology class. He's pretty classic, now that you mention it. High levels of aggression and narcissism, low levels of control. He keeps people around him, but he's isolated just the same. He probably misses the characters in his games desperately. It's likely they were his closest friends."

"He may not be capable of having normal, healthy relationships, which would be why he manipulates." Jack sighed. "Dangerous as he sounds, I have to admit I'm anxious to meet him. He's a kid. I'm good with kids. You said you could resist his 'vines' until after you deliberately dropped your defenses, so hopefully I would have the same experience."

"I've been thinking about it, and I would bet some people are more susceptible than others. The people who lost consciousness – maybe they have rotten shields, or they didn't try to resist him at all." Piper sighed, too. "If he weren't a textbook sociopath, it would be fascinating to ask him about it. I wonder if the games he played taught him to role play, to present the façade that's most compelling to the person he's interacting with?"

From the shadows near the door, Owen's voice broke in, distorted by a yawn. "Interesting as your dissection of this little shit is, I've got to cry uncle." Rustling sounds were followed by another enormous yawn. "You two carry on. I'm just going to close my eyes for a minute."

And in less than that minute, sonorous breathing told them Owen was asleep. Jack and Piper continued their conversation, in whispers now. "Gideon told us they were being cared for by their grandmother, who died in the plague. Their mother abandoned them when Gideon was just a baby, and they have different fathers, neither of whom is in the picture."

"Don't you dare try to make me feel sorry for him, Jack. Owen called it right. He's a little shit."

Jack was quiet for a moment. "I'm not disputing that. But every angry kid I ever met was a hurt kid. It always came down to fear and pain. I'm not making excuses for him. I'm just saying there's always a 'why' behind bad behavior. Layla always says –"

The air left his lungs as if he'd been kicked. He had actually forgotten, for a moment there, that Layla was dead. They had talked about kids like this for hours without number, and he missed it. Missed her, her friendship, her intelligence and wisdom when it came to troubled children. He squeezed his eyes shut and pulled in a long, deep breath, trying to loosen the pain that tightened his chest.

In the dark, Piper's searching, patting hand connected first with his bicep, then slid down to squeeze his hand. Her fingers were icy cold, and without overthinking it, he slid next to her on the cot, curling an arm around her back to cushion it from the damp stone wall. She tucked into the place against his side as if she had always fit there.

"Go on," she said softly. "What did Layla always say?"

He had to clear his throat before he could answer. "That the outer walls were always directly proportional to the inner softness. The kids with the scariest defenses, with the spikes and piercings and gauges, those kids are the marshmallows underneath."

"Well, Trent doesn't have the Goth thing going on, but we could try holding his hand and singing him a lullaby, tell him we're sorry he has abandonment issues. See if we can find that soft underbelly." Her voice dropped to a sibilant hiss. "So we can gut it."

Jack smiled, even though he knew she wasn't really joking. Then he fell silent, thinking, considering, and finally deciding. He spoke in a low voice, aware of Owen snoring on the floor a few feet away. "I want to tell you what happened between me and Layla."

He *felt* her surprise, as both an emotion and a slight stiffening of her shoulders. "Okay."

Jack turned his head to speak more directly into her ear, not wanting this to feel like a whispered intimacy, but not wanting to burden Owen with it, should he wake. "I forced Layla to respond to me sexually. I stopped short of raping her body, but I violated her mind. She and Owen were together by then, but I knew she wanted me. I could *feel* it, whenever she dropped those crazy shields of hers. And I wanted her."

Piper's breath touched the side of his face. "If you wanted each other, why weren't you together?"

His face heated, but he wasn't about to start backpedaling now. "I didn't think I could be with her, not openly, not in the bright light of day. Her spirituality was something I just couldn't accept. She was a witch, and I was a pastor. At the time, it seemed so cut and dried. She was wrong and I was right."

"Are you telling me this because you think we're going to die? Because I've gotta tell you, I'm feeling like our chances are at least 60-40. Maybe even 70-30, so –"

"I'm telling you this because of what's growing between us. You deserve to know what kind of man I am, so you can choose whether or not to continue."

Piper absorbed his words, and did not answer right away. She turned her face away from him – he felt it in the way her body shifted. In her silence, Jack could feel something gathering.

"I killed a man in cold blood."

Jack nodded slowly. On some level, he'd known. It had been there, in the words that rose from her nightmares, in her haunted eyes, in a thousand ways. "You weren't defending yourself?"

"No." She kept her face turned away from him, and in her voice, he could hear the extent of the damage she'd done to herself. "I lured him into a trap with sex. And when they told me to execute him, I did. I shot him in the head, point blank, and I was not sorry. I won't lie to myself or to you about that, even if it would make it easier."

He admired her honesty, though her words made his heart ache. He knew this woman, knew how tough she was. He also knew she was innately kind, and concerned for the fate of her fellow man. He couldn't imagine the hell she must have been inhabiting, to make such an act possible.

Piper went on. "One moment he was there, and the next moment he had ended. His name was Josh, and he was sobbing when I shot him." Finally, she turned her head back towards him, and a shift in the moon illuminated half of her face with soft silver. "But do you know what the worst thing was? It was the look on his face at the end, the terror and the total aloneness. I made sure every one of his bond lines were snuffed. All of the connections he'd built, the camaraderie with the other men – I ended those, too. Severed them. And he knew it. He could *feel* how alone he was before he died, and he looked almost relieved when I pressed my pistol to his forehead."

"Piper." Jack would have given anything at that moment to be able to take it from her. What a bitter cup she'd been given. "I'm so sorry you had to suffer that. I'll carry it with you now, and the load will be lighter."

She curled into him, warming him, seeking and giving solace. "It already is lighter. All this time, I've been wondering what I wouldn't do to survive. Everything my mom taught me, the values my folks tried to instill, the laws I believed in – none of that meant anything when it came time to choose. I didn't even hesitate. I've been so afraid that there's nothing in me but the desire to survive, nothing decent, no line I wouldn't cross." She smiled. "And then a shitty little pariah named Trent Donnelly walked into my sights, and I couldn't do it. I could not shoot him, and I would not now, not even to save my life. There's peace in that, Jack. A great deal of peace."

Then she grinned at him, and the one eye he could see glowed with something that made heat curl and lick in the pit of his stomach. "So, back to that thing you said was growing between us. Does it matter if I'm agnostic? Because I believe in a higher power, I think, but –"

Jack laughed. He might be stupid about women, but he knew how to stop her words as a wise man should, with a kiss. The thrill of brand new blended with the sensation that he'd been kissing her like this, always. The lazy heat that had warmed the pit of his stomach and the base of his spine ripped along his arms and legs, and crackled across his scalp. He pulled back just before his eyebrows caught fire, and found her wide-eyed.

"Criminey, Jack, if you could see what I'm seeing right now. It's like flaming rainbows, but not as 'Ghost Rider' as that sounds..." She trailed off, and her eyes, both dimly visible now, danced around them. She leaned into him, watching his eyes, and pressed her mouth to his once more. Jack *felt* her desire as his own, *felt* her sensations blend and heat with his. She laughed softly against his mouth. "Oh my gosh, this is going to be so *interesting*."

They drew back simultaneously, and Jack had to stand up before he prowled right over on top of her and forgot all about Owen and cellars and everything else that made this not the time, not the place. He pressed his back against the cold stone wall opposite the cot and listened to her take quick, shaky breaths. Listened, and grinned from ear-to-ear in the dark.

"So." Piper's voice had a grin in it, too. "A little more incentive to get out of this hell hole, hmm?"

"Darn tootin'," he replied, and she belly-laughed in response. He couldn't help himself, moving near enough to touch her face, feeling the pull of her like a lodestone in his blood. She tilted her cheek into his palm, and he closed his eyes.

Jack blew out a breath that should have flamed, and stepped back. So tempting, so very tempting, to fall into this fascinating newness opening up in front of him, but there was a time for everything. Now, for example, it was time to change the subject. He dragged his chair away from the cot and sat down. He was about to resurrect their earlier discussion about Trent when a rustle and a familiar, rhythmic tapping at the window brought him to his feet again.

"It's Gideon." He moved to stand under the window, his fingers finding the gritty ledge. The window slid open, halting and grating in its dirty track, and a waft of fresh, cool air hit his face. A round, dark shadow blocked out what little light was coming through.

"Hi, Jack. Can I come in?"

"Sure, buddy. I'm ready."

Gideon squirmed through the window, legs first, bringing with him a rain of Juniper needles and dirt. Jack caught his slight little body around the waist but forgot to brace himself. Momentarily blinded by Gideon's angelic posse, he set the little boy down on the ground, then cupped his eyes in his hands to help his night vision return.

Owen stirred and sat up, shaking off sleep. "Hey, it's our favorite visitor. How's it going, G-man?"

"I brought a flashlight." A rustle, then a strange, rhythmic whirring sound. "I couldn't find one with batteries. This one you have to pump with your hand, and it only lasts a little while."

A dim glow illuminated Gideon, tongue caught between his teeth, cranking a flashlight for all he was worth with his little hands. When the light glowed steadily, he looked up. "Hi, Piper. That was really good shooting." Then, he looked up at Jack. "Are you ready to go?"

"Go? What do you –" Before Jack could finish asking, a series of thumps outside the door silenced him. The bracket holding the padlock rattled, and faintly, through the door, they heard the jingle of keys. Jack barely had time to scoop Gideon behind him before the door swung open.

Reggie. And two other men. They were all holding rifles and lanterns, and the only one that didn't look scared to death was Reggie. Owen had stepped in front of Piper, and she tilted her head to peer around his shoulder. Reggie's eyes found her, and he inclined his head.

"Hope we didn't startle you too much." He looked at both Jack and Owen. "Don't know what the hell you two can do that's more dangerous than her shooting, but it doesn't really matter." Again, he met Piper's gaze. "We owe you a debt. Nobody knew, not really, how Trent was running things. Running us. It don't sit well, a boy controlling men. It don't sit well at all, even if he can see the future."

Piper nodded slowly. "I guess it wouldn't. Are you setting us free?"

"Yep." His eyes flickered back to Jack and Owen, but he continued to address Piper. "Trent's planning to kill them in the morning. Said he wanted me to do it after you'd treated our people, a public execution, so's everybody would see the consequences for disobeying him." Reggie shook his head. "I ain't going to tell you that I wouldn't shoot innocent men, 'cause I have. Didn't bother me, neither. Nothing bothers me since my daughters died."

Reggie looked away for a moment, a muscle flexing along his neck and jaw, and his deep and awful grief rolled over Jack like a wave. Then he drew a deep breath in through his nose and returned his gaze to Piper. "But like I said, we owe you, and killing your men ain't how we repay a debt." He unslung an AR-15 rifle from his shoulder and handed it to her. "Believe this is yours. We've got your bikes and your gear on the edge of town. Most of your gear, anyway." He was all asshole again for a moment, rubbing his stomach. "That bacon sure hit the spot. And we relieved you of your marijuana, too. For medicinal purposes, of course."

Jack couldn't quite stifle his disappointed sigh. He bolstered his shields, then reached behind his legs and drew Gideon forward. "For the record, the real future-caster is right here." He pitched his voice just so, and put *power* behind the words. "And he'll be coming with us."

The air around them seemed to vibrate for a moment, and the men with Reggie exchanged startled glances. One of them laughed nervously. "Did you hear that? That was a damn Jedi mind trick, that's what that was." He waved his hand in the air and intoned, "'These aren't the droids you're looking for.'"

A ripple of genuine laughter circled around the group, and Jack felt the tension in his shoulders ease. He lifted Gideon to his hip, but before he could swing him around to piggy-back position, Owen had plucked the little boy free and deposited him on his own back.

"Your head," he explained. He jiggled Gideon, making him giggle and reminding Jack that he'd been a father of three, before the plague. "I'll do the heavy lifting. You just walk a straight line, okay?"

Jack nodded, and looked towards the door to find Reggie watching him. The other man nodded at Gideon. "So he's the one who knows the future? Trent told us all he could do was *see* what others can do, who's dangerous, stuff like that." He made a disgusted sound. "Guess he lied about that, too. Kid's right at the top of my shit list, tell you what. All right, let's go. Stay quiet and stay close."

They filed out after Reggie and his men with Piper bringing up the rear, climbing the stairs and gliding through the dark, silent house. Once outside, Piper moved to Jack's side. Her fingers brushed his, but she didn't take his hand as they ghosted through the empty streets. Like Reggie and his men, her eyes scanned around them constantly and her rolling footsteps were soundless. Every once in a while, she lifted her nose to the breeze or tilted her head to listen. She made him think of a wolf, silent and lethal. Not the gypsy Naomi always named her, but something more elemental and wild.

They were within sight of the bikes when everything went south. The coughing sound of a generator starting up made them all freeze just before a bank of lights pinned them like bugs to a board where they stood. Piper and Reggie both brought their weapons to the ready, squinting in the direction of the lights, as a young voice, high with nerves, rang out.

"Nobody move! Reggie and Piper, I've got five guns on both of you – lower your weapons!"

They exchanged a glance before they both dropped their rifles to their hips. Jack knew Piper could shoot from that position, and apparently Trent knew the same thing about Reggie.

"Put them on the ground, all of you, and just stay right where you are! We outnumber you three to one!"

As if by prior agreement, neither Reggie nor Piper moved. Then, a slight, dark silhouette stepped out in front of the lights and spread its arms. Both Piper and Reggie tensed, bringing their rifles to bear on the slim figure, but

Trent spoke before either of them could act. His voice was gleeful, euphoric. "I asked you nicely to put your weapons on the ground. Now I'll *make* you!"

Instantly, Reggie and his men staggered, and Piper gasped. She dropped to her knees, her rifle landing roughly on the ground in front of her, both hands clutched over her heart. She looked up at Jack, tried to say something, but could only cry out again and pant for air. Jack spun back, praying he'd heard enough to do what needed doing.

"Stop." Thunder seemed to rumble in the air around him. He heard Owen's startled exclamation, and Trent's men swearing, but Trent just jerked his head and continued to stand, arms outstretched.

"You can't make me listen," he shrilled. "I made Gideon tell me what you can do, and I don't have to listen to you!"

Lord, if lives weren't hanging in the balance, Jack might have laughed. How many times had he heard those words, in just that tone, from an angry, broken kid? He reached deep, into the imperatives of *authority* and *control*, and let those powers course through his words. "Stop, Trent. Stop *now*."

Trent dropped to his knees, but whatever hold he had on Piper and the others did not relent. Reggie was curled up on the ground, clutching his skull and moaning. One of his men appeared to be unconscious, and the other had collapsed on his hands and knees and was vomiting helplessly.

Piper's skin was grey. She looked up at him, eyes dull, lips blue, and he *felt* the bond between them falter. She tried to say something, but he couldn't make it out.

She was dying. And it was in his power to stop it.

He looked up at Trent, and knew the word he needed to speak: *Die.*

Jack knew the place in his heart that harbored the dark power. He had touched that blackness in his soul when he violated Layla. Justifications began to hiss through his mind: This community would be better off without this dangerous young man; better to end him now, before he could mature, perhaps become more powerful; this whole, changed world would be that much safer, that much less violent, without Trent Donnelly in it.

The blackness boiled up around his feet and raced up his body, eager to be unleashed. Jack took in a deep breath of air, then...

Stopped.

His eyes found Gideon, where he was still clinging to Owen's back. His small face was ghostly white, his eyes otherworldly blue, and the terrible grief twisting his childish features stopped Jack, stopped him cold. Trent was his big brother. As surely as Jack loved his younger sister, no matter how long they'd been apart, no matter the wounds they'd dealt each other, Gideon loved Trent, faults, cruelty, selfishness and all. Jack could *feel* the bond between them. He had the power to sever that bond, and little Gideon knew it. Knew it, and was already mourning.

What had this angel-touched child *seen*?

Please. Jack sent the simple prayer to the heavens. *Please. Guide me.*

A cool calmness seemed to open up around him, giving him time to think, time to consider. His eyes returned to Piper, and he remembered what she'd said on a beautiful summer evening not so long ago: *We're all one. When one of us suffers, we all suffer. When we love, when we lift each other up, we are all lifted.* He thought about what she'd *seen* when she had killed the man named Josh, and realized she'd learned what she'd learned because of her intuitive ability. Because of her willingness to see herself honestly, without excuses or rationalizations.

And just like that, he knew. What he needed to do had always been with him. He had the sensation that a lifetime of experience and preparation had led to this very moment. He had just enough time to send a wry prayer to God that there would be life beyond this night, life with Piper's kisses in it, life with another chance to be the brother he always should have been. Then, he acted.

Jack stepped right in front of Trent and dropped his shields completely.

Words had always been Jack's gift, but the pain was something he couldn't begin to describe. He felt as if some great creature had torn his chest open with long claws and bitten into his beating heart. How could one young man harbor so much misery? How did he function, trapped under the net of such paralyzing fear? Trent's eyes met his, filled with the agony of a young creature whose needs had never been met, and perhaps never could have been. Jack had encountered kids like Trent before, kids whose need yawned black and deep, a bottomless pit of dissatisfaction and emptiness. The only thing that could fill Trent, Jack knew, was love. And that love had to come from Trent himself.

All Jack could do was understand, absorb and then reflect that pain, channeling it away from the others. The world narrowed to his connection with Trent, to a dark tunnel he feared he might never escape. When he couldn't endure another moment, he sucked in a lungful of air and bellowed Trent's pain to the sky. Then, the blackness became complete.

What might have been days or minutes later, he opened his eyes.

Piper and Owen were hovering over him, their frantic faces backed by a starry sky. "I'm on the ground," Jack said inanely. He struggled to sit up, but found himself held down on both sides. "Why am I on the ground?"

Piper and Owen looked at each other, then back down at him. "We're not sure what happened," Owen said, "But now that we know you're alive, we think it might have been a good thing."

"Somehow, you stopped him. He collapsed at the same time you did and his people hustled him out of here," Piper said. Her color had improved, though Jack still wouldn't call it good. "You broke his hold on us, but I don't know how."

This time, when Jack tried to sit up, they helped him. "I do," he said quietly.

He looked around. Reggie and his men were sitting up, looking exhausted but otherwise unharmed. Just behind Owen stood little Gideon, his hands clutched together over his chest, his eyes shining with wonder. "So do I."

Jack held his arms out, and Gideon scrambled into them, curling against Jack's chest. Jack closed his eyes, resting his cheek on Gideon's grungy, pungent hair, allowing the little boy's gift to fill him with light and strength. "I surprised you, didn't I?"

"You did!" Gideon looked up at him, then reached to rest his hands on Jack's jaw. With his touch, Jack caught a flash-forward glimpse, to a future where this sweet-hearted boy would become as dear as life and breath, a son of his heart. "You didn't kill him," he whispered. "What I saw didn't come true. It doesn't always have to come true!" He laughed, the sound pure, care-free little boy. "I don't always have to *see*!"

"This is touchin' and all," Reggie drawled, rising to his feet and gesturing to his men to do the same. "But unless you want to be here when Trent and his zombies regroup, I suggest we save the snuggling for later and get the hell out of here." He started towards the bikes, moving slowly at first, then with greater confidence. "We'll take you as far as the main road, then you're on your own. Looks like me and the boys burned a few bridges, so we're out of here."

Owen stood, then reached down to help Jack up. The whole world performed a graceful spiral, then two, then stabilized. Gideon clung like a monkey when Owen tried to take him, and Jack shook his head. "I'm okay. I've got him."

Piper picked her rifle up from where she'd dropped it, and they all followed Reggie. "We'll head to Onawa," she said, strength and determination returning to her voice, as surely as the pink had returned to her cheeks. "We'll pick up Ed and Rosemary, then I think we should make tracks. I just have this feeling." She rubbed the center of her chest, and her worried eyes met Jack's. "I'm afraid we wouldn't walk away a second time."

Jack settled onto his motorcycle with Gideon in front of him. They fired the bikes up, then followed the taillights of Reggie's pickup out of town, headed south towards Highway 30. Gideon craned his head to look back as Maple River slipped away behind them, an expression both wistful and fearful on his face.

When they reached the intersection that would take them back west to Onawa, Reggie slowed. He lifted an arm in farewell, then gunned his pickup, heading east towards a sky that was starting to lighten with approaching dawn. Jack looked down at Gideon, and once again, the little boy's eyes were sad and far away.

"What is it?"

Gideon sighed. His little hands knotted in Jack's t-shirt with surprising strength. "You let him in. You let him all the way in. Piper was right," he said, so softly Jack had to strain to hear. "Next time you see Trent, you won't walk away."

FIFTEEN
Cass: Milwaukee, Wisconsin

"Ready about!" Luc called from his position at the tiller, and Cass hopped to. She checked the area around them, then held tight to the freed jib sheet and called back.

"All clear!"

"Coming about!"

Holding the port sheet, Cass slowly released the starboard side, allowing the jib to fill on the opposite side. At the same time, Luc pulled the main sheet in and turned the bow of the boat into the wind. As the boat turned, Cass pulled the jib sheet in and made it fast. The sails flapped loudly until they were pulled in tight; with more speed and efficiency than she ever could have managed, Luc adjusted tiller and mainsail until they were once more flying along close-hauled. They'd been sailing into the wind since dawn, beating south along the Wisconsin shore, and no matter how many times they successfully completed a tack, she marveled at how easy he made it look.

Before she'd started taking lessons from Luc, she'd thought she had a handle on the basics. Veda had taught her about points of sail, how to tack and jibe, reef sails and heave to. She was even a fair hand at backing out of irons. Ten minutes into her first lesson with Luc, her ignorance felt like a flashing neon sign, complete with prominent down-arrow, hanging right over her head. He and his younger brother Bastian, who sometimes helped with the lessons, knew more about sailing than she could learn in a lifetime. Like their father, the boys had been born for water, wind and sail.

Cass had become something of a Nolette family project. In spite of Veda's predictions, she had no intention of asking Luc along on her journey. As her lessons had progressed, however, Luc's father had gotten involved, and the next thing Cass knew, both Gavin and Luc were insisting on accompanying her. From there, the plan evolved into leaving her little boat behind in favor of Luc's first-born ship-building project, a 40' custom-built sloop christened the *Grindylow*.

"We can't take your ugly little abomination," Gavin had reasoned with her, as he and Luc had exchanged smirks. Cass's beloved and homely MacGregor was a source of mockery for all the Nolette men. "It's just not big enough to be stable in rough seas. At the very least, you'll be dealing with heavy chop around the Porte des Morts. Besides, there's no way of knowing how many people we might be bringing back. If we do find your brother, chances are good he won't be alone, and I doubt he'd want to leave his companions behind. Can't safely carry that many passengers in your sad little dinghy."

So she'd been outmaneuvered, and she could admit she wasn't really sorry about that. The *Grindylow* was an elegant and lovely lady, and sailing with Gavin and Luc would be exponentially instructive. The plan was to sail from Beaver Island west towards the northern tip of Wisconsin's Door peninsula, a finger of land named for the treacherous passage into Green Bay. They wouldn't have to pass through the Porte des Morts – Death's Door – but the area had claimed hundreds of ships over the years with its notoriously unpredictable conditions. From there, they would sail south, keeping the Wisconsin shoreline in sight and harboring each night until they reached Milwaukee's McKinley Marina. Both Gavin and Luc were familiar with the marina from the lake side, and Cass knew the area from the shore, thanks to her time on Milwaukee's streets. With reasonably favorable conditions and the option to motor sail when necessary, they were anticipating a four or five-day trip.

Once there, the plan got more seat-of-the pants. Pewaukee lay about 20 miles inland from Milwaukee, and they intended to walk it. Again, conditions were everything. They could make it in a single grueling day if nothing went wrong and no detours were necessary. Cass figured on at least a full day to rest up when they reached her home – time enough to take care of her parents' remains if possible, and to leave a message for Jack – before they turned around and did it all in reverse.

And then, life had intervened.

Just two days before their planned departure, Maddie, Gavin's wife, had fainted dead away in the midst of preparing dinner for her family. When she'd come to, she'd blamed the episode on the mysterious fatigue that had gripped her the last few weeks, insisting she felt fine. But the next morning, according to Luc's account, she'd eaten three bites of scrambled eggs, then sprinted for the door, vomiting up her breakfast on the kitchen herbs she grew just off her back porch. Luc's face had been the deep, rich red of mortification as he told the story at Cass and Veda's kitchen table later that same day.

"She's pregnant." He closed his eyes, and shook his head. "Dad ran – and I really do mean ran, I think he's lost his mind – into town and traded for a pregnancy test, so you know everyone on the island knows. Mom keeps giggling, then crying, then giggling again. She and my dad – God, it's just awful." His voice alternated between a simpering falsetto and a rumbling bass as he imitated his parents. "'I told you to get snipped! Didn't I tell you to get snipped?' Then he says, 'You said you counted the days – how did this happen?' and then she laughs and says, 'How? Are you really asking me *how* this happened?'" Luc shuddered. "It's just so *wrong*."

Cass had left Luc drinking one of Veda's "restorative" teas and had gone over to see the Nolettes. Happily, she hadn't needed all the arguments she'd stacked up as she had walked: Gavin wasn't willing to leave Maddie under the circumstances. When Cass had said she'd just go back to her original plan and sail her ugly little boat solo on the course they'd planned, Gavin and Maddie had exchanged glances.

"We thought you might say that, but before you decide, you should talk it over with Luc," Maddie had said. "Solo trips are never smart if you have an alternative. If he still wants to go, he has our blessing." Then, she had raised an eyebrow at Cass. All four of the Nolettes were exceptionally adept at reading the emotions of others, with Maddie and Luc being the most sensitive. "It can be hard for a young woman to accept help, especially when she's used to making her own way. Harder than just doing it alone. Luc is as steady and reliable as they come, and he has sailed farther than what you're planning, many times. His instinct is to help people, which makes me very proud. Accepting his help is a gift to him and a lesson for you, I think."

Which was how Cass found herself on the deck of the *Grindylow* as they approached McKinley Marina. Luc started the motor, the low, churning rumble a startling, man-made sound after four days of snapping sails and lapping water. He kept the boat pointed into the wind while Cass got busy lowering both the jib and the mainsail. As they had traveled down the coast, they had switched back and forth between helm and crew, so Cass could learn both sets of responsibilities. Luc never stopped teaching, and as he had said, over and over, she needed to know how to make decisions, not just obey orders. For now, though, she was grateful beyond words that she'd taken his mother's advice and that he was the one calling the shots.

They rounded the breakwater and entered the mouth of the harbor with Cass perched on the bow of the boat watching for obstacles. Like everywhere else they'd stopped, the marina appeared to be deserted, and Cass looked over her shoulder to see if Luc was picking anything up she should know about. Under her tutelage, he'd learned to expand his intuitive capabilities. He always knew when someone was watching now, and he was getting better by the day at discerning what that person's emotions or intentions were. In answer to her silent question, Luc shrugged.

"Nobody around, as far as I can tell."

Cass nodded and turned back to her task. To the south, the slips were more than half empty; the plague had impacted this area in the early spring, just as people would have been getting their boats out of winter storage. Of those occupied slips, many held sunken or half-submerged vessels, testament to the destructive power of a winter spent in Lake Michigan ice. Cass alternated between checking the water ahead of them for debris and trying to count boats that still looked seaworthy. She came up with six. Once again, she turned back to Luc, holding up six fingers. He held up four, and repeated his shrug.

As they'd agreed ahead of time, Luc steered them to the dock adjoining the boat launch rather than looking for an empty slip. Someone familiar with the area would instantly note their presence, but, they had reasoned, someone familiar with the area wouldn't be fooled if they tried to hide in amongst the scattering of boats, either. If they returned to find Luc's boat missing or damaged, they would commandeer anything still floating and punt.

As gently as a mother laying a baby in a cradle, Luc tucked the boat in next to the dock. He kept the motor running while Cass stepped onto the dock and began making the boat fast, staggering a little as she found her land legs again. When they were securely tied up, he cut the motor. Cass started straightening and rolling the sails while Luc jogged to the adjoining docks to check out the condition of the other boats they'd spotted. He returned in time to help her with the mainsail.

"Three of them look good, and we could make do with a fourth, but only if we can get the pumps running. Only one of them looks like someone's been on board recently." He pointed to a 45-foot catamaran, rolling gently at the end of the northernmost dock. "That one. I think someone might be living on it, but there's no one there now."

When they had finished stowing the sails, they stood together on the dock, listening to the soft sounds of land. Gulls called, and the wind rose and fell in soft whistles, making the halyards ring against the mast. The soft haze didn't do much to soften the punch of the mid-summer sun, and still they stood there, staring at the dark outlines of the high-rises in downtown Milwaukee. Finally, Cass broke the silence.

"Well, I'll go ahead and admit it. I'm scared to death to walk away from this boat. You?"

Luc's head dropped forward, and he took a deep breath. "Jesus, yes. I know what I'm doing on the lake. Trouble comes up, I can usually find a way to handle it. Out there?" He gestured to the silent, dead city before them. "I'm afraid I'll be worse than useless."

Cass forced her voice to lightness and hopped back on the *Grindylow*. "Well, I'll be sure to point it out to you, if you are. How many times did you make me capsize that skiff and recover from it? What? You didn't keep count?" She drilled him with a look before she headed below. "I did."

He joined her a few minutes later, and they loaded their backpacks in silence, taking most of what they'd brought with them. If the boat was looted, at least they wouldn't lose much. Cass changed her deck shoes for her hiking boots, filled the water bladder in her back pack, resettled the baseball cap she never seemed to take off these days, then picked up the stout hiking stick she'd borrowed from Veda. She turned just as Luc attached a sling to his bow and adjusted it over his shoulder. Her surprise must have shown on her face, because he turned red and gestured to the bow.

"My dad made me swear I'd carry it. We don't use guns – well, me and Bastian don't. Dad has one, but he hasn't taught us to use it yet. I told him I'd feel like some kind of Katniss Everdeen wannabe, but he insisted."

"I think it's a good idea, actually. We're not overloaded with food. And if we run into trouble with people, maybe they'll see it and think twice."

"That's exactly what he said," Luc grumbled. "I still feel like a hick, carrying my big scary bow into the big scary city."

Cass made a sympathetic sound but didn't share what she was really thinking: That the city was probably going to be scarier than he'd even imagined. On her trip down the Michigan coast, if she'd sensed danger, she'd simply sailed on. She hadn't ventured into a city the size of Milwaukee, and she had no idea what dangers they might encounter. To her, Luc's bow seemed like a damn fine idea, especially because she was carrying nothing more threatening than a really big stick and the hunting knife Gavin had pressed on her. Veda had tried to convince her to carry a pistol – there were several people on the island who owned one and would teach her the basics – but Cass had refused. It simply wasn't in her to aim a weapon at another person, even if her life was at stake.

They left the cabin, double-checked that the boat was properly secured, then stepped once more onto the dock. As badly as Cass wanted to hesitate yet again, she didn't allow herself to, striding purposefully towards shore with Luc a half-step behind her. She was so preoccupied with faking a courageous attitude, she didn't notice the spirit until it drifted right in front of them. She stopped abruptly, and Luc had to dance to the side to avoid plowing her over.

"What the –?" He followed the direction of her gaze, then looked back at her. "What is it?" His voice dropped to a hoarse whisper. "Is it...is it...oh, Jesus, is it a ghost?"

Cass reached over and gave his shoulder a reassuring pat. "Don't worry. This is my turf. Just caught me off-guard, that's all."

Swiftly, she stilled her mind, centered, prayed for protection, then made contact. "We're just passing through.

Is there something we need to know, something you want to tell us?"

She's late. She's never late. Why isn't she here yet?

Cass stifled a sigh as her fears were confirmed. This wasn't a visitor from the world of spirit. This was an earthbound spirit, a lost soul. What had once been a young, robust man was now a frantic, frightened echo. He stared at her, radiating anguish and confusion.

She's late. We were supposed to go sailing, have dinner on the boat. Why isn't she here?

An exceptionally articulate lost soul – it was unusual to hear such complete thoughts, even more rare when the soul was confused. His voice boomed in Cass's head, making her wince. She didn't ask the obvious question; instead, she asked, very gently, "What's your name?" After a long silence, the spirit's confusion intensified.

I don't know.

"It's okay. I'll help you. Tell me what your mom called you. Hear her voice calling you, maybe to come in for supper, or to wake up for school, and tell me what name she used."

She felt the ghost's relief as a lightening in the air all around them, as if they'd been enclosed in a noxious fog without really being aware of it.

Bryce.

"Bryce. Do you remember getting sick, Bryce? Do you remember hearing news of the plague and heading out here to the marina, maybe? Maybe you had a headache, a cough, or just a little fever?"

Rage and sorrow thickened the air. *I can't die. I run triathlons! I never get sick!*

"I know, Bryce, sweetie. It's not fair. You took care of yourself, did everything right. You were in the prime of your life. A terrible number of young, healthy, strong people died." She paused. "But I need you to listen to me very carefully. Your soul goes on. Your soul is talking to me right now. Bryce, hon, your body did not survive. But your soul is eternal."

Rage, softer this time, and sorrow so deep it made her bones ache with the cold. *This is it, then? I'll just be alone here forever? This is terrible. I don't want this.*

"No, that's not how it is at all. Your loved ones are all waiting for you, waiting to welcome you to the other side." Cass reached for the connection and began naming them for him. "Your mom, your dad, your twin sisters. And a beautiful young lady. She says her name is Jenna?"

How can I get to them? I don't believe in an after-life. The worms crawl in, the worms crawl out. You're just done. Is this some kind of Heaven bullshit? Because I'd rather haunt this marina than sit on some damn cloud playing a harp.

Cass stifled her impatience. Helping earthbound spirits was not her specialty, and she wished she knew a faster way. She and Luc had a long distance to travel and they were wasting daylight, but she couldn't walk away from this. "Humor me for a moment, Bryce. Just let your mind float away from all those beliefs. Let your mind be free of this marina, of Lake Michigan, of all the physical world around you. Reach, with your heart and your mind, for your family. Picture them. Reach for Jenna. The veil is like a curtain, and they're waiting right on the other side. Just move the curtain aside and step through."

The veil. That is so hokey.

Cass gritted her teeth. "Just give it a try, Bryce my man."

The ghost's joy was a burst of light so brilliant it made her stagger back a step. She heard his voice, calling to his family, the peace and relief in it, and one last fading echo. *So beautiful...*

Cass blinked. She blinked again, rubbing at her eyes, but the spots remained. She was aware of Luc, then, hovering near her elbow. "Gonna need a minute for my vision to clear."

"Is it gone? Its name was Bryce? Did it tell you that? Was it good or evil? Were you scared?"

Cass held up a hand, stopping the deluge. "I'll answer your questions, but first, I need to get my shields up. At this rate, we'll make Pewaukee in about..." She turned to look behind her. They'd made it about 25 feet away from the *Grindylow.* "Fifteen years. Give me a second, okay?"

Cass closed her eyes and sank deep into her center. She envisioned a cone of pure white light, benevolent, impenetrable, cascading from the crown of her head to her feet. "Divine Guides and all the angels," she murmured. "Please protect us. Please help us pass without interference from the restless and earthbound dead. I will do what I can to help them whenever I can, but our journey to my home needs to be swift. I ask that this be done, if it serves the greater good. So be it, and so it is."

She opened her eyes to find Luc staring at her again, his black eyes shining with more than a little yearning puppy-love, which she thought he'd left behind. As many times as she'd found herself unexpectedly underwater during his lessons, she'd long since stopped being shy about evacuating water from her nasal cavities, enthusiastically when necessary. That, along with the perpetual drowned-rat look she'd been sporting, tended to wreak havoc on a crush.

"You can talk to God and the angels, too?"

Cass rolled her eyes and slugged him on the arm, none too lightly. "So can you, doofus. Everybody can. It's called 'prayer.' Come on, let's go."

Luc hurried to catch up to her. "That prayer – it didn't sound like the church prayers I've heard. It sounded like Tolkien, or Robert Jordan, or Patrick Rothfuss."

"I was a preacher's daughter. I grew up listening to beautiful, lavish language." Cass hunched her shoulders forward self-consciously. No way was she going to tell Mr. Literature her prayers were heavily influenced by the fantasy role-playing video games that had been her favorite down-time indulgence in the time before.

They reached the end of the dock and headed through the parking lot of the marina. Here and there, vehicles were parked haphazardly, sometimes with bodies inside, sometimes standing open, with human remains scattered about. Passing close to one such vehicle, Luc paused with a soft exclamation of dismay.

"Cass, look at this. The long bones have been split, to get to the marrow inside."

"Split by what?" She'd been so concerned about the humans they'd encounter, she hadn't given a thought to other types of predators.

Luc leaned closer, although he was obviously reluctant to touch what had once been a person. "Dog or coyote, probably. Maybe a wolf, but I don't think so, not this far south. It could be a coywolf – a coyote-wolf hybrid. They've been spotted in most of the northern states. Pretty good size, whatever it was." He straightened and looked around, shifting his bow into a more accessible position. "We need to add that to our list of things to keep an eye out for."

Cass stifled a sarcastic, "Fabulous." Snark was not going to help. She led them away from Luc's discovery and out onto the city streets, squinting up at the position of the sun. "It's mid-morning or just past - we've got to push hard, if we want to make Pewaukee by nightfall."

South on Lincoln Memorial Drive to pick up Brady Street via a little pedestrian walkway, then north on Warren Avenue, and they were at the Milwaukee River in a matter of minutes. Other than the abandoned cars, overgrown garden beds, and some obviously looted businesses, this area looked much as she remembered it. They scooted across the river on the dam just above the 690 Reservoir, then jogged up a steep set of stone stairs. What had once been a large, mowed open space in the middle of a shopping area was now a tangle of chest-high weeds, and they stuck to the streets instead of cutting across, picking up North Avenue. Cass paused and looked around.

"Okay, make sure you've got your bearings, in case you need to get back on your own. We'll follow North Avenue until we intersect with Lisbon, remember, then angle up and catch 190."

"Which will take us straight into Pewaukee," Luc said impatiently. "I know. We only went over it like 27,000 times." He hunched his shoulders and looked around. "Do you feel like we're being watched?"

"I don't," Cass answered honestly, "But I've got my shields up, thick as I can make them." Even so, the presence of the dead was nearly overwhelming. They were everywhere, thick as fog to her senses. "We need to go with your instincts on this. Do we need to re-route? Go back the way we came?"

Luc took a deep breath, and shut his eyes for a moment. "No," he said after a moment, his forehead creased in concentration. "I'm getting...curiosity. Some fear. Whoever it is, they don't want to meet us any more than we want to meet them. They're like...bears. They *feel* a lot like bears. They don't want to confront us, but they'll fight if they have to." He opened his eyes. "Let's just move through as quick as we can. I'll let you know if I pick up something more hostile."

Onward they went, swinging south around overgrown Kilbourn Park. Sometimes, they would walk for several blocks, and the only sign that the plague had passed this way was overgrown weeds in the sidewalk cracks. Then, they might travel through five straight blocks which had been leveled by fire. They crossed I-43, which was a parking lot as far as they could see in both directions, and after an hour and a half, they reached Lisbon Avenue.

Cass paused. Heat was bouncing up off the tarmac until she felt like she was being roasted from the feet up. Not a breath of wind stirred to relieve the oppressive humidity. "Do you want to rest?"

"No." Luc was as saturated with sweat as she was. "Let's just go on. All these buildings – how did people stand it? Makes my skin crawl. And it's too still. I think we're in for some weather later on today."

"Spoken like an island boy." Cass re-adjusted her pack straps and took a long drink of water. "We should stop in the next hour or so to eat something, though. Let me know if you see someplace that seems particularly safe and secure, okay?"

As it turned out, it was Cass who spotted their rest stop. They were getting close to 190 when a cemetery began to unfold on the north-east side of the street, deep and green and blessedly quiet from a psychic perspective. Cass automatically looked both ways – they'd been traveling on the south side of Lisbon – then laughed at herself and jogged across. She hopped the chain-link fence and bee-lined for the deep shade under the huge old trees. The tops of marble gravestone were just visible above the tall grass. Luc had stopped short of the fence.

He called out to her. "Uh, seriously? You want to stop *here*?"

"I so totally do. Just c'mon – trust me!"

She couldn't hear him, but the look on his face and the movement of his lips told her he was grousing under his breath. She swung her pack off and flopped down on the ground under one of the beautiful old trees, luxuriating in what felt like air-conditioning after hours in the sun. Moments later, Luc joined her, but he didn't take his pack off, nor did he sit down.

"Why a cemetery?" He looked around, eyes just a little wild, and shuddered. "This place has to be crawling with ghosts."

"Not even one." She sighed, driven to be honest, though he'd never know the difference. "Okay, there's one. Fellow died mowing the lawn just on the other side of those trees, but he's it, as far as I can tell. Have a seat. I promise you won't be haunted while you eat your lunch."

He didn't bother to keep his grousing under his breath this time. "I don't mind ghosts when they're someone I know, I guess, but these are strangers. Ghosts of strangers. Of all the places you could pick. If this is some kind of revenge for making you capsize your skiff so many times, let me remind you that you asked me to teach you, and –"

He broke off when Cass leaned over and stuffed one of his mother's cookies in his mouth. They both chewed in silence for a while. Then Cass handed him some venison jerky and went over the basics. "Ghosts don't usually hang out in cemeteries, contrary to popular belief. Usually, you find them where they lived or died, or associated with a person they were close to. And to answer your question from before, no, I wasn't afraid that Bryce was an 'evil' entity. Truly evil spirits are rare." She grimaced. "Though

I attracted my share of troubled souls when I was a teenager."

"But how did you know the difference? You said Zeb was just visiting, that he wasn't lost. How did you know Bryce was different?"

"He'd forgotten his name, for starters. Veda told me that can happen; she said it was important to reconnect the restless dead with their names, if possible. For Bryce, the idea of dying was so unacceptable, he just refused to believe it. He got stuck on the last day of his life and kept trying to make it come out the way he wanted it to."

"So the dead can convince themselves of things?"

"Yep. Just like the living. And as long as we're on the subject, they don't become all-knowing and wise, even after they've reckoned with the light. If your Aunt Sue gave you bad advice when she was living, you probably shouldn't listen to her when she's dead."

That got a chuckle out of Luc, and it made Cass realize how long it had been since she'd heard him really laugh. This was a grim and frightening task, and she felt both guilty and grateful that he'd undertaken it with her. They finished eating, then stood in the shade, contemplating the gathering clouds in the western sky. A gusting breeze had picked up while they ate, refreshing, but pushing ahead of it the smell of rain. Cass took off her baseball cap and stuffed it in her pack, then re-did her mess of a ponytail, enjoying the way the breeze cooled her sweaty head. She secured the rain cover on her backpack before resettling the straps on her shoulders.

"I guess if we get rained on, we might smell better."

Her quip earned another chuckle from Luc, and they left the cemetery, walking briskly side-by-side. "I don't know," he answered. "I know I didn't have what most people think of as a 'typical' upbringing, but I always thought it was weird, how mainland girls wore so many different layers of scent. Their hair stuff, lotion, then perfume. It's like their real scent was something to be ashamed of."

"You know, I've been thinking something similar about the end of disposable razors. What are we all going to do? Shave with a straight razor? Scavenge some Brazilian wax? Or," she clutched her chest dramatically, "Get used to the fact that grown women have hair on their bodies?"

Luc's cheeks flushed, but he laughed. "The end of civilization as we know it." He was quiet for a few steps, then spoke again, thoughtfully this time. "Does it ever seem to you that some things are better, because of the plague? I mean," he hurried to clarify, "Not that so many people died. That part is terrible. But maybe we'll be done with stupid things like too much artificial this or that, like scent and additives in our food. Maybe a world where girls have body hair and that's just normal will be better."

Hearing how closely his thoughts mirrored what Cass often thought reinforced the connection that had been growing between them through all the days of working and sailing and learning together. In the time before, Cass had enjoyed casual friendships and the occasional romantic interlude. People came and went in her life, with Veda as her only necessary constant. Now, she could see how she'd held people at arm's length. Safer, to keep relationships surface-only. No chance of rejection that way. She knew, from counseling her clients, that she had "family of origin" issues, that she felt abandoned by her parents and her brother, and had limited others' access to her heart as a result.

But now, survival was forcing people to work together whether they liked each other or not. To do that, they needed to really know each other, strengths, weaknesses and all. Relationships were no longer temporary or disposable. It was so much harder. And so much richer. Cass looked over at Luc as they walked and realized that she might very well know this young man all the rest of her days on the Earth. She'd watch him grow and mature. She'd meet his new little brother or sister, and watch that child grow. In all likelihood, she would build unique and lasting relationships with every person on the island – even the elusive "Mr. Smith." The insight made her smile and also made her heart clutch with tenderness and fear. People could be gone in a blink. Everyone left living knew that.

"I hope you're right, Luc. I hope at least some things will be better. I really want to think we didn't lose so much and gain nothing in return."

Luc nodded. "My mom thinks the plague was Nature's way of forcing us all to evolve." He nudged her with his elbow as they walked. "You know, those of us who weren't already psychic. Anyway, she thinks the plague was the Earth's way of saving herself. She lightened the load, and at the same time, made it so we would understand each other better and maybe live with more care on the planet."

"That makes as much sense as anything." Cass looked around, and knew that much of what she was seeing would fall into unrecognizable ruin in the next few years. Not only people had been lost, but art, literature, music, technology, and myriad other expressions of human creation and ingenuity. The living would retain what they could, remember what they could, but in so many ways, they would be starting over. A brutal lesson for Earth's children, to be sure. She tightened the straps of her backpack and moved forward with greater purpose, suddenly not wanting to talk. "We'd better pick it up."

Luc fell in behind her, and they pushed on through the afternoon. Occasionally, gusts of wind brought a few drops of rain, but the bulk of the storm clouds swung to the north of them. Not until they crossed the Menominee River did they see evidence of living people. On the long, sloping hill to the west of the river, on what had once been a golf course, three tents had been set up, and small campfires smoldered amid long lines of drying fish. The unmistakable carcass of a zebra hung from a tree, headless and field-dressed. Cass and Luc exchanged startled glances.

"That's right – the zoo wasn't that far south of here." Cass looked around. "There has to be someone close by, tending those fires."

Luc, too, was looking all around them. He frowned. "I don't feel attention on us. But I don't think we should stop to chat, either. Just a hunch."

"Good enough for me." Cass closed her eyes for a moment and took in a long, slow breath. The presence of the dead was especially heavy here, and she wondered if these people were unknowingly holding lost souls near. Even through her cone of white light, the confusion, hostility and despair pulled at her spirits, dragged her thoughts into the dark. She shook herself, and gestured for Luc to take the lead. "I don't want to freak you out, but there's a lot of pressure here from the lost ones. Just keep following this street and keep your eyes peeled for trouble on the physical plane. I'll just follow for a while, okay?"

Luc's eyes snapped wide, then slid from side to side as if the ghosts were sneaking up on them from behind...which, in fact, they were. One of these days, Cass would have to ask how they sensed her, how they knew she could sense them. Impatiently, she gestured again, infected by their urgency. "Chop chop. Not a spot for lingering."

They double-timed it across the bridge, past a gutted Target and a whole string of burned-out fast food places. Cass kept her eyes fixed on Luc's backpack. As she walked, she sang the doxology she'd learned as a child under her breath. The short hymn acted as a mantra, focused and soothed her. A memorial garden stretched along the south side of the road, and Luc looked at her over his shoulder, tilting his head towards the arched gate. "Need to rest?"

"Nope. Onward."

The farther west they walked, the more upscale the businesses became. What houses they could see also increased in size, many of them sporting tennis or basketball courts. Cass estimated they'd come fourteen or fifteen miles when 190 curved gently to the south to cross the Fox River. Suddenly, Luc stopped. He made a startled sound, and his hand shot out to grip her upper arm.

"Cass! Look!"

She followed the direction of his gaze. There, in the waving grass on the bank of the gentle little river, crouched a little girl. She was naked except for a pair of filthy, lime-green shorts, and her white-blonde hair was a tangled nimbus around her head. She was eating a fish raw. As if she sensed their eyes on her, she stood abruptly, dropping the fish. For a frozen second, they all stared at each other. Then, she was gone, the top of her head barely visible as she ran through the undulating grass.

"No! We won't hurt you! Please come back!" Cass looked at Luc. "She must be alone. We can't leave her."

Without a word, Luc vaulted the guard rail and ran after her. Cass followed, tripping several times when the grass snagged around her ankles, falling flat-out once and startling a pair of herons into flight. Ahead of her, she could hear Luc calling first to the girl, then back to Cass.

"Where are you? Hurry up!"

Cass blundered out of the grass and into a parking lot, breathless. Across the street, a chain link fence and a dark scoreboard marked an abandoned baseball park. "Did you see where she went?"

Luc nodded, pointing to a group of houses on the other side of the ballpark before he took off again. "I didn't see which one she went into, but I think I can track her. Hurry – she's so fast!"

Her hiking boots pounded the pavement and her backpack bounced painfully until she tightened the straps on the fly. At some point, she'd dropped Veda's walking stick. They ran down the asphalt path separating the overgrown ball fields, emerging on the other side to more grass and trees bordering a once-affluent neighborhood. Luc scanned for a moment, then pointed. "There."

He jogged through the grass towards a Tuscan-style home, following a trail too faint for Cass to see. They passed a swimming pool filled with brackish, black water, and slowed to a walk. Cass was breathing like a bellows and coated from head to toe with sweat in the thick, afternoon air. She swiped at her face with her shoulder, and put her hand on Luc's arm.

"Let me go first. Maybe she'll be less scared of a woman."

Luc nodded and pointed towards a door that led to a small courtyard. A no-longer functional fountain in the middle of the space had been planted with vegetables, though the bed looked overgrown and neglected. Cass moved towards the door into the house, which stood ajar. She stepped inside, and gave her eyes a moment to adjust before calling out.

"Hello? Little girl? We just want to help you, I promise." Cass paused and looked around. The kitchen had been a beauty, with vibrant, Mexican-themed tile and deep blue walls, but it was a disaster now. Garbage overflowed everywhere – empty boxes and cans of food, and fish bones. Lots of fish bones. They crunched underfoot as she took another step forward. "Hello?"

"You stay right where you are!"

Cass gasped and spun to the right. A woman stood in the shadows of a doorway, a pistol wobbling in her hand. Behind her, the little girl had both arms wrapped around one of the woman's legs. The woman tried to take a step forward, then swore and swatted at the little girl's hands.

"For Christ's sake, Annalise, let go!" She shoved the little girl away from her, then straightened and pointed the pistol at Cass again. "What the hell you want?"

Cass held her hands out, the universal sign for "Please don't hurt me." The woman's hair was as blonde and wild as the little girl's, and there was something very, very off about her eyes. "I just wanted to make sure your little girl was okay – we – I thought she was alone." Instinct made her conceal Luc's presence. "You said her name is Annalise? That's such a pretty name."

The woman squinted at her. "You can't have her. Told you people already, she's just fine. For fuck's sake, give a kid a little independence, a little responsibility, and it's everybody's business, how you parent. So you can stick your foster care where the sun don't shine."

"Ah." Cass had no idea what to do. "I'm sure you're a wonderful parent." She cast around desperately. Maybe if she could get the woman talking, she'd at least lower the pistol. "Your kitchen is beautiful – I love the colors."

"Not my kitchen. Well." She switched hands with the pistol, then smirked, then laughed, an awful, cackling sound. "Guess it is my kitchen now, huh? I worked here, before. Cleaned for them. They're both dead." She waved the pistol vaguely over her head, making Cass flinch. "Died in their beds, and they can rot there, far as I care. Always paid late, and the husband was always trying to grab my ass." She cackled again. "Karma's a bitch, huh? I hope he's getting his sick ass grabbed by some big, hairy con in hell. Serve him right."

Cass just stared at her hopelessly. This woman's grasp on reality was, at best, occasional. The conditions she and her daughter were living in were animalistic, and all around them, Cass could feel the dark pressure of a very strong, very angry lost soul. Not knowing what else to do, she shifted her gaze to the little girl.

"Hi," she said softly. "My name is Cass. I bet I scared you, huh?"

Annalise stared back at her for a moment, then nodded, the gesture so slight, Cass barely saw it.

"Did you catch all these fish?" Another tiny nod. "You must be a much better fisherwoman than me – I hardly ever catch anything, and I live on an island. How old are you, sweetie?"

A small, filthy hand splayed out shyly. Five. Another finger from the other hand made six, and Cass had to swallow, again and again. My God, what was she supposed to do? She couldn't leave this little girl here, in this squalor, with a mother who probably had fallen far short of wonderful before the plague and its aftermath unhinged her mind. She returned her gaze to the woman.

"Let me help you," she said softly. "Let me help you both."

The pistol, which had been drooping, jerked up again. "I told you, we don't need help! Don't need foster care, don't need your god damn rehab!" The woman's voice grew even more shrill. "It's not like I'm using now, is it? Can't even find a stupid cigarette in this town no more."

Oh, no. It all came together, then, and Cass understood the nature of the entity she could feel, pressing all around them, malevolent and greedy and gleeful. This woman was an addict, and whoever had latched onto her had been one as well. Veda had told her about this phenomenon. Before Cass's time, Veda had worked in a homeless shelter and had quietly helped similarly burdened addicts free themselves of what Veda labeled, "Cling-ons, not to be confused with 'Klingons,' who are a passionate and warlike people."

Sometimes, especially if an addict died of an overdose, they might linger and attach themselves to a person similarly afflicted, to continue their suffering vicariously. For the first time, Cass felt a spurt of pity for this dirty, unstable creature. She was trying to keep herself and her child alive, she'd lost the drugs she had certainly used as a crutch in easier times, and to make a desperate situation worse, she had this foul entity glomming onto her like a cancer. Cass couldn't fix everything, but she could relieve her of one burden, at least.

"Look, I'm not here to take your daughter or anything like that. I can...well, I can talk to the dead." Cass paused. How to proceed? "I just wonder if...well, if you feel someone close. Someone who died. Someone who was addicted to drugs."

The woman's head snapped back and she scowled. "What kind of nut job are you? Everybody died – didn't you notice? Addicts and goody-two-shoes and everybody in between. Annalise says she sees people on the river sometimes, but I ain't seen them. I ain't seen nobody, not one person but Annalise, since this all started. I don't leave this house. Buncha criminals and packs of dogs out there – that's all that's left."

Okay, on to plan B. Cass made contact with the entity, wincing at the chaotic, disorganized energy. It took her long seconds to even come up with a gender. "A man." A sense of arrogance and entitlement came through, ridiculous and unwarranted self-confidence. "Probably a pretty cocky guy. Loved to party. Good-looking." She was guessing, but the look on the woman's face told her she was getting warmer. Then, clear as a chiming bell, a name came through. "Aaron. His name was Aaron."

And all hell broke loose.

The woman's face contorted with what Cass would always know, from that moment on, was killing rage. Her complexion flushed a deep, brick red, and her eyes were suddenly magnified by tears. Betrayal, desperate loneliness, terror and grief: the woman's emotions sucker-punched Cass and left her gasping.

"That son of a bitch! That rat bastard! He's here?" She looked around wildly. "Aaron, you mother-fucker, you show yourself!" She fired the pistol, two shots in quick succession, the percussions obscenely loud. Cass screamed – she couldn't help it – and dropped to a crouch, hands over her ringing ears.

The woman spun around again, waving the pistol in an erratic arc. "You left me," she howled. "You left me alone to deal with all this, you worthless piece of shit! I needed you!" She started to sob brokenly. "I needed you, God damn you to hell!"

Cass stayed down in her crouch but held her hand out. "Please," she said, her voice nearly strangled by terror. "Please, just put the gun down. I can help you talk to Aaron."

The woman froze, then turned her head slowly, her eyes narrowing on Cass. "How do you know Aaron?" she hissed. Her chest started to heave. "Are you fucking him? Are you one of his whores? Fucking him to score smack?" She brought the pistol up again, this time pointed right between Cass's eyes. "I'll kill you, you dirty –"

Her lips never formed the curse. Instead, they rounded in a soundless "Oh," as she looked down at the bright red flower of blood, blooming in the center of her chest. She staggered, dropped to her knees, then fell forward onto her hands, the pistol clattering as it skittered away across the floor. Cass stared at an arrow, streaked with blood and quivering, lodged in the wall behind where the woman had been standing. She was aware of a curious detachment as her brain tried to come up with logical explanations for what she was seeing. There was an arrow. It was stuck in the wall. A rustle from the doorway behind her made her turn her head. Luc took one halting step, then another, his face a rictus of horror. Was he hurt, too? Should she go to him? What should she do?

The woman fell heavily onto her side, then rolled to her back. Her face spasmed in agony, but still, she made no sound. Cass crawled to her side. The woman held her hand out, and Cass took it automatically. Their eyes met, and Cass felt destiny shift and settle into a new shape around her.

"You," she whispered. "We know each other from the time before time, don't we? You brought me here. Brought us both here."

The woman nodded, her eyes clear of madness and craving, clear of fear. Beside Cass, Luc fell to his knees, much as the woman had. He placed his bow on the floor with great care, his eyes never leaving the woman's face. He was bone-white to the lips, and his whole body was shaking. He looked at Cass, his eyes vague and shocky. "She was going to...I didn't know what to...she would have...I'm sorry..." His gaze turned back to the woman's face. "I'm so sorry, so sorry. Please."

The woman's eyes returned to Cass. She coughed once, spraying blood onto the pretty tile floor. Then she smiled, and Cass saw her spirit lift free of her body. Cass bent her head and prayed, prayed for all of them in that room, the living and the dead. She felt Luc slump against her and begin to sob, awful, ripping sobs, and still she prayed. The woman lingered for no more than a breath, then lifted to the Light, her task complete. The entity called Aaron swirled and pushed a little longer, then drifted away; he might follow the woman into the Light, or he might not. At the moment, Cass didn't really care.

She opened her eyes, and gently laid the woman's hand on the floor. Then she curled an arm around Luc while destiny tore through him. He would be forever changed. Broken and new. Veda had predicted this, and Cass had dismissed it. In a different space, she would have been crippled by the guilt of that, would have convinced herself she could have prevented this if she'd listened, if she hadn't let Luc come with her, if, if, if. Here, so close to the connection with this woman, she knew a path was being forged for both of them that could not have been avoided or denied.

Luc sat up, scrubbing at his face with both hands, chest heaving as he tried to regain control. He looked again at the woman's face, and his chin gave a mighty wobble. He squinted and looked away, then startled and looked around the room frantically.

"Where's the little girl? Cass, what happened to Annalise?"

Cass knew before she looked; the little girl was gone. So was the pistol. They searched the house, then the surrounding homes. They returned to the house, and worked together to dig a grave for the woman in the back yard. Cass rummaged through cupboards until she found a soft, pretty blanket. They lifted her limp body onto the makeshift shroud, trailing a drizzle of blood across the delicate yellow flowers as they moved her. Luc was white again when they had finished. He stood abruptly, then half-ran out the kitchen door. Cass heard the sound of him vomiting, but she didn't say anything when he returned. They wrapped the woman's body, then carried her outside.

He didn't speak until they were standing over the mound of her grave. "We don't even know her name. Will she go to hell? I mean, I don't think she was a good person." Tears filled his eyes and began spilling again. Cass didn't think he was even aware that he was crying. "She seemed like a terrible mom. I'm not saying this to make it okay, what I did. I just want to know if I put her in hell."

Cass slid her arm through his and leaned her head on his shoulder, hugging his arm. "She went to the Light, Luc. I felt it. We all go to the Light, eventually."

He rested his cheek on her hair, twining his hands with hers and gripping tightly. "So there's no hell? And I won't go there for killing her?"

"No, honey, no. I know it doesn't make sense now, and it sounds like I'm just trying to make you feel better, but you two had a contract. You made an agreement, to meet in this way, in this time and place. You served each other as you agreed."

"How can you know that? You can't know that." Luc was fighting sobs again. "I killed someone, Cass! I took her life away! Anyone else would be telling me I was going to hell!"

Cass turned and cupped his face in her palms. "Honey, the only hell is the one you're in right now. The one we make for ourselves here on Earth. The Light is love, and all souls return there. I don't understand why this happened the way it did. I think we both just need to be patient and wait for that path to unfold."

Luc closed his eyes. After a moment, he reached up and gripped her wrists, removing her comforting hands. "I have to find Annalise. We can't leave her here alone."

He searched until well after dark, traveling up and down the river, then searching the neighborhood in ever-widening circles. Cass stayed at the house, in case Annalise returned, and cleaned her mother's blood off the floor. She removed the arrow from the wall and cleaned it, too, not wanting either Luc or Annalise to see, to be reminded. She tidied and straightened both the kitchen and the dining room adjoining it, where Annalise and her mother had obviously been sleeping. She walked to the river for water, and thoroughly watered the flagging garden in the fountain, then walked back and filled every container she could find, lining them up on the kitchen counters.

And then, she was out of things to do. The helplessness that took the place of doing was miserable. When Luc finally returned, silent and muddy, they slept on the plushly carpeted living room floor, avoiding the mouse-infested sofa and loveseat as well as the old death upstairs.

For two days, they searched. Cass had to force Luc to eat, and even then, he seemed too thin and harden before her eyes. Gone was the lean, healthy, strong young man she'd left Beaver Island with; a man with haunted eyes had taken his place. Finally, Cass had to call a halt.

"We're out of food, and your parents are going to be frantic if we delay any longer. We're already going to be a few days past our predictions. She's not coming back, Luc." He tried to turn away from her then, but she caught his arm. She made her voice hard, no matter how badly she wanted to be tender with his wounded, aching heart. "She's not coming back. She's either too scared or too angry. We have to go."

He followed her back to 190 silently, the way he did everything these days. When they were on the highway, he paused once to look back, and Cass saw something take shape in his face. He gazed at the river for long moments, then turned to face her. His voice was determined, matter-of-fact. "I'll never stop looking for her," he said. "Never.

We were wrong, Cass. The world isn't better since the plague, not for people like Annalise or her mom. We've just been lucky."

And so begins a path, Cass thought. They walked through the early morning fog, arriving on the outskirts of Pewaukee before the last of it had even burned off. The familiar places disoriented her, made her realize that she, too, was changed. As they drew closer and closer to her home, she began to feel a stirring excitement. Something was building, something was on the verge.

When they rounded the corner onto Hill Street, she couldn't hold back any longer, and broke into a jog. As everywhere, death was here, and destruction. Houses damaged and looted, bodies in vehicles. But there, oh there. The little white two-story house with the green roof, the pretty, spindly porch railing, the sun room above. She ran up the long, gravel driveway, and the ghosts of all her childhood selves ran alongside her. Gangly legs, flying pigtails, Sunday dresses and skinned knees. The towering walnut tree, the hydrangeas, the little pine tree they always decorated with Christmas lights, so much bigger than she remembered. Cass slowed as she neared the porch, suddenly terrified to go inside. She stood there, hands clutched over her heart, until Luc joined her.

Together, they stood there looking at the front door. Finally, she felt Luc glance at her. "Ah, is everything okay? Are we going inside?"

Cass nodded, and still, she couldn't make her feet move. They were dead. She knew they were dead. But what if? What if? The hope was terrible. She looked at Luc and had to clap her hand over her mouth to stop the sob that burst out. "I haven't been home in almost ten years," she managed. "I can't believe how scared I am. I don't want to go in there."

He picked her hand up and looped it through his arm, patting her clammy fingers. Cass had a flash-forward that made her dizzy for a moment; this sweet boy would always be her friend, steady and true, and would always offer her a strong and capable hand to hold onto. "We came all this way. I'll help you."

They walked up the porch steps – oh, familiar creaks – and through the unlocked front door. Here, the house was remarkably unscathed, no windows in the front living room or dining area broken. The dust was thick and the air was stale, but otherwise, it looked like her mom might come bustling in at any moment, carrying a serving platter with a pretty roast chicken and vegetables for Sunday dinner.

Then, she heard her father singing the doxology.

Cass broke away from Luc and ran down the hallway, bursting through the swinging kitchen door. Her dad was standing at the kitchen sink, and he whirled, startled. Sun streamed in the window behind him, haloing his tawny hair, outlining the familiar shape of his head. Dimly, Cass registered movement out of the corner of her eye, sensed people converging, but her eyes were locked on her dad. Then, she blinked. And launched herself into her brother's arms.

"Jack!"

SIXTEEN
Grace: Rock Ledge Ranch, Colorado Springs, CO

"Scarlett Johansson."

Verity tilted her head to the side, listened for a moment, then beamed at Adam. "Alive and kicking!" Then, her face dimmed, as much as Verity's face ever dimmed. "Ooh, though, in the thick of some trouble... But aren't we all? Next."

Tyler spoke. "Pentatonix."

Before Verity could respond, Adam kicked at the leg of Tyler's tilted-back chair, nearly unseating him. "Which one? You can't do five at once – that's cheating."

"Fine." Tyler shoved at Adam's shoulder, retaliating for the chair-kick. "Shakira, then." They tussled for a moment, pushing and cuffing like little boys. Or, thought Grace, like lovers who didn't think they could be open about their feelings. She walked down the porch steps and headed for her favorite bench beside the irrigation pond, leaving them to their game of "Celebrity Who's Alive and Who's Dead?" The three of them had been playing for days, with Tyler a few points ahead at last reckoning.

The evening was cool in the wake of an afternoon thunderstorm, and Grace wrapped her arms around herself, wishing she'd grabbed her jacket. As if summoned, Persephone rose from her place between Verity's feet and trotted down to join Grace. She leaped lightly to her lap, then curled up against Grace's chest, settling in with a sigh. Grace curled her arms around the little dog and leaned to bury her nose in the musty fur on top of her head, loving her warm weight and familiar scent.

By this time tomorrow, she hoped to be dead.

Their plans were set. At dawn, she, Tyler and Adam would head for Fort Carson. Levi would slip into one of the positions he'd scouted on Colorado College's campus and wait for the show that was Grace to begin. Verity was supposed to head back to Woodland Park with Persephone – Grace had begged, in spite of the futility of such a gesture, for a promise on that plan – but as soon as she thought the woman would follow through, Verity would make some comment about spending some "girl time" at the Broadmoor spa, or visiting the zoo to see who remained in residence. As with everything else about this plan, Grace could only play her role and hope the others met with success.

Her task, after all, was simple: endure. Whatever they dished out, she needed to take, until distant explosions on Fort Carson told her Adam and Tyler – "the boys" as Verity had taken to calling them – had destroyed the helicopters. If all went as planned, they would do so shortly after nightfall, just as the arena festivities were beginning on the CC campus. Their role was far more hazardous, in Grace's estimation, than her own. They wanted to live to tell the tale; Grace would rather not.

And as far as Adam and Tyler were concerned, Levi had the hardest job of all: taking out enough of the gang leadership to prevent the current regime from re-forming and keeping Grace safe while he was at it. Levi and Grace had worked out a prioritized target list, and he'd studied her sketches for hours, asking her question after question about the men, the way they moved, habits she'd observed. In addition to taking out the leadership from his sniper's nest, he was supposed to provide cover for Grace to escape. On that, though, he and Grace had a private agreement.

They'd been sitting at the dining room table late the night before, after Adam and Verity had already gone to bed. Tyler was on watch, and she and Levi had been going over some of the hiding places he might use if his escape routes were compromised. Grace had bolt holes all over the area, but only some of them were big enough for Levi to use. When they'd finished the task, Grace had asked him for a favor, as calmly as she would've asked him to pass the salt.

"Kill me, if they haven't already. As soon as the shooting starts, they're likely to kill me anyway. But if they don't, and if some of them survive, don't leave me alive."

His cold eyes had reflected neither surprise nor dismay at her request. "There will almost certainly be some of them left alive. I can take out two for sure. Maybe three. After that, they'll head for cover. Even with the night scope, I can't guarantee better odds than that."

"I know. That's why I'm asking." She gazed at him, let him see her resolve. "Don't let them make me pay for what we accomplish."

She'd waited through the still silence of his decision-making process and had been relieved to the point of tears when he'd nodded his agreement. She had risen from the table, and rested a hand on his shoulder in gratitude for a moment before going on to bed herself. It eased her, knowing her suffering would not be prolonged.

And so, all was in readiness. Grace had been staying at the ranch to let her pepper-induced hives clear, and the boys had searched the area, bringing her back stylish clothes in her size, as well as toiletries and make up. She needed to look as different from her "Stinky" disguise as possible. If someone recognized her as the "boy" that had been skulking among them for months, their cover story would blow to pieces. She had taken a bath earlier today, soaking away the last of the grime of her alter ego, and was still enjoying the green apple scent of the shampoo the boys had brought her. The men's weapons and supplies were also laid out and ready, firearms cleaned and oiled, ammunition divvied up.

The boys even had explosives they'd "liberated" from a group of "wannabe mall ninjas" in Green Mountain Falls, though they downplayed the story when Grace was in earshot. It was easy to forget sometimes, when they were laughing with Verity, whom they both now openly adored, or working together in the kitchen in quiet, companionable harmony, that they were predators. The group they'd raided hadn't been able to defend their supplies, and therefore had deserved to lose them. Neither of them would lose a minute of sleep over such decisions, either. As Grace had begun to know them over the last several days, she had come to envy them the simplicity of that outlook, even though she could never share it.

She never forgot, though, not for an instant, that Levi was dangerous.

He stepped out of the same door Grace had exited a few minutes ago. Pausing for a moment to find out whether or not Tom Hanks was still around – he was not, sadly, though Verity said his presence in the hereafter was being enjoyed immensely – Levi stepped down off the porch and headed her way. He took a seat beside her, stretching out his long legs, and they sat in silence for a long, peaceful while, listening as the game rollicked on. After a time, Grace nodded her head at the boys.

"Why do they hide how they feel? They love each other." She looked at Levi. "Are they afraid of you and what you'd think?"

Levi slid a sideways look at her, and for the first time, she got the feeling she'd surprised him. "I don't know," he said finally. "We've never discussed it."

"When this is done, you should," Grace said. "If we haven't learned that, then what have we learned? Love is love. It's stupid to turn away from it, whatever form it takes. You should let them know that it's okay with you, if that's what's holding them back."

"Yes ma'am." The faintest thread of amusement ran through Levi's voice, though his face betrayed none of it. "You left people who love you in Woodland Park. And if you make it through this, you don't intend to go back."

She didn't ask how he knew. It was moot, in any case. The probability of her living long enough to make that choice was low. "That's different. I left them because that's how I can best love them. How I can best serve them." She smiled a sad smile, remembering. "My dad used to say he showed his love for us by serving our country, by doing his part to keep us safe. I guess you could say I'm following in his footsteps."

"For argument's sake, suppose you do survive. Where would you go, if not home?"

"To Piper." She didn't know it until she said it. "I would find Piper and stay with her."

She looked over at him then, wondering if he knew how his whole body changed whenever Piper's name came up. He was rubbing absently at the center of his chest, staring into a middle distance, and Grace decided it was time.

"You're Brody."

His eyes snapped to hers, but he didn't answer right away. Then, "How long have you known?"

"Subconsciously, from the start."

They stared at each other, two people who kept secrets as naturally as they breathed, letting all subterfuge between them drop and dissipate on the cool evening breeze. Grace had thought about this moment, but she had not decided what she would say. What she should say. On Piper's behalf, on her own behalf, she should have been able to come up with something. Finally, she asked the only question that mattered to her.

"Why?"

Brody looked away. He was silent a long, long time, but she'd learned to wait. If he didn't intend to answer, he would have walked away. She'd learned much about him in the past several days, and in that knowledge lay the key to a door she needed to open. She hadn't put all the pieces together yet, but she could sense the picture forming.

"Power," he said at last. He looked at her straight on, no apology, no defense. "Control."

She thought about that. "If you could bend someone as strong as Piper to your will," she said slowly, "You could believe you were in control. Of everyone. Everything."

He nodded, sharply, once.

"And you're not sorry."

He shook his head.

Grace looked away. She didn't need or want to know more. What she'd suffered at the hands of the gang had been fundamentally the same. *Look what we can do*, had been the message. *Look at the atrocities we're willing to commit. We're in charge. You can't stop us. We have the power.* Grace, as a person, had meant nothing to them. She had just been a female body upon which they could carve their message of might for all to see.

She thought he'd get up and leave then, or at least wait for her to ask another question, but he surprised her by speaking. "I don't know how to be sorry. The path unfolds, and we walk it. We survive and learn, then move on to the next lesson. From Piper, I learned that control is an illusion. It's a trap. You think you're the puppeteer, and all along, you're the puppet." Again, he touched the center of his chest. "I won't say I'm sorry for what I did to Piper. I had a lesson to learn, and I learned it. But I wouldn't treat her so again."

Grace turned her head slowly, taking her time in meeting his eyes. "Did you fall in love with her?"

Brody closed his eyes, then opened them. "I don't think that's in me. I wanted her to...fill an emptiness. I had something very specific in mind, and when she didn't meet my expectations, I made her pay. By the time I figured out she'd been maneuvering me, that she was so much more than I had suspected, it was already ruined between us. Love can't grow where you plant hate."

He did leave then, left her sitting in the growing dark of a summer night, thinking about forgiveness and responsibility, justification and the complexities of the human experience.

They were very alike, she and Brody. They both preferred to think instead of feel, preferred to deal with data and logic. Emotions were unpredictable, feelings were frequently baseless. They were inferior as a basis for decision-making. Why, then, was Grace feeling a growing imperative in her chest to forgive Brody, to speak the words? Not on Piper's behalf; she hadn't the right. She didn't understand the compulsion, but it moved in the depths of her, a Truth that was just beyond her ability to grasp.

As with any problem she couldn't readily solve, she decided to leave it until morning. Her brain frequently sorted and rearranged as she slept, and in a day or so, she was likely to wake with the answer. She stood up, cradling Persephone in her arms, and it hit her: she might not live long enough for her brain to puzzle this question out. For the first time, the desire to live lifted its head and roared.

Grace set her teeth and forced her feet to follow the path back up to the house. She wished Verity and the boys a quiet good night, then carried Persephone upstairs to her room. She slept in the tiny room on the northwest corner of the house, what used to be the servant's room, as evidenced by the mismatched wallpaper on the sloping walls and ceiling. She didn't bother changing her clothes, just slipped her shoes off and lay down still cradling Persephone. She did not expect to sleep.

She had set this course, and she would not deviate from it. "The path unfolds," she whispered to the darkness – her last darkness? "And we walk it."

She did sleep, to her surprise, so deeply that Adam had to wake her in the dark before dawn. He took Persephone with him while she changed into the clothes they'd found for her – skinny jeans, a brightly patterned, slim-fitting top and brand new, black leather boots that rose up to her knees. She jogged down the stairs, then slipped outside to use the outhouse. Back inside, she commandeered the bathroom, where several hurricane lamps were already burning.

The makeup and hairstyling products seemed like archaeological relics. She picked the items up one by one, turning them in her hands, remembering her mom teaching her how to "make the most of her beautiful eyes," remembering the line of girls in front of the mirror in her high school locker room, heads tilted back, mouths slightly open, as they applied mascara. She remembered painting her lips with strawberry-flavored gloss and pouting those lips until William gave in with a laugh and kissed them. She looked at the mirror, at the girl there, and realized she had no idea who she was anymore.

Fifteen minutes later she left the bathroom, hair scrunched and tousled, mascara and liner neatly applied, cheeks warmed with blush and lips subtly colored with a tinted balm. She felt self-conscious, as if she was overdressed at a party. Verity, Brody and the boys were waiting in the kitchen, and Verity clapped her hands, gasping with delight.

"Oh, look! Look what a pretty dolly our Gracie is!" Her hands fluttered around Grace, touching, adjusting, smoothing, each touch accompanied by a glow of golden light and a tingle down Grace's spine. Her hands came to rest on Grace's shoulders, surrounding them both with glow and warmth. Her blue eyes were ancient and tender. "There will be no pain," she said softly, speaking for Grace's ears only. "My brother told me. When you're about to die, nothing hurts, and you will not feel fear. All your guides are with you, and the archangels as well. They will stay with you to the very end. You will never be alone."

It stirred and rumbled again, the longing for life. So much to learn. So much to do and see. Grace twisted her hands together to keep from grabbing onto Verity and clinging. "You know, you could maybe do a Divine intervention sort of thing. Just walk in there with your Heavenly Host and," Grace waved her hands, a hocus-pocus gesture. "End them. End this."

"Beloved Grace." Verity reached up to smooth a piece of Grace's hair behind her ear, and for a moment, choir-like music resonated. "It doesn't work that way. Angels don't work that way. They leave us to our dramas and lessons and contracts, and they love us through it all. They don't interfere with Soul Journeys."

She leaned to press a tender kiss to Grace's forehead, then pirouetted away to scoop Persephone up, as silly as if the moments between them had never occurred. "Give us a smoochie, Gracie, yes, smoochies for the yittle puppy."

Grace obediently kissed Persephone, and Verity twirled away. Grace blinked at the sudden darkness, shivered at the sudden chill, and looked up to find Adam and Tyler both gazing at her doubtfully. "What?"

They exchanged glances. Adam gestured to her face. "You look beautiful, don't get me wrong, but you're too...too..."

"Tasteful," Tyler finished for him. "And innocent." He ducked into the bathroom, emerging a moment later with a handful of items. "Hold these," he commanded Adam, and set to work. "Look down. Good, now look up." He smudged and layered, swirling a tiny brush around her eyes in skillful circles, his big hands deft and talented. "I started out doing my sister's makeup. Then, I did makeup for the school theatre productions." He pointed a finger at

Adam without looking away from Grace's face. "And you can shut the hell up. I can kick your ass seventeen ways from Sunday, and you know it." He held a tissue to Grace's lips. "Blot."

When he was finished, both he and Adam were nodding. "Much better."

Grace leaned to look in the bathroom mirror. It was a shock at first, but after a moment, she nodded, too. Tyler had given her a mask, a hard-edged, used-up mask. Much more suitable to the day's work than the subtle smoky eyes her mom had taught her, and her features – or rather "Stinky's" features – were obscured. She turned, and this time, found herself the object of Brody's scrutiny.

"Adam and Tyler will have to touch you," he said without preamble. She realized that he was instructing them, as much as he was informing her. "They'll have to disrespect you, handle you familiarly, maybe even hurt you, to convince these men."

"I know." She met Adam's and Tyler's eyes in turn. "It's okay. I'll be okay."

A muscle was flexing in Adam's jaw. Of all of them, he had the most trouble with this plan, with the risk Grace was taking. "I'm the oldest of five," he had told her once. "And the only boy. Four younger sisters, all of them too cute for their own good. That'll make a guy protective."

Adam gazed at her now, squinting suspiciously. "We've been through every plan and contingency plan over and over," he said, "But we've hardly talked about the rendezvous. Yes, we agreed to meet back here, but what's our secondary?"

Grace and Brody exchanged a look, and Brody answered. "World Arena. Stay for two days, and if no one else shows, make tracks. If we don't take everyone out, whoever survives will be hunting all of us."

"And does Grace know how to find the World Arena?" Adam was not going to let this go.

"She does," Grace answered, though she didn't. Not really. She looked between Adam and Tyler and made a decision. "Before we go, I need to ask you a favor."

Her eyes did not include Brody; she'd already burdened him, and in any case, this was not something he could do. "I have a daughter, in Woodland Park. She's with my friend Quinn. Her name is Lark." Her sweet name felt soft and loving on Grace's lips, so she repeated it. "Lark. She's just a baby, not even a year old. If this all goes to hell, I want whoever makes it through to get her out of Woodland Park. Make Quinn leave at gunpoint if you have to, but get her out of harm's way." Her eyes traveled between Adam and Tyler, and she knew she should feel bad, trading on the guilt they were feeling for wrongs they hadn't even done her yet. But she didn't. "Swear it to me."

Adam huffed out a humorless laugh. "Jesus, Grace, you got any other bombs to drop?"

Grace smiled, equally humorless. "Yep. One of the men we're going to kill today is her father. I have no idea which."

"Christ." Tyler's face was stricken. "What the hell, Gracie? Haven't you been through enough? Why didn't you tell us before?"

"Because this isn't about me." She looked around at all of them. "This is for Lark. We're going to give her a chance." She turned and walked out the door. "Let's go."

They walked through dead streets, past wreckage and ruin, past the corpses all their eyes had learned to slide past. As they walked, Grace fell into a kind of trance, a place of free association and drifting memory. A song beat in her head, an old Coolio tune her dad had taught her when she was no more than three or four. How it had made him laugh, to see his dainty little daughter brassin' and struttin', flashing sign and rapping in her flouncy pink dress.

Her mom had hated that song, Grace remembered. Hated rap music, hated any reminder of Martin's upbringing, of the cold and neglected childhood that had hardened him into a Marine. That had probably been the beginning of the end, Grace realized, in a small moment of clarity. How could a marriage survive diametrically opposed senses of humor? Should have seen the signs, Mom. You despised something that made him laugh. She wondered if her dad recognized how often Naomi made him laugh, hoped so, and walked on through the valley of the shadow of death.

The sun was nearing its zenith when they approached the main gate of Fort Carson. The boys had flanked her all this way, but now Adam took the lead and Tyler dropped back. Adam turned to look at her, his brown eyes locking onto hers.

"Show time, little sister." He held two fingers up under his eyes, emphasizing the connection. "You get scared, you remember this, you remember me looking at you right now, promising you that we got you. We got you, baby girl."

They walked right in, all smooth and swagger, violent men who owned a violent world. So fast, Grace thought. So easy. Just like that, they were trading military-speak, companies and battalions, fists bumping and palms meeting in whispering slides. Then, the rough hands on the back of her neck, the exclamations, the hard hand gripping her chin, forcing her head up for a better look.

"Fuck me," a man spat. "It is her. Get Thompson."

And then Sleeper was there. They didn't need to force her head up this time; she searched his features, searched for resemblance, searched for Lark. No. Not him. He gazed at her for a long time with regret in his eyes, then shook his head.

"Radio north and tell them what we got going on. Then get the truck and load her up. There'll be a hell of a show in the arena tonight." He turned away, addressing Tyler and Adam. "You boys want to ride along and watch?"

Tyler spat on the toes of her dusty new boots. "Nah," he drawled. He cupped the back of her head roughly, suggestively, and the men who had gathered around them sniggered. When he let her go, his fingers brushed her cheek in secret apology. "We've had her about every which way you can think of, and some ways I'll bet you haven't even imagined." He turned away. "I'll tell the man who buys me a beer all about it."

"Shit, if you've got beer, we'll draw you pictures and write out instructions." Adam's hand lifted as if to brush away an insect, his fingers briefly pointing to his eyes.

"Thanks for the memories, cowgirl." He, too, turned away. "Now, whatcha got that's fresh?"

A truck rumbled up, army green with a canvas tarp covering the cargo bed. Sleeper ushered Tyler and Adam away as Grace was lifted inside. A man climbed in behind her, already reaching for the buckle of his belt. "However shall we pass the time, cowgirl? Never got a piece of you before. Gonna fix that right quick, bet your sweet ass on that."

Sleeper spun around to walk backwards. "Pull up your god-damned pants, Fletcher. You're going to deliver her just as fresh and pretty as she is right now, you got that?"

"What the hell for?" Fletcher's voice was a grating whine. "They're going to fuck the life out of her before they kill her, bet your damn ass on that. Why shouldn't I take the first bite?"

Sleeper could move fast, faster than Grace would have thought. He was at the back of the truck, his hand fisted on the crotch of Fletcher's pants before the man could even get them all the way back up. "In part, because I don't like you. But mostly, because I said so. It's called an order. So you keep this –" Sleeper's hand squeezed, then jerked, hard. Fletcher gasped for air. "Zipped. If I hear you so much as got it out and waved it at her, I will make you profoundly sorry. And by the way, stop saying 'bet your ass.' It's a crass expression and it irritates me."

He released Fletcher, then walked to rejoin Adam and Tyler without so much as a backward glance. Fletcher collapsed on the seat across from her. As soon as the truck started, he began cursing, a steady, low stream of dissatisfaction and vitriol, some of it directed at Sleeper, some of it directed at Grace, most of it directed at the world in general. He kept it up until the truck ground to a stop after half an hour of swaying stops and starts. Grace rose, then crashed backwards when Fletcher's closed fist caught the side of her head, full roundhouse.

"Take that to remember me by, bitch." He grabbed his crotch in an obscene gesture, winced, then kicked at her viciously. "I'm looking forward to tonight, I really am. You're going to beg to die, and I am gonna laugh and laugh." He kicked at her again. "Bet your ass."

A blur of people's faces, staring, pointing, then Loudmouth parted the crowd, strutting towards her. He, too, grabbed her chin, cranking her head from side to side. "Son of a bitch," he crowed. "You little slut, you missed us? Back for more?" Then his eyes narrowed. "Huh. You make me think of someone. Can't think who, though." He released her chin with a hard flick of his wrist, then grabbed a handful of hair at the back of her head, forcing her along beside him. "I got it from here, Fletch. Dismissed."

Grace fought to pull air in and out of her lungs steadily. Her death must not be imminent, because Loudmouth's grip in her hair hurt, hurt so much. He gave her a shake every now and then as they walked, making her eyes sting with tears, making her gasp, which seemed to delight him. As they walked, he crooned to her.

"Thought you were so smart, huh? Thought you were so damn smart. You got any idea the problems you caused us? You got away, and people started thinking. Started talking amongst themselves." He shook her violently. "That's why we had to start with the arena. Had to up the ante, show people the consequences of thinking and shit. All because of you, being so smart."

Grace stopped walking, and ripped her head free, leaving him holding several chunks of her hair. What the hell did she have to lose? She was done just taking this. "Try 'clever.' It's a synonym for 'smart,' and it keeps your speech from redundancy."

For a few seconds, she actually shut him up. He stared at her, mouth agape, then round-housed her, fast as a snake. That hurt, too, an explosion on her cheekbone that made her spin and nearly stumble to her knees. Loudmouth caught her arm and jerked her to face him.

"Okay, *clever* bitch." He hissed the words in her face, and she watched his eyes dart from side to side. People were watching, and he knew it. "Keep it up. Sass me again. See how you like the consequences."

Grace crowded right up in his face, like she'd done with Karleigh in Woodland Park, and felt the same exhilaration seize her. "What can you do to me that you haven't already done?" She hissed back. She looked around deliberately, and raised her voice. "Are you afraid these fine people will figure out you're too stupid to know what a synonym is?" She raised her voice even louder. "Are you afraid they'll figure out they're better off without you and your scare-mongering, might-is-right posse of wannabe warlords? Are you –"

His next punch did knock her down, crunching along her jaw, filling her mouth with blood. She stared up at him from flat on her back, then leaned on an elbow to spit out a long, drooling stream of blood. She scanned the crowd around them, and shot her fist in the air. "Overthrow the grasshoppers! Long live the ants!"

She learned, then, what the expression "beat the shit out of" really meant. For as long as she could, she curled in a tight ball, covering her head from the raining kicks and punches. After a while, it stopped hurting, and everything started to fade in and out. Was this death coming? The thought was vague and not all that worrisome. Dimly, she was aware of being dragged along the ground, then into a building. She was dumped on a blessedly cool concrete floor. Then a door slammed. The darkness was broken only by a line of light under the door. Grace shut her eyes and either lost consciousness or slept.

When she stirred, hours later, her first thought was how badly she needed to pee. She tried to sit up and froze, moaning long and low. Everything hurt. She thought about books she'd read, about descriptions of surviving a beating, and put that theory into practice. Starting with her toes, she inventoried. They were okay, as were her calves – the boots had saved her. From there on up, it got ugly. Her lower back was on fire. The ribs on her left side creaked every time she took a breath. And some of the fingers on her right hand were either broken or sprained so badly, she couldn't use them. Her head was okay, though not unscathed. Her cheekbone ached dully, as did her jaw, and she had a whopping headache. She lay there, wondering if she'd been foolish to goad Loudmouth like that, and decided it had been worth it. It didn't matter whether she acquiesced meekly or went out kicking and howling. She was going out, either way. Might as well sow dissension and incite rebellion while she was at it.

She steeled herself and rolled to her hands and knees, breathing until the pain became bearable, then crawled around the room. Her eyes had adjusted to the dark, and she could see the faint outlines of things: a messy stack of football shoulder pads, a mop bucket that still smelled faintly of ammonia, a tangled pile of jump ropes, boxes filled with cleaning supplies and the kind of paper towels that went in a dispenser. A catch-all janitor's closet in the sports center, she'd bet. She pushed the bucket to the far corner of the room, then relieved herself in it. Just that simple act eased her discomfort considerably, and she sighed in contentment. It really was the little things. Then, she had to stuff her fist in her mouth to stifle wild giggles. Maybe she wasn't altogether balanced, here.

She stood up and wobbled back across the little room, then slid down the wall next to the football pads. After a moment, she picked a set off the top and buried her nose in it. Yes, there, so faint but there: skunky boy. She thought about Friday night football games and William, and wondered, for the very first time, what he'd think of all this. What he'd think of her, now. How would it have been different, if he had been the one to survive instead of Quinn? She closed her eyes and swore she could feel William's presence, his sorrow at this pass she'd come to, his loyalty to his brother, even beyond death. She could almost hear his voice. *Quinn was the one you needed, not me. Quinn is the one this world needs. You can always trust him, Grace, always.*

Grace opened her eyes and sighed, wondering idly if she was hallucinating, not really caring. She thought about Benji, then, sweet little brother, and her mom. She remembered making herself switch from "Mommy" to "Mom," because it was what big girls said. "Mommy," she whispered in the dark. She never let herself think of them, never allowed herself to remember all the people she'd lost. Her step-dad, all her friends, her teachers, William and Quinn's folks. Where were they all now? Did they know what was happening here? What the human race had become?

And what had they become? Maybe that remained to be seen. Verity always said they were inhabiting the space between "no longer" and "not yet." Grace's thoughts shifted to the living, to the ways in which people had changed. Evolved. Naomi, and the depth of her connection to the natural world via her animals. Quinn, and his communion with growing things, as if he, too, sprang from deep roots in the Earth. Her dad, and his instinct for Truth.

And Lark.

Grace closed her eyes again and pictured her daughter, every detail she could remember. Wisps of dark hair. Curving pink cheeks. Tiny hands, chubby feet. She didn't know how Lark had changed, but she knew for certain she had. The mystery of it was there in her sad, dark eyes. Grace pressed her hands over her heart and loved her daughter with all her might, and would do so with all the time she had left.

When the door was snatched open, she was ready. She smelled the fires, heard the thumping music and the crowd, and her legs wobbled. The past snapped at her from all around, memories of the violations and abuses, a rising flood that threatened to close over her head and reduce her to a wailing animal. She picked her chin up and breathed through it, rose above it. The man holding her arm – she recognized Little Man with a jolt – yanked and twisted cruelly, but it didn't hurt.

No pain. No fear. *I love you, Lark.*

They were all there, gathered around what used to be the middle of the football field, seated shoulder-to-shoulder in a half-circle. Little Man forced Grace to her knees, then took his seat with the rest of them. The stands around them were packed with screaming spectators, their faces all open mouths and blood lust.

Slowly, with as much dignity as she could manage, Grace stood. She would not face this mock court on her knees. She looked around at every face. Bean Counter and Loudmouth, Little Man and Sleeper, the Giant. And the Boss, his two Trigger Fingers standing slightly behind him. Grace ignored all of them except for the Boss, gazing at him with quiet composure. She turned to look to the west where the sun was gone, nothing but a faint, creamy glow over the mountains. Her eyes lingered on the familiar outline of Pikes Peak, and it comforted her, knowing the mountains would witness this and go on. Long after she was dead, like her beloved monoliths in Garden of the Gods, they would remain.

She swung her eyes back to the boss just as the first, distant explosions rumbled up through her feet.

It took a few minutes for the crowd to fall quiet. Somebody cut the music, and the abrupt silence pressed on her ears. All the men were on their feet now, staring tensely to the south, where a bank of low-lying clouds glowed orange, yellow, and red. Explosion after explosion vibrated the night. She lost count after a while, and just closed her eyes, hoping with all her might that both Tyler and Adam would make it through safely, that they'd live on and love each other.

She kept her eyes closed, waiting for Brody's shots to begin. On and on, time stretched, until it felt like her heart was beating once a minute. Still, nothing. Something had gone wrong.

She opened her eyes, and became aware that the explosions had stopped. The men were still all watching the southern sky, their faces grim, speaking to each other in low voices. As if he felt her eyes, the Boss turned his head to look at her.

"Do you know anything about this?"

It was the first time he had spoken directly to her, and Grace was startled by the ripple of *power* his words carried, the imperative push of them. She didn't just want to answer him, she needed to. And so she did, smiling sweetly.

"Score one for the ants."

There was a commotion in the crowd, then, a series of startled exclamations and a parting of bodies. Over the buzz, Grace heard a voice she knew well, polite, lilting, and insistent.

"Excuse us. Yes, coming through. Move aside, if you don't mind – thanks so much!"

Verity. Persephone cradled in one arm, the other arm looped through the crook of Brody's as they strolled across the field. And around them, the angels.

Grace blinked, and scrubbed at her eyes. You couldn't see them if you looked straight at them, not really. They were a suggestion, a majestic force field of shifting opalescent light that rose above and around Verity and Brody. As they walked, Verity nodded and smiled, lifting her fingers in an occasional wave. Brody looked strange. He was wearing a bulky jacket, and there was something odd about his face. It took Grace several moments to realize what it was: No tension. No calculation. Peace.

They reached the edge of the group, and Verity released Brody's arm, skipping to Grace's side. She bundled Persephone's quaking body into Grace's arms, then frowned. "Oh, honey."

She reached up and touched Grace's bruised cheek. Then her fingers coasted over Grace's ribs, slid around to her back, and ended with her fingers. Pain flashed and ricocheted everywhere she touched, making Grace gasp and flinch, but when she flexed her fingers, they obeyed. She caught Verity's wrist.

"What's happening? What are you doing? This is not the plan!"

Verity cupped Grace's face between her delicate palms. "This was always the plan. Since the time before time." She looked over her shoulder at Brody, then back at Grace. "He thought Piper would be the death of him, and all along, it was me!" She shrugged impishly. "Men can be so silly!"

"You told me angels don't work this way – why did they change their minds?"

"This isn't angelic, sweetie." She winked. "Though they did get us in the door, I have to admit."

Verity turned and looked over her shoulder, and Grace's gaze followed. Brody and the Boss were standing, staring at each other, less than a foot apart. The Boss's dazed eyes drifted to Verity, and his lips parted. His eyes narrowed, then widened, then narrowed again as he tried to understand what he was seeing. Verity twiddled her fingers at him and turned back to Grace.

"This is a reckoning. It's mercy. It's a good and faithful servant, going home." She closed her eyes and hugged herself, the joy on her face as brilliant as sunrise. "My brother. We'll be together at last." Her eyes popped back open and she laughed, Christmas bells ringing. "Can you imagine the mischief we'll get up to?"

She kissed Grace's cheeks, both of them. "For the boys. Tell them I simply adore them." She leaned to plant a final kiss between Persephone's ears, then skipped back to Brody's side. "Is there time for Grace to monologue? No? Sad day. Shall we, then?"

Brody nodded at her, then looked at Grace over Verity's glowing head. "Tell Piper…" He trailed off, then shook his head. "Never mind. Grace, run."

He said it so quietly, it took a moment for his command to register.

She whirled, and dug in. Clutching Persephone to her chest, she ran as she had never run, ran for her life, for her *life*. The joy of it burst in her chest like a super nova. Behind her, shouts arose, panic and scuffling, then a strange whooshing sound. Noise and heat and light lifted her off her feet and threw her through the air, and her ears popped painfully. She twisted her body, trying to protect Persephone, and landed badly on her shoulder and side. She lay there, stunned, while all around her, flaming debris rained down. A partially burned chair landed in the stands, scattering the screaming crowd, and acrid smoke dimmed the blazing lights.

Persephone appeared in her field of vision. Her fur was singed and she was favoring one of her back legs, but otherwise she looked okay. She licked Grace's forehead and cheek frantically, whimpering, until Grace reached up and curled an arm around her. Finally, she summoned what strength she had left and sat up.

Where Brody and Verity had been a moment before, there was a crater. Bodies, many of them torn apart and still burning, lay in a ring around the devastation. Two men appeared to have survived, one of them dragging a mangled arm as he combat-crawled away, the other being helped to his feet by people who had rushed in from the stands. Grace squinted. Bean Counter. And Little Man.

She continued to analyze the carnage, making sure, making completely sure, before she let her head fall forward, slumping in relief and grief. No one else. She looked up at the sky, at the swirling sparks, searching for angels. No one else. Grace struggled to her feet and picked

Persephone up. As people around her screamed and ran, scattering into the night, she limped into the rest of her life.

SEVENTEEN
Naomi: Woodland Park, CO

"What do you mean, 'She left?'" Martin leaned across the library desk, until his measured breaths stirred the spiky silver hair above Anne's forehead. "Where the hell did she go?"

Anne's chin gave a great wobble and her eyes filled with tears. Then she sucked in a deep breath of air through her nostrils and rose from her chair with regal poise. "How dare you speak to me using that tone! Do you have any idea who I am?"

Martin's head fell forward for a moment, and Naomi could *feel* his exhaustion, his effort to throttle it back. "No, Anne, I really don't." He looked back up at her. "Please. Where is Grace?"

Naomi stepped forward, laying a hand on Martin's shoulder and moving him to the side. She reached across the library desk to grip Anne's knotted hands. "Anne, honey, it's so good to see you. We had a rough trip." Understatement of the century. "What do you mean, Grace left? Where did she go?"

Eyes still locked on Martin, Anne reached for the corner of her desk and picked up a large manila envelope. She handed it to him, a queen bestowing her favor on an undeserving serf. "She left this for you. Now leave me at once, before I forget I am merciful."

Martin turned away and tore open the envelope, removing a stack of papers and what looked like a letter. Naomi tucked in close to his shoulder, and began to read Grace's familiar, neat handwriting.

"Dear Dad: By the time you get this..."

She finished reading, then slumped to sit on one of the tables close by, more tired and heartsick than she could remember being since Macy had died. Martin shuffled through the papers, muttering, then returned to the letter, scowling as he scanned it one more time.

"I don't understand. She's left us all of her calculations, all of her research. There's material here on the politics of gangs. On survival strategy in an 'End of the World as We Know It' scenario. She plotted out the safest course to Pagosa Springs, and one to Crested Butte, just in case." He looked up at Naomi, and she could see that logic hadn't yet penetrated his exhaustion. "Why would she leave all this? These are her projects. This is what she does, what gives her purpose."

Naomi stood up and took the papers from him, laying them aside. "She left them because she doesn't expect to be back."

The moment her words penetrated was an awful one. Martin's face locked down tight, but his eyes blazed with agony. "No. No, no, no, that is not how this is going to go." He whirled away from her, but Anne had beat a quiet retreat. "I need to talk to someone who saw her, talked to her."

"You're back." Rowan's voice. She walked towards them from the library entrance, and it struck Naomi like a fist, how much her friend had aged. The weight of their small world bowed her back and pulled her face into age lines, years before her time. "We were starting to think about sending out a search party. What took so long?"

Naomi answered. "We ran into trouble on the trail. The rains have damaged Rampart Range Road, and Shakti lost her footing, took a bad fall. Rolled right over the top of Martin – we were lucky it wasn't a lot worse. We had to let her rest for a day, then redistribute our loads and walk her in."

"I'm not a vet, but I'll take a look at her." Rowan's eyes narrowed on Martin. "What damage did you sustain in this little adventure?"

Martin ignored her question. "Anne says Grace is gone. Did you know about this?"

Rowan sighed deeply, and hung her head. "Yes. She mixed it up with Karleigh the day you two left. Tore a strip off her, off the whole community, really. Shook some people up, for sure. She left with Verity later that morning, according to the note she left for Anne."

"Verity went with her?" Rowan nodded, and Naomi's eyebrows felt like they rose to her hairline. She couldn't decide if she was comforted or terrified by this information.

"Why didn't someone go after her?" Martin started pacing back and forth, overcome with frantic energy. "What the hell, Rowan?"

Rowan's eyes sparked with temper, but she reined it in. "Quinn asked us not to."

Martin stopped pacing, and the air all around them seemed to darken and throb with menace. "He what?"

"You heard me," Rowan snapped. "He said we would only endanger her, that she had to do what she had to do. He's been on the receiving end of this with Grace before, if you'll remember." She walked towards him. "Now sit down! You bruised your damn spleen, you moron."

Martin caught Rowan's probing hands and stilled them. "I'm fine." He looked up at Naomi. "I have to go after her."

"Of course you do." They moved towards each other. "You should take one of the ATVs, or one of the motorcycles and go down 24. Go through fast, and no one will have a chance to give you trouble. What do you need me to do?"

"Nothing, honey – just get the horses back to Ignacio and tell him I'm sorry I rolled Shakti. I'll grab my gear right out of the saddlebags and go." His eyes were already far away, already searching. "If she's not at the ranch, I'll have to find a way to slip in with the gang's people, get my ear to the ground. I could be gone a while."

Her heart stuttered, but she nodded. "I know. Do what you need to do, and tell her I love her when you find her."

He stepped close and wrapped both arms around her waist, lifting her off her feet and kissing her so thoroughly, heat tingled across her scalp and down her spine, in spite of everything. He broke the kiss and leaned his forehead against hers, lowering her slowly to the ground and nuzzling her face with his. "I love you," he breathed. "Be safe while I'm gone."

She staggered a little when he let her go, and then he was striding for the door. Her head cleared, and she called after him. "Martin – wait." When he turned, she said. "If we're not here when you get back, meet us in Pagosa Springs."

That made him pause. He turned to face her fully. "You've decided, then. You're going."

"As soon as I can talk everyone into packing up. It's past time." She pressed her fingers to her mouth and tried to hide the tremble there. "I love you. Be safe. Bring our girl home – and Verity, too, while you're at it."

He nodded, and was gone, the door sighing shut behind him. Naomi turned to find Rowan watching her with wide eyes.

"So it's like that, huh?"

"Yes. It's like that." Naomi's cheeks had to be bright pink, and she decided then and there she didn't care. She and Martin had become lovers on the trail, the long nights of heat and discovery counter-balancing the long days of frustration and delay. Since she had no intention of hiding the change in their relationship, she'd better learn to ignore the raised eyebrows. "What other hell has broken lose while we were gone?"

"No hell to report, lots you need to know about, and nothing that can't wait. Come find me after you see Ignacio, and I'll fill you in."

Naomi nodded, grateful for Rowan's understanding, and hurried back out to the horses. Shakti seemed fine, but Naomi was anxious to get Ignacio's expert eyes and hands on the mare. She was just as anxious to speak to Quinn about Grace. She rode out with Shakti and Pasha on lead ropes behind, Hades trotting alongside.

They had stopped at the cabins on the way into town to drop off the supplies they'd brought, unsurprised to find Martin's cabin empty. Grace was supposed to be staying with Anne while they were gone, after all. For the first time, it occurred to Naomi to wonder where Persephone was. She made contact with Hades and *felt* the question. "Do you sense her, boy? Where is she?"

Hades' ears pricked, and his head turned this way and that as he sampled the summer afternoon breezes. Through him, Naomi was aware of a sense that went beyond sight, smell or hearing. Much as she was connected to Piper, Hades was connected to Persephone, but there was more; he was, in fact, connected to a vast, unified energy beyond that, which she'd barely begun to understand. She had just touched the edges of it, had just become aware of it on a conscious level. One of these days, she thought, she'd have a chance to sit and contemplate it all. Right now, she just wanted to know where little Persephone was.

Hades looked at her and whined. *Far.* Naomi pressed a hand over her heart, aware of the newness that was Martin, aware of Piper, aware of Grace. All of her loved ones, far from her and probably far from safe. And now Persephone missing. Tears heated her eyes and she blinked at the sky, not wanting to give in to them. If she started crying now, she would never stop. And there was too much to be done. She blew out a huge breath of air, then pointed a finger at Hades. "Don't even think about going anywhere! You're with me, you got that, bub?"

She had thought her heart would stop when Shakti had fallen. One minute they'd been riding along, and the next minute the air was full of terrified squeals and flailing horse's legs. Martin hadn't made a sound, though he'd probably lacked the wind to do so. The soft ground had certainly saved both horse and rider from more serious injury, but they'd been lucky. So damn lucky. Naomi had since decided that she hated luck.

That fast, he could have been gone. Didn't they all know that now, how fast life could be lost? She thought about that a lot these days, particularly in the dead of night, when she couldn't sleep and thoughts were never good. She thought about her life before, about how cozy and protected she had felt, how insulated from death and loss. She knew now it had all been an illusion. Given the chance, would she go back to the beloved fantasy, even knowing what she now knew?

Naomi shook her head and laughed a sad laugh, remembering the words Isaiah had spoken to her in the grip of his strange vision: Life lived to the fullest isn't lived only in comfort and safety. No, she wouldn't go back. She had learned to hold paradox in her heart. She'd lost a life she had loved, would always have loved, and she had gained the chance to be so much more. To be something she never could have imagined.

She rode up to Ignacio's ranch, the horses' loud, nickering neighs announcing their arrival. Ignacio came out of the barn, wiping his hands on a rag, trailed by Sam and Beck. In the garden behind the house, Quinn was bent over a small bush covered with white, daisy-like flowers, explaining something to a young woman Naomi didn't know. On a blanket in the shade, Lark lay quietly, either napping or contemplating the fluttering aspen leaves above her. Quinn lifted a hand in greeting, then returned to his explanations. Naomi rode into the stable, dismounted, and was seized in a fierce hug by Ignacio.

"We were that worried! Quinn and I both had the heebies – what kind of trouble did you run into?" His eyes went to Shakti. "Ah. I see part of it. Let me look at you, sweetheart."

While his hands coasted and examined, Sam and Beck led the other horses away. Ben craned his head back to send her an anxious whicker, and she sent a pulse of love to him. "I won't leave without saying goodbye, boy." Then she turned back to Ignacio. "I hardly know where to start."

She went over it, all of it, including the exodus of the Bear Creek people, what Isaiah had said, and what she had decided. "I know you don't want to leave here, Ignacio. Neither do I. But even if by some miracle Grace is successful in crippling the gang or disrupting their plans, she can't wipe them out completely. We're just too close to Colorado Springs here." She sighed, and rested a closed fist on her heart. "I could go through all her arguments with you, and all of mine, but it comes down to this: we need to go, if we want to survive. I *feel* it, in my heart and in my gut."

Ignacio listened without interrupting, then led Shakti back to her stall with Naomi trailing behind. She leaned a shoulder on the stall door and watched as he began brushing Shakti with a soft brush. He murmured to her as he worked, a low, soothing sound that lulled the mare into a doze and made Naomi's eyes droop, too. Finally, he gave Shakti a pat and left the stall, closing the door behind him. Their eyes met, and Naomi felt hers fill with tears.

"You're not coming with us."

Ignacio looped their arms together, and strolled them out into the beautiful summer day. Finally, he began speaking. "I *feel* my course, too, Naomi. You and I don't talk about religious matters, but I have a deal with our Creator. I listen, and He guides me. My place is here." Ignacio stopped walking, pausing in the shade by the stable. He nodded his head towards Quinn and Lark, his brown, lined face soft and broken with love. "Just like their place is with you. Quinn won't want to leave, but he will, for Lark's sake. Same with Ethan and Elise – they'll go for the twins." He patted her hand, stopping her protest before it could start. "I won't be alone. Andrea will stay with me. Not sure yet about her brother. She seems to think we can mount some kind of defense, but I know better. We can slow them down, maybe sting them a little, but we can't stop them. My bones will lie here with my family's and my ancestors', and that brings me a great deal of peace."

Naomi stared at his profile. "After all this, you're opting out? It's suicide, Ignacio. You're right – we don't talk about religious things, and I'm not a religious woman. I respect you too much to trot out a bunch of mumbo-jumbo about suicide being a mortal sin." The tears she'd been fighting flooded over, and her face twisted like a child's. "I've lost so many people I love, Ignacio. Help me understand why, so I don't hurt us both by trying to change your mind."

"Nature teaches us all of it, Naomi, everything we need to know. My wife, she put a lot of store by the church and its teachings, and I went with her because it meant that much to her. But for me, God speaks through nature, through the animals I love and the passing seasons, the ways of living and growing things. You and I, we understand the hearts of His creatures, whether they're tame or wild. We *feel* the Creator through them. You know what I mean, don't you?"

Naomi nodded slowly, thinking about the vast connection she sensed through Hades, the network of energy that felt like it had no end. "With dogs especially. They love us, not because we're worthy or we deserve it. They simply *love*, purely. I've always thought dogs are as close to Divine love as we can get on Earth." She smiled a watery smile at him. "But I've never said it out loud before. Cats and Shetland ponies, not as Divine. Less evolved, maybe."

Ignacio smiled in return, and squeezed her hand. "They sure don't think so, especially cats." He gazed at her quietly for a moment, from eyes that were sad and peaceful. "Seasons pass, Naomi. Animals know when their time here is done. Just like I know." He reached up, and with his gnarled, brown thumb, smoothed the tears off her cheeks. "I'm so glad to have known you. I don't think I would have made it this long without the life and love you brought to me after I lost my family. You brought Quinn and my sweet little Lark to me, too. That's your gift, just as much as your way with animals. You bring people together. You create love and comfort, wherever you go. You make strangers into family. And I have surely appreciated it."

She leaned her head on his shoulder, and together, they watched life bloom and buzz and thrive on a summer afternoon like any other, an afternoon that felt endless, though they both knew it was one of the last. The end of a season. Finally, she sighed, looking over at him, letting her eyes trace and memorize his dear, weathered features. "I will miss you so much."

"And I'll miss you. You'll take the horses with you, of course, all of them. I won't have them here for those bastards that are coming, and Ben's your boy, now and always. I called that one, didn't I? You two are peas and carrots."

Naomi nodded. "It will be my joy to take care of them." She reached up to kiss his cheek. "Could you let everyone know we're having a community meeting at the church tonight? A couple hours before sunset, I think, so we have plenty of time to talk it all out and make plans."

"Ethan and Elise are hunting, but I expect them back soon. I'll pass the word."

Naomi gave his arm a final squeeze and headed for the garden, and Quinn. She nodded politely at the young woman as she approached. "I'm Naomi. We haven't met – are you a newcomer?"

"Just visiting from Limon. I'm Aly." She held out her hand and they shook. "Quinn has been helping me learn about medicinal herbs." She slid a brief, admiring glance in his direction, but Quinn was oblivious. "He's so knowledgeable."

Naomi smiled. "He sure is. Aly, if you'd excuse us, I need to talk to Quinn in private for a moment."

Quinn gave Aly some quick instructions, then walked with Naomi to the blanket where Lark was drowsing. They sat down on either side of her, and Naomi dove right in. "You told people not to go after Grace. Why?"

Quinn looked away. "Even if they had been able to find her, she wouldn't have listened to them. She wouldn't listen to me."

"You knew what she had planned?"

"Not until the day she left. But I wasn't surprised. I knew she wouldn't be able to stay here."

"Why, Quinn? I thought, with time, she would start to heal."

"They broke something in her. It hurts her to feel, and Lark makes her feel. In time, I hope she learns how again. But she needs to be away from all of us to do that, so she can take the time she needs. We push her too hard."

Naomi felt her stomach tighten. "What about her dad? Does she need to be away from him, too?"

Quinn looked down at Lark, tracing a finger along her tiny, plump forearm, then stroking her cheek before he answered. "Martin wants Grace to feel things she's not ready for. He's ready to love Lark. I think he already does, and it hurts him, that Grace can't. Not yet, anyway. That's a big distance to cross."

Naomi, too, reached out to stroke Lark's butter-soft cheek. So badly, she wanted to scoop the sleeping baby up and nuzzle her close, feel her warm, living weight safe in her arms, listen to her breathe. She contented herself with straightening Lark's little yellow jumper and smoothing the dark down of her hair. When it was long enough, she would teach Quinn how to do a French braid. "It is," she sighed at last. "A very great distance. Thanks, Quinn."

She left on one of Ignacio's ATVs with Hades tucked in a small trailer behind her. She needed to continue spreading the word, and she wanted some time to gather her thoughts and look through Grace's notes before everyone came together. She thought about Quinn as they rode, and realized he was part of the future she very much wanted to experience. He was such a sweet-natured young man, so kind. And Lark, oh, that baby girl could own Naomi's heart without an ounce of effort. Not the family she'd lost, but the family she'd gained, with the potential to grow just as dear, just as beloved, with the passage of time.

As Rowan had requested, Naomi tracked her down when she arrived back in Woodland Park. Rowan offered her an early dinner, which Naomi accepted gratefully. They walked to Rowan's small cottage, and Rowan filled Naomi in on the events that had transpired in the community in her absence.

The girl Quinn had been working with, Aly, was part of a larger group visiting from Limon. They were led by a man named Brian Weaver; he and his "emissaries" had arrived a week ago and were staying with Rowan. Aly had been spending time with both Rowan and Quinn, learning all she could about herbal and other natural medical treatments. Greg, an older man, spent all his time with Alder, talking about wind turbines.

"I'll let Brian fill you in on the rest – I don't want to steal his thunder," Rowan said, as she held her front door open for Naomi. She grinned. "He's a silver-tongued devil, but he's so darn nice about it, you can't dislike him. Believe me. I've tried."

In Rowan's small living room, the man named Brian rose to his feet. "Greetings from Limon, and from your daughter," he said, with a smile so beautiful Naomi was instantly charmed, whether she wanted to be charmed or not. "I see now where Piper gets her beauty."

Naomi gasped. "You've seen Piper!"

Brian nodded, then walked to pick up a thick plastic envelope from a side table. "We brought copies of her maps and notes, as well as a letter for you. She told us to tell you she'd send runners whenever she could find people interested in creating a network." He grinned again his gorgeous grin. "It's an honor to be the first participants in the Piper-net."

Naomi took the packet from him and opened it with eager fingers. She read Piper's note again and again, tracing each letter with her finger, absorbing her girl. "Loki," she whispered. She hadn't seen the raven since the day Piper left, now that she thought about it. She remembered the dreams she'd had, the strange perspectives, the places and people she hadn't recognized, and finally understood. "I'll be damned," she breathed. "Wow, that sure would have come in handy when she was in high school."

Over a simple meal, she visited with Brian and Greg, asking about their community, what they'd seen, what they'd heard about the outside world. Aly returned partway through the meal, and joined in the conversation eagerly. Shortly after they'd arrived in Woodland Park, Brian had spoken with Quinn, explaining the misunderstanding in the wake of the plague and delivering his father's apologies. Brian was determined to wait until the situation with Grace was resolved before he left, hoping to make peace with her as well. The people of Limon, he told Naomi, were interested in helping Woodland Park address the gang issue.

"It's not really our problem yet," he said. "We haven't seen hide nor hair of the helicopters, thank God. But it will be our problem, if we don't do something. It's only a matter of time. I guess if the plague taught us anything, it's that we're all more closely connected than we thought."

Naomi agreed. So many of his ideas were intriguing; watchers, for example, who could provide an early warning system if the gang was on the move, perhaps via intuitive channels. "We've got people who can just about read each other's minds, they're so attuned to each other. Doesn't matter how far apart they are. With practice, maybe that could be refined. Piper said you two have a connection that you can both always feel. Do you know where she is right now?"

Without hesitation, Naomi pointed to the north-east. "That way. And very, very far away."

Brian's face fell, and he sighed theatrically. "I should probably confess that I've got a crush on your daughter," he said, eyes sparkling. "She doesn't return my regard, but I'm a patient man."

They finished their meal. Naomi returned to the library to ready herself for the community meeting while Rowan, helped by Brian and his people, began spreading the word. Through all her preparations, through a tough conversation with Anne, who was devastated at the thought of leaving her beloved library, through the community meeting that followed, which went much as Naomi had anticipated, she kept a corner of her attention fixed on Martin, on the bond that glowed steadily in her heart. He was alive and he wasn't in mortal danger; those were the only two certainties she had.

Fourteen people were choosing to stay, including Ignacio, Andrea and her brother Paul, and a group that had traveled together from Colorado Springs earlier this summer and settled on Turkey Creek near Ignacio's ranch. The rest of them, ninety-six people not counting Martin, Grace and Verity, would travel the 230 miles to Pagosa Springs, crossing rivers, gorges, canyons, and four mountain passes, including Wolf Creek Pass at nearly 11,000 feet. They would use motorized transportation only for the elderly; otherwise, they would travel at the speed of their slowest walker. Twenty horses and a scattering of goats would help carry their lives away from the old and into the new, and Naomi had already assigned work crews to help Anne pack up the library. They needed to bring as much of their knowledge base with them as they could possibly manage. If Grace's projections were correct, the journey would take them at least two weeks, and that was assuming bridges were still intact and passes were still open.

Naomi had set their departure date for a week from today. She didn't like the itch she felt to move that up, but she wanted to give Martin and Grace as much time as possible to return. Her announcement to the gathered community had been met with a minimum of shock and dismay, and Naomi knew she had intuition to thank for that. Several people had spoken to her after the meeting of nightmares, of the sense of impending danger they'd been suffering.

The sun had set by the time she finally wound her way home, the headlights of her ATV cutting through the rapidly thickening dark. Hades was tucked once again in the trailer, curled up against the cool mountain air. She sensed his tension when they rounded the curve by the meadow where they usually saw mule deer, but tonight, there were no deer to be seen. His head lifted, sampling the night wind, and she *felt* his low growl just before the information came to her via his senses: *mountain lion.* She looked around automatically, though she knew it wasn't close, and wondered how Ares was faring with a bigger kitty in the neighborhood.

She pulled up close to the cabin and cut the engine, then let herself in, locking and barring the door behind her. A few seconds later, she had a hurricane lamp warming the stale interior. They hadn't been gone that long, so maybe it was just her state of mind, but it felt like the cabin was already starting to decay around her. Naomi shook the sensation off impatiently and hustled through the nighttime routine of filling a bucket of water for Hades and Ares, should he deign to return, and bringing in a load of wood in case weather moved in. Hades was already snoring on the floor when she carried the lamp into her bedroom, then crawled into bed with a near-sob of relief. She was so tired she ached, so tired, she barely remembered to blow out the lamp, so tired, she had mere moments to think of Martin and miss his warmth beside her before sleep took her down, hard and fast.

It was the light that woke her. Naomi blinked, then blinked some more. She could have sworn she had blown out that lamp. Maybe she hadn't snuffed it all the way in her weariness. She sat up to blow it out again, and finally registered that the light was coming from behind her. She turned, and saw them, sitting on the edge of her bed.

Scott and Macy.

Naomi collapsed back against her pillows, clutching the covers to her chest with fists that shook, afraid to breathe, afraid to move. She stared at them, drinking them in, her eyes racing over their beloved features. She'd dreamed of them both, of course, but never so clearly. Never so vividly. The light was coming from behind them, a light that reminded Naomi distinctly of Verity. As she stared, they looked at each other and grinned.

"She thinks she's dreaming, doesn't she?" Scott's voice. Had she really forgotten the exact timber of his voice?

The realization came as a shock, so much of a shock, it took her a moment to realize what he'd said.

"Yep. But she's getting there. In five, four, three..."

Macy's voice, Macy's sweet voice. Naomi sat bolt upright and clapped both hands over her mouth, but she couldn't stifle her cry of inarticulate, indescribable joy.

"Scott, love, Macy, honey! You're here! You're really here!" She stretched her hands out to them. "Can I touch you? Oh, please, can I touch you?"

"No, honey." Scott shook his head. "We're just visiting."

"We can't stay," Macy chimed in, "But we wanted you to know it's okay, you leaving Woodland Park and the cabin and all. You'll be fine, and Piper will find you."

"Have you visited her, too? Is she okay? Where is she?" Naomi's words tumbled one over the next. "Where are you? What's it like there?" She couldn't take her eyes off them, their faces mobile and animated once more, instead of locked in the stasis of her memory. "I miss you both so much. Why haven't you visited before now, if you can?"

Again, Scott and Macy traded smiles. "I told you she would get to that question sooner rather than later," Macy said. "You weren't ready for us to visit, Mama."

"You needed to figure some things out," Scott added. "As Verity would say, you needed to find your path and set your feet on it. We didn't want to interfere with that process."

Naomi was startled. "You know Verity? How is that possible?"

Scott grinned. "Are you kidding? Everyone here knows Verity. I don't understand how it all works yet, but she's a special case – she could cross back and forth at will, until she came over to stay."

"Wait – to stay? Are you saying Verity is...?"

"Yes, Mama," Macy nodded gently. "She's here now, reunited with her brother." That sly smile. Naomi's heart tore right in two at the sight of it. "The guides are pretty flustered, trying to keep up with them, but the angels keep her in line. Sort of."

Naomi absorbed this, wondering why Verity had chosen – and there wasn't a doubt in her mind that she had chosen – this particular time to leave them. Why now, just as they were getting ready to start a new life? The loss ached in Naomi's chest, but there was a rightness about it, too. She thought about Verity, remembering her particular brand of nonsensical wisdom, her silly, irrepressible joy, and smiled. Even if Verity had chosen to stay, her practical input couldn't have been relied upon, now could it? She'd given them her gifts. It was up to them, to figure it out from here.

Naomi looked back up at Scott and Macy. They both looked so healthy, so vibrant and damn it, alive. "Are you sure I'm not dreaming?"

"You're not dreaming, but you're not fully awake, either. It will all make sense, one day." Scott was gazing at her with such love. "I can't tell you how proud I am of you. What you've survived, what you're helping this community accomplish, what you've taught Piper about life, and living, and love. She'll be back, honey. You'll see Piper again. We can tell you that much."

Relief, a treasure to look forward to. But... "You have to leave soon, don't you?"

"Yes." Macy's smile, the curve of her cheek, the tilt of her pert nose, all of her sweeter than Naomi could bear. "You need to rest, and sleep will help you understand all this."

"Will you come back? Will you visit again?" She knew the answer, before they exchanged looks, before they returned their eyes to hers, filled with the first sorrow she'd seen in either one of them. She held her hand up to stop them from talking. "No, don't say it."

She scooted down in her covers, snuggling back against the pillows. Her eyes were so, so heavy, she could hardly keep them open. "Just let me watch you until I go to sleep, okay? And I'll pretend, just for a little bit, that you're both here. Scott, you're sleeping here beside me. Macy, you're on the trundle." Her eyes slid to slits, and still she fought, just a little longer. "In the morning, I'll make blueberry pancakes, and we'll go down to the lake, see if we can find any wildflowers for Macy's book..."

Her eyes shut. She smelled Macy's favorite shampoo, felt her soft lips brush her cheek. "Love you, Mama. We'll be here, when you're done. Right here, in the sweet by and by."

EIGHTEEN
Grace: Rock Ledge Ranch, Colorado Springs, CO

Grace would never be able to remember a single detail of her trip back to Rock Ledge Ranch. She slept somewhere, a deserted house or a shed maybe, slammed into the ground by exhaustion and grief. Persephone woke her at dawn, and they continued on their way with Persephone leading her one stumbling step at a time. Not until she found her father standing by the dining room table at the ranch did things come back into focus.

Martin had found the notes and diagrams she and Brody had left, and was hunched over them. He looked up sharply when she entered, his features ancient with worry. He took one look at her face, and covered his own face with his hands. Terrible, harsh sobs ripped out of him. He dropped his hands and came towards her, not trying to hide his tears.

"Gracie," he breathed. He gathered both her and Persephone in his arms, then sat down in one of the dining room chairs and just rocked them both until Grace fell into a doze. She was vaguely aware of him lifting her, of being settled on the bed in the front bedroom. Then nothing once more.

Raised voices woke her hours later. She sat up and had to swallow a surge of nausea. Hungry, she thought, and dehydrated. She stood up and moved towards the kitchen, using the walls as support, and heard her father's Marine voice.

"I don't care who you say you are, or how you claim to know Grace. You look an awful lot like members of that gang to me. So move along, or I'll risk the sound of a couple of shots."

Grace ducked down and looked out the dining room window, to the grassy rise outside the kitchen door. Tears rose in her eyes, and she covered her mouth with her hand. They'd made it. Adam and Tyler had survived.

"Dad." Her voice was a froggy croak. "Dad, it's okay. They're friends."

Martin's head snapped in her direction, but he didn't lower the rifle he had pointed at the boys from behind the shelter of the kitchen door. "Honey, I can't tell if you suffered a head injury, so take a really good look. Be sure."

Grace looked to appease him, then nodded, which made her head throb. "Their names are Adam and Tyler."

They filled the kitchen moments later, vibrating with victorious energy and looking around. "The others aren't back yet?" Tyler asked. His eyes swept over Grace, and he frowned. "It looks like things didn't go exactly as planned. You need to sit, Grace, before you face-plant."

Her dad was there in a heartbeat, supporting her elbow. "Bed or couch?"

"Couch." She let him settle her in the sunny front room, what she and Quinn had always called the sewing room. The boys followed. Adam leaned back against the wall and slid down it with a sigh, scrubbing filthy hands over his face, combat-booted feet sprawled in front of him. Tyler dragged a delicate antique chair closer to the couch, then perched on the edge of it.

"I'm not a medic, but I've patched a few folks up." He started to reach for her cheek, then looked up at Martin. "Sir?"

Her dad nodded, and Grace had plenty of energy to roll her eyes. "Long live the patriarchy," she muttered. The corner of Tyler's mouth twitched up, then he frowned in concentration as he pressed along her cheekbone. Grace's eyes stung and watered, but she didn't complain.

"Your cheekbone isn't broken, but this cut should have a stitch or two. Maybe we can scare up some butterfly bandages." His eyes cataloged the bruises starting to darken her arms, took in the filthy state of her clothing, and he started firing rapid questions. "What did they beat you with?"

"Fists and boots."

"Any signs of concussion? Double vision or puking?"

"No. I have a headache and I'm dizzy, but I haven't had anything to eat or drink since we left here."

Her dad disappeared at that and Tyler went on with his inquiry. "Any trouble breathing, or coughing up blood? Cold sweats or abdominal tenderness?"

"For someone who claims to not have medical training, you ask a lot of questions." She shook her head. "No, none of those. I thought he broke some of my fingers, but..." She trailed off. She couldn't explain. Not yet.

Her dad returned with a glass of water and of all things, a Hershey Bar. He handed both to her. "Been saving that candy bar, just for you. Naomi sends her love. I've got some jerky and fresh vegetables when you're ready."

Grace nodded at him, and Tyler slid the next question in before she even had a chance to dread it. "Did they rape you?"

"No." Her dad slumped against the wall and covered his face again. Meanwhile, Grace took a moment to appreciate the strength of her own voice. "No, they did not." Her face twisted of its own accord, and she had to lift her fingers to discover something between a snarl and a smile there. "They were too busy kicking my ass for verbally castrating them in front of their groupies."

Complete silence met her pronouncement; then Adam barked out a laugh. He leaned forward, his big fist extended for her to bump. "Hooah, little sister."

Tyler scooted his chair back, tipping it against the wall next to Adam. Again, silence fell. They were both watching her with sad eyes, eyes that knew the message she had yet to deliver. Grace looked away, while something huge and monstrous tried to claw its way free of her chest. "I saw the explosions. Tell me."

Adam started. "Well, we didn't accomplish anything as kick-ass as verbal castration, but we did complete our mission."

Without looking, Tyler held his hand out to Adam. Their palms cracked, slid and twisted together in a complicated congratulatory handshake. "No birds left to fly, Gracie. Not a one."

"I had a little trouble with pilot-boy, though." Adam nudged Tyler's leg with his elbow, then left his elbow resting on Tyler's knee. "He wanted to bring that last Apache home in the worst way. All this blah blah about how we'd use it for good and shit." Adam's voice fell to a deeper baritone, and he spoke with a passable British accent. "'But through him, the ring would wield a power too great and terrible to imagine.'" Adam dropped the Gandalf imitation and grinned. "So I blew it to smithereens when he went to take a piss."

Grace found herself grinning, too. "Any other damage? Their fuel? Any tanks?"

"Their avgas is up in smoke, unless they were smart enough to store some elsewhere and let's be honest, 'smart' is not the operative word going on there these days. With a little more time to plan, we could have either destroyed or taken control of all their munitions. But that wasn't the mission, and Brody doesn't take kindly to improvisation."

His name dropped like a bomb in the room. Her dad straightened slowly, his eyes examining all their faces, coming to rest on Grace's. "Did he say 'Brody?' The same man that brutalized Piper and kept her against her will?" His eyes returned to Adam and Tyler, once again narrowed with hostility. "Which would make you the men that colluded in her abuse."

Grace felt a sigh rise up from her very bones. Nothing, absolutely nothing, could be easy. She took a deep breath, and held her hand up to her father. "Dad, please sit here beside me. You need to hear all of it. Then, if you want to be angry with me, that's your choice."

And so she told him, all of it, all the way back to the beginning. She told him about a message from a dying president, and finding in that call to action a reason to go on. She told him how she had considered leaving the neighbor boy behind, the same boy that would one day save her life and the life of her daughter, because she was afraid he'd be a burden she couldn't carry. She told him she'd found her breaking point, and it hadn't been at the hands of rapists. A tiny newborn with her brother's eyes had shattered her, sent her plunging into the most dangerous situation she could find, in an effort to atone for her failure as a mother. She was still trying to atone, she recognized that, and accepted that she probably would be for the rest of her life.

Then, she told him about meeting someone who understood her, in a way no one else ever had. She told him about a man whose cool logic and analytical mind matched her own, and a relationship that became a place of safety. In Brody's company, she was not unemotional. Not cold. She simply was. She'd known who he really was from the very beginning, though she'd tried to delude herself out of loyalty to Piper. She was still working on that and would give just about anything to talk it out with Piper herself. She told her father of strategies and hope, realizations and justifications. She told him about the door she sensed but could not open.

And then, she told all of them about the end. The angels. The peace on Brody's face. Verity's healing touch. To the boys, she delivered Verity's words verbatim. When she was finished, Adam's head was hanging between his bent knees, and Tyler was staring at the ceiling, his eyes brilliant with unshed tears. Grace rose and went to them each in turn, giving them the kisses Verity had left in her keeping. Then, her legs simply went out from under her. She crumpled there on the floor beside Adam, leaning into him, and felt Tyler's strong arms close around them both. Her heart cracked open, and her loss rose out of her on a long wail.

She cried for Verity, because the world was so much colder and so much less ridiculous without her, and that was a tragic thing. She cried for Brody, because she knew with absolute certainty no one else on this Earth would. Persephone burrowed into her lap and snuggled close, licking Grace's chin in comfort and love. They stayed there, bound together in their grief, while the world around them altered and changed and spun on. Finally, Grace sat up and wiped her face. Her father had disappeared. She gave both the boys another kiss on the cheek, from her this time, and went to find her dad.

He was in the kitchen, working at the stove. He turned when he sensed her and gestured at the small table. "Sit. I've got a soup started. Can you eat a granola bar with that jaw, or do you need something softer?"

Grace sat, relieved that they could both take refuge in the practical. They would talk, eventually, but for now, this was so good. "Where did you find a granola bar? Wait —" She held up a hand. "Same place you found a Hershey bar, and there is no amount of money I wouldn't bet that Naomi had something to do with both."

Her dad smiled, and there was something different in the expression, something private. Interesting. He brought her another glass of water and a peanut butter granola bar that tasted so good it brought more tears to her eyes. Taste of the past, soccer games and track meets. While she ate, he filled her in on what they'd learned. They discussed the Bear Creek people and their plan to settle near Monte Vista, which Grace considered adequate but vastly inferior to Pagosa Springs. He told her about Naomi's plan to organize the relocation of Woodland Park as quickly as possible, and once again, Grace found herself in tears. She lay her head down on the table and just gave in to them.

"I'm sorry," she whispered to her dad, when he crouched beside her and started rubbing her back. "I guess I've just held it all in too long."

"I know someone else who struggles with that tendency."

She shut her eyes, and pillowed her head on her arms, enjoying his nearness and his soothing touch on her back. During the long winter days of her pregnancy, Quinn had often comforted her like this. She missed him suddenly, the ache so deep and lonely, it brought on still more tears. Her dad scooped her right out of the chair, just like he used to do when she was a child, and took her back to the front bedroom. He settled her on the bed and pulled a light cover over her, then moved a chair to sit beside her.

"Sleep," he said simply. "Rest your heart and your mind, Gracie. I'll be right here."

She slept through most of that day, waking only to eat and use the bathroom, and right through the night. She slept most of the next day as well, and the next, until she started to think there was something wrong with her. She said as much to Tyler, when she woke to find him keeping vigil. One of them was always with her, most often her dad.

"You're healing, inside and out," he said. "Sleep is the best thing for you. For now, there's no rush. Just let your body tell you what it needs."

She was out of it, but not that out of it. "What do you mean 'for now?'"

Tyler rolled his eyes. "Missing Brody right about now," he muttered. "He was the only one who could stay ahead of your brain. Let it go, Grace. Just let it go."

She made herself get out of bed the next day. While she'd rested, her dad and the boys had developed routines, dividing chores so efficiently, it left Grace at loose ends. They'd also begun to form friendships. More and more, Grace would hear them talking about things that had nothing to do with the tasks of everyday living, like hobbies and interests, or speculation on conditions elsewhere in the world. That conversation had stopped Grace right in her tracks. Here they were, fighting their battles in their little tiny corner of the world. How was it different elsewhere? In rural China, say, or Australia? Curiosity for the sake of curiosity woke in her, long dormant, and she welcomed it as an old friend.

When she felt up to it, she went down to the old Gallagher cabin. Animals had been inside, and therefore the weather, and much of what Quinn had left behind was ruined. From the stack of books he'd left, she salvaged all but the fifth book of the *Harry Potter* series, lugging them back to the Chambers house. She read the entire series over the next week, and was overjoyed when Adam surprised her with a copy of *Harry Potter and the Order of the Phoenix*. The boys had once again been out scouting, and the conversations between them and her father began to lower in volume, taking on an urgency she didn't want to hear. They stopped talking whenever she walked in the room, which was just fine with her.

Until it wasn't. Grace woke up on the tenth morning since they'd returned, and knew it was time. She sat at the dining room table in the exact same spot she'd spent so many hours the winter before and began to write. She captured all of it, what she had observed and what she had heard. When she completed the document, she made a copy. She finally finished late in the afternoon two days later, and went to find her dad and the boys.

Martin and Adam were in the kitchen, preparing a rabbit Persephone had caught for dinner. Grace looked around. "Where's Tyler?"

Adam looked up. "He went to find you some new clothes. I brought some back the other day, but nooo. Not good enough. He said they were old woman clothes and went to find you something more 'stylish.'"

"And I found some, too, you hopeless slob." Tyler stepped in the kitchen door, which had been left open for the cross-breeze. He pulled off his backpack and took it to the kitchen table to begin unloading its contents. "I found some new boots and a pair of tennis shoes in your size, a couple pairs of jeans, and some shorts and t-shirts. I also found some sundresses - comfortable and cute - and they'll look great on you."

"'Comfortable and cute,'" Adam mimicked, then laughed when Tyler straightened and glared. "Oh, chill, you fashionista. I'm just glad Grace has another girl around to bond with."

"Spoken by the man who joined the army so he could wear cammies 24-7." Tyler nudged Grace, pointing at Adam conspiratorially. "He wouldn't know 'style' if it climbed up his leg and chewed on his ass."

"I hunt. I fish." Adam saluted. "I ranger, or at least I used to. Camouflage isn't a fashion statement, it's a way of life. Besides," He waved the bloody knife he was wielding in a side-to-side, up-and-down fashion, indicating Tyler's camouflage pants and shirt. "Pot criticizing the kettle."

They bantered like this all the time, and Grace loved it. She and her dad exchanged grins. Then she turned to the pile of clothes Tyler had set on the little kitchen table. She held up one of the sundresses, a gorgeous tie-dye in blues and greens, and looked up to find her father gazing at her.

"Your mom used to wear sundresses all the time," he said. "Even before it was 'stylish.'"

"I remember."

Grace held the dress up to herself and smoothed it, then looked around at all of them. She sighed. She'd stalled long enough. "I need to know what's going on out there."

It was almost comical the way they all exchanged glances. Adam's eyes got big, and he looked for all the world like a five-year-old trying to hide a contraband cookie behind his back. Tyler was suddenly very busy re-folding the clothes he'd brought her. But her dad gazed at her steadily. "Let's go in and sit down."

They gathered around the dining room table, and her dad started. "The men you called Bean Counter and Little Man survived. Bean Counter lost an arm, but it looks like he's going to make it."

Grace nodded. "I thought I saw them both. Are they taking command of the gang?"

"Little Man is," Adam answered. "And he's a man on a mission." He shifted to reach into the back pocket of his pants, and Tyler put a hand out to stop him.

"Don't show her," he said in a low voice. "There's no need."

For the first time ever, Grace saw true disagreement between them. Adam shook his head at Tyler, disapproval on his face. "That's not right, and you know it. She took a hell of a beating for the mission and would have died for it. It was her plan, and it was genius. Not even Brody could do better. She's got a right to know and make her own decisions."

Their gazes stayed locked for long moments. Then Tyler sighed and dropped his hand. Adam reached into his pocket and pulled out a square of paper, which he unfolded and handed to Grace.

"Well," she said, when she worked up enough saliva in her suddenly dry mouth to speak. "Looks like they've got a police sketch artist lurking around there somewhere. And a copy machine hooked up to a generator, I bet." She tossed the paper, a flyer with all three of their likenesses on it, onto the table. "These are posted around?"

"Everywhere," Adam answered. "They didn't get Tyler right at all – this looks like a constipated pug, you ask me – but you and I are dead ringers. I've only been going out at night since they scattered these around. People won't hesitate to turn us in, believe me. We screwed up their gravy train, and they're not too happy about it."

Grace shook her head sadly. She'd done what she could. People would change if they could. "Any word on whether they're still planning to raid outlying settlements?"

"Full speed ahead. Taking out the helicopters changed their attack plan, but they've still got tanks and Humvees on Carson." Adam glanced at Martin. "They tried to recruit your dad for the crew clearing Highway 24. They don't seem too worried about keeping secrets anymore."

Grace looked at her dad. He nodded confirmation. "Whenever you're ready, we need to get you out of here. Tyler and Adam are welcome in our community, if they're interested." He glanced to the side, speaking almost to himself. "I'll have to talk to Naomi, level with her about the Brody connection. It could take some time to bring her around, but considering what they've done for you, for all of us…" Then he returned his eyes to Grace. "When will you be ready to travel?"

"Tomorrow." She reached across the table and took both his hands in hers. "But I'm not going to Pagosa Springs."

Martin dropped his head forward and started swearing, long and low. Grace let him wind down, then squeezed his hands hard when he looked up at her with anguished eyes.

"They know my face, Dad, and they will not forget this. Not for a long, long time. Little Man hated me before, and he'll never stop hunting me. I'd lead them right to Lark, to Quinn, to Naomi." She shook her head. "After everything I've been through, that is the last thing I want. Pagosa Springs is safe enough as long as I'm not there."

"You and I will go farther, then," her dad began. "There is a limit to how far they'll go, Grace. At the end of the day, they're trying to survive, just like we are. Their resources aren't unlimited."

"I don't want you to go with me."

As one, Tyler and Adam scraped their chairs back, preparing to stand. "We should just let you two talk this out," Tyler began, but Grace held her hand out to both of them.

"Stay. Please." She looked at her dad. "Do you remember what you used to tell Benji and me, whenever you deployed?"

Martin shook his head at her, looking hunted. "Don't, Gracie. Please."

"You told us that your service showed your love. You told us that you had to leave us because it was your job to keep us safe." She leaned closer. She had to make him understand, because she simply did not have the strength to do this if he fought her. "Daddy, I can't be her mama. But I can keep her safe by leaving. Let me show her my love the only way I can."

Her dad's face was quivering with his effort to maintain control. "I'll go with you," he said. "I'll take you wherever you want to go."

"I want to go to Piper. I kept my own set of notes on their trip, and I can find Jack's home in Pewaukee." She took a deep breath. "And I want you to go to Lark. I want you to help Quinn raise her, and I want you to be with Naomi. Please, dad."

"If you think for one god-damned minute I'm going to let you take off cross-country alone –"

"Excuse me, sir," Adam interrupted, a hard edge in his voice. "But if *you* think for one god-damned minute we would let her take off cross-country alone, you are seriously mistaken. We'll take her to Piper." He looked at Grace, and lifted his chin. "It would be an honor."

Tyler nodded his agreement, and silence fell around the table. In her father's face, Grace saw acceptance, even if he was struggling with the words. She rose. "Dad, will you come walk with me?"

Arm in arm, she led him along still-usable trails, into the heart of the Garden of the Gods. How she would miss the majesty and peace of this place, the beauty and scope of time that never failed to take her outside of herself and her tiny, short-lived, human problems. They spoke of little things, pointed out wildlife and blooming plants, named the monoliths, then found a bench and settled on it, watching the sun sink slowly towards the top of Pikes Peak. Deep shadows fell, cooling the day. Finally, her dad spoke of consequential things.

"Do you know which one was Lark's father?"

Grace stilled. The eyes had given him away. Sad and fathomless, just like his daughter's. Grace had recognized those eyes only minutes before he died. She kept her face turned away so he wouldn't see her knowledge. She just couldn't see any reason to burden him with it. "Quinn's her father. And you're her grandfather." She looked at him then, and smiled. "Are you going to be 'grandpa,' or 'grandad,' or 'papa?'"

To her delight, he blushed a little. "'Papa' I think. It's less old."

They laughed softly together. Grace leaned her head on her dad's shoulder, snuggling close. They were losing the light and would need to head back soon. Plans needed to be made and provisions needed to be packed. The thought left her both bereft and excited. What would they find on their travels? Who would they meet? Part of her yearned for her father and his shelter, but even stronger rose the desire to leave all this behind. To start anew. She grinned at herself in the gathering dusk. In a minute, she'd be singing, "Just around the riverbend..."

"I made a record of what happened here for you to take back to Anne," she said. "I'll take a copy to Piper. Crazy to think we're writing our own history, isn't it?" Grace thought about that for a moment, and felt a resonance in her chest. A noble calling indeed, recording the history of a devastated people. Something a long-dead president would approve of. "Make sure people know what Adam and Tyler accomplished here, dad. There's just about no way to overstate the importance of it. Their names should be remembered. Verity, too, and Brody. I know it doesn't make up for what he did to Piper, but he's a hero, dad. They all are."

She looked up to find her dad gazing at her, his face alight with love and pride. "I know who to name 'hero,' Gracie. Don't you worry about that."

NINETEEN
Piper: Beaver Island, Michigan
October

Piper slogged up the dune face, shuddering as the wind cut right through her parka and snapped at her bones. She'd never known a wind like this, penetrating and damp, relentless and downright hateful. No matter how many layers she put on these days, she felt chilled to the core. Not for the first time, she questioned whether or not she was tough enough to make it through a Michigan winter, particularly since winter hadn't even arrived yet. She reached the top of the dune, took the full brunt of the sand-slinging wind in the face, and knew with certainty: She was doomed.

The object of her search stood on top of the dune, bare-headed and coat open to the elements as he stared out over the heaving grey waters. Luc had obviously been gifted with some kind of insulation Piper didn't possess. His eyes were turned to the west, as they almost always were, searching. Piper trudged to his side, blinking away tears the cold stung from her eyes.

"There are no cuss words obscene enough to describe this wind," she said. "Tell me you're not thinking of going out in this. Tell me you're not that nuts."

Luc's lips lifted in a brief smile, the only kind she'd ever seen touch his face. Word around the island was that his trip to Pewaukee last summer had changed him, but word didn't know what had occurred. Only a select few knew the details, Piper among them, and they knew how to keep their own counsel.

"No. We won't be going out again until spring. Not far, anyway. The mainland would be the farthest." Luc nodded at the restless Lake Michigan waters. "That's a dead roll. Heavy weather's coming in. Feels like a November witch."

He turned and headed down the dune face, and Piper slipped and slid after him. "Wait? A witch of November? Like the shipwreck song? That's an actual thing?"

Luc turned to look at her, and this time, his smile was more of a smirk. Her Colorado-native ignorance of the ways of water often amused him, and she played to that. Anything to lighten the boy up and give him a moment of forgetfulness.

"It's an actual thing. Technically, it's a storm system caused by low atmospheric pressure over the Great Lakes which pulls cold air down from the north and warm air up from the south. The two air masses collide, and a November witch is born."

"It's October. Okay, yes, it's the last day, but still."
A particularly strong gust of wind slugged her right between
the shoulder blades. "Jesus," she gasped. "Did she hear
me? Should I apologize?"

Luc chuckled at that, which she considered a
triumph. "Witches can happen anytime during the autumn
months," he explained. "This isn't even all that early. Is the
party starting?"

"Soon. People are starting to trickle in. Your mom
sent me to get you so you wouldn't be late." Partial truth,
which both of them knew. Maddie had sent Piper because
otherwise, Luc wouldn't have shown up at the community
center at all. Community gatherings, he had told her, made
him feel sick to his stomach.

"Is Annalise surrounded by people who care about
her? No. Is she at a celebration? Is she participating in a
feast? I seriously doubt it. I don't deserve to go to a party."
Luc had hurled the bitter words at Piper months ago, in
early August, when she had hunted him down during the
combination "Lammas / Welcome, newcomers, to Beaver
Island!" party Veda had organized. Then, like now, Piper
had found him on the western shore, staring out over the
rolling waters of Lake Michigan. And then, like now, his
worried mother had sent her. Luc listened to Piper, because
he sensed she understood him. That day, she had told him
why.

"I murdered a man." She'd dumped the words on
him with deliberate roughness, no preamble. "I shot him
execution-style, in cold blood. And I didn't do it to save
anything but my own ass." When his startled eyes had

found her, she'd dropped her shields and let him *feel* some of what she carried, what she would always carry. "You're not the only one with images in your mind you can't stop seeing, Luc. You're not the only one who feels like the remorse will drown you sometimes. Annalise is still out there. And though I can't believe I'm quoting Verity, she's always right about this stuff. If it's your path to find that little girl, you will. So do what you can on that front, and in the meantime, stop moping around and channeling Heathcliff. You're worrying your prego mother half to death. You want to feel guilty? Go look at the lines you're putting on her face, pal."

Luc had stared at her for the longest time that day, analyzing her words, *feeling* her truth. Then he'd stomped down the dune ahead of her, muttering. "Heathcliff, my ass. I hate the Brontes."

He tugged at her heart, this bookish and brave young man, and had since the first day she had met him. When he and Cass had shown up at the Kiel family home in Pewaukee, he had still been in shock. Cass had told them what happened, and on their way back through the area the next day, they had all looked for little Annalise for hours. Intermittently, Piper would pick up a faint red bond-line connecting Luc to someone, but it wasn't consistent enough to navigate by. Five days later, they had arrived on Beaver Island. The very next day, Luc had left a note for his parents and sailed the *Grindylow* back to Milwaukee. He was gone for nearly two weeks, and by the time he returned, his mother was hysterical with worry.

By then, Piper had already been struggling with a growing restlessness. Jack, with little Gideon tucked by his side, had stepped right into the center of island life by opening a school for the six surviving children. Owen was quietly breaking the hearts of every woman within a decade of his age by fixing all things broken and giving his strong back to any task that needed doing. Ed and Rosemary were Veda's constant companions in the garden, and Cass was rarely separated from Jack, whether she was teaching alongside him at the school or dragging him along on sailing lessons with Bastian, Luc's younger brother. The two talked non-stop, catching up on years of separation, and Piper could literally see the healing taking place for both of them in the multi-colored, nuanced bond-lines that grew and strengthened between them every day.

Piper helped wherever she was needed and provided medical care in the rare instances where Veda's teas and tinctures didn't suffice. She hunted as well, though the bows and traps of the Nolette family were just as effective and more practical, given the limited supply of ammunition. But she had no true purpose. No calling. Luc's return had clicked something into place for her, had answered a question she'd just begun to ask. While Luc had been gone, Piper had visited the Nolette family daily to read their bond-lines, offering them what reassurance she could. On the day of his return, she gave the hullabaloo time to die down, then marched over and stuck her nose right in their business.

"Please don't try to stop him from searching for Annalise," she had said to the Nolette parents, especially his teary-eyed mother. "He has to do what his heart tells him to do. When you think about it, this is a healthy response to a tragic occurrence. He's trying to do something to make it right, instead of curling up in a corner crying, 'Poor me.' Besides," she had straightened authoritatively, catching Luc's eye and holding it. "You won't be going alone, ever again. You'll promise your mother that. I'll go with you, to watch your back and gather information about what's happening out there. I don't like to brag, but I've only met two people who can out-shoot me. One is a sociopath in Iowa, who I pray you'll never meet, and the other is a housewife in Colorado, who also happens to be my Mama." She had turned back to his parents. "I'll keep him safe or die trying. We'll make a good team."

And they did. They had sailed back and forth to the Milwaukee area four times since that day. They had made contact with the group Luc and Cass had seen evidence of on the banks of the Menominee River, a tight-knit, resourceful and suspicious group composed of people that had been homeless in the time before. They had also connected with a tiny handful of survivors in Pewaukee, a group of four: three twenty-something siblings and their mother, who was more terrifying and formidable than all three of her children put together. One of those children, the middle daughter, was considering a trip to Colorado the following spring, intrigued by the idea of forming a network of runners to share information and hope.

Finally, on their last trip, they'd found two more orphans for Jack to foster, twin brothers who had not yet spoken a word, but who had at least stopped trying to bite any adult that approached. They thought the boys were around seven, and they refused to be separated for even an instant. Cass and Veda were certain they were communicating telepathically; their eyes would meet for extended periods, whereupon they would act in eerie unison to complete a task or – less frequently now – make a break for freedom. Little Gideon had been invaluable in caring for them, greeting them as old friends and chattering to them both non-stop as he coaxed them into play with a train set Jack had found and set up.

They had not found Annalise yet, though. Not even a trace of her. In spite of this, both Luc and Piper believed she was still alive. The red bond-line connecting Luc to that mysterious someone had grown stronger as time had passed, which fascinated Piper. She had no explanation for the phenomenon. It almost had to be Annalise – the line clearly indicated someone on the outskirts of Pewaukee, and Luc didn't know anyone else there. But how? Intention, perhaps? The simple, printed notes Luc always left on Annalise's mother's grave and in the house? Whatever bound them had grown stronger without Annalise's involvement or consent, without any further interaction between them.

It was so interesting, and at the same time, disturbing. Piper had spent many an hour thinking and writing in her tattered journal about the nature of human bonds, both seen and unseen. She thought about her mother, and the rock-steady bond she had come to view as foundational to her mental well-being. She thought about Trent, and the twisted, unhealthy bonds he had forged; no doubt he was forging them still. She thought about Jack, and the vibrant bond she'd *seen* between them when all she knew about him was his name. And, of course, she'd thought about Brody.

He was dead. Piper had felt him die, the day after they arrived in Pewaukee back at the end of July. One moment he'd been there, a heaviness in her chest and a bond-line she couldn't shake, and the next he'd been gone. She hadn't said a word to anyone; there had been plenty to keep her busy and distracted during those eventful days of reunions and introductions. She had felt certain enough, though, to leave information at the Kiel family home on where to find their group, should anyone from Colorado come looking.

At the time, she hadn't known Cass well enough to ask her to confirm her conviction that Brody was dead, though she intended to do so tonight. According to Veda and Cass, this was a night to remember and honor the spirits of the dead, the night of the year when the veil between this life and the next was thinnest. Accordingly, another combo-celebration had been planned: a "Harvest Festival" for the folks with Christian beliefs; "Samhain" for those of pagan or wiccan persuasion; and all of it united by the decorations and traditions of "Dia de los Muertos," which had been celebrated on the island by families of Mexican descent since long before the plague.

Piper was looking forward to it, all of it. Veda and Ed had been baking for days, and Jack had been singing snippets of the sing-along songs he'd prepared. Cass and Veda would both be giving readings throughout the afternoon and evening, and Piper had heard rumors of other skits and dramatic presentations. In today's world, this was as close to field study as a thwarted sociologist could get. "Celebration as an expression of localized values, norms and mores," she said as she followed Luc off the dune. "That would have made a kick-ass thesis."

Piper had brought the community's Kubota RTV to fetch Luc. The luxury utility vehicle had just been raffled off when the plague struck, and the lucky winner had not survived to claim it. It had become a part of the community center by default, and no one would even consider gainsaying a pregnant Maddie when she commandeered it for Piper to fetch Luc. They piled inside the snug, covered interior just as another gust of wind picked up half a dune and sent it hissing against the windows. Piper sighed with relief and started the motor, putzing them towards the east side of the island on Donnegal Bay Road.

She peered out at the lowering sky and gave an exaggerated shudder. "So if the witch of November is a real thing, what about other northern legends? Like the wendigo? Or that thing where a pond can freeze so fast it can trap a whole flock of ducks, and they fly away with it?"

"Wendigos are nonsense, and so is the duck thing. Only Canada geese can fly away with a pond." Luc didn't smile, but there was something mischievous about the crinkled corners of his eyes when he squinted at her. "Everybody knows that."

Piper nodded solemnly and bit the inside of her cheek, rewarded when he chuckled a moment later. She laughed along with him, then brought up the subject that had been troubling her. "So, no more trips to Milwaukee until spring. How do people stay busy during the winter months, then?"

More than concern for Luc motivated her question; in her soul, Piper was a wanderer. The thought of being trapped on the island for months on end was already making her just a little breathless. She glanced at Luc as she drove, noting that his face had flushed a dull red.

"A disproportionate number of people on this island have fall birthdays," he said. "Do the math."

"Okay," She was both amused and mortified to feel her face flush, too. "So, how do those of us without a love life occupy our time? Are we just stuck here on the island?"

Luc gazed at her, and she could *feel* how badly he wanted to ask about Jack. Piper kept her eyes stubbornly ahead, concentrating on the deserted road. She wasn't going to discuss her relationship with Jack until she and Jack had discussed it themselves. And certainly not with a teenage boy. The kisses they had shared in Trent's dungeon hadn't been repeated, and though Jack was warm and relational when he was with her, he didn't seek to be alone with her. They saw each other all the time, but always in the company of others.

Veda's kitchen table had become a hot spot for discussion and debate, and though Piper loved the far-reaching and speculative conversations about the how and why of what had happened to them as individuals and as a species, in her heart of hearts, she yearned for more from Jack. Sometimes, she'd catch him watching her in a way she wanted to call him out on. Damn it, she knew what that look meant, and the bond-line she could *see* between them was stronger and brighter than ever. But at some point between that basement in Iowa and here, he'd obviously had second thoughts.

What would a community-builder like Jack want with a gypsy like Piper? She sure as hell wasn't preacher's wife material, and then there was the kid thing. If she'd ever met a born father, it was Jack. And Gideon, bless his little otherworldly heart, had casually mentioned that motherhood wasn't in Piper's cards.

"You'll never have a baby," he'd announced one day as they'd sailed north on the *Grindylow*. His heaven-blue eyes had been ancient and innocent as he'd gazed at Piper, and she'd been intensely aware of the eyes of every one of her companions swinging her way, especially Jack's. "No, you'll never be a mama. But you'll guide hundreds. You'll see."

She could *feel* the truth of little Gideon's words and wasn't all that surprised; her mother had struggled to conceive and carry children. Hearing it in such a way had been a shock, though, and all of them had been working with Gideon on the concept of "discretion." For Piper, though, there was some peace in the knowledge. She could not fathom what her mother had gone through trying to protect Macy and losing her anyway. Then, when she and Luc had found the twins and brought them here, she'd felt a path solidify beneath her feet. *You'll guide hundreds*. Well, she already had the first two under her belt.

Beside her, Luc shrugged, his all-purpose "whatever" gesture. "Winter used to be the time Bastian and I would work on more extensive research projects with mom, or work with dad, making repairs and learning more about the boatbuilding craft. Doesn't make much sense to build more boats, though. We already have more than we need." He drummed his fingers on his knee, thinking. "We used to fly to the mainland once a month, and that helped break the winter up, but we don't have any pilots left. Snowmobile groups used to go to Mackinac Island or the U.P. over the ice, and years ago, people walked it to deliver the mail."

Interest sparked. "Really? It's safe to travel over the ice like that?"

"Safe?" Luc snorted. "Not hardly. People died, but they did it anyway. Is it safe to summit a fourteener?"

Piper sighed. "Point taken. I guess I'll just have to get used to the idea of being here until – what – March?"

"April, at least."

Piper drummed her fingers on the steering wheel. They were approaching the east side of the island, passing people who were walking or riding bikes towards the community center, many of them carrying packages or plates of food. A few of them were dressed in Halloween costumes, and one woman had beautiful, sugar skull makeup covering her face. She waved at them as they went by, and Piper recognized Cass with a start.

"Huh. I wonder if that helps her communicate with the dead," Piper mused, and that was when the idea hit her. "Luc, does anyone on the island have a short-wave radio?"

"Well, sure," he said. "Mr. Smith does. We have one, but it's broken. Dad was going to order a part, but, well.

And I'm sure there's one at the community center. Wouldn't be surprised if others had them, too – it was a pretty popular hobby, before."

"No one has tried to reach out, see who's out there?"

"We did, at first. Then a boatload – ha, no pun intended – of people showed up, and Miss Veda told us to turn them away. After that, it was decided to keep our location on the down-low. Then, there was so much to do, I guess people just lost interest."

Piper nodded, her mind already buzzing with excitement over the prospect of a new project to fill the winter months. She'd talk to the elusive "Mr. Smith," she'd talk to Gavin Nolette, she'd learn what she needed to learn, maybe find her niche here as the island's new communications specialist. Re-establishing regional and then world-wide communication should be a priority for survivors everywhere, or crucial knowledge would inevitably be lost. It wasn't enough to survive. They needed to analyze what had happened to them as they adapted and remember the lessons their species had learned. Most importantly, they needed to teach future generations. Piper laughed softly at herself as they pulled up in front of the community center. Lofty goals, to be sure, but with her degree at UNC suspended indefinitely, what better did she have to do with her time?

They hopped out of the Kubota and hurried towards the door. The wind was less intense here on the east side of the island, but the bay was still rough with white-caps and heavy chop, and the clouds had brought with them a grey and dreary early twilight. Before Luc reached for the door, though, he turned to Piper and rested his hand on his heart.

"Is she still alive?"

Piper didn't have to ask who. Luc never left her company without asking after Annalise. Piper let her vision go unfocused for a moment, and there the bond-line was, strong and vibrant red. "She is."

He nodded once, then sighed. Then he reached for the door and pulled it open, releasing a flood of warmth, light and life. Piper spotted Maddie across the large, open, common room, waved, and gave Luc's shoulder a shove.

"You're my good deed for the day. Go give your mom a kiss and tell her she owes me."

He gave her a refreshingly teenaged eye-roll and did as he was told, weaving his way through small groups of party-goers to give his rounded mother a gentle hug and a peck on the cheek. Piper watched the bonds between mother and son deepen and flare – green, pink, violet, bright white. She broadened her scope of vision and just enjoyed the light show for a few moments. What a vibrant community this was, connected, committed, growing. And how lucky she was, her life woven into this tapestry of colors and lives.

"Just once, I wish I could see what you see."

Jack's warm voice sent delicious tingles down her spine. Because she didn't know what to do with that, she didn't look at him right away, smiling instead at Ed and Owen across the room. When she was braced, she turned and gave him a tighter, more controlled version of her smile.

"It's beautiful. I was just thinking how lucky I am to be a part of it."

"We're all lucky. Every single person in this room."

Piper nodded her agreement, and silence fell between them. They stood side-by-side, greeting people as they passed by. Piper counted; every single person on the island was here. The room was festive with eclectic decorations: slightly tattered tissue paper flowers and garlands, beautifully painted sugar skulls, pumpkins and gourds, and candles, which blazed and sparkled everywhere. A long table was artfully arranged with the offerings of food, the air rich with scents both savory and sweet. In a far corner, separated from the rest of the room by dividers draped with colorful scarves and beads, both Cass and Veda had set up shop, offering their unique talents and skills to the people lined up waiting. In the opposite corner, Bastian was playing his guitar, a soft, lilt of music underlying the buzz of conversation and laughter. And still, the silence between them grew, and grew, until Piper had to start laughing at both of them.

"For Pete's sake. It shouldn't be this hard, Jack. We're both all intuitive now." She met his eyes and stopped worrying about protecting her heart. More than anything, she wanted this man's friendship. "I don't know why we can't talk anymore, but I can try to clear up my side of it. I don't have any expectations. If you're sorry you kissed me, can't we just chalk it up to the heat of the moment and be friends again? I miss you." She covered her heart with her hand and warmed the bond between them. "No one else here wants to talk sociology. They start glazing over, and nodding, and pretty soon they've got a deer to skin or something –"

"Is that what you think? That I regret kissing you?" Jack shook his head slowly. "You're right – it shouldn't be this hard, but it is. Piper, you are such a beautiful, free spirit. I can't stand the idea of stifling that. I'm a homebody. Unless I have to go chase down my baby sister again, I may never leave this island. I love it here, and I want to build a home here." His eyes dropped to her mouth, and his voice slid into a lower register, weaving a curtain of heat and intimacy around them. "I go to sleep, thinking about kissing you, and when I wake up, it's the first thing I remember – what your mouth felt like. And you can just stop looking at me like you want me to elaborate, because I'm not going to."

Piper's skin was flushing with heat and chills from head to toe, and her heart was tripping out a rapid beat. She turned so that her back was to the crowd and couldn't stop herself from taking a step closer to him. She felt their energy blend together as an all-over tingle of desire, and thought she might go a little crazy when she heard his breath catch, when his eyes dropped to her mouth, unmistakably hungry. "Why not?" she said. "Because I'm interested in hearing all about that, especially when you use that voice thing you do –"

"Piper. Stop." He interrupted her a second time, but his heart wasn't in it. She could *feel* that, plain as plain. "I'm nine years older than you. And I'm old-fashioned. No, don't you dare laugh, I am! You college kids and that 'hooking up' thing you do – that is not for me. I don't want casual. And I don't particularly want a 'girlfriend' since I'm being honest."

Well, then, that was a bucket of ice water. Piper reeled a little, blinking, and took a step back. "I see. Okay. I understand. So –"

"I want a wife."

More blinking. Then Piper squinted at him. "Jack? I'm lost. Could we regroup? I'm having trouble keeping up..."

Jack laughed, and hung his head for a moment. Then, in front of the entire population of Beaver Island, he swooped her into his arms and kissed her until she was cross-eyed and dizzy. A scattering of applause started around them, quickly spreading through the room until it was accompanied by cheers and catcalls. Cass's laughing voice cut through the chaos a moment later.

"Hey, Jack! There's someone here named Scott, and he says you better straighten up and ask his daughter to marry you *properly*, so he can give his permission and get on with his afterlife!"

TWENTY
Jack: Beaver Island, Michigan
February

The distant sound of the kitchen door thumping shut yanked Jack out of a nightmare. Fog, and fire, and someone screaming. Someone he wouldn't be able to help. He blinked in the dim, early-morning light, trying to orient himself while he listened to stockinged feet run lightly up the stairs. Moments later, swift rustling sounds were followed by a waft of frigid air, and Piper was burrowing under the covers towards his warmth.

"Sweetheart," he said hoarsely. "I love you with my life, but if you stick your cold feet on me, I swear I'll...okay, I can't come up with anything. Just have mercy."

She snuggled her cold face into the crook of his neck instead, then pulled back, reaching up to touch the sweat that hadn't yet dried on his forehead. She frowned, her eyes meeting his in the dim light. "Was it a bad one?"

"Nah." He pulled her face back where it belonged, then wrapped around her with his arms and legs, avoiding her icy feet. "Not even a 3 on the Richter scale. So, is there a new little person in the world?"

He felt her smile against his throat, and joy filled her voice. "Micah Alexandre Nolette was born in the wee hours of whatever dark February day we've got going on here. He weighed in at 8 pounds 3 ounces, give or take, according to the kitchen scale. I haven't the faintest idea how long he is, but mom and baby are doing very well. Dad was both elated and weepy when I left, and his big brothers are jazzed, though Bastian is a little green around the gills. They were there for the entire production, and I'll tell you what – I could present a strong argument for birth attendance as birth control for teenage boys."

Jack grinned against her forehead. "You're wired."

"Yep, for about fifteen more minutes, probably." Jack started rubbing her back, long, soothing strokes, and she sighed, speaking around an enormous yawn. "Make that ten. I haven't slept, not a wink."

"Then sleep." He pitched his voice just so, murmuring against her temple of his love for her, his pride in her, his deep contentment in their lives together, *soothing* her as only he could. In under two minutes, she was limp and snoring her soft, purring snore of complete exhaustion. Jack smiled, smug. She slept so restfully when he put her out like this, and was always appreciative when she woke up. Often *very* appreciative. Jack's smile turned to a grin.

He drifted off with her, ignoring the rising sun. Everyone here seemed to sleep a lot during the winter months, and he was no exception. He was skirting around the edges of another dream, a benign, nonsensical one this time, when a sound began to penetrate his sleep, a sound he recognized but shouldn't be hearing. He woke with a start when Piper sat bolt upright, then launched out of their bed and began dressing swiftly. Their eyes met, and they spoke in unison.

"Helicopter."

She beat him down the stairs and out the door, feet hastily stuffed in her boots, parka flapping open as she tucked her rifle against her chest and ran. Jack cursed steadily under his breath, calling after her as he snatched up her shotgun and slammed out the door behind her.

"Piper, darn it! Wait!"

Their cottage was situated on the north shore of Font Lake, just a hundred yards east of the Nolette's. Jack looked towards their property and saw Gavin and Luc running through the trees towards the lake as well, Gavin armed with a pistol, Luc with his bow. They converged where Piper had tucked herself behind a stand of trees, watching an orange and blue helicopter hover over the frozen lake. Jack squinted.

"Flight for Life? Seriously?" They all exchanged glances. Piper was scowling, looking from her chest to Jack's, and back at the helicopter.

"It's someone we know," she said. "I think. The bonds are tentative."

"Bonds? More than one?"

Piper didn't answer, just shrugged, her total attention focused on the helicopter. It settled onto the ice as delicately as a bird perching on a tree branch, and the pilot cut the rotors. Jack could see three dark figures inside moving about as they pulled on outer wear. Then the door popped open, and a very large, very armed man stepped out. Piper tensed and brought her rifle to her shoulder, sighting in. Even in the bitter cold, sweat beaded her upper lip.

The man examined the wind-swept ice at his feet and around the helicopter, nodding to the occupants still inside. Then he turned, scanning the shoreline, his gaze coming to rest on the very stand of trees they were concealed behind. Moving with deliberation and care, he slung his rifle over his shoulder, then held his hands up and to the sides, and called out.

"I know you're there, behind those trees, and I know you're armed. I can *feel* it. We're not here to cause trouble – we're looking for Piper."

Piper squinted and lowered her rifle a fraction. "Tyler? Is that you?" Then she made a low, distressed sound that made the hackles on Jack's neck rise, and her rifle snapped back to the ready. "Who's with you? Who the fuck is with you, Tyler? Answer me now!"

Tyler froze. "Piper, he's not here. Brody is not with us. Do you hear me? Brody is not here."

She sagged, her face white as the snow around them, and would have gone to her knees if Jack hadn't caught her around the waist and braced her against his side.

"We hear you," he called, as he lifted Piper's rifle out of her slack hands and engaged the safety.

Gavin stepped to Jack's side and took the rifle from him. "You know them?"

"I do," Piper said. She took a deep breath, and some color began to return to her face, though she still clung to Jack's supporting arms. "The last time I saw Tyler, he was with Adam and Brody." She squinted again at the helicopter. "So, if that's not Brody, who is it?"

Tyler helped a much smaller figure descend from the helicopter. The person began taking short, uncertain steps across the ice towards the shore. "Piper? Are you there?"

"Oh my God!" Piper pulled away from Jack and floundered to the edge of the lake, stepping carefully onto the ice and scooting forward with her arms open. "Grace! Gracie, what on Earth are you doing here?"

They were both giggling wildly by the time their slow-motion, "run across the meadow" greeting met in the middle. They skidded together and almost fell, laughing as they clung to each other and rocked in joyous embrace. An even larger man than Tyler exited the helicopter, just as heavily armed, and all of them started across the ice. By the time they arrived on the shore, Jack was shuddering with the cold, and he'd at least managed to get his parka closed. Piper was beaming, arm in arm with Grace, but her lips were blue.

Jack pulled Grace into a bear hug, rocking her just as Piper had. "My God, sweetie, it is so good to see your face!" He kissed both her smiling cheeks, then let her go, and gestured. "Quick introductions, then I have to get my wife inside before she turns into an icicle. Gavin and Luc, this is Grace, the daughter of a dear friend in Colorado Springs, and —" He only hesitated a moment over the word,

"Friends of Piper's, also from Colorado. Sorry, fellas, we only met briefly, so you'll have to do the honors."

"I'm Tyler," Tyler reached out and shook hands with Gavin and Luc, then stepped to the side so the other man could do the same. "And this is Adam." Then, he zeroed in on Piper and grinned. "Wife?"

"Lots to tell, guys. Lots to tell. Come to our cabin – we'll feed you, settle you in." She looked at Gavin and Luc. "I'm guessing you two will want to get back to the new baby?"

Gavin nodded, but Luc looked at Piper. "I'd like to come with you, if that's okay. I want to hear the news."

"More the merrier, if it's okay with your dad."

Gavin clapped his hand on his son's shoulder, grinning. "The new daddy is going back to bed." He nodded to the newcomers. "Looking forward to hearing that news myself when I'm not so tired I could fall over. Welcome to Beaver Island."

Piper linked arms with Grace again, and they headed towards the cabin, Adam and Tyler a few steps behind, Jack and Luc bringing up the rear. Their little cabin felt even smaller as they tried to find spots for everyone to shed their gear and find a seat. Luc built up the fire in the wood burning stove while Tyler slipped out to secure the helicopter. Jack and Piper distributed food and hot drinks all around, and, finally, the stories began.

Grace began, with Tyler and Adam interrupting to elaborate, or occasionally, to tease. The closeness between the three of them was obvious, as was the relationship between Adam and Tyler. They touched each other easily and often, the warmth between them tangible. Grace was more at ease than Jack had ever seen her, teasing right back when one of the men ribbed her. When Piper asked how they'd ended up landing on the lake instead of at the airport, Grace answered.

"Tyler wanted to land at the airport – we're low on gas – but Adam insisted on heading north. He was positive he could *feel* where we needed to be, even though statistically speaking –"

Before she could finish speaking, both Adam and Tyler threw their hands in the air, groaning and hooting. Adam stood up and caught Grace in a gentle head-lock, scrubbing her hair with huge knuckles. "What did I tell you would happen if you ever used the phrase 'statistically speaking,' ever again? What did I tell you, baby girl?"

He released her, and she sat back, laughing, disheveled and pink-cheeked. Emotion swamped Jack, seeing her like this, so youthful, so playful and free. He had to turn his face away and swipe a hand over his eyes. Piper turned her head and met his gaze. Her pretty green eyes were bright with unshed tears as well, and they smiled at each other in perfect accord.

Grace explained how she and "the boys" had come to be together, then met Piper's gaze, sobering. "Brody was with them. He told me his name was 'Levi,' but I knew. I knew it was him, Piper, and at first, I told myself I was using him as a means to an end." She paused, and her throat worked as she swallowed. She seemed to shrink into herself, and both Adam and Tyler leaned closer to her as she gazed at Piper. "But he became my friend. He understood me, and I understood him. I cried for him when he died. I'll understand if you can't forgive me."

Piper leaned forward and gathered Grace's hands into her own, never breaking eye contact. "We'll talk, just you and me, but there's nothing to forgive. Nothing at all, Gracie." She paused. "He is dead, then."

"Yes."

Piper turned her head to look at Jack. "I knew. I meant to ask Cass to confirm, the night of the Harvest Festival celebration." She grinned at him for just a moment, that grin that always made all of his nerves wake up and pay attention. "But someone distracted me with a marriage proposal." She turned back to Grace and the boys. "How did it happen?"

Tyler cleared his throat. "I know it may be hard to believe, Piper, but he died a hero. He took the core of the gang leadership with him." He hung his head for a moment. "And Verity. She went with him, too."

"Wait, what? What did you say?" Jack leaned forward. "Verity's dead?" Grief tightened his chest, then, to his surprise, red hot rage followed. "Well, what the fuck? She could have said goodbye, at least! Don't tell me she couldn't have, her of all people!"

Stunned silence greeted his outburst, and he looked around. To a person, their eyes were wide, and Piper's mouth was hanging open. Adam reached out and grasped his shoulder, squeezing hard. "I know, right? I felt the same way. But here's what I also know, thanks to her – I'll get a chance to bitch her out for it one day."

Jack nodded, gave Adam's hand a brief squeeze, then stood and took a few minutes, gazing out the kitchen window while the conversation went on behind him. A few minutes later, Piper's warm arms slid around his waist. "You okay?"

"No. I will be, but not right now." He had to struggle to keep his throat from closing up. "To borrow one of your sayings, she made me bat-shit crazy, most of the time. I've never worked so hard to understand another person in my life, not even Layla." His voice did break then. "I grew to love her. I'm so sad she's gone."

Piper squeezed her arms around his waist, and he lifted an arm around her shoulders to tuck her close to his chest. "Two swear words in a single day," she said softly. "Who are you and what have you done with my husband? I'm sorry you're hurting, love. What can I do?"

"Just keep breathing, sweetheart. That's all."

They rejoined the group, and Jack set his grief aside for the time being, listening with great interest as Grace and the boys described what they'd seen on their travels here. They had walked out of Colorado Springs, stopping in Limon for a few days, then walked on. Over and over, they'd tried to start one of the innumerable abandoned vehicles, but to no avail. Fuel left in vehicles was simply no longer usable. They passed through a few settlements where survivors had possessed the foresight, knowledge and necessary supplies to gather and stabilize fuel, but without any goods or skills to barter for that fuel, they were stuck walking.

"Eleven hundred miles, I figure, every damn step of it on foot. We walked every day, rain or shine, and I will tell you what – this girl here?" Adam nodded his head at Grace. "She is relentless. She walked us both into the ground. She wanted to get to Pewaukee before the snow flew, and we made it by the skin of our teeth."

"We arrived at your folks' house in mid-October," Grace said. "We thought we'd winter over there, but then Tyler found the helicopter while he was out scouting. He said this clear spell of weather *felt* like it was going to last, and it was starting to get tense in Pewaukee, so we decided to go for it."

"Tense, how?" Piper asked. "We met a small group of survivors there, a mom and her grown kids – were they still around?"

"They were when we first got there," Adam said grimly. "Eva and her kids – geez, I can't remember their names now. Then they just poofed. Disappeared like they'd never been there. We found what we think was the son's body about a month later, but he'd been pretty thoroughly, uhm, eaten. So we had no way of knowing for sure."

For the first time, Luc joined the conversation. "Eaten? By what?"

Grace answered. "Some kind of large coyote, we think. We only caught glimpses of them. We've got big coyotes in Colorado, but I've never seen any this size. They might have been wolves, but I don't know anything about the wolf population in this part of the country. Gray wolves were making a comeback in the northern Rockies, up in

Montana and in Yellowstone. Could they have spread this far east already?"

"They wouldn't have to. The Fish and Wildlife Service has been monitoring comeback populations of the Eastern Grey Wolf in Michigan's upper peninsula and Minnesota, and even a few hundred in northern Wisconsin."

"Really? I would not have guessed that, in such a densely populated area." Grace's ears were practically perked; clearly, she sensed a fellow researcher. "Do you think they would already be taking over areas formerly inhabited by humans? The little I know of the wolves in the Rockies indicates they avoid human contact unless they're starving – they're very shy and wary."

Luc leaned forward, vibrating with enthusiasm for his favorite subject when he wasn't consumed by his search for Annalise: wildlife. "They could have been coy-wolves, a coyote-wolf hybrid. I've studied them extensively, and they're amazingly adaptable animals. I wouldn't be surprised at all to see a population explosion, given the sudden absence of humans. Unlike wolves, they're not afraid to penetrate populated areas, and abandoned homes would make outstanding dens. Statistically speaking –"

Luc didn't get to finish, interrupted by shouts and jeers from both Tyler and Adam.

"Oh my God! He did not just say that! He did not just say, 'statistically speaking!'"

"Are you kiddin' me? There are two of them? Un-freaking-believable!"

Laughter burst and bubbled around the room, warming them all, and Luc blushed. He kept sliding sideways glances at Grace, and Jack made a mental note to just keep an eye there. A little guidance, a little support, and a friendship could very well blossom. Given time, who knew what else?

Luc returned to the subject when the laughter died down, frowning at all three of the newcomers. "You don't think wolves or coy-wolves preyed on this whole family, do you? Because in my opinion, that would be highly unlikely."

"Oh, no, we know what – or should I say 'who' – the initial predator was. Somebody with opposable thumbs." Adam popped himself in the middle of the forehead with his first two fingers. "Gunshot wound, close range. Burn marks on the skull, back half of his head totally gone. When we first talked to Eva and her kids, they'd been hearing rumors of people being kidnapped, or killed if they resisted, by groups of armed men from cities to the south – Chicago, primarily, but they'd also heard Indianapolis and Cleveland were best avoided. They had an in with a group in Milwaukee, and that group had learned to stay on the move. They didn't settle anywhere permanently, so they were less likely to be captured. They lost all but two of their women and children last fall, Eva said."

Piper looked at Luc. "I hope that wasn't the group we met," she said. Then, her eyes swung to Jack. "Do you think this information has anything to do with your nightmares?"

Jack grimaced, then nodded. "It strikes a chord, I have to admit." His nightmares no longer featured Cass, thank God, but they'd kept right on coming. Invariably, when he caught a broader glimpse, the setting was urban. He knew the dreams were a type of premonition, but he suspected they were possibilities, rather than certainties. Or at least he prayed so, every single day of his life. He looked at Adam and Tyler. "Military groups?"

"Para-military, from what we've gathered, and often rag-tag." Tyler blew out a deep breath. "We think they're slavers, if you can believe that. All the indications point that way."

Grace seemed to shrink in on herself again, and again, Tyler and Adam both moved closer to her. Adam draped an arm across the back of her chair and tapped her opposite shoulder with his fingertips. When she looked at him, he pointed to his eyes, and spoke for her ears only.

"Who's got you, little sister?"

She leaned into his shoulder. "You do."

"Damn straight."

Luc watched this whole exchange, and the expression on his face made Jack think of Grace, when she was putting together one of her "mental puzzles." The pieces were coming together, and young Luc did not like what he was seeing. Again, he leaned forward. "Slavery? To what end?"

"Mal-adaption to the current crisis," Piper said. "Exploitation and a hierarchal society worked for us before, why not now? The strong will always seek to use the weak. It's the way the human species is constructed."

Nods and sounds of agreement circled the room, but Luc frowned. "I don't agree," he said slowly. "Or, I don't want to agree. Obviously, I can't know for sure, but it seems to me we're poised to be something different. So many of us have evolved – there's no other word for it. And intuitively at that. We understand each other better. Why? Why would we change as a species in just that way?"

Silence met his question, the only sound for several moments the pop of the fire. Then, Grace spoke, her voice tentative at first, then gaining strength. "We needed to recognize the interconnectedness of life," she said. She looked at Piper. "Of all life. What you learned, Piper. What hurts one of us, hurts us all. When we help someone, comfort them or offer a kindness, we are all comforted and supported." She kept her eyes fixed on Piper. "I thought I hadn't evolved. Verity kept trying to tell me differently, but I didn't believe her. She told me I was always in my own way. Over the past few months, as we traveled, as I started to feel safe, I let myself feel again."

Sudden tears swam in Grace's dark eyes, and the punch of her emotions caught Jack off guard. She certainly was feeling again; he wasn't used to shielding around her. She had always been so cool and contained, so logical. What he felt from her now wasn't illogical, but it was strong and deep.

"I was so afraid to feel," she went on, clinging now to Piper's hands as well as her eyes. "Ever since my mom and Benji died. I thought if I started crying, I'd never stop. Then, the gang. And Lark." A great sob shook her. "It wasn't safe to feel. I couldn't keep functioning. So I didn't. I just used my brain and kept doing what needed doing. But after Brody and Verity died, I just couldn't keep the walls up anymore. As we traveled, I just let it come. I cried whenever I needed to." She slid a rueful glance between Adam and Tyler. "I cried a lot."

"And raged. And screamed." Tyler's hand had landed on Grace's back, rubbing in soothing circles. "But we're big, tough rangers. Can't scare us."

"I haven't worked it all out, but I did learn this – the more I feel, the more information becomes available to me, intuitively. My brain is making these leaps I couldn't have made before – it's crazy. The more I feel, the more I *know*. I can't explain it, but I know it has to do with integration of emotion and intellect. With allowing myself to be human, and fallible." She leaned even closer to Piper, her eyes intense, and Jack was sure she'd forgotten the presence of everyone else in the room. "I have been dying to talk to you about this – you're the only one I could think of who would understand. I know who it was. Lark's dad. I saw his eyes before he died, and I know what I have to do. I don't know how to do it, but I know: I have to forgive. Somehow, I have to get there, to forgiveness. How do I get there?"

Grace bent her head, and the sobs that wracked her made Jack's heart ache with misery, right through his shields. Piper gathered her up and helped her to her feet, shepherding her towards the stairs. "I've got you, honey, you just let it all out. Let's go find a bath and a bed for you, tuck you up all warm and cozy. We'll get some lunch and just chat..."

She sounded so much like her mother, Jack had to smile through the pain in his chest. Luc's eyes followed Piper and Grace up the stairs. When they were out of sight, he leaned back, a thoughtful frown on his face. Adam leaned forward and dropped a heavy hand on his shoulder.

"So, Luc? What you heard right there – that's what we call 'privileged information.'"

Tyler's hand landed on the opposite shoulder. "Yep. As in, 'if you keep your yap shut, you earn the privilege of keeping your balls.'"

To Jack's great pride, only a spike of fear escaped Luc before he locked it down. He looked between Adam and Tyler, then straightened in his seat, shrugging off both their hands. "She's not the only one with secrets. Statistically speaking," his teeth flashed, white and sharp in the dimly lit kitchen. "She's in the majority. I don't think there's a single person alive today who hasn't had to compromise their values or learn something terrible about themselves in order to survive. So don't sweat it. And leave my balls alone."

A moment of silence. Then Adam and Tyler both shook with guffaws. "I like you, kid," Adam said. "Even if you're as bad as Grace. Both ya'll sound like you swallowed a college syllabus."

A soft rapping on the kitchen door made all of them look up, and Jack stood, hurrying to let Cass and Veda in. It had just occurred to him that others would have heard the helicopter and would be wondering what was happening. He should have sent a runner around with reassurances. Introductions went around the room, and Veda planted herself happily between Tyler and Adam, patting their cheeks in welcome.

"It is about time. I have been waiting on you two for-eh-ver! The spirits have been fluttering about 'the boyz' for months – Verity says 'hello,' by the by."

Jack grinned as Adam and Tyler floundered around with that greeting and hugged Cass. As always, a sense of rightness settled inside him, a sense of being complete whenever he was in her presence. "Sorry, I should have sent word that we have visitors. Are the villagers armed with torches and pitchforks?"

"No, no thanks to you." She squeezed him back, then linked her arm with his, as she was wont to do. "Gavin sent Bastian around with the news that they were friends, not foes, as well as word of sweet baby Micah. Veda and I dropped by their place with a pot of soup and a loaf of bread before we came here. Mama, daddy and baby were all sleeping, so we just left it all in the kitchen. Where's Piper?"

Jack explained in a low voice about Grace, and Cass nodded thoughtfully. "When she's ready, I may be able to help her. Piper, too, if she wants. They've both got unfinished business with the dead."

"Verity's gone," he said, and felt his throat tighten with fresh grief. "I'm so disappointed. I wanted you two to meet in the worst way, though I've never been sure what the cosmic consequences of such a meeting might be. Now, we'll never know."

"If she has reason, she may visit. I suspect she won't. From what you've told me, she was almost certainly an advanced soul – the silly ones always are. She did what she needed to during her time here and is enjoying some well-earned down time, I hope."

In this, Cass was the teacher, Jack the student. He was still working on integrating what he'd been learning from her, as well as what he'd learned from Verity, with the religious teachings he'd been raised with. He probably always would be. "Why would she go with Brody? I can't think why she'd waste her life on such a despicable man." Jack's lip curled without his volition. "And if you give me some pat answer like, 'All souls return to source,' I'll swat you. That's great in theory but not in this reality. Make it make sense to me, Care-bear."

She smiled at his childhood nickname, but the expression was touched with sorrow for his loss. "The pat answer you don't want is that they had a contract. They agreed to perform that task together in the time before time. What I suspect, though we'll probably never know for sure, is that they were light and dark sides of the same coin. Soulmates, perhaps even parts of the same soul. They needed each other, for balance. I know this may be hard to hear, and it's just a theory, but I've begun to believe that all of us are servants of the Divine, even when we're involved with evil acts. Even when we hurt each other. We serve, no matter what we're called to do, and sometimes, the greatest servants among us are called to do the most disturbing tasks."

"You're right. It's too far for my puny little brain to go, at least right now." He patted her hand, where it rested in the crook of his arm. "I'll keep working on it."

For a moment, they listened to the conversation that was going on across the room – Tyler was every bit the movie buff Veda was, and a quotation contest was under way – then Cass looked up at Jack. "Do you suppose this will make Piper want to stay here now? I mean, her short-wave radio project is going so well. She told me she reached someone from Georgia the other day. And with Grace here now, maybe she'll give up her gypsy ways."

Jack smiled down at her. "Not my Piper." His Valkyrie, though he called her that only in the privacy of his mind. She'd either laugh or be embarrassed, so he kept that part of his admiration to himself. "She's a wandering spirit, Cass. I knew that when I married her and accepted it, just like she knows I'm going to keep putting down roots right here on this island, thank you very much."

"If the ground ever thaws."

Jack laughed. "Spring's coming. And when the weather is warm, Luc and Piper will be back out again. If they find Annalise, it won't surprise me if she ranges farther. She'll want to visit her mother, sooner rather than later, gathering her information as she goes. Maybe Adam and Tyler will go with her – they seem to make outstanding escorts."

"And you?" Cass's voice was higher pitched than normal, and Jack realized she was clutching at his arm, digging her fingers into his forearm. "Will you go with her, if she decides to do that?"

"No." He freed his arm from her grasp, then looped his arm around her shoulders, hugging her and kissing the top of her head. "No," he repeated. "I'm not leaving you. Never again. I promise."

She clung to him, hard, for a moment. When she moved back, her eyes were luminous. "I know I'm supposed to be all chill about death, but I'm not. Not with you. If you left and never came back, I don't know how I'd go on. I always loved you, of course I did. You were my big brother, and you hung the moon. Even when we were apart, I loved you. But now that we're back together, and we're friends, not just siblings, I don't want to even think about you leaving. You're a gift to me."

Jack felt a shiver slip down his spine and heard the long-ago echo of Verity's words. "You're a gift to me, too," he said, not altogether steadily. He hugged her again, and kissed her temple. "And I may sound all chill now, with the lake frozen solid and eight feet of snow, but when Piper goes, I am going to be a disaster. I'll be looking to you, to keep me steady and sane."

"You are each other's place of refuge, you and Piper," Cass said in a faraway voice. Her eyes were glazed, the pupils dilated, and a soft, golden glow suffused her features. Jack felt the hair on the back of his neck rise. "She is your haven, and you are her sanctuary, in a hard, brutal world."

Across the room, the conversation abruptly ceased. "The Sight's on her," Veda whispered. "Just let her be."

Cass was silent for long moments, swaying a little as she clung to Jack's arm. Then she took a deep, shuddering breath and looked at Jack. "Piper will leave, Jack. Over and over. She'll bring children here, for years to come. But she'll return to you, always."

"Always," Veda intoned happily. "A love like Snape and Lily Potter."

Tyler snorted, and muttered, "Yeah, except, you know – reciprocated."

Cass laughed, and Jack heard Christmas bells. He'd only seen that golden light surround one other person. "And by the way? Verity says she loves you, too."

LAST
Naomi: Pagosa Springs, Colorado
July

Naomi was struggling to hold onto a squealing, splashing Lark in the Crick Tub pool when Karleigh found them. She'd clearly run some distance, poor girl, and she bent over, bracing a hand on her knee and holding up a finger while she tried to catch her breath. Naomi didn't need to hear what she had to say. She met Hades' gaze, and his senses confirmed what her heart had already told her. With a scrambling splash, she was out of the pool, bundling Lark into a towel and plopping her in Karleigh's waiting arms. She snatched up her clothes and took off in a precarious, skidding run.

Piper was here.

Naomi had known she was close for days, and the anticipation had been just about more than she could bear. With Hades on her heels, she dashed past the mostly empty soaking pools and the cascading, multi-colored mineral formations. She yanked her clothes on over wet skin as she went, hopping as she jammed on her shoes. Then she ran up the steps Karleigh had just run down. Past the bath house and into the parking lot beyond, where a crowd had gathered, and there, there was her girl.

With an inarticulate cry, Naomi barreled through the onlookers, not stopping until she had Piper wrapped in her arms. Sobbing and laughing, they rocked and swayed together. Naomi pulled back and took Piper's face in her hands, kissing her forehead, the sweet curves of her cheeks, her eyelids, her darling nose, her laughing mouth. Then, she looked deep into her daughter's beautiful, teary green eyes.

"Goodbye, travel safe, I love you with all my heart and all the breath in my body," she said. "And don't you ever, ever leave without me saying that again!" She hauled Piper back into her arms, rocking her more gently this time. "And welcome home, my baby, my girl, my love."

"Mama, I missed you so much, so much." Piper pulled back this time, and taking Naomi's hands, held her mother's arms out to her sides. She scrutinized her from head to toe, nodding. "You've rounded out some. Looks good on you." She hugged her again, joyous, exuberant. "Feels good, too – almost like my old, squishy mom."

"Well, you're downright scrawny," Naomi retorted. She wrapped her arm around Piper's waist, and for the first time, looked around. "Did Jack come with you? Or Ed and Owen?"

"No, Jack stayed behind on the island with his sister and the kids. As for Ed and Owen – oh, my gosh, there's just so much to tell you, I hardly know where to start." She wrinkled her nose. "Is now a good time to tell you I married Jack?"

Naomi shut her eyes for a moment. Her only daughter, married. She could safely bet there'd been no fairy-tale wedding day, no perfect white gown, no gorgeous flowers or fancy cake. She sighed deeply, let those things go, and opened her eyes. "Are you happy?"

"So happy, Mom. And get this – Dad gave his blessing. I'll tell you all about it, but first, you need to meet some people." She stepped back, and two enormous, heavily-armed men stepped forward. "Adam and Tyler, my dear friends, and the men who were responsible for destroying the helicopters on Fort Carson last summer. They also helped Grace get to us safely, and me get back to you."

"Well, then." Naomi brushed right by their rifles and knives, and wrapped her arms around them both in turn, kissing the cheeks they bent to offer her. "Martin told us about the helicopters, so your reputation precedes you. Welcome, and blessings on you both for keeping my girls safe. Plan on being spoiled rotten while you're on my turf."

A disturbance in the crowd made her turn. Martin was hurrying towards her with Lark in the crook of his arm, Karleigh trailing behind them. When he saw Piper, his face lit with a brilliant smile. He swooped her into a hug, then pulled back and looked around. "Grace?"

"Safe and sound with Jack. She wanted to make the trip, but we overruled." Piper reached for his hand, and squeezed it. "Martin, she's doing so well. She's healthy, sleeping so much better, and healing by the day. The safety of the island has so much to do with that, so we insisted she stay, this year at least. She didn't fight us too hard, so we knew it was the right decision. She sent letters – a huge one for you, one for Anne, one for Quinn." Piper's eyes landed on the toddler on Martin's hip, currently squirming to get down. "And one for you, little bean. Gracious me, but you do look like your mama."

Lark, suddenly shy, dove to hide her face against Martin's chest. After a moment, she peeked at Piper, then stuck her finger in her mouth and gave her a gooey smile. Her sweetness lasted about ten seconds. Then she was twisting and wiggling to get down again. Martin looked over his shoulder. "Karleigh, can you please watch her for me while I catch up? I'd really appreciate it."

"Sure, Mr. Ramirez." She took a ready position. "Go ahead and set her down. I'll chase her until she wears out."

Martin set Lark on her feet, and she was off, dark curls bouncing as she ran back towards the pools. Karleigh scooted after her, and Piper looked at Naomi. "Where's Quinn?"

"Delivering a baby," Naomi said. She put her arm back around Piper's waist, squeezed, then began walking towards the buildings so many of them now called home. "We've got a lot to tell you, too."

Most of the travelers from Woodland Park had settled in what was formerly known as the Springs Resort and Spa, spreading out among the old Spring Inn Motel building, the Mountain Suites and the luxurious, 100% geothermal heated, EcoLuxe hotel. The surviving inhabitants of the town, numbering only nineteen, had welcomed them after a period of uncertainty and negotiations, and the two communities had blended with only a few bumps in the road. Most of the original inhabitants had stayed in their own homes, but the Springs Resort grounds had become a central gathering point, much like Jack's church back in Woodland Park.

Naomi and Martin shared a suite with Quinn and Lark on the ground floor of the EcoLuxe building, with Ethan, Elise and the kids in a nearby suite. Cries of welcome greeted Piper when they entered the building, and she stopped to hug people frequently as they traversed the busy lobby, a popular gathering spot. Martin met Naomi's eyes and tilted his head at the bar, raising his eyebrows in question. Naomi nodded, grateful, and Martin peeled off with Adam and Tyler in tow.

"How long has it been since either of you had an iced drink? It's just water – the liquor's long gone, and we've been so busy harnessing geo-thermal forces, we haven't gotten around to building a still yet. A few folks have tried their hand at brewing beer, but the words 'horse piss' come to mind..."

Naomi hurried Piper to their rooms, shooing Hades inside and shutting the door behind them. Hades trotted over to his customary place by the fireplace, settling in with a groan. Naomi gazed at her girl in the sudden peaceful silence, then lifted her hand to touch Piper's hair. Not quite real, yet, that her baby was here. She wanted to wrap around her and absorb her with all her senses. "You're letting your hair grow again."

Piper nodded, and touched Naomi's braid in return. "So are you. I've never seen your hair so long."

"Or so grey," Naomi groused, though the complaint was nothing more than an echo from the past. If she was honest, she rather liked her mostly-silver braid. She reached for Piper's backpack and rifle, taking both and urging her towards the couch. "Sit, and let me fuss. Are you hungry?"

"Mama, even if I wasn't hungry, I'd want to eat. I dream of your cooking, and wake up all weepy." Piper sank onto the sofa with a sigh, and looked around. "This sure is different from the cabin," she said, and Naomi heard the longing in her voice. "It's almost like before. Luxury living, at its finest."

"It sounds ungrateful, but I miss home. I miss the familiarity of the cabin, the way your dad always felt so close there, Macy's grave. I still feel like a hotel guest here – it just doesn't feel like home yet. In time, I'm sure that will change." Naomi went to the tiny kitchen and began pulling out food. "Still, the hot springs provide tremendous advantages, and the river is so close, for both fish and power. Alder has been in his glory, creating and installing alternative energy sources. We've got it so good I worry others will hear and try to take it for themselves."

Piper looked up sharply. "The gang? Are they still a threat?"

"Yes and no." Naomi carried plates out to the living area and set them on the coffee table, then sat down beside Piper. "We heard the old leaders – the ones who tried to take over after the explosion – got overthrown. Then we heard the over-throwers got overthrown, and so on. When you see Gracie, you tell her she ripped the guts right out of those rat bastards." She held up a plate. "Want a cookie?"

Piper just stared at her for a moment. Then she shook her head and laughed, and tears shone in her eyes. "I missed you so much, Mom. Yes, I would kill or die for one of your cookies right now. So if the gang is dead, who are you worried about?"

"Well, that's the 'yes' part. They're not dead. They've just changed form. Mostly they've become nomadic, raiding up and down the front range. They've got at least one tank from Fort Carson, but last we heard, fuel was an issue. We've got watchers stationed between here and there, people who can communicate with a partner telepathically – that's how we get our information." She grinned. "And how weird does that sound?"

"Not nearly as weird as it would have sounded a couple years ago." Piper spoke around a huge bite of cookie. "So, Grace was able to thwart the gang's attack plans. I can't wait to tell her."

Naomi bent her head. "Well, about that." She looked up. "They did attack. They didn't have helicopters, but they managed to get their tank up the pass, and they brought plenty of soldiers as well. Everyone who stayed behind either scattered or was killed." She knit her fingers together, squeezing hard. "Ignacio is gone. Andrea and Paul, too."

Piper curled close, pressing into Naomi's side and slipping her hand into the knot of her mother's fingers. "I'm so sorry. He was a good man, and your friend. Did you lose any people on your way here, or last winter?"

"Judy, one of our older folks, died on the trail. I think it must have been a relief to her. She saw possible futures, and I think she spent all her time trying not to be terrified." Naomi sighed deeply. "And Rowan had what we're pretty sure was a stroke, just this past spring. We kept trying to get her to slow down, but she wouldn't listen. She survived, but she needs round-the-clock care. Elise is with her now, and the twins help out a lot. Quinn had already been training under her, and you can't believe how he has stepped up. It breaks my heart, how mature he has had to become. He should be a senior in high school this fall, not the father of a toddler and healer of his community."

"Oh, Mama, you know better. If we start up with 'shoulds,' we'll never stop."

"I know." Naomi attempted a watery smile, but failed. "To Hades' great joy, Ares did not make the trip with us. I'm not sure if he was still alive or not. I never saw him after we got back from the Springs. But I like to imagine him there, undisputed king of all he surveys. I've been romancing a feral cat here, a lovely, sleek black lady I think I'll call 'Demeter,' if I ever win her over."

"Speaking of Greek goddesses, where's Persephone?"

"She's either with Rowan, or with Anne – depends on who needs her the most on any given day. Anne has really struggled with the transition. She misses Grace so much, and the library here just isn't the one she left behind. Martin and I are both hoping she'll take a more active role with our kids, but right now, she's still channeling her queens a lot. I took Lark over there this morning for a new story book, and I think Anne Boleyn helped us find one. She definitely had a saucy gleam in her eye."

They laughed together softly. Naomi was so grateful to Martin for this time with her girl, for the chance to just soak in her company without distraction or interruption. "Oh, I've been so excited to tell you – we've had four runners already this summer, all part of the Pipernet. First was a young woman named Lara from Pewaukee. She said she met you last summer, and that she and her mother just barely escaped a group of what she called slavers. Her brother was killed, and her sister was taken. Her mother insisted she make the trip – I take it she's a pretty bossy soul – and she didn't linger. She turned right around a few days later and hurried back to her mom."

"We wondered what had happened to them. It's not as bad as we thought, but it's bad enough. Where were the others from?"

"A young man named Timothy all the way from Florida – he said he talked to you on the radio. And cousins from a little town in Iowa –"

"Michaela and Christopher! Is it them? Are they still here?" At Naomi's nod, Piper clapped her hands like a little girl. "Oh, excellent, I'll be so happy to see them! Jack will be so tickled to hear about them, too. I think I better start taking notes, so I remember everything when I get home."

Home. Naomi had to turn her face away for a moment, so Piper wouldn't see the dark cloud passing over it. Her daughter's home was thousands of miles away now, in a world where that was a formidable distance indeed. Naomi made an impatient sound, irritated with herself. Dwelling on such thoughts helped her how? She pushed the dark away and turned back to her light. "Tell me about this island – is it really an island? Like in the middle of water?"

Piper laughed. "I know a young man who would have fun teasing you. Before I forget, though, I have to ask – did Loki make it back to you? I haven't seen him since we were in Iowa."

"And I haven't seen him since the day you left Woodland Park. He sent me images in dreams, but I didn't know what they were until long after the fact. I wish I'd been quicker on the uptake, there." She was quiet for a moment, and this time, her smile was more determined than watery. "I'm going to imagine him back at the cabin, watching sunsets and irritating the dickens out of Ares by disrupting his hunts. Now. About this island..."

She settled in and just listened to her daughter talk, just watched her familiar gestures, more content than she could ever recall being. Piper had almost brought her tale up to the present day when Martin and the boys returned. Martin walked over to her and leaned to kiss her lightly.

"There's a big old party gearing up out there to celebrate Piper's homecoming. You up for that?"

Naomi made a face, but nodded. "I guess, if I have to share her." She peered around him at Adam and Tyler. "Did Martin get you settled in a room? Good." She rose, and bustled them towards cushy chairs. "Now sit down here and let me get you something to eat. Cookies, anyone?"

Through the long, festive evening, and through the too-short days that followed, she and Piper were rarely parted. They chased Lark along the river walk and visited Anne in the library. They sat beside Rowan's bed, filling her in on the happenings around town. They went with Quinn to check on the new baby and her young mother, bringing food and tiny clothes with them. They spoke of Brody and Verity, of journeys and paths. Through it all, people continued to bring their problems to Naomi, looking for advice or resolution. One afternoon, after she'd settled a dispute over a bicycle tire repair kit, Naomi looked up to find Piper watching her, a strange expression on her face.

"You're the leader here. Not Martin, or anyone else. These people look to you."

Naomi shrugged, pleased that Piper had noticed, but strangely embarrassed as well. "I suppose I am. It's not leadership, really. It's more like common sense. People just need help thinking it through. For example, we've got enough clothes to last us a lifetime if we salvage what was left behind. What we need is food and medicine, and that means gardening, fishing and hunting. So why are people wasting their time knitting socks, when they should be weeding the beans?"

Piper laughed and pushed at Naomi's shoulder playfully. "You used to knit us socks – you made all of us a pair every Christmas. We used to call them the Weasley socks, you know, like Mrs. Weasley and her sweaters in Harry Potter."

Naomi smiled. "I remember, both the socks and the nickname. And I don't knit them anymore. I'm too busy making herbal tinctures. Just don't burst my bubble and tell me you hated them, okay? Leave me that much."

"You got it." Then, Piper sobered. She caught Naomi's hand as they walked along, lacing their fingers together and making Naomi's heart clutch. Piper had started refusing to hold her mother's hand when she was eight years old. The easy affection between them these days meant the world to her. "I'm proud of you, Mom. Really proud. I wasn't always respectful to you while I was growing up, and I didn't value you, not like I should have. Not like I do now. Then, I wanted to be your opposite in everything. Now, I'm proud to say I'm your daughter." She grinned at her mom, flickers of Macy and of Scott in her sly smile, and swung their hands. "Although that Suzy Homemaker gene seems to have passed me right on by."

Naomi laughed, and in her chest, the curled, dormant bud of potential she'd been through all her sheltered years broke free, stretching in the sun of Piper's regard. The energy of it moved down her spine and spread through her limbs like springtime sap, but it wasn't a thing of youth. It was maturity and survival, loss and growth. It was gratitude in the face of change she hadn't chosen.

In a few weeks, Piper would be gone, with no assurance they'd ever see each other again. Naomi didn't know when she and the boys planned to leave for the return trip, and she didn't want to know. She didn't want to count down days or start labeling "lasts." Last meal. Last hug. Last kiss.

So she looked over at Piper and memorized this moment, the perfection of it. The late afternoon sunlight on her daughter's golden, softly curling hair. The wind, pushing high clouds across a bright blue sky. The scents of high mountain pine and shy wildlife, filtered to her through Hades' senses. The soothing mutter of water tumbling over rocks in the river below. It was just a moment, like any other on a summer afternoon, sweet and transient. Not a guarantee in sight. Just life, and the living of it.

Made in the USA
Middletown, DE
27 December 2016